Praise for *Afte*

"A deliciously distracting thriller . . . Scottoline illuminat[es] the landing strip of revelations and truths in a deliciously slow and intense way." —*The Washington Post*

"Filled with plenty of twists and complex characters, this entertaining story builds to a satisfying conclusion." —*Publishers Weekly*

"A nail-biting thriller." —*Kirkus Reviews*

"Scottoline, a master at crafting intense family dramas, expertly twists Maggie's reality with a page-turning mix of guilt, self-delusion, and manipulation." —*Booklist*

"Scottline's expertly plotted stand-alone book moves at a rapid-fire pace." —*RT Book Reviews*

"Once again, Scottoline has written a gripping stand-alone psychological thriller." —*Library Journal* (starred review)

Praise for Lisa Scottoline

"Entertaining . . . This fast-paced read culminates in a daring chase that would play well on the big screen." —*Publishers Weekly* on *One Perfect Lie*

"Scottoline slams the plot into reverse at midpoint and accelerates at full speed." —*Library Journal* on *One Perfect Lie*

After Anna

Also by Lisa Scottoline

One Perfect Lie
Most Wanted
Every Fifteen Minutes
Keep Quiet
Don't Go
Come Home
Save Me
Look Again
Daddy's Girl
Dirty Blonde
Devil's Corner
Running from the Law
Final Appeal

Rosato & DiNunzio Novels
Feared
Exposed
Damaged
Corrupted
Betrayed
Accused

Rosato & Associates Novels
Think Twice
Lady Killer
Killer Smile
Dead Ringer
Courting Trouble
The Vendetta Defense
Moment of Truth
Mistaken Identity
Rough Justice
Legal Tender
Everywhere That Mary Went

Nonfiction (with Francesca Serritella)
I See Life Through Rosé-Colored Glasses
I Need a Lifeguard Everywhere But the Pool
I've Got Sand in All the Wrong Places
Does This Beach Make Me Look Fat?
Have a Nice Guilt Trip
Meet Me at Emotional Baggage Claim
Best Friends, Occasional Enemies
My Nest Isn't Empty, It Just Has More Closet Space
Why My Third Husband Will Be a Dog

After Anna

LISA SCOTTOLINE

ST. MARTIN'S GRIFFIN
NEW YORK

Published in the United States by St. Martin's Griffin, an imprint of St. Martin's Publishing Group

AFTER ANNA. Copyright © 2018 by Smart Blonde, LLC. All rights reserved. Printed in the United States of America. For information, address St. Martin's Publishing Group, 120 Broadway, New York, NY 10271.

www.stmartins.com

The Library of Congress has cataloged the hardcover edition as follows:

Names: Scottoline, Lisa, author.
Title: After Anna / by Lisa Scottoline.
Description: First edition. | New York : St. Martin's Press, 2018.
Identifiers: LCCN 2017053395 | ISBN 9781250099655 (hardcover) |
    ISBN 9781250185235 (signed edition) | ISBN 9781250099679 (ebook)
Classification: LCC PS3569.C725 A69 2018 | DDC 813/ .54—dc23
LC record available at https://lccn.loc.gov/2017053395

ISBN 978-1-250-88303-2 (trade paperback)

Our books may be purchased in bulk for promotional, educational, or business use. Please contact your local bookseller or the Macmillan Corporate and Premium Sales Department at 1-800-221-7945, extension 5442, or by email at MacmillanSpecialMarkets@macmillan.com.

Second St. Martin's Griffin Edition: 2023

10 9 8 7 6 5 4 3 2 1

For Francesca, with love

Three can keep a secret, if two of them are dead.
—Benjamin Franklin

You can't believe people when they look you in the eyes.
You gotta look behind them.
See what they're standing in front of.
What they're hiding.
—Sam Shepard, *Curse of the Starving Class*

After Anna

Chapter One

Noah, After
TRIAL, DAY 10

Dr. Noah Alderman watched the jurors as they filed into the courtroom with their verdict, which would either set him free or convict him of first-degree murder. None of them met his eye, which was a bad sign.

Noah masked his emotions. It almost didn't matter what the jury did to him. He'd already lost everything he loved. His wife, Maggie, and son, Caleb. His partnership in a thriving medical practice. His house. His contented life as a suburban dad, running errands on Saturday mornings with Caleb. They'd make the rounds to the box stores and garden center for whatever Maggie needed. Potting soil, deer repellent, mulch. Noah never bought enough mulch and always had to go back. He actually missed *mulch*.

The jurors seated themselves while the foreman handed the verdict slip to the courtroom deputy. Noah would finally know his fate, one way or the other. It had been hanging over his head every minute of the trial and the almost seven months prior, in jail at the Montgomery County Correctional Facility. He'd done what the inmates called "smooth time," becoming a jailhouse doc, examining swollen gums, arthritic wrists, and stubborn MRSA infections. He'd kept his head down and hidden his emotions. Pretty soon he was hiding them from himself, like now.

Judge Gardner accepted the verdict slip, causing a rustling in a gallery packed with spectators and reporters since the horrific crime and its unlikely defendant had drawn media attention. Judge Gardner put on his glasses and read the verdict slip silently. His lined face betrayed no reaction.

Noah felt his lawyer, Thomas Owusu, shifting next to him. Thomas had put on a solid defense and been a friend as well as a lawyer. But Noah's best friend was his wife, Maggie. Or at least, she had been. Before.

Noah turned around to see if she'd come to hear the verdict. The spectators reacted instantly, recoiling. They hated him. He knew why.

He scanned the pews, looking for Maggie. He didn't see her, so he turned back. He didn't blame her for not coming, of course. He wished he could tell her that he was sorry, but she wouldn't believe him. Not anymore.

"Will the defendant please rise?" Judge Gardner took off his reading glasses and set the verdict slip aside.

Noah rose, on weak knees. The courtroom fell dead silent. He could almost hear his heart thunder. He was about to know. Guilty or innocent. Prison or freedom. If they convicted him, he could be sentenced to death.

Noah wished he could run time backwards, undo every decision until this moment. He'd made so many mistakes. His life had exploded like a strip of firecrackers at a barbecue, igniting the patio furniture and spreading to the house until everything was blazing out of control, engulfed in a massive fireball.

His entire world, destroyed.

It had all started with Anna.

Chapter Two

Maggie, Before

"Anna, is it really *you*?" Maggie felt like shouting for joy. She couldn't believe it was really happening. She'd prayed she'd hear from Anna someday. It was her last thought every night, though she kept it to herself, a secret heartache.

"Yes, it's me. Uh, hi—"

"Oh my God, I'm so happy you called!" Maggie felt tears spring to her eyes. She grabbed a napkin from the drawer and wiped them, but the floodgates were open. It was a dream come true. She couldn't wait to tell Noah. He was in the backyard with Caleb, planting rosebushes.

"I hoped you'd be happy I called."

"Of course, of *course* I would be! Wow, it's so great!" Maggie's throat thickened, and her nose started to bubble, which she hated. She was Queen of the Snotty Cry, which was even uglier than the Ugly Cry.

"I know it's kinda random, to call out of the blue."

"It's not, it's wonderful, it's *amazing*! You're my *daughter*! You can call me *anytime*!" Maggie held the napkin to her eyes. She hadn't seen Anna since she was an infant, only six months old. That was seventeen years ago, the darkest time in Maggie's life, when she'd entered the hospital. It started coming back to her, a dark counterpoint to her elation.

I can't sleep even though I'm exhausted.

"Uh, Mom, I wasn't even sure what to call you. Is Mom okay?"

"Yes, Mom is okay! Mom is *more* than okay." Maggie wanted to jump up and down, but held it together. She had just been called *Mom*. She never dreamed she'd hear Anna call her Mom. She'd never been called Mom before, by anyone. Caleb called her Mag.

"Good, great. I hope it's okay I called on a holiday."

"It's fine!" Maggie dabbed at her nose, trying not to make weird noises into the phone. "So, Happy Easter!"

"To you, too."

"What did you do for the holiday? Are you at your dad's?" Maggie kept her tone light, even though she hated her ex, Florian. She knew he was behind Anna's decision never to see Maggie, estranging mother and daughter permanently.

"No, I'm at school."

"Oh." Maggie felt a pang for her, spending the holiday without family. "Did they do anything special?"

"No, mostly everyone's still away for Spring Break."

"I see." Maggie tried to collect her thoughts, sitting down at the kitchen island. Sunlight glistened on the granite countertop, which was white flecked with black and gray. Caleb's Easter basket of Cadbury eggs and jellybeans sat next to the Sunday paper, and the air still smelled like banana pancakes from breakfast.

I'm losing weight but I'm not dieting.

"So Anna, tell me, how are you? How have you been? Can we catch up on your whole entire life?"

"I don't know." Anna chuckled. "If you want to."

"I do, I'd love to!" Maggie's heart lifted. "We can try, can't we?"

"I guess."

"Of course we can! So tell me how you are!" Maggie would give anything to reconnect with Anna. Maggie had fought for shared physical custody, but Florian had enrolled Anna in a fancy French boarding school, and the French courts had ruled against Maggie.

She'd tried to establish visitation, but then Anna herself had written Maggie, saying she didn't want to see her. Maggie had honored the request, though it had broken her heart.

"I guess I'm fine. My life is . . . fine." Anna giggled.

"Mine, too! What a coincidence!" Maggie joined her, laughing. "How's the new school?"

"Not as fine. And it's not new."

"You started there for high school, right?" Maggie had gotten a notice from Florian two years ago, which was required by the court, telling her that Anna had come stateside to Congreve, an elite boarding school in Maine. It drove her nuts that Florian had won custody of Anna, only to send her to a school to live. Maggie sensed he didn't visit Anna much, because what little Maggie could see of Anna's social media never mentioned Florian, not even on Father's Day. Maggie always checked Mother's Day, too, torturing herself.

"Yes, but that was, like, three years ago. I wanted to come to the U.S. for high school."

"So what's Congreve like? I saw on the website, it's so pretty!"

"There's not much to tell. It's school." Anna fell momentarily silent, and Maggie rushed to keep the conversational ball rolling.

"So you're only a year from graduation! Tell me, what's next for you? College?"

"Totally, they're obsessed here. Congreve is a feeder for the Ivies. My grades are pretty good. I have a 3.7."

"Wow, I'm so happy for you!" Maggie felt new tears come to her eyes, a mixture of joy and guilt. Anna deserved the brightest future ever.

I hear sounds and voices.

"It's good, but it's not, like, valedictorian good."

"But still! I'm proud of you!"

I feel guilty and ashamed of myself.

"Thanks." Anna perked up. "I like your letters. It's so old-fashioned to get a real letter, instead of email."

"I'm so happy you read them!" Maggie wrote Anna once a month, figuring that one-way communication was better than none at all. She had no choice other than snail mail, since she didn't have Anna's email address or cell phone number.

"I'm sorry I didn't write back. I should have."

Maggie felt touched. "It's okay, you didn't have to."

"No, totally. It's rude."

"It's not rude, honey!" Maggie heard the *honey* escape her lips, naturally. "No worries!"

"And thanks for the birthday cards, too."

"I'm happy to. I celebrate your birthday, in my head. It's crazy!" Maggie cringed, hearing herself. *Crazy.*

I can't tell my husband how I feel.

"I save the cards."

"Aww, that's so nice. That's really sweet." Maggie swallowed hard, thinking of Anna's birthday, March 6. The labor and delivery had been difficult, an unexpected Cesarean, but Maggie didn't dwell on that or what came after. All her life, what she'd wanted most was a baby girl.

"And you know that navy fleece you sent me, last Christmas?"

"Sure, yes! Did you like it? Did it fit?" Maggie always sent up Christmas and birthday gifts. She'd had to guess at the correct size, so she bought medium. Anna's social media had moody shots of Congreve, but the privacy settings were high and the school's website said it frowned upon selfies and the like.

"Yes, I wear that fleece all the time. My Housemaster thinks it walks by itself."

"I figured, Maine, right? It's cold." Maggie wondered who Anna's Housemaster was and what her dorm was like, her classes, her friends. It felt so awful being shut out of her daughter's life. It was like having a limb amputated, but one nobody knew about. Maggie looked complete on the outside, but inside, she knew different.

I never thought I would feel this way.

"Also, congratulations on getting remarried."

"Thank you." Maggie assumed Anna knew from her letters. She didn't know if Anna felt uncomfortable about Maggie's remarrying, but it didn't sound that way. "Noah is a great guy, a pediatric allergist. I work part-time in his office, I do the billing, and I have a step-son, Caleb, who's ten."

"It sounds great."

"It is," Maggie said, meaning it. She was so happy with Noah, who was loving, brilliant, and reliable. He'd been a single father since the death of his first wife four years ago, from ovarian cancer. Maggie had met him at the gym, and they'd fallen in love and married two years ago. And Maggie adored Caleb, a bright ten-year-old who was on the shy side, owing to a speech disorder, called apraxia.

"Caleb's supercute and—uh-oh. I just busted myself." Anna groaned. "I stalk you on Facebook."

"Ha! I stalk you, too!" Maggie laughed, delighted. She had thought about sending Anna a Friend Request so many times, but she didn't know what Anna had told her friends about her mother.

My baby would be better off without me.

Anna cleared her throat. "Anyway, I should get to the point. I was wondering if you wanted to, like, maybe, see each other? I mean, for dinner or something? Either here or in Pennsylvania?"

"I would *love* that!" Maggie dabbed her eyes. It was more than she could have hoped for. "I'll come see you, to make it easier! Anytime, anywhere, you name it!"

"Um, okay, how about Friday dinner?"

"This week?" Maggie jumped to her feet, excited. "Yes, totally! I'm so excited!"

"Cool!" Anna sounded pleased. "I didn't know if you would want to. Dad said you wouldn't."

"Of course I would!" Maggie resisted the urge to trash Florian. She was trying to be better, not bitter, like her old therapist had said. It wouldn't get her anywhere anyway, so late in the game. Florian had cheated her of her own child, exploiting her illness to his advantage.

I have thoughts of harming myself.

"I'm glad I asked, you know? And I kind of want to know, like, what happened. With you."

"Of course." Maggie flushed. Her shame was always there, beneath the surface of her skin, like its very own layer of flesh. "Anna, I'll tell you anything you want to know. You must have lots of questions and you deserve answers from me."

"Okay. There's a place in town that's vegetarian, is that all right?"

"Vegetarian's great!" Maggie felt her spirits soar. "Anna, I give you so much credit for making this call. It couldn't have been easy. You're very brave."

"Aw, thanks. I'll text you the address of the restaurant. Okay, bye, Mom."

Mom. Maggie's heart melted again. "Bye, honey."

I have thoughts of harming my baby.

Maggie ended the call, jumped to her feet, and cheered. "Noah!" she yelled, running for the back door.

Chapter Three

Noah, After
TRIAL, DAY 9

Noah waited alone in the bull pen, a secured detention area of room-like cells on the bottom floor of the courthouse. The jury had been deliberating for two days, and it was eating him alive. Thomas had assumed the deliberations would take a day at most and hung with him from time to time, which Noah appreciated, not knowing how much longer he'd be in civilized company. Maybe not for the rest of his life. If he got convicted, he wasn't going back to the smooth time at Montgomery County Correctional Facility. He'd be doing hard time in a maximum-security facility like Graterford. Assuming he didn't get the death penalty.

Noah tried not to think about that now. He had to be hopeful. He didn't know which way the jury would go. They could find him innocent. It happened. People walked every day. He couldn't control what the jury did, so he was trying to get to *a place of acceptance,* a favorite phrase from the overworked MSW at the jail, who did med checks and ran group therapy sessions. Noah had been given a *coping toolkit* to help him come to a *place of acceptance*. Problem was, the tools weren't working now.

Suddenly the door opened, and a deputy admitted Thomas, filling the small room with his massive frame. He was six-foot-five and built like the linebacker he used to be at Cheney, and his presence and personality commanded attention in any courtroom. Right now his big features—round eyes, large nose, and oversized grin—were alive with animation, and he clapped his meaty hands together. "Great news, dude!"

"What?" Noah shifted on the metal bench, bolted to the wall.

"Lovely Linda is very nervous. Ask me why. Answer? Because I *crushed* that closing." Thomas grinned broadly, his chest expanding, and he opened his arms to reveal a wingspan that strained the seams of his tailored charcoal suit.

"What's up?" Noah felt a tingle of hope. Lovely Linda was what Thomas called the Assistant District Attorney, Linda Swain-Pettit. Thomas had nicknames for everybody in the courtroom, including the jurors.

"She's worried the jury's been out this long. She wants to make a deal."

"No deal. I said already." Noah didn't know what he'd expected. The cavalry?

"No, this time, you'll listen. I got her to sweeten the pot." Thomas sat down next to him. His grin vanished, and he turned to Noah, his eyes narrowing with intensity, like a microscope focusing.

"No deal."

"Wait." Thomas held up his palm. "You're charged with murder of the first degree. You're looking at life without, or death. That's possible."

"I know that." Noah had gotten used to the lingo. *Life without* meant life without possibility of parole, or LWOP.

"But if you plead guilty to third-degree murder, she's offering twenty years."

"No."

Thomas's eyes flared in disbelief. "Noah. I got her down from forty years, the max."

"No." Noah didn't even have to think about it. He knew how he felt.

"Noah, you're not listening. Sure, I gave a great closing, but don't lose your damn mind. The fact that they're still out doesn't mean they're going your way. Maybe somebody doesn't want to go back to work. It's snowing, maybe somebody doesn't want to go home and shovel. You don't know. You can't risk it. Take the deal."

"No."

"She destroyed you on the stand. It was like watching a major-league hitter swing at your head. I couldn't believe you even stood up after that. I wanted to send you a *stretcher*."

"Still, no." Noah had underestimated how hard it would be to be cross-examined by an experienced prosecutor. He'd thought he could just tell his story.

"It's like you have a death wish. Do you have a death wish, Noah?"

"No," Noah answered, but the truth was yes, or at least, maybe.

"Noah." Thomas took a deep breath, inflating his barrel chest, trying to calm himself down. "I'm *begging* you to take this deal."

"I can't."

"Why not? Because of the plea? Who cares? Like I told you, whether you're guilty or innocent doesn't matter. The only thing that matters is whether Linda convinced the jury you did it, and I assure you, she did that."

"Still." Noah had heard Thomas's lecture before. "Thomas, on a firing squad, they always put blanks in one of the guns. And you know the reason? So that everybody on the firing squad can sleep at night, saying to themselves, 'There's a chance I didn't do it.'"

"So what's your point?"

"If I plead guilty, Maggie will never be able to sleep again. It will ruin her life. I can't do it to her."

"But you've got to think of yourself now. She's not thinking of you. *You* have to be thinking of you."

"I couldn't sleep at night knowing what I'd done to her."

"They're going to *convict* you, man!"

"But at least she can say to herself, somewhere, that I didn't do it. She'll never have heard from me that I did it. The same goes for Caleb. I can't do it to him, either. He already gets bullied."

"But what if it means you get out sooner? Caleb's only how old now?"

"What makes you think he'll want to see me, after I plead guilty to murder?"

"He might not want to see you anyway!" Thomas threw up his heavy arms.

"Pleading guilty ensures it. If I plead guilty, well, I explained it. I just won't do it."

"It's your *life*."

"Mine isn't the only life to consider. I have to think of Maggie and Caleb."

"You're being noble."

"I'm being a husband and a father."

"Exactly why I'm single." Thomas snorted. "Noah, you're going against my express legal advice. What would you think of a patient who did that?"

"My patients are eight years old. If a mom or dad didn't take my advice, I'd figure they'd had their reasons." Noah encouraged his parents to get second opinions. He understood it, himself. Caleb had been late to babble as a baby and as he reached a year and a half, he'd shown difficulty repeating words like mommy and daddy. Noah had suspected he had childhood apraxia of speech, which was hard to identify in pre-school children. The pediatrician had disagreed, but Noah had been right.

"If this came up on appeal, I'd be considered negligent."

"You're not. I'm not appealing anything. Thank you for trying. I appreciate it."

"Damn, you're tough!" Thomas folded his arms.

"You need to come to *a place of acceptance*," Noah said, without elaborating.

Chapter Four

Maggie, Before

"Noah, great news!" Maggie raced across the dappled lawn to Noah, planting rosebushes along the back fence. She hustled past Caleb, who was taking videos of their tabbycat, Wreck-It Ralph, near the swingset on the other side of the backyard.

"What?" Noah turned, pushing back his hair, a thick sandy-blond thatch glinting silver at the temples. He was forty-three, and she loved the signs of age on him, like the crow's-feet crinkling the corners of his eyes, which were a seriously intelligent blue, set wide apart. He had a straight nose and a grin that came more easily once he knew you better.

"Guess what?" Maggie reached him, bursting with the news. "Anna called! I'm going up to see her on Friday!"

"*Anna* called?" Noah's face lit up. He stuck the shovel in the ground. "My God, that's wonderful, honey!"

"She wants to see me! Like, I got a shot!"

"That's awesome! Come here!" Noah scooped Maggie up and swung her around.

"It's amazing, isn't it? Woo-hoo!" Maggie did a little dance, holding on to his hands. "It's everything!"

"We have to celebrate! How about we go out to dinner? Order a bottle of champagne!"

"On Easter?" Maggie laughed again.

"Oh, right, I forgot!" Noah hugged her close to his sweatshirt, which smelled of peat moss. "Honey, I'm so happy for you. You deserve this, you really do."

"I hoped it would happen, and it did! I can't even deal. It's a miracle, I swear." Maggie buried her face in his chest, trying not to cry all over again. "I always hoped she'd come around."

"I know, babe. I'm so glad." Noah rocked her back and forth slightly, and Maggie let herself be cuddled in the sun, breathing in the comfort of his arms, his familiarity, his *husbandness*. She loved that Noah was always on the same page as she was, especially about the big things. About the backyard, they had different views. She'd fallen in love with Zephirine Drouhin roses, but he would've planted ivy.

"I really want her in my life. I hate that she's not. And I hate why." Maggie hid her face, ashamed. The only thing worse than being a bad mother was being an unfit mother, like her. She'd even been *adjudicated* unfit. She didn't tell most people that she even had a daughter, to avoid the explanation. Her best friend, Kathy, knew because they had gone through it together, but Maggie hadn't told her other friends or anyone at the office. She'd told Caleb, but it had been too abstract for him to really understand.

"Honey, don't be so hard on yourself." Noah let her go, looking down at her tenderly.

"It's just awful. Now I have to tell her everything."

"You didn't do anything wrong. You got sick, is all."

"But she grew up without a mother. I have to answer for that."

"You don't have to answer for anything." Noah frowned sympathetically.

"Yes, I do." Maggie felt guilty, despite years of therapy. After Anna's birth, Maggie had developed postpartum psychosis, an extreme form of postpartum depression. It had begun with sleeplessness, anxiety, and profound feelings of inadequacy as a mother, then progressed to bouts of crying, hearing voices, and intrusive thoughts of hurting herself.

"If you had cancer, you wouldn't feel that way. You had a mental illness, you got treatment, and you got better."

"But Anna's young. She won't understand. I wouldn't have, at her age." Maggie had always thought that postpartum depression was just the baby blues and she'd never even heard of postpartum psychosis. She wouldn't have believed it was possible if she hadn't lived through it, and there were so many other women who weren't as lucky, mothers who committed suicide or drove their car into a lake, with their babies.

"You can deal with it, and so can she." Noah leaned a forearm on the shovel handle, a lanky, six-footer in a faded gray T-shirt and old jeans. He was in good shape since he never overate, which Maggie couldn't relate to.

"I hope so."

"She'll understand. When you see her, just tell her the truth."

"That I went to a mental hospital?" Maggie hated the words, then she hated herself for hating the words. *Crazy, bonkers, batshit, nuts, psycho.* She and her friends used the terms all the time, but she never told them that she qualified. She'd started to wonder if she had postpartum psychosis after she'd taken a quiz in a parenting magazine. **I have thoughts of harming myself.** She'd checked all twelve boxes. She'd gone to her OB/GYN, and he'd diagnosed and treated her, but she wasn't improving. It had come to a head one awful night, and she dreaded telling that story to Anna.

"Don't blame yourself." Noah put an arm around her. "Your ex took advantage of you because you were in the hospital. He deprived you both of the relationship you could have had."

"I know. It's true." Maggie still needed to hear Noah say it, like a reassuring call-and-response. After she'd been admitted to the hospital, Florian had divorced her and won custody of Anna, asking that Maggie be declared unfit. Maggie had neither the ability nor the money to fight him until a year later, but by then, Florian had sold his start-up, gotten mega-rich, and taken Anna to his parents in Lyon, France, creating a jurisdictional nightmare that defeated her suit.

Florian had deposited Anna with them and started flying around the world, but that didn't matter to the courts, which was when Maggie learned that money could buy anything, even children.

"Dad, Mag!" Caleb came over with a buttercup on a flimsy green stem, and Wreck-It Ralph trotted after him, his tail high.

"What, honey?" Maggie said, turning to him. Caleb called her Mag because kids with apraxia had trouble pronouncing longer words, to the point where it was hard to understand them. But he got great grades, and his speech was getting clearer after years of practice. He had an IEP and received some services at school, but Maggie took him three times a week to a speech pathologist, who gave them target words to practice at home. They were given ten at a time, and the idea was to use them in normal conversation. Caleb had cut his knee on the playground at school on Wednesday, so this week's target words were about accidents. They made it a game, like family Mad Libs.

"Ralph likes butter." Caleb grinned, a smile that lit up his face. His eyes were a warm brown, and he had a cute nose with a smattering of freckles, from his late mother, Karen. His intensity was pure Noah, and it helped him cope with the teasing at school, due to his disorder. Even when his speech was understandable, it could sound halting and robotic, since he had to think about the words before he said them.

"He does?" Maggie smiled. "How do you know?"

Caleb hoisted the wilted buttercup. "I held this under his chin. It turned yellow. I got it on my phone."

Maggie smiled. "So you figured it out by *accident*?"

"Good question," Noah chimed in, with a wink. "It must have been by *accident*. Was it an *accident*, Caleb?"

"Yes." Caleb rolled his eyes, knowing what they were doing. He paused, thinking, and Maggie knew he was forming his motor plan, rehearsing in his head the way he was going to make the sounds for the word *accident*. It killed her that talking, which came so naturally to other kids, was something that Caleb had to fight for, every day.

"Caleb, don't forget your 'tippy T,'" Maggie said, which was a trick their pathologist taught them, to remind him to put the tip of his tongue behind his upper teeth to form the *T* sound.

Caleb nodded. "Yes, by ac-ci-dent."

"*Accident!* Way to go!" Maggie ruffled Caleb's reddish-brown hair with long bangs.

"Great job, Caleb! By *accident*." Noah grinned down at him. "Say it again. Was it by *accident*?"

Maggie held her breath. Caleb was supposed to repeat the word three times, which was difficult for kids with apraxia. If he couldn't, they were supposed to let it go. The pathologist didn't want them turning every conversation into a drill. They needed to encourage Caleb to talk, not shut him down.

Caleb answered, "It was an *ac-di-dent*."

Noah smiled. "Try it again, buddy. *Accident*."

Caleb pursed his lips, thinking again. "*Acc-di-tent*."

Noah touched his shoulder. "Good enough for now, buddy."

"It sure is," Maggie added, but she could see that Caleb was disappointed. "Caleb you don't have to learn that word. It's not an *emergency*."

"Ha!" Caleb smiled slyly at Maggie, knowing it was another of their target words. "No, stop! That's too hard."

"Caleb, it's an *emergency*!" Noah grabbed Caleb and gave him a hug. "It's an emergency! I need a hug!"

Maggie laughed. "Yes, an emergency hug!"

"Dad, no!" Caleb shoved Noah away playfully, and father and son started laughing and wrestling, falling onto the grass as Ralph sprang out of the way.

Maggie watched them with another surge of happiness, feeling lucky in them both. Caleb was more than she ever could have asked for, and she'd treated him as her own since the day she'd met him. She wondered if she'd ever get that close to Anna or if it was too late to make up for lost time.

Maggie felt the sunshine warm her shoulders. It was finally April, after a long Pennsylvania winter. Spring was a time of rebirth, and it was Easter, so it didn't get any better. Maybe this was a new beginning, for her and Anna.

Starting Friday.

Chapter Five

Noah, After

Noah arranged his features into a mask at counsel table, shifting in the gray suit that Thomas had bought for him. Thomas was standing in front of the jury box, about to deliver his closing argument. The prosecution had just finished, and Noah knew that Thomas's closing was his last chance.

"Ladies and gentlemen," Thomas began, his voice booming with a hint of a Philadelphia accent. "Thank you for your time and the attention. I won't keep you longer than necessary. But a man is on trial for his life here, and though you have heard one side of the story, you need to hear the other. I hope you'll keep an open mind because my client, Dr. Noah Alderman, has been wrongly accused of the murder of his stepdaughter, Anna Desroches."

Noah cringed, hearing it said aloud. It still seemed so unreal to him, despite the fact that he had lived it. Yet he had only himself to blame.

"Let me remind you that Dr. Alderman is a prominent pediatric allergist in the suburbs. He graduated from Yale University, Tufts Medical School, and he took an oath to never harm anyone. He raised his only son Caleb on his own, after the death of his first wife from ovarian cancer."

Noah hated that Thomas was playing the sympathy card. Karen had suffered so much. He shuddered to think of it now.

"Dr. Alderman is a person just like you and me, and I say this because you saw him on the witness stand. Some of you may have thought that he was not telling the truth, simply because of the way he acted. If you recall, he seemed to forget certain facts, he got confused, and he even appeared evasive at times."

Noah tried not to cringe. He could see one or two of the jurors nodding in agreement.

"But here's what I want you to remember when you go into the jury room and recall Dr. Alderman's testimony. First, he did not have to testify at all. The United States Constitution guarantees that he is innocent until proven guilty, and the burden to prove him guilty always rests with the Commonwealth. You know from TV and the movies that very few defendants take the stand in their own defense. Dr. Alderman did that very thing, and that should tell you something about him and his integrity."

Noah swallowed hard, watching the jurors. An older Asian man in the back, VFW Guy, nodded, but a chesty white woman in the front row, Victoria's Secret, folded her arms. The Terminator, a steroidal pipe fitter, glanced at Noah with approval, which gave him some hope.

"Secondly, I would like you to ask yourself how *you* would have done under cross-examination by Linda Swain-Pettit, one of the most experienced prosecutors in the city, if not the country." Thomas gestured at the prosecutor. "You've seen her in action, so you know that the woman is a heat-seeking missile. She talks fast and thinks faster. She's been in the courtroom almost every day for the past twenty-two years of her life, which is remarkable considering she looks only thirty."

Noah smiled at the unexpected joke, and even Linda chuckled, caught off-guard. The jury laughed, and Noah could feel them warming to Thomas's argument.

"If you ask yourself honestly, couldn't she make *you* look like a fool on cross-examination? I know if she had me in that witness stand, I'd get nervous. I might forget what I said or didn't say. And look at me, nothing scares *me*." Thomas wisecracked, and the jurors laughed. There were seven African Americans on the jury of twelve, five women and seven men. "And Dr. Alderman has never been in the courtroom before. He never testified before. He has no criminal record. He's never even been sued civilly." Thomas waved his hands in the air. "Consider that, and take a moment. Look around you at this grand, intimidating courtroom. I mean it. Look around, right now."

Noah scanned the courtroom, one of the largest in the Montgomery County Courthouse, ornate with crown molding and a paneled mahogany dais, witness stand, and jury box. Portraits of Pennsylvania judges in gold-filigree frames blanketed the plaster walls, next to polished-bronze sconces that were original. The walls had marble trim, and the pews were antique, also mahogany. Modern concessions like overhead fluorescents, computers, microphones, and an overhead projector and screen had been uneasily retrofitted. Equally incongruous was the sign taped to the plaster wall: **YOU MUST BRING A TICKET TO BE SEATED. Allocation of Seating in Courtroom: Members of the General Public, 60. Reporters, 30. For Use of the Commonwealth, 12. For Use of the Defense, 12.**

"Ladies and gentlemen, I ask you. Weren't *you* intimidated the first time you walked into this courtroom? Aren't you sometimes *still*? Now, can you imagine being on the witness stand, having questions fired at you like a machine gun, with your fate in your hands? Can you imagine facing that gallery, with all those people, reporters, everybody looking back at you, hanging on your every word, watching every move you make?" Thomas pointed an accusatory finger at the gallery, and Noah could hear them shuffling behind him.

"What normal person would *not* get nervous in such dire straits? *That's* the reason you don't have to testify at all, in this great country of ours. The Constitution embodies America and the values we hold dear. I was born in Philly, but my parents emigrated here from Nigeria and became citizens. Our freedoms are a beacon for countries all around the world. They protect all of us, including people accused of a crime. So ladies and gentlemen, when you go in the jury room and judge Dr. Alderman for the way he testified, please, think again. Put yourself in his position. Because that's what the Constitution and our great forefathers require from you. As Americans."

Noah could see it had an effect on the jury. Victoria's Secret unfolded her arms, and an older African-American woman in the front row smiled. Thomas called her Mama because she looked like his mother.

"And there is a third point I want to make. You have heard the term 'reasonable doubt,' and I want to explain to you why that matters. Under our legal system and our wonderful Constitution, the Commonwealth always has the burden to prove guilt beyond a reasonable doubt. It's as simple as that." Thomas opened his hands in appeal. "It's nowhere more important than in a first-degree murder case like this one, because convicting Dr. Alderman could result in the death penalty. There is no greater punishment, ladies and gentlemen. Nor is there any greater power. The last thing you ever want to do is to convict an innocent man. As the saying goes, 'Better to let a guilty man go free than to convict an innocent man.'"

Noah watched the jurors, their attention completely focused on Thomas, and he started to believe that he might actually be found not guilty.

"And that is the very reason for the presumption of innocence and the requirement that the Commonwealth establish guilt beyond a reasonable doubt. What is reasonable doubt? If you recall, the Commonwealth put on four witnesses, a police officer, a detective, a criminalist, and a coroner. Did you notice what is missing from their case?" Thomas lifted an eyebrow. "A witness. The Commonwealth did not produce a witness to this crime. Now, you might be thinking to yourself, 'Thomas, that's a lot to ask. How often do you get an eyewitness to a crime?' And you would be right about that, except in this case."

Noah had no idea where Thomas was going, and he could see an older juror in the back row frowning.

"The murder of Anna Desroches occurred at night, on a driveway that wasn't that far from the street, on a property that *anybody* could have access to. It was just a normal driveway in a residential area. Neighbors, passing cars, and pedestrians could have seen a beautiful young girl getting out of a car, and any *one* of those people could've killed her. Not only that, you also heard from the defense about the one lead that the police didn't even bother to follow up on."

Noah straightened in his hard wooden chair. Hope filled his chest. Thomas was delivering, and the jury was in the palm of his hand. Noah allowed himself to believe that he might walk away from this nightmare, after days of going back and forth, up and down, witness after witness.

"In my view, the *Commonwealth* is the guilty party in this case. They're guilty of confirmation bias. They got their man at the scene and they stopped looking. Their case is completely circumstantial, riddled with *more than enough* holes to create reasonable doubt." Thomas cleared his throat. "So if I may, let me detail the deficiencies in the Commonwealth's case, starting with the first witness . . ."

Thomas launched into the remainder of his argument, and Noah kept his game face on. Sometimes the jurors would look over at him for a reaction, but he stayed stoic, his thoughts racing. He didn't know which way the jury would go, but he knew the truth in his heart.

He wasn't an innocent man.

Chapter Six

Maggie, Before

Maggie got out of her Subaru at the Lenape Nature Preserve, arriving before her best friend, Kathy Gallagher. Every morning, they walked two miles, subject to their kids' schedules. Kathy had sixteen-year-old twin boys at the local parochial high school, and the Preserve was midway between their houses, a meadow with a path mown around the perimeter. They used the exercise as an excuse to see each other, calling it their Walk & Talk, though it was more accurately a Talk & Talk.

Maggie inhaled deeply, scanning the lovely meadow, empty except for a few runners. The grass was tall and green, and the oak trees at the far side were in full leaf. A bluish-pink painted the sky, lightening where the sun was beginning to rise. Maggie couldn't wait to tell Kathy that Anna had called. Last night, she'd texted her she had big news, but wanted to tell her in person.

Kathy's Prius pulled into the parking lot, and Maggie walked over, trying to contain her excitement. Kathy turned off the ignition with a grin that Maggie loved, easy and wide. The two women had been roommates at Penn, and Kathy's sense of humor had gotten them through the hard times, like their endless papers, final exams, and mutual divorces. Plus Kathy possessed the congenitally upbeat nature of a teacher, though she only substituted lately.

"Hey honey!" Kathy got out of the car, hugging Maggie. They were dressed alike in a fleece pullover and pants, except that Maggie's fleece had cat hair and Kathy's had dog.

"Guess what?" Maggie couldn't wait. "I got a phone call yesterday from Anna and I'm going to meet her on Friday for dinner."

"Wait, *what*?" Kathy's rich brown eyes flew open. "You mean *Anna*? *Your* Anna? Called *you*?"

"Yes, can you believe it?"

"I'm so happy for you! You must be over the moon!" Kathy gave Maggie another, bigger hug.

"I am! Come on, I'll tell you everything!" Maggie hit the walking trail, Kathy fell into step beside her, and they talked during the first leg of their walk, the west side of the meadow. The chirping of birds filled the air, a lovely natural soundtrack. Maggie finished the story by the time they turned onto the south side, and the sunbeams spread like melting butter across the sky.

"I'm so happy for you, honey!" Kathy grinned, pushing her short, dark hair from her eyes. "Anna was just a baby the last time I saw her. She was all eyes, that pretty blue!"

"Right? Hold on. I have some pictures." Maggie slid her cell phone from her pocket as they walked along, then scrolled to her photos, and showed Kathy a picture of Anna at six months old, sitting in her lap. Anna's blue eyes were large and round, and her toothless smile took up her entire face. She had dimples that matched Maggie's. Maggie was smiling in the picture, too, but she knew it was forced, masking her depression.

"How cute is she?" Kathy leaned over, without breaking stride.

Maggie eyed the photo, which brought back so many emotions, both good and bad. Kathy had gone to Connecticut to take care of her sick mother during Maggie's postpartum psychosis, and they had stayed in touch, even if Maggie had soft-pedaled how bad it was getting, not wanting to alarm Kathy when she had so much on her plate already.

Kathy swiped the screen to the next photo of Anna, dressed up in a pink ruched dress with puffy sleeves. "And look at this one! She's beyond!"

Maggie remembered the day, when she'd taken Anna to a friend's gender-reveal party. All the other moms had been so happy, but she'd felt miserable, then felt guilty for feeling miserable, a double-whammy of self-loathing.

"And look, when she was really little." Kathy swiped to the earlier photo of Anna in a diaper, sleeping in her crib. She had on a yellow onesie that matched her yellow-plaid bumpers. "Ah, I remember bumpers. You're not supposed to use them anymore, did you know that? You're supposed to let the baby sleep in a box." Kathy looked over, then frowned. "Are you okay?"

"Sure, fine—" Maggie started to say, then stopped herself. "Not really. I'll have to explain to Anna the whole postpartum thing. I don't know how much she knows, if anything. She said she wants to understand what happened, with me."

"Oh, honey. She'll understand." Kathy touched Maggie's shoulder, with a sympathetic frown. "Don't worry about it. Just be happy about this, it's great. Show me another picture."

"I don't have any more. Florian said he would give me copies but he never did."

"Oh, what a jerk! He's unforgivable." Kathy loved to hate on Florian, and Maggie used to love dishing with her, but she was beyond that now, supposedly.

"Let's not start on him."

"Why not?" Kathy shot back. "Getting custody of Anna was just about power for him. That's why he dumped her in boarding school and went flying around the world with his girlfriends. It would be one thing if you had still been sick and he was truly afraid for her welfare, but you had recovered by then. Did Anna tell him that she was going to call you?"

"Yes. He didn't think that I would come."

"How dare he! Of course you would! You're her mother, whether he likes it or not." Kathy scowled. "I wonder what he's up to these days."

"Being rich, I assume. He didn't work after he sold the app." Maggie remembered Florian had been so driven, then he hit the techie's dream, an IPO jackpot. She'd put him through business school by working in Penn's registrar's office, delaying her plans to go to law school. But she had never been more than a means to an end for him, and she was more alone married to him than she had been single, especially after the baby came along.

"Did he get remarried?"

"I don't know."

"Don't you stalk him online?"

"Not anymore."

"You're not the woman I thought you were." Kathy smiled. "I still stalk Ted. It's fun. Remember when he broke his ankle skiing? I couldn't stop laughing. I was *delighted*." Kathy slid the phone from Maggie's hand. "Gimme."

"Why?"

"I'll get his address, and we'll make him give you back those pictures." Kathy scrolled through Maggie's phone, logging into the Internet.

"I'm not going to write him."

"If you don't, I will." Kathy typed into the phone.

Maggie looked away, walking along. The sun was peeking over the treeline, bathing everything in amber. Bees, butterflies, and white moths fluttered over the tall grass in the meadow. Birds chirped, and a goldfinch flew by, its wings flapping to reveal a bright yellow body. There was so much life in nature, it surprised her every time. And she was about to reconnect with Anna. Mother and daughter together, the way it was supposed to be.

Kathy gasped. "Oh no. Look."

"What?" Maggie turned to see Kathy holding up the phone screen. Online was a news story dated last month, March 8, with the headline:

TECH MOGUL FLORIAN DESROCHES AND FAMILY
KILLED IN PLANE CRASH OUTSIDE LYON

Chapter Seven

Noah, After

Noah watched as Linda hustled to the jury box, all five-feet-three inches of her, short but nonetheless powerful. Her navy-blue suit was tailored closely around her superfit frame, and she must have been a runner because she had fast-twitch muscles in her calves, which Noah identified from his days running cross-country.

"Ladies and gentlemen, my name is Linda Swain-Pettit and I represent the Commonwealth of Pennsylvania. In other words, I represent the citizens of this great state, or *you*. The purpose of a closing argument is to review the important testimony you have heard in this courtroom. The judge will tell you when he charges you on the law that the Commonwealth retains the burden to prove the defendant's guilt beyond a reasonable doubt. I believe we have more than met that burden and I will set forth the testimony and evidence that supports my statement. Excuse me a moment."

Linda strode to the trial exhibits, slid one out, and placed it on an easel. It was a whimsical selfie of Anna, grinning down against a clear blue sky, enlarged to poster-size. She had been such a pretty girl, with large blue eyes, prominent eyebrows, a longish nose, but a small mouth with full lips. Her light brown hair tumbled to her shoulders, revealing a fresh young face that was shaped like a Valentine's Day heart. She smiled in a sweet way that showed her dimples, which normally reminded him of Maggie. Today Noah felt unsettled by the photo. It was directly in his line of sight, as if it were watching him.

"Ladies and gentlemen, this beautiful young woman was Anna Desroches and she was only seventeen years old. She attended Lower Merion High School, where she was a junior. Anna is the reason we're all here today, and I want to remind you that she could've been any of our daughters, sisters, friends, or neighbors. She was a typical teenager in every way."

Noah kept his face a mask. Anna wasn't a typical teenager in *any* way. He could never explain that to Maggie, but it was true. And only he knew *how* true.

"And her young life was cut cruelly short, in the most heinous way you can imagine. She was murdered . . ."

Noah felt himself slipping away, unraveling time backwards, wondering how he could've missed so many cues, denied what was before his very eyes. He recalled the first time he'd thought to himself about Anna, *that's weird*. He and Maggie had been in the kitchen after dinner. He was taking off his tie, and Maggie was loading the dishwasher.

Noah, I have news. I didn't want to bring it up in front of Caleb. Maggie had been rinsing a plate. They'd had spaghetti for dinner, and tomato sauce ran red in the sink.

Bad or good?

Florian is dead. Maggie had put the dish in the dishwasher with the others. *He died in a plane crash, of his own plane. Somewhere outside Lyon.*

Are you serious? Noah had set down his beer bottle. He'd never wish death on anybody, even though he'd felt angry at Florian for what he had done to Maggie.

Yes, he remarried, and his wife's name was Nathalie. He had two kids, boys, Michel and Paul. Five and three years old.

And the whole family died in the crash? That's horrible. When did this happen?

March 8. Maggie had rinsed off another dish.

How'd you find out?

Online. I was walking with Kathy, and we looked him up.

What was the reason for the crash?

They think pilot error. Maggie had put the last dish in the dishwasher. The bottom of the sink had reddish globs of tomato, like human tissue.

Did he fly when you were married?

He was taking lessons. Maggie had hosed down the sink with the sprayer.

How long had he been flying for?

What difference does it make? Maggie had frowned, closing the dishwasher door. *How would I know? What's with the questions?*

Right. Noah had caught himself gathering the facts, as if he were interviewing a new patient before he began skin, blood, or patch tests. It was an occupational hazard. *My God, that's terrible. You'd think we would hear about that.*

How would we? Maggie had met his eye directly, and Noah had felt oddly challenged.

I don't know. Forget it.

Maggie had softened, leaning on the counter. *I mean, I thought the same thing, but how would we? I have no contact with him, and it's not like it made the news over here. He's just one of those rich guys who died in a private plane. Maybe the tech journals reported it, but I don't read them anymore.*

Noah had sipped his beer, eyeing her. *How do you feel? You upset?*

It's an awful thing. Maggie had shaken her head. *Nobody deserves to die, especially that way. And it must be so hard for Anna.*

Right. Noah had put it together already. *Do you think that's why she called you?*

Yes, and I understand that. I mean, it makes absolute sense that she would reach out to me after her father died.

But she didn't say anything about his death to you?

No.

That's weird.

Maggie had frowned. *I don't think so. I think it makes perfect sense, and so does Kathy. Anna doesn't know if I knew or not and she probably didn't want to tell me over the phone. You're being critical, aren't you?*

Noah had let it go, but that was the first time he thought Anna had done something weird. Not wrong, not terrible, just weird. Since then, there had been times after that, each one slightly worse, and looking back now, he realized that those early incidents were like a case history of a patient. The first exposure to an allergen could result in a faint rash, a single raised bump, a brief shortness of breath. But then would come a second exposure with another symptom, more noticeable but dismissible by someone who didn't understand its significance. Ultimately there would be a third or fourth exposure, with a symptom each time, incrementally worse, but the human body wouldn't realize it was under lethal attack until it was too late.

Noah felt his gut twist. He had missed the diagnosis, and before he realized what was happening, Anna had destroyed him and his family. Yet he was on trial for her murder.

He should've claimed self-defense.

Chapter Eight

Maggie, Before

Maggie looked at her reflection in the hotel mirror. She was about to see Anna, all grown up. Maggie had on an outfit she had bought for the occasion, a white blouse under a navy V-neck with gray-wool pants, looking every inch the suburban mom. Her dark curls were reasonably well-behaved, falling wavy to her shoulders. Her eyes were an earthy brown and wide-set, emphasized by the good eyeliner, not the CVS brand, for tonight. She had a short, wide nose and dimples that punctuated chubby cheeks, since she was ten pounds over goal weight, which was no longer her goal. She felt nervous and excited, both at once.

Maggie grabbed her down coat, left the inn, and hurried down Main Street, adjusting to the cold. She passed the Maine Savings Bank, and its digital sign read 6:15 P.M. and 39°. The waning sun cut through the crisp air, and traffic moved at a civilized pace through the charming town of Congreve. The sidewalk bustled with young people and families going to upscale boutiques, funky restaurants and coffee shops, and an independent bookstore.

Maggie's step quickened. She craned her neck to see if Anna was coming the other way. She wondered if she would recognize her, but she knew she would. She felt her heart hammering, and her mouth went dry. Suddenly she spotted a young girl hurrying down the street toward her, and her heart knew her on sight.

"Anna!" Maggie found herself running to her daughter, arms outstretched.

"Mom!" Anna's eyes lit up, and she smiled, causing both dimples to pop, which melted Maggie's heart.

"Honey!" Maggie reached Anna, scooped her up, and held her close, squeezing her like she'd never let her go. "It's so good to see you!"

"You, too, hi." Anna chuckled, uncomfortably, and Maggie held her away to look at her, trying not to cry or snot up.

"Look at you! You're so pretty, you're *gorgeous!*"

"Ha!" Anna shrugged it off, with a giggle.

"Yes, you're lovely! God, look at you!" Maggie squeezed Anna's shoulders, blinking wetness from her eyes as she took in her daughter with a loving gaze. Anna truly had grown into a lovely young woman, her blue eyes large with thick eyebrows, like Florian's. Her nose was perfect, and her cheeks were prominent, like Maggie's, and her mouth curved into a broad smile. Light brown hair flowed to her shoulders, and the sun brought out her reddish highlights.

Anna chuckled. "You're just going to look at me?"

"Exactly!" Maggie burst into laughter, feeling the warm rush of a happy memory, out of nowhere. "I remember combing that hair with a baby brush and clipping it with a pink plastic barrette! A bunny!"

"Aw."

"It didn't hold much hair, but it was cute." Maggie laughed with joy. She was here, with Anna. It was too much. She wiped her eyes with her coat sleeve. "Sorry, I'll get it together soon."

"It's okay." Anna's eyes shone sweetly. "It's nice."

"Thanks, well, it can't be helped. It's the Italian part." Maggie wiped her eyes and got her emotions in control. She didn't think she would ever stop smiling. She felt great, whole again, thrilled to the marrow. Anna seemed pleased, if subdued, by contrast, but Maggie had expected that. Anna really was beautiful and tall, maybe five-eight, which she'd gotten from Florian's side of the family. She had on a black down coat with an oversized Coach purse and a cobalt-blue totebag, with a CA for Congreve Academy.

"We should go inside. This place fills up fast." Anna turned away, opened the door of the restaurant, and made a beeline for an empty table by the window, with Maggie behind her, composing herself. They reached the table, and Maggie took her purse off her shoulder.

"This place looks great," Maggie said, looking around, getting her bearings.

"It's good." Anna shed her belongings, bunching her coat behind the chair, and sat down.

"This is just wonderful!" Maggie sat down opposite her, finally settling.

"Thank you for coming."

"I was thrilled to, obviously." Maggie wiped her eyes with a cloth napkin. She needed a sip of water but there wasn't any.

"I'm glad you did."

"No, really, it was very brave of you, emotionally brave, to ask me!"

"Not really." Anna pursed her lips, growing serious. Her smooth brow furrowed. "It's just that I have so many questions, you know, about what happened with you. And why it happened, when I was little. I would really like to hear it from you."

"Of course." Maggie felt newly nervous, skipping the small talk.

"That's why it's hard to, like, throw myself into your arms."

"Sure, right."

"I mean, there are questions."

"Right, yes, totally." Maggie nodded, sniffling. She had to get a grip. "And I want to explain everything."

"Good."

The waiter came over, an older man, he looked down at them with a professional smile. "Would you ladies like tap or sparkling?"

"Tap is fine, please," Anna answered, looking up. "And I'd like a Greek salad."

"Me, too," Maggie said, to get rid of the waiter.

"You ladies are easy. I'll be right back."

Maggie waited until he was gone, tense. "Well, I guess I'll begin at the beginning. I was so happy when you were born, I really wanted a baby girl and I couldn't believe how lucky I was. But fairly quickly, I developed postpartum psychosis. Have you heard of it?"

Anna frowned slightly. "I've heard of postpartum depression. Is it the same thing?"

"No, postpartum psychosis is less common, and I didn't know what it was, either. Before I go on, I want you to understand this is not a reflection on you, because you deserved all the love in the world, and I did love you very much." Maggie had been about to say *and I still do*, but stopped herself. It was too much too soon for Anna, and Maggie didn't know if she could explain to such a young person what it felt like to be a mother, how it was something that never left you, even if you lost your baby.

"And to make a long story short, what happened was that one day I just felt in such despair and I thought I was such a terrible mother that you would be better off without me." Maggie fell silent as a busboy came over, poured two glasses of water, then left. "I heard voices saying 'let her go, just let her go.' And that voice came to me one night, when I was alone, standing on our deck in the backyard. You were in my arms, crying. You had colic. I was at the rail." Maggie felt her heart begin to pound, going back to that evening. "And the neighbor saw me, she called to me and I didn't hear her, I was in some kind of a trance. I was fighting with the voice, and the voice was telling me to let you go, to drop you. But there was still a healthy part of me that knew that I loved you and could never hurt you, and I knew that the voice was an illness that I had. A mental illness."

Anna's eyes widened as she listened, though she said nothing.

"Before I knew it, the neighbor was standing next to me and I said, 'please take this baby, she'll be better off without me.'" Maggie felt tears come to her eyes, but she blinked them away. "And I told her to call the police and have them come get me. I knew I needed professional help. I committed myself that very night."

"Is this true?" Anna tilted her head, skeptical.

"Absolutely."

"Where was Dad, that night?"

"He was working on his app, coding around the clock, when he wasn't at school. He hadn't sold it yet." Maggie didn't add that Florian was never around, ever. It was as if she and the baby didn't exist. She used to wonder why he'd married her, until she knew. He'd dumped her as soon as he got his graduate degree. He'd looked gleeful in the pictures.

"Can you, like, prove what you're saying is true? About the postpartum psychosis?"

"Yes." Maggie hid her dismay. It was obvious Anna didn't believe her, for some reason. "I had extensive treatment, inpatient, and then outpatient therapy and meds. And finally it resolved. It took almost a year."

"And is that why you abused me? Why you hit me?"

Maggie gasped, shocked. "What? No, never. I never *abused* you."

"You never hit me? You never beat me?" Anne's eyes widened, an incredulous blue.

"No, never!" Maggie recoiled. "What makes you say that?"

"Dad said you used to beat me. He said that's why you lost custody. The judge said you were unfit because you abused me."

"That's not true!" Maggie shot back, appalled. She'd assumed that Florian would have told Anna that she was crazy, but this was far worse. This was a total lie. "Anna, your dad really told you that?"

"Yes."

"It's not true."

"Why would he lie?" Anna's eyes narrowed.

"I don't know. To win some power struggle?" Maggie knew Florian. He always had to win. It was about ego and vanity. "Did he even mention the postpartum psychosis?"

"No, this is the first I heard of it."

"Honestly, I was found unfit, but it wasn't because I hit you. I *never* hit or abused you. I was ill, but I swear I *never* hurt you. I needed help, but I never physically hurt you or even neglected you."

"Really?"

"Yes, really, I have court papers and medical files, too." Maggie felt panicky to defend herself. She couldn't bear to have Anna think she'd been abused, not for another minute. "The custody papers show I was treated for postpartum psychosis. There were no allegations of any physical abuse, not even a single one! I didn't—"

"Could I see those papers?"

"Of course! I could have them emailed to you, if you want. Anna, I never hurt you. I loved you."

"Do you swear?" Anna bit her lip, uncertain.

"Anna, yes, I swear. I loved you from the day you were born and I love you still." Maggie touched her hand. "I'm very, very sorry that I wasn't with you, that you grew up without me, but I swear to you, I tried. I can show you how hard I fought for you in court. You sent me that letter, remember? You said you didn't want me in your life."

"Yes, but that was because you hit me. Dad told me you hit me."

"But I didn't. Ever. I only wanted to be in your life, to be your mother. Your mom. I promise you that, Anna."

Suddenly the waiter materialized with a tray bearing the salads. "Chow time!" he said brightly.

Chapter Nine

Noah, After

Noah watched as Thomas called their witness to the stand, hoping that he could help the defense, which badly needed it. Thomas had told Noah to keep the faith, but it was almost impossible. Still he held his head high as the witness was sworn in and sat down, adjusting the black microphone.

"Please, state your name and address for the record," Thomas said, from in front of the witness box.

"My name is Richard Weissberg and I live at 474 Marlin Road, in Haverford, Pennsylvania."

"Mr. Weissberg, do you know Dr. Alderman?"

"No."

Noah had never met Weissberg, who was of average height and build, with horn-rimmed frames that looked bookish on his round, friendly face, framed by dark brown hair cut in layers. He had on a dark wool suit and a silk tie, and Noah felt encouraged that Weissberg made a nice, reliable appearance on the stand.

"Mr. Weissberg, did there come a time when you became aware that Dr. Alderman lived around the block from you at 460 Howell Road?"

"Yes."

"Please tell us where your apartment is located, using this map,

Defendant's Exhibit 52." Thomas gestured to an enlarged diagram of two blocks of Noah's neighborhood, including his carriage house and in front of it, the main house, where Noah's landlord lived.

"I'm at the bottom of my street, there." Weissberg pointed to south Marlin Road. "I live on the first floor of a duplex. Most of the other houses are single homes."

"What do you do for a living?"

"I'm a teaching assistant in linguistics at Temple University."

"Now, let's turn to the events of the night in question, Wednesday, May 10. What time did you get home from work that night?"

"Almost nine o'clock. I worked late."

"And what did you do then?"

"I walked my dog."

"What time did you leave to walk your dog?"

"About 9:15 P.M."

"Please tell the jury which route you took. Feel free to use this map."

Weissberg pointed to the map, generally. "I took a right at the end of my street, onto Devonette Road, then I took a right and walked up Howell."

"Did you walk on the same side of the street as Dr. Alderman's house or the opposite side?"

"The opposite."

"And was Howell Road dark or well-lit?"

"It was dark. It's generally a dark neighborhood. There are so many big trees. It's residential, and the houses are big."

"Are there streetlights on Howell Road, if you know?"

"No, I don't think there are."

"Were there any parties or anything like that, on the night in question?"

"No. People go to bed early. It's the suburbs, with families and kids. They're inside, watching TV and doing homework."

"Did you see anyone on your walk that night?"

"No."

"While you were walking along, were you doing anything else?"

"Yes, I was talking on the phone."

"May I ask with whom you were talking?"

"My then-girlfriend. I called her when I left the house with the dog. She worked at NYU, and we were long-distance."

"And what, if anything, happened on your walk?"

"I heard a shout."

"What did the shout sound like?"

"It was abrupt, like someone yelling 'no' or 'oh!'"

Thomas cocked his head. "Was it 'oh' or 'no'?"

"It was 'oh.'"

"Was it a woman's voice or a man's voice?"

"A woman's."

"Adult or child?"

"Adult."

"Where did the shout come from?"

"From Dr. Alderman's house, across the street."

"Mr. Weissberg, do you know at what time you heard that shout?"

Weissberg nodded. "I heard it at 9:28 P.M."

"And how do you know?"

"Because I happened to look at my phone."

"Where were you when you heard the shout?"

"Near Dr. Alderman's driveway, like, fifty feet away, it was up and to the left, like this." Weissberg pointed on the exhibit.

"From your vantage point, did you have a view of Dr. Alderman's house?"

"No, there were trees in the way."

"Did you have a view of Dr. Alderman's driveway?"

"Yes."

"Did you see anything in the driveway?"

"Yes, a black Range Rover."

"How did you know that, if it was dark?"

"I saw it clearly. It's a distinctive car, and I got a good look, uh, because of what happened next."

Thomas paused. "Was there any other car in the driveway at that time?"

"No. Only the one."

Noah knew it was a good point for him. It was already in the record that Anna had a black Range Rover and Noah drove an Audi SUV.

"Mr. Weissberg, what happened after you heard the shout?"

"My dog pulled against the leash, and I dropped the leash and he took off running."

"Did he run toward the shout?"

"Yes, at first. He ran across the street, but then he ran back to the same side of the street. He zigzagged, and then he was running away from me, up Howell Road. He's a beagle, a scent hound." Weissberg shook his head. "He'll dig in everybody's trash cans for scraps."

"So then what happened?"

"I started running after him."

"And did you run with the phone call connected to your girlfriend during this time?"

"In the beginning, but then I told her I had to hang up because I was worried I would lose him."

"And did you catch him?"

"Yes, it took me twenty minutes."

"Where did you catch him?"

"He was at the top of Howell Road."

Thomas paused. "How did you get such a good look at the car in Dr. Alderman's driveway?"

"Because I ran toward it when I was chasing the dog."

"When you heard the shout, how did you feel?"

"Alarmed, I mean, I sensed it was a bad thing. Instinctively." Weissberg frowned. "I still feel guilty about it. It's just that I got so distracted when the dog ran away. I didn't want him to get hit."

"Your Honor, may I approach the witness?" Thomas returned to counsel table when Judge Gardner nodded, and he slid three copies of a document from atop his legal pad, then handed one each to the judge, Linda, and finally to Weissberg. "Mr. Weissberg, I'm showing you a computer printout and I'm asking you, does this represent the phone calls you made that evening?"

"Yes."

Thomas nodded. "Your Honor, I move this printout into evidence as Defendant's Exhibit 32."

Linda waved her hand, dismissing it. "No objection, Your Honor."

"It's admitted." Judge Gardner nodded, and Thomas faced the witness stand.

"Mr. Weissberg, does it show the phone call with your girlfriend commencing at 9:02 P.M. and ending at 9:47 P.M.?"

"Yes."

"Did you tell her that you heard a shout?"

"No."

"Do you know how long you stayed on the phone with her after you heard the shout?"

"No."

"Now, after you caught the dog, did you walk back down Dr. Alderman's street?"

"Yes."

"And did you pass Dr. Alderman's house?"

"Yes."

"And did you look in Dr. Alderman's driveway?"

"Yes, I did. I remembered about the shout."

"And what did you see in Dr. Alderman's driveway the second time?"

"I saw that another car had pulled in behind the Range Rover."

"And what type of car was that?"

"It was a gray Audi SUV."

Noah breathed a relieved sigh. Weissberg's testimony had gone beautifully. Thomas had made his point. Noah's Audi SUV hadn't been in the driveway when the shout was heard, presumably from Anna.

"I have no further questions. Thank you, Mr. Weissberg."

Thomas returned to counsel table as Linda shot up, brushed off her suit, and powered to the witness box.

"Mr. Weissberg, my name is Linda Swain-Pettit and I represent the Commonwealth of Pennsylvania. Thank you for your time today."

"You're welcome," Weissberg answered with a warm smile, not realizing it was a formality.

"You said you were certain that you heard the shout coming from the direction of the defendant's house, isn't that correct?"

"Yes."

"But you also said it was a nice night, is that correct?"

"Yes."

Linda turned to Judge Gardner. "Perhaps Your Honor would take judicial notice of the fact that it was clear and temperate at that hour of the evening, 72 degrees and low humidity. I verified this information with accuweather.com."

"Fine, go ahead." Judge Gardner nodded.

"Thank you, Your Honor." Linda turned back to the witness stand. "Mr. Weissberg, do you recall whether any residents had their windows open that evening?"

"No, I don't."

"But you testified that people were inside watching television, didn't you?"

"Yes, I did."

"Mr. Weissberg, didn't you know that because you saw flickering TVs?"

"Yes. You can see inside the houses, and people had TVs on."

"So it's certainly possible the windows were open, given the temperate weather, isn't it?"

"Yes, I suppose so." Weissberg blinked behind his glasses.

"And isn't it also possible that the sound you heard was coming from a television?"

"No, I think I heard it from the driveway." Weissberg shook his head.

Noah remained impassive, but he felt like cheering.

Linda frowned. "But you can't be absolutely 100 percent sure that's where the sound came from, can you?"

"I think I'm pretty sure."

Linda shot him a look. "Mr. Weissberg, you *think* you're *pretty* sure, but you were on the phone at the time, were you not?"

"Yes."

"And if your dog is a beagle, he pulls when you walk him, doesn't he?"

"Yes, the whole time."

"Doesn't he pant when you walk him, too?"

"Yes."

"Mr. Weissberg, so we're clear, you're walking him, he's tugging and panting, and you're talking with your girlfriend, isn't that correct?"

"Yes."

"Mr. Weissberg, what was the subject matter of the conversation?"

At counsel table, Thomas shifted in his seat, but didn't object. Noah's heart began to sink. Linda appeared to mull it over, but he knew she already had a plan.

Weissberg hesitated. "It was about our relationship."

"Was it a calm or emotional conversation?"

"Emotional."

"Were either of you raising your voices?"

"Yes."

"Were either of you crying?"

Weissberg blinked. "She was."

Linda cocked her coiffed head. "So you're walking down the street at night, your dog is panting and pulling, and you're on the phone having an emotional conversation with your girlfriend, who is *crying*, and the televisions are playing in the houses, isn't that correct?"

"Yes."

"In fact, weren't you *so* distracted that you dropped the dog's leash, isn't that correct?"

"Yes."

"Yet despite *all* of these distractions, the dog pulling and panting, your girlfriend crying, the TVs playing through the windows that could have been open, you feel *positive* that you heard the sound coming from the defendant's house at exactly 9:28?"

"I did notice the time on my phone screen," Weissberg answered, newly defensive.

"Mr. Weissberg." Linda looked at him like he was nuts. "You saw those *little tiny numbers* on the top of the screen in the dark, with all of those distractions?"

"The, uh, screen was lit."

"You saw them exactly at the very moment your beloved dog ran away, your girlfriend cried, and you were distracted, is *that* your testimony?"

"I thought . . . I had, but maybe I didn't," Weissberg answered, faltering.

"So isn't it *possible* that you were wrong?"

"I guess it's possible." Weissberg swallowed hard.

"I have no further questions, Your Honor." Linda turned on her heel.

Chapter Ten

Maggie, Before

"Anna, tell me what it's like at Congreve," Maggie asked, trying to recover from the revelation that Anna had been lied to about being abused. It had thrown Maggie off-balance, but she couldn't let that ruin their dinner. She would set the record as straight as she could, but it was hard to prove a negative. She worried Anna would always wonder whether Maggie was telling her the truth.

"Before that, I have bad news." Anna pursed her lips, looking down and pushing her salad away. "I didn't want to tell you over the phone. Dad died, in a plane crash."

"I'm so sorry, I did know that." Maggie felt a pang, seeing the change come over Anna's face, as her lovely features fell into grief-stricken lines.

"It's horrible." Anna's big eyes glistened. "I don't know how it happened. He was a good pilot. He loved flying, but they think he had, like, a heart attack. He wasn't even that old."

"I'm so very sorry, truly." Maggie patted her hand. "I saw an article about it online, after you called."

"So then you know. They were all killed, my stepmom and my stepbrothers."

"I know, it's so awful." Maggie could see Anna's pain at losing the entire family.

"And my stepbrothers were so *little*." Anna grimaced. "I didn't know them that well, but still. They were so cute. They were nice kids. It's so awful. Michel and Paul. And my stepmom Nathalie was nice, too."

"I bet." Maggie heard Anna pronounce the names in an authentically French way, though her English was flawless. "It really is, and it's hard for you to lose them, I know."

"It shouldn't be. Like, I don't want you to get the wrong idea, it's not like I saw Dad so much, or them." Anna frowned, blinking her eyes clear. "I hardly knew Nathalie. I met her for the first time when Michel was born. They flew me home for the christening. It was a big deal."

"Oh?" Maggie kept her surprise from her tone. "But what about the wedding? You must have met her then."

"No, Dad didn't invite me. They had it in Morocco. He told me it was on impulse, like, they eloped? But I saw the pictures later. There were three hundred people there."

"Even so, it's hard for you to lose him." Maggie simmered but tried not to let it show. It was Anna who mattered, not Florian.

"Yeah, it is, hard. It was a month ago, but it still, I don't know, it messes me up. Ellen, my therapist, says that can be worse because conflicted emotions are harder to grieve. She says it's normal to be depressed and crumbly."

"Of course, that's very normal, honey." Maggie patted her hand again. "I don't think you ever truly get over the death of a parent. My parents were gone before you were born, and I still miss them every day. I wish they got to meet you."

"You only got to meet me today, for real."

"That's true." Maggie let the awkward moment pass, though she felt proud of Anna for her honesty. "Well, it's good you have a therapist to get you through something this difficult. And your friends."

"Honestly, I don't have that many friends." Anna shrugged. "Congreve isn't such a great place if you're a boarder. Most of the other boarders are international and they're not that friendly."

"There must be some Americans who board."

"Not that many. Congreve is popular with European families. American kids go to Andover or Moses Brown because they're coed." Anna shook her head. "I wanted to come stateside, but Dad said he would only let me go to Congreve."

Maggie wondered if Florian had picked Congreve because it was so far from Pennsylvania, but whatever. "You make friends in your classes, right?"

"Not so much. And they separate themselves from the Parkers."

"Parkers?"

"That's what they call us." Anna's eyebrows slopped unhappily down. "The boarders live in Parker Hall, like, we're parked."

"That's so mean."

"But it's true. I'm *parked*."

"No, you're not." Maggie felt tears come to her eyes, hearing how lonely Anna must have been. Guilt made her heart feel heavy and hurt.

"Yes, I am," Anna shot back, without self-pity. "Dad totally parked me. I talk about it in therapy. He wasn't capable of more. My grand-parents weren't either. I wish I could leave but I don't know where to go."

"You mean leave Congreve?" Maggie blinked, surprised. "You're seventeen, almost finished. You only have one year left before col-lege."

"I know, but I can't make it here another year." Anna brushed a strand of hair from her troubled forehead.

"What do you mean, 'make it'?" Maggie worried that Anna was depressed. She herself had that tendency and wondered if Anna inherited it from her, like dimples.

"Dad was the one who wanted me to stay, but now that he's, uh, gone, I wish I could leave. If I could get out of here today, I would." Anna sipped her water. "I already talked to James about it. He's our lawyer. He runs the trust that pays my bills. He said I could go to any boarding school I wanted and the trust would pay. But I can't believe that it would be any better than here. Wherever I go, I'm parked."

"Anna, listen." Maggie was formulating an idea. "If you wanted to, you could live with me. Would you consider that? Because I would do it in a second."

"I have to admit, I *was* wondering about that." Anna smiled, cautiously. "Like, if living with you and your family was an option for me."

"Of course it is! I'm your *mother*!" Maggie's thoughts raced. "I could get back in touch with my lawyer, and I may have to go to court, but I never lost legal custody of you, only physical, and that was way back when."

"I mentioned it to James, and he said that would be a formality, but that's all." Anna shifted forward, with a new frown. "But first you should talk to him. His office is right in town. I already talked to him about you, and I talked to Ellen about you already, too. They think you abused me when I was little. You have to tell them what really happened, just like you told me."

"I will. I can send them the papers from your custody case. I'll call my husband and have him scan and email them, right now. But if we can explain it to them, I would *love* to have you live with us! Please consider it, I would really love it so much and so would Noah." Maggie felt her heart open at having Anna at home with her, a part of her and Noah's family, with Caleb and Wreck-It Ralph.

"For real?" Anna's smile broadened. "I think it would work, I can tell from your letters and from Facebook."

"It would be great!" Maggie bubbled over with excitement. "We have a lovely house, and the high school is only twenty minutes away, it's terrific!"

"I know, Lower Merion. I researched it online."

"Please come live with us!" Maggie laughed, giddy. "I know you'll be happy. You're young, and this should be the happiest time of your life."

"What about your husband? Would he be okay with it?"

"Of course! No doubt! He'd *love* to have you at our house! He always wanted me to reconnect with you!"

"Okay, great!" Anna beamed, her blue eyes glistening. "Thank you so much!"

"Are you kidding? Thank *you* so much!" Maggie felt her own eyes brimming again. She was getting the second chance she'd hoped for, prayed for, dreamed of.

"Could we leave tomorrow, if James and Ellen say it's okay?"

"You're damn right we can!" Maggie jumped up, joyful. She threw open her arms. "And now you're getting a big Italian hug!"

Chapter Eleven

Noah, After

Noah hadn't realized that there were times in a murder trial when nothing was happening, even though everyone remained in the courtroom in a state of suspended animation. Thomas and Linda were conferring with Judge Gardner, and Noah sat at counsel table, his thoughts cycling over the past. He was haunted by what-ifs, and the one that haunted him the most was the first. What if he'd told Maggie no, when she'd called that night from Congreve?

Noah, I just had dinner with Anna and it was wonderful! She's adorable and great!

That's great, babe! I knew it would go well. Noah had been in the car, heading home from the gym. He'd gotten their sitter to take Caleb to the speech pathologist and he'd be home in time to make dinner or, more likely, order pizza.

And Noah, guess what, I asked her to come live with us and she said yes!

Wow! Really? That's amazing! Noah had braked, stuck at the traffic light on Lancaster Avenue behind a string of cars, a TGIF crowd if he ever saw one.

I know I'm springing this on you, but it got sprung on me.

No, it's okay, it's great!

She's just really unhappy at Congreve and she's been seeing a shrink, and she seems depressed to me. She's grieving for her dad, who told her that I beat her and that's why I lost custody!

What? That's terrible! Noah had felt shocked. The light had turned green, and he'd hit the gas, snaking along.

I know! I need you to scan and email me my court papers, you know the ones? They're in the file drawer.

Sure, I'll be home in five minutes. Why do you want the court papers?

I have to prove that I didn't abuse her, can you believe that? I'm going to meet with her therapist and her lawyer tonight. She's inside the restaurant, contacting them. She gave me their email addresses, and I'll email them the papers. If I can convince them I'm not an abuser, I can take her home tomorrow.

Tomorrow? Noah had asked, surprised.

Yes, and I know you think this is happening fast, but sometimes you have to move quickly.

I think it's a great idea, babe. I'm psyched. Noah had read between the lines. Maggie always said he was too cerebral and deliberate, and he thought she was too emotional and impulsive. This time, he understood. She'd always wanted to get Anna back. It hung over her head.

This is going to be so great, honey! We'll be a family. You'll love her. Caleb will, too. She's just the kind of girl he likes.

You mean pretty? Noah had laughed.

Exactly! Maggie had laughed, too. *But I don't know where to put her. We only have your office and the train room.*

I'm on it, don't worry. You sound so happy, honey. Bring her home. We'll make it work.

I just know it will be great, honey!

We're a family of four. Presto!

Okay, I gotta go. See you tomorrow!

Love you! Noah had said, but Maggie had already hung up.

Chapter Twelve

Maggie, Before

Night had fallen, and Maggie and Anna walked to Parker Hall on the elegant Congreve campus. Every building was of colonial vintage, perfectly restored, and Anna pointed out a dining hall that looked like Hogwarts and the First Meeting House, a white-clapboard chapel with a pristine spire. The trees and shrubs were perfectly maintained, and the footpaths were lit by authentic gas lights. Schoolgirls passed them in noisy groups, carrying totebags, covered coffee cups, and phones.

Anna waved to one group, and they waved back. A trio of long-haired girls in navy-blue blazers hurried past, flashing automatic smiles, but Anna didn't wave to them, nor did they acknowledge her.

"Who were they?" Maggie said, when they'd passed.

"Mean girls on parade."

"What's with the blazer?"

"The Senior Blazer. They never take it off. We *get* it, ladies."

Maggie smiled, and they reached Parker Hall, an imposing colonial mansion with a brick façade, tall white columns, and windows with bubbled-glass panes and thick muntins.

"Home sweet home," Anna said, with a smile that Maggie could tell was forced. "I'd take you inside, but they don't know you, okay?"

"Absolutely, and I don't want to keep Ellen waiting."

"Okay. Her office is in the Graham Center, at the end of the path. You'll see the sign. Just go that way." Anna pointed down to the left, down a path through the campus.

"I got it."

"Want me to walk you?"

"No, I'm fine. You go inside and pack."

"The walkway ends in the Graham Center, which is the counseling services. Everybody calls it Graham Crackup."

"Not exactly enlightened. I always thought the crazy people were the ones who never went to therapy."

"Agree!" Anna laughed. "Bye now."

"See you later." Maggie waved as Anna turned away and headed up the brick path to the dorm.

Fifteen minutes later, Maggie was sitting in the Graham Center's beautifully appointed reception area, which was empty. There was a cushy navy-blue rug on the floor, patterned club chairs around a cherrywood coffee table, and walls covered with black-and-white photographs of Congreve dating as far back as 1810.

"Maggie Ippoliti?" said a voice behind her, and Maggie turned to see a trim woman who was maybe sixty-five or so, with plastic rimless glasses perched on a fine nose, sterling silver hair cut fashionably to her chin, and a gray-wool pantsuit, worn with graduated pearls and black flats.

"Yes, thank you for seeing me on such short notice."

"You're welcome." Ellen smiled warmly, then gestured at the chair and sat down, crossing her legs. "Please sit down. We can chat here, since we're alone."

"Great." Maggie sat back down. "First things first. Anna told me that her father told her that I abused her, and that's not true. Nothing like that is true. In fact, I lost physical custody when she was a baby because I had postpartum psychosis. Did you get the papers I emailed you? They explain why I lost physical custody."

"Yes, I reviewed them."

"There were no allegations of physical abuse, you saw that."

"Yes." Ellen nodded. "I have a good handle on the situation now.

I'm familiar with postpartum depression and psychosis, which are more common than most people realize."

"Yes, they are. I hate that Anna thought that of me, all these years. Or that you did."

"Not to worry." Ellen pursed her lips, which were thin. "I will say, I often suspected that Anna was not being told the truth. I think Anna had her doubts about its veracity, as well."

"Thank God," Maggie said, relieved.

"It didn't stand to reason, for me. I've counseled victims of child abuse, and Anna shows none of the signs. In addition, I've seen custody battles across oceans, so I know the mud that gets slung around. Families tell lies for a variety of reasons, and I don't think it's for us to speculate about your ex-husband's reasons for so doing."

"I agree." Maggie eased into the chair. She felt better, now that Ellen believed her. "I appreciate your seeing me."

"I do it all the time with the student's permission."

"How long have you been seeing Anna?"

"I've been working with her since she arrived. Anna has been unhappy at Congreve for some time, and since her father died, she's been wanting to make a change. I assume she told you that."

"Yes."

"She has a remarkable degree of insight. I think that her father's death, unfortunately, was the impetus she needed."

"I'm so excited that she wants to come live with me. What do you think about the idea?"

"I think it's a fine idea, now that the allegations about you have been resolved in my mind. Anna is on the reserved side, and though she has so many talents, her self-esteem has suffered here. She's made very few friends."

"She told me that."

"We try to foster a sense of community and we follow an antibullying curriculum. That works when the girls are younger, but as they get older, it's hard to force them to include others." Ellen sighed. "I saw Anna twice a week during the difficult times. We have scaled down to once a week, on Mondays. I think she'll need to adjust to the move and I can refer you to some excellent child and adolescent therapists in the Philadelphia area."

"Thanks." Maggie paused. "Is there anything you think I should know about Anna? Ways that I can help her?"

"It gladdens my heart to hear you say that." Ellen smiled with approval. "Anna has been on her own for some time. She's compliant, a people-pleaser, perhaps too much so. She is a high achiever and functions well within the rules, but she tends to get lost in the shuffle. You're thinking about a public high school for her?"

"Yes. She wants to give it a try."

"Good, that's what she told me too. I think it's her attempt to live a normal, teenage life. She didn't see her father more than once a year, and she's here during holidays when most of the boarders are away."

"Oh no." Maggie felt a stab of guilt, like her heart hurt. She remembered so many Christmases and birthdays when she'd thought of Anna, wishing she were home, with her. It could have been so different. All that lost time.

"You may be wondering if there is a diagnosis for her, but I don't pigeonhole my patients. Not everybody fits into the categories in the DSM. More often, they fit into several. That said, I do think she has a tendency toward mild depression. However, it's a reasonable reaction to her situation. She has no family to rely upon and she's profoundly lonely."

"That's so sad." Maggie's chest tightened.

"Isn't it?" Ellen's lined face softened. "It may sound like a cliché, but there is such a thing as a poor little rich girl. That girl is Anna."

Maggie felt tears brimming in her eyes. Hearing it from a professional made her feel even worse.

"Please, take a tissue, right in front of you." Ellen gestured at a Kleenex box on the coffee table.

"Thanks," Maggie said, thickly. She tugged a tissue from the box, wiped her eyes, then blew her nose before the snotslide. "Sorry."

"Not at all."

"I know I can change things for her." Maggie spoke from the heart, wiping her eyes again. "I know I can do better than before."

"I believe you can, but be patient with her during the transition."

"I will, of course. I'll do anything she needs." Maggie gave a final sniffle, holding on to the Kleenex.

"If you don't mind, tell me about your home life and your marriage, if you would."

"I remarried two years ago, very happily, and I have a stepson, Caleb, who's adorable." Maggie felt her chest ease, on a happier subject. "My husband, Noah, is a pediatric allergist, and I work in his group's office doing billing part-time, which enables me to take Caleb to his speech pathologist in the afternoons. He has childhood apraxia of speech."

"I'm familiar with it. CAS." Ellen nodded. "So you feel Anna could fit in well with your family?"

"Yes, truly. My husband is as excited as I am. And Caleb will love her. He can be shy around new people, but she seems quiet and non-judgmental."

"She is." Ellen smiled. "Anna told me she's been following you on Facebook. She may have a tendency to idealize your family life, in the way we believe in the beautiful images we post for each other. Social media has made counseling adolescents and children much more difficult. They believe wholesale in what others post about their lives, their boyfriends, their parents, and the like."

"Oh, I'm sure. Every time I feel good about myself, if I go on Facebook I feel instantly inferior."

Ellen chuckled. "Yes, that's exactly what I'm talking about, and you're an adult, your personality fully formed. But imagine if it isn't yet, and that's doubly true for girls, who get the societal message that physical appearance is paramount. I helped write the school policy regarding posting, which is admittedly strict. Congreve privileges face-to-face interactions over virtual ones."

"Sounds like we're on the same page."

"But, to return to the point, you should note that Anna is mourning her father, as well as the loss of the fantasy of her father. And she's conflicted and angry because it doesn't square with what she has, or had."

"I understand."

"She held out hope that someday he would realize that she was wonderful and be a true father to her." Ellen paused. "I never saw that happening. I reached out to him several times, and he never responded."

Maggie felt even more angry at Florian, if that were possible. If he hadn't been dead already, she would have killed him.

"So her mourning and her grief are complicated."

Maggie remembered Anna telling her that at dinner. "Do you worry that she's suicidal? Because that concerns me."

"No, I don't. She has never had suicidal ideation."

"That's a relief."

"Anna does have abandonment issues. She felt abandoned by you, her father, and her grandparents." Ellen frowned. "My work with her has been to help her not blame herself. It's deleterious for her self-esteem."

"I feel terrible for her. It's just so sad. How can I help her?"

"I think it's important for you and your husband to demonstrate that you are there for her. She will expect you to leave her, let her down, or disappoint her."

"I would never do that."

"You can earn her trust and love bit by bit, day by day. I'm optimistic."

"Me too." Maggie knew she could turn it around. She owed it to Anna. She would make it her mission.

"So." Ellen checked her watch, then rose. "I'm afraid I'm late. Feel free to call me anytime. I told Anna the same thing."

"Don't you want to say good-bye to her?" Maggie stood up and got her purse. "We can swing by tomorrow morning before we fly home."

"No, we said our good-byes." Ellen's eyes twinkled. "Your response is exactly the one we hoped for, now that the abuse allegations have been debunked. By the way, Anna has no recollection of any abuse by you."

"What does she remember?" Maggie asked, her curiosity piqued. "Can a child even *have* memories from infancy?"

"Not often, but her sense memories are happy ones, and her recollection is feeling loved and safe with you."

"How great!" Maggie felt a warm rush of happiness.

"Tell her to stay in touch. She's a lovely girl, your daughter."

Your daughter. Maggie hadn't heard those words, in such a long time. "So she had this planned?"

"Not a plan, a dream."

"Of mine, too," Maggie said, thrilled.

Chapter Thirteen

Noah, After

TRIAL, DAY 4

"Hi," Noah said, as Thomas entered the attorney's conference room carrying a brown bag that filled the air with the aroma of French fries.

"You're about to have the best cheesesteak in the jurisdiction." Thomas set the bag on the table and unpacked Cokes, French fries, and cheesesteaks wrapped in greasy waxed paper.

"Thanks." Noah slid his share over and unwrapped the warm sandwich with his free hand, since the other one was handcuffed to his stainless-steel chair, which was bolted to the floor, like the table. The attorneys' conference room was a secured room near the courtroom, where they went for breaks or lunch, usually shorter than bullpen stays.

"Where do you stand on the best cheesesteak in town?" Thomas sat down and opened the cheesesteak, releasing a steamy cloud. "Pat's v. Geno's?"

"I'm a Geno's guy. You?"

"Pat's."

"Tourist."

"Wannabe."

"Can we still be friends?"

"We never were friends." Thomas smiled, taking the tinfoil top off the French fries. "Also Jim's Steaks on South is awesome."

"Agree."

"And Sammy's in West Philly, where the white people never go."

"I never go," Noah said, and they laughed.

Thomas slid his phone from his pocket, placed it on the table, and took a massive bite of his cheesesteak, tilting his head to the side, the way Noah's father used to. It brought back a warm feeling that Noah hadn't had in years. Jonah Alderman had been a bricklayer, a stoic Pennsylvania Dutchman. The only time Noah had seen him cry was with happiness, the day Noah graduated from college.

"So how do you think it's going?" Noah took a bite of his sandwich, which tasted delicious.

"It's going," Thomas answered, chewing away.

"I want to testify."

"You'll get killed up there." Thomas took another big bite, turning his head again.

"I'm ready. We went over and over it. I'm good to go."

"I prepared you, but you're not bulletproof. And she can't wait for me to put you up there. She'll eat you alive." Thomas squirted ketchup on the French fries.

"But we don't have anything else." Noah finished the first half of his cheesesteak, wolfing it down.

"They have the burden of proving their case beyond a reasonable doubt, and I hurt their witnesses on cross. That's the way we're going to do it." Thomas picked up some French fries.

"But we need witnesses."

"No, we don't, I told you. I've won on the burden plenty of times. I always say it, 'bank on the burden.' I tell my associates, 'bank on the burden.' My secretary even put it in a needlepoint pillow." Thomas chewed away. "It's not like on TV, Noah. Most defendants don't have witnesses unless they're alibi witnesses. And there are very few character witnesses, which are never effective. Juries discount them. Every time I see them on the witness list, I think, that's not a witness list, it's a witless list."

"Lawyer humor."

"Hey, it's all I got."

"So put me up. We've rehearsed it."

Thomas cringed. "We didn't *rehearse*. We *prepared*."

"What's the difference? Rehearsed, prepared? Coached, studied—"

"*Never* say coach. I didn't *coach* you. I *prepared* you."

"Whatever." Noah straightened as much as he could with one hand cuffed to the chair. "I'm going to testify on my own behalf. I'm good to go."

"We've been over this."

"But we never resolved it. Now, we have to. I'm going up there. You take me through the direct examination we *prepared*, then I can deal with Linda on cross."

Thomas shook his head, exhaling a heavy sigh that expanded his broad chest. "What's your blood type?"

"B negative. Why?"

"Write it on your boots. You're gonna need a transfusion." Thomas's phone pinged with a text alert, and he swiped the screen. "Oh, yes! We caught a break. Isn't this your wife? My paralegal spotted her."

"Where?" Noah leaned over, and Thomas passed the phone across the table. On the screen was a photo of Maggie, sitting in the driver's seat of her car, her head turned away like she was on the phone.

"She's in the garage across the street, right now." Thomas shifted forward, urgent. "Noah, I should put her on the stand. She's already on our witness list. She's already been served with a subpoena. She can't be forced to testify against you, but she can for you."

"No," Noah answered, firmly. "She wouldn't be a good witness for us anyway. She hates me now."

"I can *make* her into a good witness for us. I could get her to say that she isn't totally sure you did it. I could get her to say what a great guy you are, a good husband and father. She thought that once, and I know I could get her to say it. That would be a home run!"

"You just said they discount character witnesses. She's my wife."

"But she's also the *mother*. All the difference in the world. If she said she didn't think you did it, you could walk out of here a free man. Noah, please!"

"But Linda would get to cross-examine her, right?"

"Yes."

"Then the answer is no." Noah felt his gut clench. "You're worried about how *I'm* going to handle the cross-examination, how do you think *she's* going to handle it? Anna was her *daughter,* Thomas. She *loved* her. And she *loved* me." He looked down at the photo of Maggie with a pang. He'd been inside that car so many times. She called it her office on wheels. She kept everything in the side doors, gum, napkins, perfume, and moisturizer. He'd even caught her putting Cetaphil lotion on her legs at a stoplight. They'd laughed and laughed. It hurt to see her, even in the photo. "What's she doing?"

"Who knows?" Thomas glanced at the wall clock. "Dennis is waiting to hear from me. He can escort her over. We can even send over a deputy if need be."

Noah looked up, recoiling. "You're out of your mind if you think I'd let you—"

"Maybe she wants to testify, you never know." Thomas threw up his hands in frustration. "She's here, isn't she?"

"That's not why she came."

Thomas's phone pinged again, another text coming in, and reflexively, Noah swiped the screen to see it. It was a second photo, taken from a different vantage point. The view was of Maggie's car through the windshield, and Noah realized what Maggie was doing inside the car. She wasn't on the phone at all. She was crying. The realization stabbed like a knife. Noah had done this to her. He had ruined her life.

"Thomas, call your paralegal off. Tell him to stop taking pictures of my wife. She deserves her privacy." Noah sent Thomas's phone skidding back across the table. "Put me up. She wants to see me testify. She wants to hear what I'll say."

"If she returned my effing calls, I'd tell her!"

"She wants to hear it from me, in court. That's why she's here." Noah knew it was true. "Put me up or you're fired."

"Noah, really?"

"It's the least I can do for her."

Chapter Fourteen

Maggie, Before

Maggie knocked on the front door, buoyed by her meeting with Ellen. She was one step closer to taking Anna home with her, with the last hurdle to go. **James R. Huntley, Esquire,** read a brass plaque affixed to a distinctive clapboard house, painted a darkly dramatic eggplant color, its shutters and front door enameled black. Amber lights glowed from within, through more beautiful colonial windows, each bubble in the glass attesting to its authenticity. Congreve was Puritan Heaven.

The front door opened, and a portly silhouette stood in the threshold, extending a hand. "You must be Maggie, Anna's mom. Come in."

"Thank you, Mr. Huntley."

"Please, call me James." James guided Maggie inside, shutting the door behind her. "I see the resemblance."

"Thanks." Maggie smiled.

"Let me take your coat, please." James reached for Maggie's coat and hung it on a brass coatrack in the entrance hall, which had wafer-thin Oriental rugs, mahogany Chippendale chairs against the walls, and Currier & Ives prints above the wainscoting, their pastel hues colorized in an old-timey way.

"Can I get you coffee or tea? I'm addicted to green tea these days."

"No, thanks, I just had coffee." Maggie had stopped in town at a drive-through Starbucks.

"Follow me." James lumbered ahead of her into his office, his oxford shirt creased in back, which he had on with baggy suitpants and a rep tie. He waved a meaty hand at a Windsor chair across from his cluttered desk, and they both sat down. Another lovely Oriental rug covered the floor, and more Currier & Ives prints lined the eggshell walls next to glass-covered bookshelves containing the Internal Revenue Code, copies of *Trusts & Estates* magazine, and the Heckerling Institute on Estate Planning. The lighting was soft and elegant, shed by lamps with crystal bases.

"Thanks for seeing me on such short notice," Maggie said, setting her purse down.

"Not a problem. Anna told me she would be contacting you." James frowned, tenting his fingers on the desk. "Of course, I was troubled by what she'd been told about abuse by you. However, I read the custody order and supporting documents you emailed me, and they contained no reference to physical abuse or neglect. I see the sole reason for your losing custody was your postpartum disorder. They allayed my fear about physical abuse."

"Yes," Maggie said, relieved. "I never abused her, I swear."

James frowned. "My condolences on the passing of her father Florian. I never met him, by the way. He hired my partner, who has since retired. When I went solo, Florian retained me to stay with Anna's matter."

"How often did you see her? I don't really know how this works or what you do vis-à-vis Anna."

"Allow me to explain. Anna's father created a trust for her benefit, and I am in charge of the trust." James opened his hands. "Trusts and estates law can be technical, and I'm not one of those lawyers who likes to keep the mystery. So I'll break this down for you."

"Great." Maggie settled back, happy to listen.

"I meet with Anna generally once a year, and I'm a trustee. I am responsible for managing the trust assets, keeping accounts and other necessary records, filing income tax returns, and following the terms that Florian established in making distributions to Anna. I have discretion to use the trust assets for Anna's health, education, and support."

"So you pay her bills?"

"Yes. I'll contact Congreve Academy to inform them that she will not be finishing this semester. I'll ask for a refund of the second semester tuition, but I may have to settle for prorating it. The tuition for boarders is $65,000."

"Wow."

"You get what you pay for. I'm not cheap, either." James smiled. His teeth were perfect, if tea-stained. "By the way, the trust pays my fees, too. But your issue isn't about the trust, it's about custody. I reviewed the documents that you emailed me, and your parental rights to her have not been terminated. In other words, your postpartum disorder rendered you unfit for custodial purposes at that point in time, but did not terminate your legal rights as her mother."

"I thought so," Maggie said, encouraged.

"The law in Maine, and undoubtedly jurisdictions including Pennsylvania, is that with the death of Anna's father, her legal and physical custody go to you. Nevertheless, I think you should go to family court in Pennsylvania and ask them to award you custody."

"Do I have to do that before I take her?"

"No. It's just a formality. You have the absolute right to make legal decisions about her future. Anna is not legally emancipated, so until she's eighteen years old, she's under your legal authority. You have the authority to take her, and I think that is reasonable and certainly desirable in the circumstances."

"Great!" Maggie felt like cheering, but didn't.

"Excellent." James opened a manila folder on his desk, thick with correspondence. "Now let me explain something about the trust. A trust is simply a fund. I can continue to make expenditures from the fund, or trust, on Anna's behalf until she's eighteen. I don't think you need to retain a different lawyer in Pennsylvania. I can do that from here, easily. Continuity of representation benefits Anna, and she would like me to remain with her after she moves."

"Okay, I'm fine with you staying as the trustee."

"Thank you. I will copy and send you these documents." James gestured at the folder. "The trust will support Anna in the future, even when she lives at your home. Her trust pays for her expenses or ones that you incur on her behalf. Food, clothing, books, mani and pedi, hair, gym membership, or if she buys a car, which she didn't need here. She wants one, she's mentioned that to me already. She has a valid driver's license here because Congreve has driver's ed. You'll have to check the driving laws in Pennsylvania."

"Okay," Maggie said, not having thought that far ahead.

"Anna will go to college, and Pennsylvania law is unsettled as to a parent's obligation to pay her tuition. Not a problem in her case. There's more than enough money in the trust to cover her tuition and related expenses."

"How much money is in the trust?"

"Florian started the trust, but over time, the investment manager we hired, Dave Cummings at Kennebunk Investors, has invested it in curated blue-chip stocks. The trust is probably worth three mil, which Anna may withdraw at eighteen, but we need to discuss that."

"Three million dollars?" Maggie had thought it would be a lot, but that was higher than she thought.

"In addition, more money will be added to the trust because of her father's passing. I've been on the phone back and forth with the French lawyers over the past month or so. Anna is her father's only heir, but I think it's very unwise for her to receive the full amount so young."

"Oh, right." Maggie should've thought of it before. Florian had sold his business for $30 million, way back when.

"Anna stands to inherit a great deal of money from her father. According to the French lawyers, his estate is worth almost $50 million after taxes and expenses."

"What?" Maggie gasped. "Are you telling me she's going to get $50 million when she turns eighteen?"

"Yes, and that's bad news, believe it or not." James's expression soured, his jowls draping around a downturned mouth. "I tried to tell Florian that, but it was difficult to get him to return my calls or emails."

"But $50 million? That's a fortune!"

"You seem surprised."

"I am." Maggie felt nonplussed. "This is news to me."

"But you had to know that your ex-husband would provide for her in his will, didn't you?" James raised his palm. "Please, don't be offended. I'm not accusing you of an ulterior motive, by the way. Your intentions are demonstrably good."

"Thanks, I just didn't think that far ahead. I was so excited about reuniting with her, and I didn't know she'd want to come live with me, so her money was academic. I hadn't thought about it."

"So we're clear, Anna is a wealthy young girl, and her money is hers, not yours or your husband's."

"Of course I understand that." Maggie tried to process the information. Anna had way more money than she and Noah, which seemed topsy-turvy.

"By the way, I had nothing to do with the drafting of the will or the trust. It's completely valid here, however."

"Okay." Maggie collected her thoughts. "So what happens to that money now? It stays somewhere?"

"Yes, it does, and it will take months until we transfer it into the trust. But I would not have provided for Anna to receive the entire sum at eighteen. It's like winning the lottery, too young. Or let's say she meets a boy and he finds out she's coming into money. She could be taken advantage of. I've seen it happen." James shuddered. "When I set up an estate, I provide that the first disbursement isn't until age twenty-five and amounts are transferred every five years, spreading them out as much as possible."

"Can we do it that way now?" Maggie was trying to think ahead.

"Yes, but not yet. We have no right to change the terms of the trust unless the trust says so, which it does not. But when Anna turns eighteen, she has the legal ability to create a trust for herself and she can change the terms of her trust. I have already advised her to do so, so that the disbursements begin when she is twenty-five and occur at the intervals I suggest."

"What did she say when you suggested that to her?"

"She agreed. She usually does. She's prudent with money. I had already begun to set up a schedule for disbursements and draft the appropriate papers. She doesn't turn eighteen until next March, so we have time to sort this out, and probate takes ages for an estate this size, especially one that's international."

"That's good."

"I'll work in connection with her and you, going forward. So you and I will be in good touch." James rose, smoothing down his tie.

"Thanks." Maggie stood up, too. "I'm just happy that she's back in my life."

"Of course you are, and she must be, too. Every girl needs a mother, doesn't she?"

Chapter Fifteen

Noah, After
TRIAL, DAY 5

Noah braced himself as Linda strode toward him to begin her cross-examination. He hadn't seen Maggie enter the courtroom during his direct examination, which worried him. He hated to remember her crying in the car. He had done well on direct and had testified for three hours, which they had timed in rehearsal. Thomas believed it was the perfect length for testimony, since the attention spans of most jurors were conditioned by watching movies.

Linda squared off against the witness stand. "Dr. Alderman, my name is Linda Swain-Pettit, and I represent the Commonwealth of Pennsylvania. I have a few questions for you."

"Understood." Noah told himself to remain calm, that he could handle her. He and Thomas had rehearsed cross-examination, going over every possible question she could throw at him. Noah had his story down pat and he had just told it on direct, so all he had to do was not undermine himself. Thomas has drilled into him, *Answer only the question. Don't volunteer or explain.*

"Let's begin with Commonwealth Exhibit 26." Linda flipped through exhibits leaning against the dais, pulled out an enlarged photo of Anna, and set it on an easel. Anna looked beautiful in the photo, which Noah had taken from the shoulders up, her long hair grazing her lovely neck, her blue eyes cool, her smile oddly sly. Now, he knew why. Too late.

"Dr. Alderman, you took this photo of Anna during a family vacation at Stone Harbor, isn't that correct?"

"No, not a vacation *per se*. We went down the shore for a day."

"*Per se?*" Linda smirked. "Is that *Latin?*"

"Yes. It means 'as such.'"

"I know what it means. My question is, you took this photo, didn't you?"

"Yes." Noah felt off-balance. One of the jurors chuckled. Thomas told him he was a know-it-all, and it was true. Noah used to think he knew it all. Before.

"Dr. Alderman, please direct your attention to the screen while I show you Commonwealth Exhibit 15, and ask, you took this photograph of Anna, too, didn't you?"

"Yes," Noah answered, while the screen came to life with a picture of Anna in a flowered bikini, posing at the water's edge. Even in the sexy bathing suit, she looked sweet, innocent, and modest. None of these were qualities she possessed, but she had everybody fooled.

"Please keep your attention on the screen while I show you *ten* more photos of Anna, Commonwealth Exhibits 16 through 25, and ask, you took them as well, did you not?"

"Yes," Noah answered, as the series flipped by, of Anna striking different poses in the bathing suit at the water's edge. The jurors craned their necks, shifting in their seats.

"Dr. Alderman, your wife and son were with you at the beach that day, weren't they?"

"Yes."

"You didn't take any pictures of your wife, did you?"

"No." Noah didn't explain because Thomas had told him not to volunteer. Maggie didn't like to have her picture taken because she always felt fat. He disagreed, but photographs never captured the liveliness in her, the spirit or humor in her eyes. The first time he met her, he thought to himself, *she has so much life in her, her eyes actually dance.*

"You didn't take a picture of your son that day, did you?"

"No." Noah thought back. Caleb had never stood still for a minute at the beach, and they'd been busy making sandcastles and finding sand crabs. The water had been cold, but Caleb had gone in anyway. Noah had wrapped him in a SpongeBob towel, his knobby shoulders shivering, his lips blue from a snow-cone. His perfect imperfect son.

"Your wife wasn't present when you took these photos of Anna, was she?"

"No." Noah didn't explain. The explanation would only sound worse. He could see Thomas's eyes flare, warning him off.

"Where was your wife while you were taking these photos?"

"She had taken my son Caleb to get lunch."

"Isn't it true that you waited until they had gone to ask Anna to pose for you in her bathing suit?"

"No, that's not true." Noah had to say something. He had taken the stand for a reason. "Anna asked me to take those pictures. It wasn't my idea, it was hers. She wanted them for Facebook. She couldn't decide which one to use, that's why there were so many."

Linda's eyes flared in disbelief. "Dr. Alderman, are you trying to tell us that Anna, a teenager, couldn't take a *selfie*?"

"No."

"If Anna asked you to take the photos, why didn't she give you her phone to take them?"

Noah realized the answer, but couldn't say it. Thomas would kill him. "I don't know."

"But you never sent Anna the photos so she could post them, did you? I can show you your phone, if you need your recollection refreshed." Linda gestured at the evidence table, where exhibits were bagged and tagged.

"No, I never did. I must have forgotten to." Noah got the implication. The fact that he hadn't sent them made it look as if Anna hadn't asked him to take them.

"Dr. Alderman, didn't there come a time when you became aware that Anna was the sole heiress to a 50-million-dollar fortune?"

"Yes."

"You were very friendly to Anna when she moved in, weren't you?"

"Yes." Noah could see that Linda was making a connection for the jury, but he had to fight back. "I was trying to be a good stepfather, that's all."

"Isn't it true that you offered to give Anna a driving lesson?"

"Yes."

"Isn't it also true that she already knew how to drive?"

"Yes." Noah hated not defending himself. The truth was, Maggie had wanted him to take Anna out so they could get to know each other.

"Dr. Alderman, isn't it true that you found out about Anna's vast wealth before you offered to take her on a driving lesson?"

"Yes." Noah heard the jury rustling.

"During the driving lesson, it was just you and Anna, alone in the car, isn't that correct?"

Noah couldn't keep it in any longer. "Yes, but that doesn't mean anything. It's normal."

Linda pursed her lips. "Dr. Alderman, Anna was young, beautiful, and rich, wasn't she?"

"Yes."

"Isn't it true that as soon as you met Anna, you decided to make sexual advances on her?"

"No."

"But you were attracted to Anna, were you not?"

"No." Noah had to lie.

"You weren't attracted to this lovely young woman, whom you took so many photos of, in a bathing suit?"

"No."

"Dr. Alderman, didn't you attempt to seduce Anna?"

"No, I was a married man, and we had a great marriage before—" Noah stopped himself, mid-sentence. It wouldn't sound right. It would sound terrible.

"Before what?"

"Before. Just before."

Linda's eyes bored holes into him. "Before *what*, Dr. Alderman? Answer the question."

"Before all this happened." Noah's throat went dry.

"But Anna is what happened, isn't that true?"

"No."

Linda pursed her lips. "Isn't it true that Anna moved into your home on Saturday, April 22?"

"Yes."

"And she was murdered on Wednesday, May 10, only a few weeks later?"

"Yes."

"Dr. Alderman, your marriage was good before Anna moved in, wasn't it?"

"Yes."

"Please direct your attention to Commonwealth Exhibit 35 on the screen." Linda was about to signal to her paralegal when Thomas stood up.

"Objection, Your Honor. I have a running objection to the admission of the Commonwealth Exhibit 35 under Pennsylvania Rules of Evidence 404. Under Rule 404, evidence of prior crimes, wrongs, or other acts are inadmissible and unduly prejudice the jury."

Linda whirled around to the judge. "Your Honor, Commonwealth Exhibit 35 is admissible under 404(b) as a permitted use, in that it tends to prove motive and intent. Defense counsel's argument has been rejected by the Superior Court in *Commonwealth v. Drumheller* and more recently in *Commonwealth v. Ivy*. The PFA Petition is certainly relevant to the case at bar, and not only that, is also admissible under the *res gestae* exception because it forms the history of this matter."

Judge Gardner pursed his lips. "I'll overrule the objection. Commonwealth Exhibit 35 is admissible."

"Thank you, Your Honor." Thomas sat down heavily.

"Yes, thank you, Your Honor." Linda signaled the paralegal, then turned to face Noah, and the screen changed to a document he knew very well, unfortunately.

PETITION FOR PROTECTION FROM ABUSE, read the top, and under that was a form with boxes for Plaintiff and Defendant, which had been filled out Anna Desroches and Noah Alderman, in Anna's handwriting, and under that was a bolded **CAUTION**, with boxes for **Weapon Involved, Weapon Present on the Property, or Weapon Requested Relinquished**, the only boxes that remained mercifully unchecked.

"Dr. Alderman, this is a Petition for a Protection From Abuse filed against you in the Common Pleas Court of Montgomery County on May 8, is it not?"

"Yes." Noah nodded.

"In Pennsylvania, a Protection From Abuse order, commonly referred to as a PFA, is sought by victims of sexual abuse when they are trying to protect themselves from their victimizer, isn't that correct?"

"Yes."

"Dr. Alderman, who filed the Petition against you?"

"Anna."

Linda paused, lifting an eyebrow. "Isn't it true that this Petition was filed only seventeen days after Anna had moved in?"

"Yes."

"And isn't it also true that this Petition alleged that you attempted to sexually abuse Anna on two separate occasions, on April 27, in a car during her driving lesson, and on May 6, in a bathroom?"

"Yes."

"Dr. Alderman, aren't these the specific allegations regarding the two occasions?" Linda signaled to her paralegal, and the screen changed.

> **Set forth the facts of the most recent incident of abuse, including date, time, and place, and describe in detail what happened including any physical or sexual abuse, threats, injury, incidence of stalking, medical treatment sought, and/or calls to law enforcement.**

My stepfather Noah Alderman tried to kiss and fondle me in a powder room at home on Saturday, May 6, at about 10:45 pm.

If the Defendant has committed prior acts of abuse against plaintiff and/or minor children, please describe these prior incidents, including any threats, injuries, or incidents of stalking, and indicate approximately when such acts of abuse occurred.

My stepfather Noah Alderman put his hand under my dress during a driving lesson on Thursday, April 27, at about 8:30 pm.

Noah read with a sinking heart. "Yes."

"Anna testified in support of her allegations at an emergency PFA hearing on May 8, did she not?"

"Yes."

"And you testified as well and denied those allegations at the hearing, didn't you?"

"Yes."

Linda's dark eyes glittered. "Is it *normal* for a stepfather to be called to testify at a PFA hearing regarding sexual abuse against his step-daughter?"

"No."

"Is it *normal* for a stepfather to make sexual advances against his stepdaughter?"

"No," Noah answered, hiding his dismay.

"Dr. Alderman, isn't it true that you tried to seduce Anna but she spurned your advances?"

"No."

"But after Anna filed for a PFA, your wife asked you to leave the home, did she not?"

"Yes."

"So what you meant earlier in your answer was 'before Anna,' wasn't it?"

"Yes." Noah felt his throat go dry. He was off to a bad start.

"Dr. Alderman, isn't it true that Anna was murdered only two days after she filed the Petition for a PFA against you?"

"Yes," Noah had to admit, and still on the screen was the PFA petition, next to the beautiful photo of Anna on the easel. He knew this was all calculated, an opening tableau against him.

"Dr. Alderman, let's move to the night in question, May 10, shall we?"

Noah took a deep breath.

Chapter Sixteen

Maggie, Before

Maggie climbed the staircase at the Congreve Inn, and Anna rolled her overnight bag behind her. Maggie had been delighted that Anna had decided to spend the night with her rather than in the dorm, and they had already packed the car. They reached the door, and Maggie got out her key. "Anna, I'm starved, aren't you? How about we get room service?"

"Sweet." Anna lugged the roller bag onto the landing. "The room service here is supposed to be great. They make eggplant parm with local cheeses. All the Parker parents stay here."

"Well, you're not a Parker anymore." Maggie entered the room and flicked the light switch, which illuminated old-fashioned crystal lamps on the night tables. The hotel room had two queen-size beds with dotted-Swiss canopies, and chintz chairs matched the faded flower wallpaper. The far wall had a long panel of windows flanked by chintz curtains, and the effect was charming.

Anna rolled her bag inside. "Canopy beds! I love those."

"Make yourself comfortable, and I'll order us two eggplant parms. How about a salad to go with?"

"Great!" Anna shed her coat and sat down on one of the beds.

"Let's have dessert, too." Maggie crossed to the dresser, which had a printed menu under glass. "The choices are lemon poppyseed cake, chocolate cake, bread pudding—"

"Bread pudding!"

"Carbs, coming right up!" Maggie loved bread pudding, too. She was going off her diet, but it was a special occasion. *It's a girl!* she thought, but didn't say.

"Want to watch a movie? We can get a free one." Anna picked up the remote, turned on the TV atop the dresser, and flipped through the choices. "It's not a school night, and anyway, I'm out of school."

"Sure." Maggie pressed a button on the phone for room service. "I'll look into getting you registered at Lower Merion on Monday. I don't want you to lose too much time."

"I'll be the new girl." Anna frowned, worried.

"You'll do fine." Maggie told room service the order, then hung up. "My mother always said, 'When one door closes, another one opens.'"

"My grandmother said that?" Anna blinked, with a smile.

"Also 'don't sing at the table' and 'don't put so much on your fork.'" Maggie hadn't thought of that in ages. Having Anna was summoning those memories, and Maggie felt the spirit of her mother with her, sharing her happiness.

"What was her name?"

"Cecilia Theresa Macari Ippoliti. Sounds like an entrée right?"

Anna laughed. "Can I see pictures of her when we get home?"

Home. "Sure." Maggie felt her heart swell. "Now find us a movie, and we'll start our slumber party."

"How about this one?" Anna highlighted *Top Gun* on the screen. "I always wanted to see this."

"If you haven't seen *Top Gun*, your education is incomplete."

"Ha! Suck it, Congreve!" Anna clicked for the movie.

"Let's flop around until they feed us." Maggie kicked off her shoes and plopped into the center of her bed.

"Here we go." Anna sat on her bed, and the movie credits started, playing the *thumpa-thumpa* theme music.

"Turn it up, girl! You need the full effect."

"For real?" Anna glanced back, shyly.

"Yes, crank that thing!"

"Ha!" Anna did, moderately, then lay back in her pillows and pointed at the dotted-Swiss canopy. "Those dots are like stars in a white sky. Or snow in a storm."

Maggie looked up, thinking Anna was right. "That's poetic. Do you like poetry?"

"Yes. Do you?"

"Yes, but I don't always understand it."

"Me neither, but I write it anyway. I tried to get on *The Zephyr*, that's the poetry magazine at Congreve, but I didn't make it. I showed some of my poems to Ellen."

"I'd love to see them, someday."

"Okay, oh, we're missing the movie." Anna shifted up in bed, watching the TV, and Maggie looked over at the screen, an aerial battle between fighter jets. Suddenly she remembered that *Top Gun* was a movie about a pilot and one of the pilots died. She kicked herself, wondering how Anna would react to the movie, given Florian's death.

"Anna, maybe we should watch a love story or something."

"No, this is so cool," Anna shot back, riveted to the screen. "Who are the bad guys they're shooting at?"

"It's about a jet-fighter school. They're exercises." Maggie shifted up in the pillows, worrying. Anna was biting her nails, engrossed by the aerial battle in which a pilot named Cougar had a panic attack.

"Way to go, Maverick!"

"Tom saves the day." Maggie got more nervous as the next scene came on, Maverick getting chewed out with his partner Goose, the pilot who died.

"I get it. He wants to be number one. Because testosterone."

Maggie kept her eye on Goose. "Anna, I'm still wondering if we should watch a different movie. This has sad parts. It's a movie about pilots."

Anna looked over, getting the message. "I'll be okay. I'm not a little kid."

"Okay, good," Maggie said, but she worried as the movie progressed, one iconic scene after the next. Room service arrived, filling the air with the delicious aromas of tomato and mozzarella, but Anna never took her eyes from the screen as she set her tray on the bed.

"Jester seems like a jerk." Anna sipped her soda, and another aerial battle came on.

"He is." Maggie took a bite of her eggplant parm. Anna seemed to be having fun, giggling when the scene changed to beach volleyball.

"These guys have sick bodies!" Anna ate hungrily, and so did Maggie, and they both finished their meals, wisecracking through the movie, then falling uncomfortably silent when the love scene came on. Maggie couldn't believe how dumb she had been to pick a movie with sex *and* death for her first night with her daughter. The scene finished, then inevitably, the fatal aerial battle filled the screen.

"Oh no." Anna watched the fighter jet whirl in the sky, corkscrewing downward, losing altitude. The scene was so realistic that even Maggie imagined Florian during his crash, wondering what his last moments had been like as their plane hurtled toward earth.

"Oh no!" Anna gasped as Goose ejected, then limp and lifeless, parachuted down toward the sea. Anna turned to Maggie, stricken. Her lips parted, and her blue eyes brimmed.

"Anna, I'm so sorry." Maggie got up quickly, went to Anna, and hugged her as she burst into tears.

"I know . . . it's only a movie . . . but . . ."

"It's okay, honey," Maggie said, holding Anna close and rubbing her back as sobs wracked her body. Maggie could feel all of Anna's sorrow as the girl cried hard, and Maggie made a vow that she'd never let Anna go again.

No matter what.

Chapter Seventeen

Noah, After

TRIAL, DAY 5

Noah's gaze swept the gallery, but Maggie still hadn't appeared. He felt relieved that she would be spared his testimony.

Linda stood in front of the witness stand, her legs planted like a human sawhorse. "Dr. Alderman, let's return to the night Anna was murdered. You testified on direct that you left work at 6:30 P.M., did you not?"

"Yes."

"You drove directly to the gym, did you not?"

"Yes."

"It took you approximately twenty minutes to get to the gym, isn't that correct?"

"Yes, that's correct."

"You had your cell phone with you, didn't you?"

"Yes."

"You didn't have any phone conversations on the way to the gym, did you?"

"No, I didn't."

"Did you attempt to have any telephone conversations on the way to the gym?"

"Yes, I attempted to call my wife. Rather, I called her, attempting to speak with her."

Linda smiled slightly. "You're a precise man, aren't you?"

Noah assumed the question was rhetorical. He was a precise man, as a pediatric allergist. He didn't know anybody who wanted a careless doctor.

"But your wife didn't answer your call, did she, Dr. Alderman?"

"No."

"You didn't leave your wife a message, did you?"

"No."

"You weren't living with your wife at the time, were you?"

"No."

"You moved out at your wife's request, isn't that true?"

"Yes." Noah remembered every minute, but even when it was happening, he'd thought he could turn it around. He knew Maggie loved him the way he loved her, deep inside. He knew her love was still there, hunkering down through a bad spell, the way love does in marriage. Embedded, sinking into your very bones. Changing who you are forever, reconfiguring your very DNA. Noah was a different man, after Maggie.

Linda cocked her coiffed head. "So you arrived at the gym at approximately 6:50, isn't that correct?"

"Yes, it is."

"And you parked in the lot behind the gym, isn't that correct?"

"Yes." Noah had been over this with Thomas, who had warned him it was treacherous territory.

"Dr. Alderman, let me show you an item marked Commonwealth Exhibit 42." Linda set Noah's iPhone in front of him, which the police had confiscated the night of Anna's murder. He hadn't seen it since then, and it struck him as an artifact of his former life, with its calendars, photos, pollen trackers, and playlists full of classical music.

Linda gestured at the phone. "Please examine it to make sure it's yours. It's fully charged."

Noah picked up the phone and pressed the home button, which brought the screen to life with a photo of a beaming Maggie and Caleb. The speech pathologist had given Caleb a homemade certificate and graduation cap to mark his progress.

"Isn't that your phone?"

"Yes." Noah set it down. It was his old life, gone as the Jurassic. Extinct.

"Please scroll to your text function, while I summon Commonwealth Exhibit 43 to the screen."

Thomas rose quickly. "Objection, Your Honor. I'm renewing my objection, made during the prosecution's case, that the text message is inadmissible because it is not properly authenticated under *Commonwealth v. Koch* and is hearsay."

Linda faced Judge Gardner. "Your Honor, as before, *Koch* does not preclude the admission of this text. The Superior Court and *Koch* make clear that texts can be authenticated by circumstances, such as those present, where others do not routinely use the phone and the phone was not kept in an accessible place. And it is not hearsay because it is not being admitted to prove the truth of the matter asserted."

Judge Gardner looked down at Noah. "Dr. Alderman, did others routinely use your phone with your permission?"

"No, Your Honor."

"Thank you." Judge Gardner nodded. "The objection is overruled, and the text is admissible."

Thomas sat down heavily, and Linda signaled her paralegal. Onto the screen flashed a text, grossly enlarged:

> Anna, will you meet me at my house @915 tonight? I'm sorry
> and I want to work this out. Please don't tell your mother.

"Dr. Alderman, isn't this the last text on your phone?"

"Yes, it is."

"And that text was sent on May 10, the night Anna was murdered, was it not?"

"Yes."

"The text was sent at 6:55 P.M., the night Anna was murdered, was it not?"

"Yes."

"And the name at the top of the screen is Anna, is it not, signifying the text was sent to Anna?"

"Yes."

"You didn't receive an answer to this text, did you?"

"No."

"Let me show you Commonwealth Exhibit 44, which has already been admitted and is a copy of the records from Anna's iPhone." Linda signaled her paralegal, and the screen showed Anna's text history. "Dr. Alderman, can you see that it shows that Anna received the text from your phone approximately one minute after it was sent?"

"Yes."

Linda signaled the paralegal, who reverted to the previous screen showing the text. "Dr. Alderman, didn't you send this text to Anna in order to lure her to your home so you could make another sexual advance on her?"

"No."

"But doesn't the text read, 'Anna, will you meet me at my house at 9:15?'"

"Yes."

Linda frowned. "I'll ask you again, didn't you send this text to Anna in order to get her to your home?"

"No." Noah blinked, waiting for the next question. He couldn't see Thomas because Linda was standing in front of him, blocking his view. He suspected she was doing it intentionally.

"Then what did you mean when you texted Anna, 'Anna, will you meet me at my house at 9:15?'"

"I didn't send this text. It came from my phone, but I didn't send it."

"*Pardon* me?" Linda's mouth dropped open. Spectators in the gallery looked surprised, and the courtroom sketch artist started scribbling. Thomas hadn't wanted him to go here, but he had no choice.

Maggie still was nowhere in sight.

Chapter Eighteen

Maggie, Before

Maggie drove home with Anna, who looked fresh and pretty with her hair in a ponytail. She had on a cute blue-checked sundress that matched her eyes, with a jeans jacket. Maggie had never been happier. She never would've believed she was driving home with her daughter.

"This is the street," Maggie chirped like a tour guide. "Merion Avenue."

"Oh, it's so nice! And there's so many trees."

"Wait'll you see my garden."

Anna looked over with a smile. "I always wanted to learn how to garden."

"Me too," Maggie said, and they both laughed. She steered downhill toward the house, passing the old stone homes and massive oak trees. Her neighbors were clipping hedges, mulching beds, and unloading SUVs. None of them knew she had a daughter, but they would find out soon enough.

"Is our house on the right or the left side?"

Our house. "The left. There, with the yellow shutters."

"And let me give you the heads-up about something. Caleb has apraxia, which means that his speech might sound a little slow or halting."

"Oh." Anna looked over. "I saw something about that on your Facebook page. When he got that award."

"Right." Maggie thought back to the ceremony, which their speech pathologist had organized. "He's doing really well. Just be patient with him. He can be self-conscious around new people."

"Of course, no problem."

"Thanks." Maggie steered the packed Subaru into her driveway, noticing the front door opening. She had texted Noah when they had landed at the airport, and he'd texted back his characteristic **OK**.

"What a nice house!" Anna looked around.

"There's the boys." Maggie cut the ignition as Noah and Caleb came out of the house. "Hey guys, come meet Anna!"

"Welcome home, ladies!" Noah hustled toward them with a huge grin, and Maggie got out of the car, seeing as Anna must, the perfect suburban stepdad in a white polo and pressed khakis, like a Dockers ad, but sexy.

Noah gave Maggie a big hug. "Babe, I'm so happy! This is a great day!"

"Isn't it?" Maggie let him go, gesturing to Anna. "Noah, meet Anna. Anna, Noah and Caleb."

"Anna, welcome, it's wonderful to meet you!" Noah extended a hand, and Anna shook it with a grin.

"Thank you so much for having me."

"Mag, we got pizza!" Caleb shouted, wrapping his skinny arms around her. "It's a surprise!"

"Not anymore." Noah laughed.

"Great idea!" Maggie hugged Caleb back, realizing she hadn't had a chance to prepare him to meet Anna. "Caleb, this is Anna, my daughter. I told you about her. She's going to live with us."

"Anna, do you like pizza?" Caleb looked up at her, with a shy smile.

"Yes, pizza is my favorite." Anna grinned down at him.

"What toppings do you like?" Caleb asked, his speech remarkably smooth.

"I like it plain."

"Me, *too!*" Caleb practically exploded with happiness, and Maggie and Noah exchanged looks. Maggie could tell that Noah had drilled Caleb on the sentences, which was another trick they'd learned, anticipating phrases and sentences that would be needed with new people. Plus, Caleb loved pizza, which was undoubtedly why Noah had ordered some to be delivered. Maggie felt a pang of gratitude for her husband and touched his arm.

Noah put his arm around Maggie. "Come inside, we have something to show you."

"That's a secret!" Caleb ran ahead toward the front door, pumping his arms, and Maggie knew he was showing off for Anna, which she thought was adorable.

"Come on in," Noah said, holding open the door, and Caleb, Anna, and Maggie trundled inside, then Noah closed the door behind them. "Caleb, let's give her a quick tour before the surprise."

"Okay." Caleb deflated.

Maggie took the lead. "This is the family room," she said, gesturing. The room was large, with a warm pine floor, a navy-patterned Karastan, and navy-plaid couches grouped in front of a fireplace with a brick surround. The ceilings were high, and the room was light and airy, owing to a panel of windows in the front and side.

"Here's the dining room, which we never use." Maggie walked them through the dining room, dominated by an Irish farm table she had bought in New Hope. It had a rustic finish and matched a pine credenza under a panel of windows on the right.

"Love the table." Anna ran a fingertip along the surface.

"Now for the kitchen." Maggie led them to the kitchen, ringed by white windowed cabinets and white-granite countertops. The back wall had a sunny southern exposure. "We added the windows over the sink so I can see the garden."

Noah interjected, "It took forever."

"Only five months." Maggie patted the kitchen island, where they ate most of their meals. It had only three stools, so she made a mental note to get another one. "And we added the island, which has bookshelves for cookbooks. How cool is that?"

"Very cool." Anna peeked at the cookbooks. "Lidia Bastianich. My Housemaster watches her TV show."

Caleb shifted his feet. "Can we show the surprise now?"

Maggie and Noah started to answer, but Anna stepped forward with a grin.

"Caleb, I want to see my surprise! Lead the way!" Anna held out her hand, and Caleb tugged her out of the kitchen toward the staircase.

"Right behind you." Maggie looked over at Noah, who put an arm around her.

"We're off to a good start," he whispered in her ear.

"I know," Maggie whispered back, and they headed toward the stairs after Anna and Caleb. Maggie and Noah reached the second floor to find Anna and Caleb in the hallway and went to them, looking inside the room. It used to be Noah's home office, but it was completely empty, and on the wall was a poster handmade by Caleb with crayoned letters that read: ANNA'S ROOM!

Maggie felt so touched. "Honey, when did you do all this?"

Noah shrugged with a smile. "Last night. Caleb and I did it together."

"Where's all the furniture?"

"In the basement. It made sense to give her my office since it has a bathroom and the train room doesn't."

Caleb ran to his poster. "Look, Anna!"

Anna burst into delighted laughter. "This is so sweet! I love my poster and room. This is twice the size of my old room at school!"

"And look!" Caleb pointed at the border of the poster, where he had drawn small beds, chairs, lamps, and Wreck-It Ralph. "This is our cat. He sleeps on my bed. That's how he is."

"Thank you." Anna grinned. "I didn't know you had a cat. I love cats!"

"Look. Your bathroom." Caleb ran to the bathroom to turn on the light switch. "I have a bathroom. We both have bathrooms."

"I have my own bathroom?" Anna caught Maggie's eye with a surprised smile. "At school, I shared with three other girls."

"Eeew!" Caleb screwed up his nose, and looking on, Maggie couldn't remember the last time she had been this happy, feeling everything come together. She owed a big hug to Noah, who had put Caleb and Anna first, which was so like him.

Anna frowned slightly. "Noah, I hope I didn't cause too much trouble."

Noah waved her off. "Not at all. We had a good time, and the basement is finished."

Maggie interjected, "This is only one of the reasons why my husband is the greatest guy in the world."

Anna's forehead eased. "Well, thank you. I really appreciate it."

Maggie asked, "Do you want to paint the walls? The white is boring, don't you think?"

"I'd love to! What color?"

"Whatever you want! We'll get the bedspread and see what you think. It's your room, so it's your decision. I can stop by the paint store and get some samples."

Caleb grabbed Anna's hand, beaming up at her. "Come see my train room!"

"Did you say training room?" Anna looked down at him with a puzzled smile.

"No! Come and see!" Caleb tugged Anna out of the room and down the hall.

"I'm glad you're happy, babe." Noah smiled down at her, moving a curl from her eye. "I love you."

"I love you too," Maggie said, meaning it more than ever.

"You got what you wanted, huh?"

"I fished my wish!" Maggie said, borrowing a line of Caleb's.

Laughter came from down the hall, and Maggie and Noah walked to the train room, where Noah and Caleb had built a setup for model trains, with a town surrounded by fake trees and a lake that Ralph used as a water dish.

"Anna, look!" Caleb twisted the dial on the transformer, switching the model locomotive to new track.

"Amazing!" Anna glanced back at Maggie with a grin.

"Isn't it great?" Maggie appreciated that Anna was being so nice about Caleb's trains. Noah had started Caleb on them to build his self-esteem, because it was a nonverbal activity.

Caleb tugged Anna's jacket. "Want to try? I can show you how. It's easy."

"Thanks." Anna accepted the box, and Maggie edged back, taking Noah with her into the hallway.

"I think he likes her, don't you?"

"Absolutely."

"Isn't she pretty?" Maggie smiled.

"She's beautiful." Noah touched Maggie's cheek. "Like her mom."

Maggie nodded happily. "She has my dimples, did you see?"

"I sure did," Noah said with a smile.

Chapter Nineteen

Noah, After

TRIAL, DAY 5

"I didn't send Anna that text," Noah repeated, firmly.

Linda motioned to the screen, which read, **Anna, will you meet me at my house @915 tonight? I'm sorry and I want to work this out. Please don't tell your mother.** "Dr. Alderman, is it seriously your testimony that you didn't send this text to Anna?"

"Yes."

"Oh, are you merely being *precise* again? Did you write the text but not send it?"

"No. I neither wrote nor sent the text."

Thomas jumped to his feet. "Your Honor, objection as to authenticity and hearsay. This is the problem that *Koch* was intended to prevent. Dr. Alderman is testifying that he is not the author of the text."

Linda faced Judge Gardner again. "Your Honor, these are two separate issues. It's clear under *Koch* and the rules of evidence that the text is authentic and it is therefore admissible. Dr. Alderman is free to claim, as he just has, that he is not its author. That does not go to its admissibility, but rather to its weight."

Judge Gardner nodded. "The objection is overruled."

Thomas sat down, and Linda turned to Noah, her eyes flashing darkly. "Dr. Alderman. I remind you that you are under oath, and ask you again, did you or did you not send this text?"

"I did not."

Linda stepped back. "If you didn't send the text, who did?"

"I don't know," Noah answered, but that was a lie. But he was trying not to get into that, per Thomas's instructions.

"Are you *really* trying to convince this jury that you did not send a text that clearly came from your own phone?"

Thomas rose. "Your Honor, objection, asked and answered. The prosecutor is badgering the witness."

Linda whirled around to face Judge Gardner, whose lined forehead had buckled with confusion. "Your Honor, cross-examination is a time-honored engine of truth—"

"The objection is overruled. Please proceed, Ms. Swain-Pettit."

"Thank you, Your Honor." Linda turned on Noah. "Dr. Alderman, are you trying to suggest that someone else sent this text from your phone?"

"I believe that's what happened."

"But didn't you just tell Judge Gardner that no one else uses your phone?"

"I told him that no one else *routinely* uses my phone."

Linda's eyes narrowed. "Was your phone out of your possession at the time this text was sent?"

"Yes."

"Where was your phone at the time this text was sent?"

"In my car, parked at the gym."

"Is it your testimony that you left your phone in the car while you went to the gym?"

"Yes."

Linda signaled to her paralegal. "Allow me to show you Commonwealth Exhibit 47, which has been previously admitted. Please take a moment to examine it."

Noah eyed the screen, which changed to an entry log at the gym, with his name next to the time he swiped in. "I've examined it."

"Dr. Alderman, this document shows that you swiped in at 7:10 P.M. on the night Anna was murdered, does it not?"

"Yes."

"You testified that the text was sent at 6:55 P.M., the night Anna was murdered, did you not?"

"Yes."

"Yet your testimony is that you did not send the text, though you had time to do so before you swiped in to the gym?"

"Yes."

Linda pursed her lips. "Why did you leave your phone in your car while you were at the gym?"

"There's never any free lockers at that hour, and there's no reason to risk it being stolen in the gym."

Linda's eyes narrowed. "Are you about to tell us that you didn't lock your car that night?"

"No, I locked my car." Noah didn't need to look at the jury to know that they were turning to each other in confusion, because the gallery was doing the same thing. No one in the courtroom had heard this yet because none of the previous witnesses had heard Noah's story. Thomas hadn't asked him about it on direct because he thought it was ridiculous. Maggie wasn't in the courtroom, for which he was grateful.

"Dr. Alderman, was your phone stolen from your car that night?"

"No. It was still in the console when I got back to the car. I pulled it out after I left the gym."

"Did you check to see if you had received any calls or texts?"

"There was no banner, so I assumed I hadn't."

"Did you check to see if your phone had *sent* any texts?"

"No."

Linda threw up her arms. "How did someone send a text from your phone at the time it was locked in your car?"

Thomas rose again. "Objection, Your Honor. The prosecutor is badgering the witness. Dr. Alderman has been completely forthright—"

Linda faced the judge. "*Forthright?* Your Honor, the witness's testimony is nonsensical, at best. I'm merely trying to understand it. I'm entitled to press him to explain. Did the text write and send *itself?*"

"Ms. Swain-Pettit, please." Judge Gardner looked down at Noah, leaning forward. "Dr. Alderman, do you know how the text got on your phone?"

"No, I do not," Noah answered the judge. He realized that the final time he'd hear directly from Judge Gardner was when he was sentenced to life or death, if he was convicted.

Linda cleared her throat. "Your Honor, may I proceed? I'm not sure how you ruled on the objection."

"Overruled."

"Thank you, Your Honor." Linda turned to Noah, squaring her shoulders. "Dr. Alderman, do you have *any notion at all* how this text got on your phone?"

"I can speculate, but I don't know for a fact."

"Objection!" Thomas shot to his feet. "Your Honor! What's the point of having the witness speculate? This is improper!"

Linda turned to Judge Gardner. "Your Honor, this text is a critical piece of Commonwealth evidence. The jury has a right to know how he believes the text got onto his phone from inside a *locked* car."

"Counsel, I'll allow it." Judge Gardner leaned back in his chair. "Dr. Alderman, you may answer."

Noah didn't hesitate. "I believe that Anna wrote the text and sent it to herself."

"*What?*" Linda's eyes rounded like marbles, and Noah heard the jurors shifting in their seats and the spectators murmuring.

"Order, order!" Judge Gardner called out, reaching for the gavel.

Linda took a deep breath. "Dr. Alderman, did you just say—"

Judge Gardner interrupted, "Counsel, we heard. Ask your next question."

"Dr. Alderman, how in the world did Anna get inside your car to send *herself* the text?"

"I have a second set of car keys that I keep at home, in the basket in the family room." Noah could hear the jury shifting, but kept going. "She could have found out I went to the gym. She could have seen my passcode. I keep it on a pad. The text was sent after I left the car but before I got into the gym, where I swipe in. I believe she took the second set of car keys, unlocked the car, and sent the text to herself from my phone."

"If this insane story is true, why did you not *see* Anna do any of this?"

Noah swallowed hard. Thomas had begged him not to tell the story. "When I got out of the car that night, there was a young woman walking across the lot from the grocery store in the same strip mall. She dropped her bag of groceries in the parking lot, and I stopped to help her pick them up, bending over. The lemons rolled everywhere. I was facing away from my car. I couldn't see what was going on behind me. I believe that's when Anna unlocked the car, sent the text from my phone, and left undetected."

Linda shook her head, incredulous. "Why in the world would Anna send that text to herself from your phone?"

"Uh, well, I don't know why for sure. I only know that she did. I believe that she did, maybe to make me look bad or frame me."

Linda's eyes flared, her disbelief theatrical. "So is it your testimony that Anna knew she was about to be murdered and did nothing about it except to frame you for it?"

"Yes, well, I don't know about all of that, but I think she sent it to make me look bad." Noah was getting into the weeds.

"Did she also *murder herself* and frame you for it?"

"No." Noah heard rustling from the gallery.

"But what would be the point of her framing you *for her own murder?*"

"I don't know." Noah blinked, fumbling.

"Dr. Alderman, which is more likely, that *Anna* sent the text framing you for her own murder, or that *you* sent her the text and are lying about it through your teeth?"

"Objection, argumentative!" Thomas jumped up again.

"I withdraw it, Your Honor," Linda sniffed, having accomplished her purpose.

Chapter Twenty

Maggie, Before

They pulled up in front of the furniture store, and Maggie reflected that they were like any other family of four, filling up the car. She'd made spaghetti for dinner, and mealtime had been easy and fun, with Caleb talking more than usual. He'd spent the meal telling Anna about his train trestle, a conversation full of old target words he could pronounce with ease. Maggie and Noah had let him have the spotlight, since it didn't happen often.

Noah looped an arm around Maggie's shoulder as they strolled to the store entrance behind Caleb and Anna. Night had fallen, and the air felt cool and crisp. The strip mall was closing up, and only a handful of cars were left in this end of the lot. The bright lights of the furniture store spilled onto the asphalt like glowing parallelograms.

Maggie smiled as she watched Caleb and Anna hustling ahead, their silhouettes backlit. "Look at them. My mother would have said, 'Mutt and Jeff.'"

Noah chuckled. "Everybody's mother would have said 'Mutt and Jeff.'"

Maggie felt another burst of happiness. "Is this really happening? Are those our two kids, ignoring us like a real family?"

"And is she a good sport or what?" Noah smiled. "I've never seen him yap like that. No more Coke at dinner."

"I'm going to show Anna!" Caleb shouted, hustling toward the store entrance.

"Wait up!" Anna hurried after him. "I want a bed with a canopy!"

"Great idea!" Maggie called after Anna, thinking of the Congreve Inn. It was hard to believe that was only last night, but she sensed that *Top Gun* was forgotten.

"A canopy bed?" Noah moaned, under his breath. "I don't have to build it, do I?"

"No. Those days are over."

"Promise me. No more Allen wrenches." Noah held open the door for Maggie, and they entered the store, which was empty. "Meanwhile, this is our new life. In a furniture store on a Saturday night."

"I didn't want to let it go until tomorrow." Maggie watched Caleb lead Anna from family room to family room within the vast space, trying out sofas. A sign hanging from the ceiling above read, NOW DELIVERING SEVEN DAYS A WEEK!

"I agree, but we haven't had a minute alone."

"I know, and there's so much I have to tell you."

Noah shot her a sly look. "That's not what I was thinking, but okay. It's Saturday night, if you get my drift."

"Ha!" Maggie laughed, her eye on the kids.

"I'm getting a rain check, aren't I?"

"You got that right. Gimme a year. She'll be in college then." Noah smiled. "How are we gonna do this, with two kids in the house?"

"Quietly." Maggie slid her phone from her jeans pocket and scrolled to her list. "Now here's what we need to get, after the bed. A makeup mirror that lights up, makeup bag, hair dryer, rolling bath cart—"

"This does not sound like sexy time."

"No, it's Bed Bath & Beyond time. There's one in this mall and it's only open until 9:30." Maggie checked her watch. "8:35. That means we have to move fast, and you know the paperwork here takes forever."

"If you want, you can run over to Bed Bath & Beyond and I'll stay here with Anna and Caleb."

"No, let's play it by ear. Maybe we can get both done together." Maggie watched Anna in the background, taking a selfie with Caleb on an oversized recliner.

"Whatever works. I don't mind spending time with her alone. I can get to know her one-on-one, like you did with Caleb."

"Great, and guess what, I haven't even had a chance to tell you the big news. It's about her inheritance." Maggie kept her eye on Anna, still out of earshot. "Try not to react because I don't want her to know what we're talking about."

"Okay." Noah nodded, his face remarkably impassive.

"Wow. You have a good poker face."

"What's her inheritance?"

"It's a fortune." Maggie leaned close to Noah's ear. "Florian left Anna $50 million, which she's going to get when she turns eighteen."

"Whoa." Noah nodded, eyebrows lifting. "Not that I'm surprised."

Maggie felt taken aback. "How can you *not* be surprised? I said, *$50 million*."

"Florian sold his startup for $30 million, years ago. He should have an estate that size. I was already thinking that she should see Mike."

"The guy who did our will?" Maggie watched Anna and Caleb, who were taking the escalator upstairs. "But she already has a lawyer. James Huntley."

"She should have a local estates lawyer, and in my opinion, eighteen is too young for her to come into that kind of money. How good a lawyer can he be if he set it up that way?"

"He didn't. He said the same thing. He's changing it already and she agreed."

"Still, we need to get her a lawyer here. Mike can change it. Pennsylvania law and Maine law may not be the same."

"But she likes James." Maggie felt a tug. "I already told him we wouldn't switch."

"So, tell him you changed your mind. We should switch her."

"But she should have a say."

"Fine, but how much weight can you give her opinion? She's a teenager."

"I'll have to ask her. It's her money."

"I know that, I'm just trying to help." Noah shrugged. "We're responsible for her now. She's our kid."

"*Our kid*. It does have a nice ring." Maggie put her arm around him as they walked to the escalator. "You're amazing."

"Do tell. I'll pretend it's foreplay." Noah squeezed her closer, his arm around her shoulder.

"Mag, Dad!" Caleb scooted over. "Come take a selfie! Anna wants us!"

"Okay." Noah let himself be tugged away, and Maggie followed him to one of the fake family rooms, where the furniture was pseudo-English Manor House, with a British tea table in front of a damask quilted couch.

"Dad, sit down!" Caleb called out, pointing.

"Caleb, settle." Noah sat down with a chuckle. "Who wound you up?"

Anna looked at Maggie. "Come, sit with me!"

"Too cute!" Maggie sat down. "Our first family photo, huh? The Ippoliti-Desroches-Aldermans!"

"Totally, this is perfect!" Anna grinned, holding the phone out in her right hand. "Here we go."

"Say cheese!" Caleb bounced next to Noah, jostling everyone.

"Everybody, here we go, smile!" Anna sang out, and Maggie smiled for the picture. She wasn't sure she would ever stop smiling, given how happy she felt.

Caleb jumped up. "Anna, we gotta go upstairs. Come on!"

"Here I come!" Anna slipped her phone in her purse. "He's fast!"

Noah rolled his eyes, standing up. "Caleb, please!"

"He's fine." Maggie waved him off, smiling, and Anna hustled to catch up with Caleb, who was already heading for the escalator. Noah fell into step with Maggie, and she encircled his waist with her arm. "How great are you?"

"Great." Noah grinned crookedly. "But tell me why."

"I sprang her on you, and here you are, all in."

"She's your daughter." Noah smiled over at her.

"And *your* stepdaughter. How does it feel?"

"Great. It'll be fun to get to know her." Noah let Maggie go first on the escalator as Caleb motioned to them from the second floor.

"Dad! Mag! Hurry!"

Maggie and Noah reached the second floor to see Anna resting on a beautiful canopy bed with a bedspread of white polished cotton with pink piping. The bed sat in the middle of a fake bedroom that contained a matching bureau, mirror, and armoire of enameled white.

"Wow, that's lovely!" Maggie called to her.

"Isn't it!" Anna smiled, with a Windsor wave. "I feel like a princess."

Noah picked up the oversized tag hanging on the bedpost. "I think it will fit. The room is large."

Caleb opened and closed the dresser drawers. "These work good!"

"*Well*," Noah corrected. "They work *well*."

"Whatever, Dad." Caleb rolled his eyes, glancing at Anna, who smiled back.

Maggie felt happy to see them connecting. "So you think this is the one, Anna? You don't want to look at any others?"

"I think this is perfect." Anna sat up on the bed. "Should we get the dresser, too?"

"Yes. You need a dresser and a mirror. Maybe even the armoire because the closet in that room is small."

"That's what I was thinking." Anna nodded. "Plus they have a 10 percent discount if you buy the set."

"Right, and they spread out the payments."

"I'll put it on my charge. James will authorize it."

Maggie smiled. "Anna, you don't have to pay for this. We're paying for it."

"You are?" Anna blinked.

"Of course," Noah interjected. "You don't have to pay for your own furniture."

"But I can afford it."

Caleb looked over, his eyes wide. "Anna, *you* can buy this? How much money do you have?"

"Caleb," Noah interjected, "don't ask personal questions."

Anna waved it off. "That's okay. Caleb can ask me anything. He's my bro."

Caleb's eyes went wide. "Anna, can you buy a *car*?"

Anna grinned. "Actually, I'm going to. A Range Rover, in black."

Maggie looked over, surprised. "Really, Anna?"

"I need a car, don't I?" Anna shrugged happily. "I have to get to school somehow, and I'm not going to take the bus. I'm sure nobody takes the bus."

"*Nobody* takes the bus," Caleb repeated, though he took a bus.

Maggie wasn't sure about this car business. "You're not an experienced driver, are you?"

"No, but I have a legit Maine license and I'll practice once I get the car." Anna shrugged again, happily.

"I'm not sure you should be buying your own car. We have to talk about that." Maggie knew Noah would hate the idea, but she didn't want to fuss about it now.

"I agree." Noah nodded. "We can help you out with that, and I bet we can find a good used car that'll get you to school."

"But I want the Range Rover. I already picked it out online."

Maggie caught Noah's frown, but this wasn't the time or the place. "Noah, we can sort this out later, can't we?"

"Sure." Noah gestured at the bed. "We need furniture."

Maggie smiled. "Right. We're on a schedule here." She turned to Anna. "Anna, we still need to get the stuff on the list. The Bed Bath & Beyond is on the other side of the parking lot. Are you up for that or too tired?"

"I'm up!" Anna jumped to her feet.

"Me, too!" Caleb chimed in.

Maggie touched Noah's arm. "Noah, why don't you take Anna and Caleb to Bed Bath & Beyond? Anna has the list, and I'll do the paperwork here, then come join you guys."

"Sure. Let's go, guys!" Noah pretended to start jogging. "Beat you there!"

"No, you won't, Dad!" Caleb sprinted after his father, but Anna lingered, looking at Maggie.

"You don't mind if we go?"

"Not at all," Maggie answered. "I'm going to try to get the furniture delivered tomorrow."

"Thanks, Mom!" Anna said, then skipped off, her ponytail swinging.

Mom.

Chapter Twenty-one

Noah, After

TRIAL, DAY 5

Noah was bracing for the next set of questions when he noticed the door opening at the back of the courtroom, and Maggie entered, wearing sunglasses. She slipped inside and sat in the back row, where he lost sight of her behind the other spectators in the gallery. Her hair had been pulled back in a ponytail, and she had on a jeans jacket that he recognized as Anna's.

Noah felt a wrench in his chest, but tried not to react openly. He didn't want to draw attention to her. She'd probably pulled her hair back as an attempt at a disguise, since her dark curls were so characteristic in the newspaper pictures. And she must have been wearing Anna's jacket as a memorial, but only he would know that.

The jeans jacket made Noah remember that first night when Anna had moved in. They had gone shopping to buy her a bed, and then he'd taken her and Caleb to Bed Bath & Beyond. Anna had worn the jacket over a blue-checked sundress, and Caleb had hustled to the candy counter at the checkout.

Noah had had the Things To Do list on his phone and had gone into the store with Anna, wending his way through the cramped aisles of every conceivable home good. *Anna, what do you want to do first?* he had asked her. *Towels or sheets?*

Sheets.

Where's the sheets?

There, in the back. Anna had skipped ahead of him, her ponytail swinging. Noah had thought it was cute and carefree until he'd realized, later, that nothing Anna did was carefree. On the contrary, everything she did was calculated to produce an effect. She may have been seventeen, but she was the most manipulative woman he had ever met.

Noah, here they are, and they even have a sample, so you can feel the thread count.

Which ones do you want? Your call.

I want whatever feels the softest. This feels soft. Anna had fingered the material of the first sample, her lips curving into an oddly suggestive smile. *Don't you want to feel it, Noah? Don't you want to see how soft it really is?*

What? Noah didn't know if he heard her correctly, though her facial expression had turned suddenly seductive, her blue eyes glittering.

Noah, don't you want to see if I'm as soft as you think?

Noah still didn't think he'd heard her correctly, but Caleb came running up rattling boxes of Sugar Babies, and Anna's features had rearranged themselves back into a sweet, innocent mask.

Noah felt his gut clench at the memory, another red flag that he'd ignored. In retrospect, he'd gotten a glimpse of who Anna really was then, manipulating them all. The craziest thing was that he *had* been wondering how soft she really was. Not consciously, but in the primal part of his brain where he wasn't a suburban husband and father, but a man. There had been something about the way her jacket kept opening and closing over her dress, teasing glimpses of her cleavage. The pinkish skin of her breasts swelled over the top, and she was so young, and it was Saturday night. He'd been looking for sheets, but what he really wanted was sex.

Noah should've known to watch himself, after that. But he hadn't, and that was the reason he was on trial for murder today, with Linda approaching the stand wearing the smirk she had on after Noah's testimony about the text.

"Dr. Alderman, what time did you leave the gym, do you know?"

"At about 8:15."

"You didn't go straight home after you left the gym, did you?"

"No, I did not."

"What did you do?"

"I went to the car to get my wallet and phone, then to the grocery store to pick up some prepared food for dinner."

"By the way, whoever sent this text did not steal your wallet, isn't that correct?"

"Yes."

Linda signaled her paralegal, who recalled a grocery store receipt to the projector screen. "Dr. Alderman, I'm showing you Commonwealth Exhibit 45, which has been previously admitted. You see that receipt, don't you?"

"Yes."

"The receipt shows that you left the store at 9:03 P.M., does it not?"

"Yes."

"Dr. Alderman, you then drove directly home, did you not?"

"Yes."

"Dr. Alderman, how long did it take you to drive home?"

"About twenty minutes. I pulled into my driveway at 9:30 behind Anna's car."

"You weren't surprised to see Anna's car in your driveway, were you?"

"Yes, I was."

"Why were you surprised if you had sent a text asking her to meet you at your house?"

"I didn't send the text."

Linda mock-slapped her forehead. "So that's your story and your sticking to it?"

Thomas rose. "Objection, Your Honor. The prosecutor's comments are improper and prejudicial."

"Sustained." Judge Gardner waved Thomas back into his seat. "Ms. Swain-Pettit, you're on notice."

"Thank you, Your Honor." Linda turned to face Noah, folding her arms. "Dr. Alderman, what happened when you returned home?"

"I got out of my car with the groceries, and Anna's car was in my driveway. I looked inside the car and she wasn't there." Noah had told this on direct, so he summarized it now. "I kept going to the house, and it was dark. The porch light was off. I looked around since I knew that Anna didn't have a key, so she would be outside."

Linda kept her arms folded, letting him speak without interruption, and Noah realized that this would be the first time that Maggie would hear his story from start to finish. He prayed she would believe him, and so would the jury. When he'd told it on direct, they had listened attentively, but Noah knew Linda was having him tell it again so she could destroy him.

"I saw that she was lying on the porch floor, and I thought she had fallen asleep, so I set the grocery bag down and said, 'Why are you here?' But when she didn't move, I went over to her and realized that she was dead."

"How did you realize she was dead?"

"She didn't move or answer, then I touched her arm and there was no response, so I went closer to her and I looked into her face. My eyes adjusted to the darkness, and I could see her eyes were open." Noah realized he was volunteering but he felt shaken, knowing that Maggie was hearing every word. "I felt for a pulse at her neck, then at her wrist, and there was no pulse, but the skin on her neck was warm, so I tried CPR. I began chest compressions, and at the same time I got my phone out of my pocket and called 911 and put them on speaker while I did the compressions."

Linda frowned. "How did you determine she had been strangled if it was dark?"

"Oh, right. I had my phone in my hand and I turned on the flashlight and shined it on her face."

"Why didn't you mention the flashlight just now?"

"I forgot about it. I said it before, when I testified on direct."

Linda arched an eyebrow. "You mean, you mentioned it when your lawyer took you through your questions, but not now?"

"Objection." Thomas rose, frowning. "That comment is testimony, Your Honor."

"Sustained." Judge Gardner waved Thomas back down. "Counsel, please rephrase."

"I'll withdraw the question," Linda said, though she had made her point. "Dr. Alderman, are you saying that you examined her on the porch?"

"Well, not examined, but I looked at her, and I could see that she had been strangled."

"You hadn't seen the corpse of a person who had been strangled before, had you?"

"No, I hadn't. But it was obvious." Noah told himself to stop volunteering. He realized he was trying to explain to Maggie, his audience of one. But he was getting himself in deeper and deeper.

"Isn't it true that you knew Anna had been strangled because you strangled her?"

"No."

"Then how specifically did you know she had been strangled?"

Noah hesitated. He didn't want to say it in front of Maggie. "I just knew. It was obvious. Her body was still and her eyes were fixed. She was motionless, as in death."

"But if you were only going by the stillness, couldn't she have died of a heart attack or an aneurysm?"

"No, that wasn't what it was." Noah knew he sounded evasive, because he was being evasive. He had to say something. "The vessels were broken in her eyes. The petechiae, the capillaries in the whites of her eyes, had burst."

"So *now* we're hearing that her capillaries were broken, but you didn't mention that before, did you?"

"Uh, no, I guess not." Noah couldn't imagine how Maggie felt right now.

"Dr. Alderman, aren't you making this up as you go along?"

"No."

"But you didn't mention it in your direct testimony, did you?"

"No." Thomas hadn't thought it was necessary. They hadn't gone into detail about Noah's actions on the porch. It wouldn't have helped him.

"Why didn't you mention that before?"

"I . . . must have forgotten."

"You're so *forgetful* today, aren't you?"

"Objection, Your Honor." Thomas rose. "Is this a question or harassment?"

Linda snorted. "It's cross-examination, Your Honor. It's within the bounds of permissible."

Judge Gardner nodded. "Overruled."

"Dr. Alderman, didn't you observe anything on her neck?"

"Not at first. I saw her eyes first, but then I turned on the flashlight on my phone and then I saw some pinkish swelling around her neck and that confirmed it was strangulation."

"So, you find your beloved stepdaughter strangled on the porch, and what you do is take out your flashlight and visually examine her?"

"Yes." Noah knew it sounded bad. It had sounded better on direct. Thomas had ordered it for him, chronologically. He was getting confused, and Maggie must have been heartbroken, hearing this testimony.

"But didn't you cry out in horror?"

"No."

"Didn't you shout for help?"

"No, I'm a doctor. I am help." Noah felt good saying it, and he saw a flicker of an approving smile from Thomas.

"Dr. Alderman, do you recall what you said to 911 or do I need to replay the 911 tape to refresh your recollection?"

"No, I . . . recall." Noah felt himself falter, though he remembered exactly what he had said. He didn't want to say it in front of Maggie. He reached for his plastic cup of water. His hand shook, and he knew the jurors noticed.

Linda signaled to her paralegal. "I'll replay the 911 tape and ask you some questions about it."

"No . . . I can recall it." Noah wanted to spare Maggie. She never listened to 911 tapes when they came on the news. She thought it was sad and invasive. Now this 911 tape was about her daughter's murder. She would never have heard it before. Noah repeated, "I can recall it, you don't have to—"

Linda waved Noah into silence, as the 911 audiotape began to play.

Chapter Twenty-two

Maggie, Before

It was midnight by the time Maggie closed the kitchen, pressing the dishwasher's Start button, like the period at the end of a busy day. They had stowed Anna's towels and toiletries in her room upstairs, and the bedroom furniture was getting delivered tomorrow. They had used the new sheets to make a temporary bed out of the couch in the family room, and she was in there now, watching *Saturday Night Live.* Noah was upstairs, tucking Caleb in. It was way past his bedtime, but he'd been excited to help with Anna, and neither Maggie nor Noah wanted to discourage him.

Maggie left the kitchen and entered the family room, where Anna was on her laptop, propped up on the couch. "How are you doing, honey?"

"Great, thanks." Anna smiled. "I love my new sheets."

"They're pretty, even on the couch." Maggie sat down on the chair catty-corner to Anna.

"You don't think the canopy is too little-girl, do you?" Anna bit her fingernails.

"Not at all. It's feminine."

"Do you think I'll start school Monday?"

"I doubt it, but I'll email tomorrow. I'm sure we can get a meeting on Monday or maybe it's a shadow day."

"I got their calendar online. They're just coming back from Spring Break. I already figured out my classes."

"Wow," Maggie said, impressed at her initiative. "Can I see?"

"Sure." Maggie looked over as Anna hit a button and a spreadsheet came on the page, with a course load of AP Gov, AP Spanish, Honors Algebra 2, AP Language/Comp, Honors Environmental Science, Honors Psych. "Yikes, that looks hard. Maybe you should take it easy in the beginning?"

"I can't for college." Anna bit her nail. "It's the same courses that I took at Congreve, roughly. Some of the textbooks are different, but I can deal with that. I made a new Facebook profile, too. I just posted. Wanna see?"

"Sure." Maggie watched as Anna hit another button and a Facebook profile came on. The first picture was the four of them on the couch in the furniture store, with the caption:

Here I am with my family—my mom Maggie, my step-father Noah, and my adorable little stepbrother Caleb. Missing from the photo is Wreck-It Ralph, our cat. Because they wouldn't let him in the store . . .

"That's so cute!" Maggie felt pleased. Somehow seeing it on Facebook made them a real family, a thought even she realized was ridiculous.

"I posted some other pics of us. It's fun." Anna scrolled down, showing a photo of Ralph looking out the kitchen window. "He always looks thoughtful."

"Really he's just wishing treats would jump into his mouth."

"I know, I gave him some. Caleb showed me where you keep them."

Maggie burst into laughter, thinking of the two kids in cahoots. "I really appreciate how nice you're being to Caleb. You couldn't have been interested in trains at dinner."

"I was! It was cute."

Maggie sighed, happily. "Well, I'm beat. You're going to go to bed sometime, aren't you?"

"Soon. I'm just doing some research. I'm trying to learn as much as I can about my class. You know, scope out some friends."

"That's a good idea."

"And you know what? I don't really have any clothes for school. Remember, we had a uniform at Congreve, and the only things I have are weekend clothes." Anna made a sad-emoji face. "Do you think we can go shopping?"

"Of course." Maggie remembered her own school days, out of nowhere. It was funny how having Anna around was bringing back a lot of memories. "I used to have a new outfit every first day of school. My mom and I went shopping for it every year."

"Aw, you sure you don't mind? I know you have work and everything."

"Not at all. I'm taking the week off to get you situated. I missed years of going clothes-shopping with you and I'm happy to make up the time."

"Great." Anna's gaze returned to her laptop. "I'm starting a new Insta and Snapchat, and I was looking on Facebook, and you can see the clubs at school that have Facebook pages."

Maggie looked over as Anna clicked to the Poetry Club page, which showed a group of long-haired girls and boys with man buns relaxing on the lawn behind the school. "They look nice. That would be perfect for you."

"I know. The poetry magazine is called *Phrases*. They also have clubs for the literary magazine, the newspaper, and the yearbook. They have tons of clubs." Anna clicked through a bunch of Facebook windows, all of which had been open. "There's the musical theater club, choir, select chorale, then there's all the girls' sports. Since it's spring, it's tennis, lacrosse, and track."

"Do you play any sports?"

"No, I'm an indoor cat." Anna wrinkled her nose. "What about you?"

"I walk, but Noah works out religiously." Maggie smiled. "I'm the one with the Dad Bod."

Anna smiled back. "You guys are so much fun. I mean, you're really happy together, right?"

"Right."

"It's cool, there's three last names and four people in this house. But I like that your last name is my middle name. Anna Ippoliti Desroches."

"I like it too." Maggie had insisted on it, way back when. "And don't worry about school. You'll make friends."

"I didn't at Congreve." Anna shot her a skeptical look.

"You will here. People are more open." Maggie kept her voice gentle, so Anna didn't feel criticized, just encouraged.

"Still. These girls are pretty, and pretty girls are the same everywhere." Anna opened a Facebook page from *Phrases* magazine, which showed a group of artsy Goth girls. "This is my tribe."

"You *are* pretty, and you're not Goth."

"I had a Goth friend at Congreve. I liked her, but she left school. This is her." Anna hit a few buttons, calling to the screen a window that showed a head shot of a wan-looking girl with matte-black hair, black eye makeup, and a red-paper crown. "Jamie Covington. She called herself a Visigoth. She said that was a Goth with contact lenses."

Maggie smiled. "Why did she leave school?"

"Same reason I did. It is hard to fit in there if you're different. She tried to start a Wiccan club." Anna shifted her gaze, with an ironic smile. "You can't see a Wiccan with a Congreve totebag, can you?"

"No." Maggie laughed, getting the picture. Anna had been on the outside and identified with the outsiders.

"She went to Ellen too. We both liked her." Anna glanced over. "And you know what, I don't think I need to start with a therapist down here."

"Really?" Maggie wasn't sure she agreed, but kept a pleasant expression. "Why?"

"I don't know, I just don't feel like I need it." Anna shrugged. "If I need to, I'll call Ellen. She said I could if I wanted to."

"I told her that we would get you somebody here. You're going to have a lot of changes to go through, and it might be good to have someone to talk to."

"I'll have you, won't I?"

"Of course," Maggie answered, touched. "And I think we need to get you a lawyer here, too."

"What about James?" Anna frowned.

"Noah thinks you're better off with someone down here and he's probably right."

"You guys want to fire James?" Anna recoiled. "I don't. He hasn't done anything wrong and he knows me. You liked James, didn't you? You said you did."

"Yes, I did." Maggie kicked herself for bringing it up, so soon. "Okay, I'll talk it over with Noah, okay?"

"Okay." Anna hesitated. "Hey, can I talk to you about him? You can't tell him about it, okay?"

"Okay," Maggie answered, suppressing her discomfort.

"I don't think he likes me. When we were picking out the sheets at Bed Bath & Beyond, he was, well, cold."

Maggie cringed. "He doesn't know you that well, Anna. He can be on the reserved side."

"No, that wasn't it." Anna shook her head, her mouth a flat line. "I tried to get him to help me with the sheets, but it was all about Caleb. He was with him the whole time. It was like I didn't even exist."

"Oh no." Maggie felt a wave of guilt. Caleb had been an only child for so long, and they both lavished a lot of attention on him. It was possible that Noah had inadvertently paid Caleb more attention than Anna. "I'm so sorry that happened."

"You don't have to apologize, but what if he doesn't want me living here?"

"Yes, he does, Anna." Maggie covered Anna's hand, with its

beleaguered fingernails. "He wants you here, I know he does, you'll see."

"Are you sure? Because we can always change it, like I could board at another school." Anna's tone strengthened, newly distant. "I don't have to live here, I just wanted to."

"And I want you to," Maggie rushed to say, her heart speaking out of turn. She couldn't lose Anna when she had just found her again. "Noah wants you to live here, too. Whatever happened at Bed Bath & Beyond was a misunderstanding."

"Please don't say anything to him. Do you promise?"

"Yes, I promise." Maggie squeezed Anna's hand. "Don't worry about it. Everything is going to be just fine."

"I hope so." Anna smiled. "I should get to bed, huh?"

"Yes. Good night." Maggie kissed Anna on the cheek, but she was wondering what to do about Noah.

Chapter Twenty-three

Noah, After
TRIAL, DAY 5

The courtroom fell silent as the 911 audiotape reverberated through the speakers:

This is 911, what is your emergency?

My stepdaughter isn't breathing. CPR isn't working. I'm a doctor but it isn't working. You're not supposed to do mouth-to-mouth anymore, are you? Just chest compressions?

Yes, just chest compressions, Doctor. Is there any injury? What happened?

I think she's been strangled. Please send an ambulance. The address is 460 Howell Road.

It's on its way. Keep up the compressions. How old is your daughter?

Stepdaughter. She's seventeen. The compressions aren't working. I think I'm pressing hard enough. Listen, is the ambulance on its way?

Yes, it's en route. Stay on the phone with me. I'll talk you through it—

I can't, I have to go. I can't stay on the phone and do the compressions. Please send the ambulance. Thank you.

Noah didn't remember the tape sounding this bad when Thomas had introduced it during direct testimony, because Thomas had set it up the way they'd planned. But now Noah was hearing it through Maggie's ears. He couldn't see her in the gallery, but he knew this would be killing her.

"Dr. Alderman, let's circle back to the moment that you discover the body of your stepdaughter, strangled on your porch. You must have been shocked by that awful sight, were you not?"

"Yes."

"And surely you were horrified, were you not?"

"Yes."

"And you must've been grief-stricken upon realizing that such a young girl, your own stepdaughter, was dead, were you not?"

"Yes."

"But you expressed none of those emotions in the 911 tape, did you?"

Noah hesitated. "No."

Linda half-smiled. "There's no excited utterance of the type one would expect from a shocked, horrified, and grief-stricken step-father, is there?"

"Well, no."

"You didn't say, 'oh my God!' or 'oh no!', did you?"

"No."

"You didn't cry, did you?"

"No."

"You spoke in complete sentences, did you not?"

"Yes."

"You asked coherent questions, did you not?"

"Yes." Noah could hear the jurors shifting behind him. Thomas would have warned him against it, but he had to offer some explanation. "I had those emotions but I kept them inside. I'm a professional, a doctor. I think I reacted as a doctor would."

Linda recoiled. "You mean that it didn't make any difference to you that this patient, this *dead body,* was your *stepdaughter*?"

"No, I mean, uh, that isn't what I meant. I meant that I went into doctor mode. I felt those things, those emotions, but I went into doctor mode."

"Yet for a man in 'doctor mode,' you seemed to forget how to perform CPR, didn't you?"

Noah blinked. "Uh, maybe I needed reminding. I knew the procedure had changed. I hadn't performed CPR in the field. I'm not certified."

"It's interesting, don't you think, that there is no sound of you grunting or breathing hard, as someone would while they were performing chest compressions to resuscitate the body of his own stepdaughter?"

"I don't know why I wasn't grunting." Noah was forgetting to answer only yes or no. It wasn't so simple.

"Dr. Alderman, didn't you text your stepdaughter, lure her to your home, and when she spurned your sexual advances yet again, kill her with your bare hands?"

"No."

"Right, I keep forgetting, you found her strangled and you were shocked, horrified, and grief-stricken, correct?"

"Correct."

"Dr. Alderman, you testified earlier that after Anna's Petition for a PFA was filed against you, your wife asked you to leave the house, isn't that correct?"

"Yes." Noah couldn't think about Maggie now. He understood that she had been caught in the middle.

"Isn't it true that after word got around about Anna's Petition for a PFA, some of your patients stopped seeing you?"

"Yes." Noah cringed. He had gotten cancellations the next day. Social media had spread the word.

"So isn't it true that after Anna's Petition for a PFA, you lost your wife, your house, and some of your patients?"

"Yes." Noah didn't want to relive it, or make Maggie relive it, but there it was.

"Your wife is not testifying on your behalf in this trial, is she?"

"No."

"Nor has she come to court to stand by you, has she?"

"No, she's not here." Noah didn't hesitate. Maggie was still in the courtroom.

"So." Linda crossed her arms. "Isn't it true that after Anna filed her Petition for a PFA against you, you were angry at her?"

"No."

"Are you seriously asking this jury to believe that despite the fact that Anna cost you *so much,* you had *no* negative feelings toward her?"

"Yes." Noah didn't know what else to say. He was damned if he did and damned if he didn't. He couldn't see Thomas at counsel table. Linda was blocking him again.

Linda bore down, narrowing her eyes. "But you said Anna was a liar, correct?"

"Yes."

"Are you saying that you were fine with that?"

Noah could see the gallery looking at each other. Maggie would know he was lying. "Well, uh, no, not fine with it."

"So you had some negative feelings toward Anna, didn't you?"

Noah hesitated. "Some. Yes."

"You were angry at her, weren't you?"

"Some." Noah knew it was the wrong thing to say as soon as Linda's eyes lit up.

"You had more than *some anger,* didn't you?"

"No."

"Dr. Alderman, weren't you *furious* with Anna for filing that Petition and lying about you?"

"No."

"And weren't you *furious* with Anna for rejecting your sexual advances?"

"No."

Linda stepped closer to the stand. "Didn't you lure Anna to your home by text?"

"No."

"Didn't you make yet another sexual advance on her on the porch of your house?"

"No."

"And when she spurned your advance yet again, didn't all that anger come to the fore and you strangled her with your bare hands?"

"That's not true!" Noah raised his voice, but even he could hear the anger in his voice.

"Let's move on from your 911 audiotape." Linda walked back to counsel table, and Noah saw the faces staring back at him, their expressions angry, disapproving, judgmental. Maggie was among them but he couldn't see her.

Suddenly Noah thought he saw someone in the back of the gallery pushing back her hair, a gesture that seemed so much like Maggie's, moving a curl from her eyes. It took him back to that first night, the night that should've told him everything. They had been to the furniture store, then Bed Bath & Beyond, and Maggie had come upstairs after saying good night to Anna.

You okay? he had asked, because of her worried expression.

Fine.

Great. Noah had kissed her good night, but she had returned his kiss in a perfunctory way, which wasn't like her. She called herself the Makeout Queen.

Did you guys have fun at the store?

You mean Bloodbath & Beyond?

What's that mean? Maggie had frowned.

It's a joke. Noah had been slipping off his shirt, which normally would've drawn a compliment from Maggie about his arms or chest.

Would you take Anna out driving?

She knows how to drive.

I'm talking about just to practice. To make sure she feels comfy behind the wheel. And safe.

What about this car business? She wants to buy a Range Rover? What she needs to do is get a valid Pennsylvania license. She shouldn't drive without one. I don't think a Maine license is valid here at her age.

I'm not talking about the car or the license, I'm talking about practicing driving. Would you take her? It might be a nice way for you guys to spend time. Get to know each other, like you said.

Okay.

I'll keep an eye on Caleb.

Or he could come with.

No, I think it would be good if you went alone. Just you and Anna. Is that okay with you?

Noah had said yes, and it had turned out to be his second big mistake.

The first mistake was allowing Anna to move in.

Chapter Twenty-four

Maggie, Before

"Hi!" Maggie answered Kathy's call on her way downstairs to get snacks for Noah, Anna, and Caleb, who were setting up Anna's bedroom, since the furniture had been delivered. It was already Sunday afternoon, but she hadn't had a spare moment to call her best friend and fill her in.

"Hey, girl, I'm dying to hear what happened with Anna."

"You're not going to believe it." Maggie hurried down to the kitchen. "I brought her home. She's here."

"Who is? Anna?"

"Yes! She's living with us now."

"Wait, what?" Kathy gasped in delight. "Are you serious?"

"I am, and you know what, Florian told her that I abused her and that's how I lost custody. Can you believe that?"

"Oh my God! But wait, is she really there? Right now?"

"Yes!" Maggie launched into the whole story as she fetched sodas, a bag of popcorn from the cabinet, and the gleaming copper tray that she reserved for special occasions. If this wasn't a special occasion, she didn't know what was.

"Oh my God, this is amazing! I'm so happy for you!"

"I know, isn't it incredible! I have her back again! My baby girl!"

"This is so exciting! So you've got to get her in school and everything."

"I know, I'm going to take her tomorrow and get her registered. She'll start classes Tuesday." Maggie opened the freezer door and filled the glasses with ice.

"I can't wait to meet her! What does she look like?"

"She's pretty and smart, but she doesn't have much confidence."

"You mean she's insecure?"

"Kind of, yes."

"Guess where she gets that from."

Maggie laughed, at herself. "She's getting along great with Caleb."

"Of course she is! How can you not?"

"It makes me really happy." Maggie lowered her voice. "She's worried Noah doesn't like her, but of course he does."

"How do you know that?"

"She told me. She thinks he favors Caleb." Maggie arranged the glasses on the tray, then went for some napkins.

"That would be natural, wouldn't it? Caleb's his son. He doesn't even know her."

"I know, but I don't think he does anyway. We're a family of four now, can you believe it?"

"Good luck." Kathy snorted. "I'm at a lacrosse game, and Josh is at travel basketball. You each take a kid. Divide and conquer."

"There you go."

"You want to walk tomorrow?"

"No, if you don't mind, let me get her situated." Maggie wondered if Anna might prefer some healthier snacks, so she went to the refrigerator, rummaged around the produce drawer, and found some oranges and an apple. She put them in a separate bowl on the tray, making a note to herself to ask Anna what kind of fruit she liked.

"I get it. Stay in touch. Congratulations! Love you!"

"Love you, too. Bye." Maggie hung up as she heard the sound of footsteps coming down the stairs, the tread too heavy to be anybody but Noah, who entered the kitchen and crossed to the base cabinet, where they kept a few tools, a tape measure, and steel wool.

"Of course I need an Allen wrench. My days of Allen wrenches will never end."

"How's the bed?"

"Great."

"Does Anna like it?"

"Loves it." Noah found the Allen wrench and stood up, eyeing the fancy copper tray. "Look at you. The hostess with the mostest."

"I know, right?"

Noah glanced over his shoulder, then lowered his voice. "Anna is telling Caleb that she's buying a Range Rover. Are you just going to let her go buy a car? Doesn't she have to ask our permission?"

"I don't know, I haven't thought about it." Maggie liked to be more spontaneous than Noah, who did everything step-by-step. Their difference in temperaments was by now a well-established fact, in the way of marriages. He was The Scientist, and she was The Italian, though she suspected that sometimes it sold her short.

"Don't we have to figure that out? She's under our roof, so she has to follow our rules, doesn't she?"

Maggie smiled. "It's not like we have any rules about cars."

"We don't let Caleb buy anything he wants with his money."

"He has $37."

"That's not the point. It's the principle. Can she just buy a car without our permission, even if she has the means? We're a family. We should function like one."

"Can't we talk about this later?" Maggie glanced upstairs.

"She shouldn't get a Range Rover. I think there are used cars that are a better value, and even if she has the money, it might make sense to finance a car. The rates are low now, and it will teach her how to pay a monthly bill."

"We'll see." Maggie reached for the tray, but Noah stopped her.

"One more thing. Did she have a boyfriend at school?"

"I don't think so."

"She must have dated, some."

"No, she didn't." Maggie didn't understand why he was asking. "It's a girls' school, remember? It's not like she had a lot of opportunities."

"You sure? Because it seems like she would have boyfriends. She's pretty."

"I know, but she didn't date. I even talked to her therapist about it. She barely had any friends except the one. Jamie." Maggie leaned closer, not to be overheard. "I don't think she's had sex yet."

Noah's lips parted in surprise. "You think she's a virgin?"

"Shhh." Maggie glanced at the staircase. "Don't make a big thing of it."

"I didn't."

"Yes, you did. You looked surprised."

"I am, but I'm not making a big thing of it."

"Lower your voice, okay? And please don't say anything to her."

"Of course I wouldn't." Noah rolled his eyes, looking like Caleb. "But I don't think she's a virgin."

"Why not?"

"I just don't," Noah shot back, then seemed to catch himself.

"What makes you say that? Do you know something I don't?"

"No, not at all."

"She's only seventeen years old, Noah."

"Honey, lots of girls have sex before they're seventeen these days. This is the age of selfies and duck lips."

"How do you know?"

"I just do." Noah looked away again, and Maggie sensed the conversation was making him uncomfortable, which was odd. He didn't shy away from sex talk, and if anything, he was more sexual than she was. Or maybe less tired. Or maybe a man.

"What's up with you?"

"Nothing." Noah put the Allen wrench on the snack tray. "I'll take this for you."

"Thanks."

"Not a problem." Noah left the kitchen with the tray, and Maggie followed, wondering why he was acting so strangely.

Chapter Twenty-five

Noah, After
TRIAL, DAY 5

Linda strode back to counsel table, picked up an exhibit, then returned to the stand, holding it close to her chest. Thomas had warned him that her holding-the-exhibit trick was intended to make him nervous, but it didn't work because he was already nervous. He tried to see Maggie in the back of the gallery but he couldn't. She had to be hiding from him. He didn't blame her.

"Dr. Alderman, isn't it true that you told the 911 dispatcher that you didn't want to stay on the phone because you had to administer chest compressions?"

"Yes."

"But isn't it true that after you hung up with the dispatcher, you called your lawyer?"

Noah blinked. "Yes."

"So you were able to make another phone call and continue compressions, even though you told the 911 dispatcher that you could not?"

"Uh . . . yes."

"Dr. Alderman, I am going to show you Commonwealth Exhibit 48, which has already been introduced into evidence, and ask you, is it a copy of the phone calls you made from your phone on the night in question?"

"It is." Noah looked down at the log with a sinking heart.

"And this phone record shows that you spoke with 911 dispatch for one minute and ten seconds, isn't that correct?"

"Yes."

"The phone record also shows that *one minute after* you hung up with the 911 dispatcher, you called your lawyer, isn't that correct?"

"Yes." Noah had given this testimony on direct, but again, under Thomas's questioning, it had sounded better, more reasonable.

"Your lawyer was present counsel Thomas Owusu, isn't that correct?"

"Yes."

"Isn't it true that the real reason you wanted to get off the phone with 911 was to call your lawyer?"

"No."

"But you called your lawyer one minute after you hung up with the 911 operator, so you must have been thinking of calling your lawyer while you were talking with the 911 operator, isn't that correct?"

"No."

Linda arched her eyebrow again, and Noah realized it was her tell, when she was about to tear into him. "So when you told the 911 dispatcher that you wanted to get off the phone, you had absolutely no idea you were going to call your lawyer next?"

"Yes." Noah felt confused, and suddenly beaten. Maggie was witnessing this disaster. It would haunt her forever.

"Dr. Alderman, didn't you lie to the 911 dispatcher so you could get off the phone and talk to your lawyer?"

"No."

"Didn't you lie to the 911 dispatcher when you told her you were doing chest compressions?"

"No."

"But you did lie to her when you told her why you were hanging up, didn't you?"

"No."

"But you called your lawyer *one minute* later, didn't you?"

"I was just reacting."

"Right, like a doctor, as you testified?"

"Yes."

"A doctor who calls his criminal lawyer?"

"Objection, Your Honor." Thomas rose. "Is that a snide comment or a question?"

"Your Honor, I'll withdraw it," Linda said without pausing. "Dr. Alderman, isn't it true that you made up that bit about the compressions, lying to the 911 dispatcher, because you knew that the 911 tape would be evidence later?"

"No." Noah had to help himself. "As you point out, if I were trying to make a fake story, I would've acted upset or said 'oh my God' and things like that, as you said before. But I didn't."

Linda arched an eyebrow again. "Isn't it also true that if you knew you were going to try to sell this phony-baloney story of the doctor-reacting-as-a-doctor, you wouldn't exhibit any of those behaviors?"

"No, no." Noah didn't elaborate. He couldn't. There was nothing more to say. He'd tried to score but it had backfired.

"You weren't too shocked, horrified, and grief-stricken at Anna's murder to call your lawyer, were you?"

"I was horrified. I had those emotions."

Linda crossed her arms. "But nevertheless you carried on somehow and called your lawyer, did you not?"

Thomas shifted uncomfortably back at counsel table, and Noah took it as a signal. They had discussed how to deal with these questions. Their defense was that the prosecution's case was circumstantial, and Noah was supposed to remember to use the term *circumstances*.

Noah cleared his throat. "As I said in my direct testimony, I called my lawyer because, given the *circumstances*, I knew it could look like I killed Anna even though I didn't do it."

"So you admit you were thinking of yourself at that time, weren't you?"

"Partly, yes." Noah had no choice but to admit it. He and Thomas had decided that was the best strategy.

"You weren't concerned with Anna anymore, were you?"

"I still was, but I had determined that she had no pulse. There was nothing I could do."

"But you tried chest compressions earlier, after you had determined she had no pulse, did you not?"

"Yes."

"So, there *was* something you could do, wasn't there?"

"Okay, yes."

"I'm confused, were you or were you not administering chest compressions at the time you called your lawyer?"

"I was, I said I was." Noah didn't believe for one minute that Linda was confused.

"Dr. Alderman, when during the twelve minutes of that conversation with your lawyer did you stop administering chest compressions?"

"I don't know."

"Between one and five minutes, or between five and ten minutes?"

"Between one and five."

"Did you have a hard time talking with your lawyer and compressing Anna's chest, is that why you stopped?"

Again Noah couldn't say yes or no. "I stopped because it was futile. She had passed."

"But you said she had passed before you even called 911, didn't you?"

"Yes."

"The phone record shows that you spoke with your lawyer for twelve minutes, isn't that correct?"

"Yes."

"So your conversation with your lawyer was twelve times as long as your conversation with the 911 dispatcher, isn't that correct?"

"Yes." Noah got the implication, and so did the jury. He could hear them shifting. He had to fight back.

"And isn't it true that you spent a minute and ten seconds on the phone trying to save Anna's life and twelve minutes trying to save *yourself*?"

Noah's mouth went dry. "I called my lawyer, and that's how long we spoke. I was concerned for Anna the whole time and I was also concerned for myself. Both things can be true."

"Dr. Alderman, after five minutes into that conversation, you weren't doing any chest compressions for Anna, were you?"

"No."

"Yet you were continuing the conversation with your lawyer about yourself, were you not?"

"Yes."

"Dr. Alderman, although the 911 dispatcher had offered to stay on the phone with you until the police arrived, you in fact stayed on the phone with your lawyer until the police arrived, isn't that correct?"

"Yes." Noah heard the jury shifting in their seats.

"You didn't call your wife after you hung up with 911, did you?"

"No."

Linda frowned, telegraphing disapproval. "So you did not call your own wife, the mother of this child, to tell her that you had found her only daughter dead on your porch?"

"No."

"Isn't it true that you didn't call her because you couldn't face her?"

"No." Noah felt the pressure to answer building inside him. Maggie would want the answer.

"Dr. Alderman, isn't it true that you didn't call her because you knew that your wife, the woman who knows you best, would know that you had killed her daughter?"

"No, I didn't call her because I knew she wouldn't answer. She wasn't taking my calls."

"But you called her from the car after you left the gym, did you not?"

"Oh. Yes, I did." Noah had forgotten he did that. It was a habit. Maggie always left work before he did. He always called her on the way home. It had been when he missed Maggie the most, the in-between times, the interstices of his life that she filled in, connecting everything. He had never known that until he'd lost her. And then it was too late.

"So you called her after the gym, knowing that she wouldn't take the call, yet later, holding her precious daughter dead in your arms, you didn't call her?"

Noah didn't know what to say. He knew Maggie would be listening to every word. He couldn't see her face. He knew what it would look like. Devastated.

"Dr. Alderman?"

"I forget the question," Noah blurted out, and there was shifting in the jury box behind him, but he didn't dare look over. He knew what their expressions would look like too. Distant. Incredulous. Furious.

"Isn't it true that you didn't call your wife because you wanted to call your criminal lawyer?"

"No."

"But as you testified, you were worried that you were going to be suspected of Anna's murder, weren't you?"

"Okay, yes, I was." Noah was confusing himself, his mind on Maggie. The gallery. The jury. The judge.

"Dr. Alderman, isn't it true that when the police came, you declined to answer any questions?"

Thomas rose. "Objection, Your Honor. The jury is not permitted to draw any adverse inference regarding Dr. Alderman's exercise of his constitutional rights."

Judge Gardner nodded. "Sustained."

Thomas rose. "Your Honor, this cross-examination has gone on quite some time. May I request a brief break, Your Honor?"

Linda frowned. "Your Honor, I don't think that's necessary."

"I do, Ms. Swain-Pettit." Judge Gardner reached for the gavel. "We'll recess for fifteen minutes, ladies and gentlemen."

Noah breathed a relieved sigh, avoiding Linda's eye. He was looking for Maggie.

Chapter Twenty-six

Maggie, Before

"So this will be fun!" Maggie cruised down the street with Anna, seeing her neighbors inside their houses, the kids hunkering down to homework in the family room and the parents getting ready for the work week, fighting off the Sunday night gloom. She knew that feeling, but she didn't have it tonight. Everything felt like a new experience, with Anna.

"Agree!" Anna smiled.

"And King of Prussia is a great mall. It has every store imaginable. J. Crew, Abercrombie, Free People, Nordstrom." Maggie left out Neiman Marcus, since that may have been in Anna's price bracket, but not her and Noah's.

"There's a pop-up store there, too. I saw it online. It's called Circa. It sells really cool stuff, like vintage. Boho."

"Okay, sounds great." Maggie felt suddenly cool and hip. Pop-up stores. Mall trips. Girly fun. She wasn't an odd duck anymore, with a secret daughter. She was a full-blown mom.

"And I want to pay for this, okay?" Anna looked over, her ponytail swinging. "These are my expenses. James approves them. I never even spend that much."

"I know, but let me treat you tonight." Maggie turned onto Montgomery Avenue, taking the back roads.

"Then let's split it, okay?"

"Okay." Maggie wondered if Noah would agree. "You know, Noah and I were talking about house rules, and how to make rules for you."

"Rules?" Anna looked over, blinking.

"Nothing too onerous. We're not really strict with Caleb. But we should probably have some rules for both of you."

"Okay," Anna said, slowly enough to make Maggie wonder if she was pushing the point.

"I don't want to make a big thing of it. I'm just thinking that with respect to purchases, whether it's the clothes or the car, we might discuss those things as a family."

"If you want to, I will." Anna shrugged. "You're right, you guys should make the rules and I'll follow them. I followed the rules at Congreve."

"What rules did they have? Curfews?"

"Yes, but I never went out. I don't think following a curfew is going to be a problem here, either." Anna shot her a sideways glance. "It's not like my social calendar is going to be crazy busy."

"I know you'll make friends, and like my mother used to tell me, 'it only takes one.'" Maggie hadn't remembered it until this very moment.

"Did you have a lot of friends, growing up?"

"Yes, I did, but it wasn't easy. I was insecure." Maggie realized she had stumbled onto something. Maybe a way to get Anna to talk about herself was to be open about her past. "I used to be fat. My dad always said 'pleasingly plump,' and in an Italian family, plump is always pleasing. I never thought it was a bad thing until I got to school. I got bullied and called names."

"Fat-shaming."

"Right." Maggie stopped at a traffic light, the red burning into the increasing darkness. "So I felt shy, but there was one girl in my Latin class and we became best friends."

"So it only took one."

"Yes, but it's not like I had a lot of dates." Maggie felt a twinge, surprised she carried the dumb high-school hurts, even now. She was fifty-two pounds lighter, but a fat kid inside. "I got asked to the senior prom by a guy I liked, and his friends called him a chubby chaser."

"That's so mean!"

"I know, and he was a great guy."

"It'll be strange to go to school with boys," Anna said, after a moment.

"You didn't have a boyfriend at Congreve, did you?" Maggie asked, trying to keep her tone casual. She was asking for Noah.

"No."

"You could meet a guy this week who could ask you out. Or you could even ask him out."

Anna waved her off. "No one will ask me out."

"You don't know that. You're beautiful and smart and any guy would be lucky to date you." Maggie steered through the night, heading toward Route 202. "And if a guy happens to ask you out, and you like him, you should say yes. You could have a date this weekend."

"You *think*?" Anna squealed, which made Maggie laugh.

"Of course! You're assuming things will go badly. Why not assume that they'll go well?"

"Because they never have?"

"Things are changing." Maggie thought a minute. "And listen, I have to bring this up because I'm the mom. You know we can talk about sex, right?"

"Oh my God, really?" Anna burst into laughter. "Are you serious right now?"

"Yes. That's the one thing I want to do differently from my mom." Maggie felt her smile fade. "It took a lot of growing up and therapy for me to feel comfortable talking about sex, much less having sex."

"Really." Anna's tone turned surprised.

"Yes." Maggie hesitated. "May I ask you, have you had sex?"

Anna covered her face, giggling. "I can't believe you!"

"It's okay, you can tell me. No judgment."

Anna's hands slid from her face. "I feel weird talking about this."

"I'll go first, then. I had sex for the first time when I was seventeen, just your age."

"Whoa! Okay. We're jumping right in." Anna laughed again.

"There was a guy I had a crush on. He was in my Latin class, he was a swimmer. Little-known fact, they have the best bodies. Take it from me."

"Ha!" Anna giggled.

"We went to a party where everybody was drinking. He told me he wanted me to be his girlfriend, which he didn't, and we had sex in the basement. Then he dumped me and started calling me Meatball."

"Oh no!"

"Let me tell you, being Meatball Ippoliti is no fun. The sex lasted five minutes, but the nickname lasted until graduation."

"I'm sorry." Anna groaned.

"It's okay, it happens." Maggie glanced over, but couldn't see Anna's expression in the dark. The only light was backlighting, emanating from the townhome developments.

"Do you regret it?"

"Not really. I learned from it, and it wasn't the end of the world. I fell in and out of love a few times with some wonderful men until I got it right."

"Like with my father?"

"Yes," Maggie answered, though she had been thinking of Noah. "But it's not what I would want for you. So, you see where I'm coming from? How about you?"

Anna paused. "I haven't really had sex yet."

Maggie kept her hands on the wheel, cruising past the homes. She knew she had been right. She couldn't wait to tell Noah. She loved being right.

"There was this one guy, from our brother school, but we didn't have sex. He wrote poetry, too. I showed him my poems, and he said they were 'pedestrian.'"

"Oh please. What a jerk."

"Anyway, it never came to anything. I never even went on a date with him."

"His loss."

"Thanks." Anna giggled again. "This is kind of fun, hanging with my mom."

"Aw, I feel the same way about my daughter." Maggie spotted the lights of the King of Prussia Mall and aimed for the exit ramp.

"I think I'm going to like living here."

"I think you are, too," Maggie said, hopeful.

Chapter Twenty-seven

Noah, After

TRIAL, DAY 5

Linda gestured to the projection screen, where the Petition for Protection From Abuse was showing. "Dr. Alderman, that hearing on the Petition for the Protection From Abuse took place on an emergency basis on Monday, May 8, did it not?"

"Yes."

"The hearing lasted only a single morning, isn't that true?"

"Yes."

"And there were only two witnesses, isn't that correct?"

"Yes."

"And isn't it true that Anna testified at that hearing on her own behalf?"

"Yes."

"And you testified on your own behalf, isn't that correct?"

"Yes."

"You had your present counsel, Thomas Owusu, represent you at this hearing, didn't you, Dr. Alderman?"

"Yes."

"However, Anna relied upon legal services, did she not?"

"Yes." Noah suspected he knew why Anna had used a legal services lawyer, but Thomas had told him to keep that to himself. Anna's trust fund never came into the record at the PFA hearing, and using legal services made her look helpless and sympathetic, in contrast to the rich, powerful doctor.

"You were present when Anna testified, were you not?" Linda strode to counsel table, picked up a packet, and returned to the stand with them.

"Yes."

Linda turned to face Judge Gardner. "Your Honor, may we approach the bench for a sidebar?"

"Certainly," Judge Gardner answered, and Thomas shot up and barreled toward the dais. Noah was close enough to hear whatever they were going to say, though he assumed the jury couldn't, in theory.

Linda cleared her throat. "Your Honor, the audiofile from the PFA hearing has become available and I would like to move it into evidence and play that to impeach Dr. Alderman."

Judge Gardner blinked. "Ms. Swain-Pettit, are you saying that you have the victim's actual testimony on audio?"

"Yes, exactly."

Noah held his breath. It would be terrible if they played Anna's PFA testimony, her voice echoing throughout the courtroom. She had testified that day, so credibly. It would kill Maggie and convict him, for sure.

Thomas scowled. "Your Honor, I object. This is outrageous. It's hearsay and it violates an array of my client's constitutional rights, including the confrontation clause. In addition, why wasn't I notified about this audiotape? I haven't had a chance to review it and neither has my client. It's been almost seven months since he was arrested. Does the prosecutor expect us to believe that she happened to locate it *just now*?"

Judge Gardner shifted his gaze to Linda. "Ms. Swain-Pettit?"

"Your Honor, I only got this case four months ago. Nobody before me even asked about getting the audiofile. You know how this courthouse works, some of the courtrooms have the systems working and some don't and—"

Thomas interjected, "Your Honor, if you're believing this, I have a bridge I can sell you."

Linda ignored him. "—then they had to find the transcription specialist, and we've outsourced some of it, so it was a slog. The audiotape was just found two days ago. I would've notified defense counsel, but I didn't know that he was going to call his client to the stand."

Noah saw the jury craning to hear, which wasn't difficult since Linda was intentionally raising her voice.

Thomas shook his head. "Your Honor, the prosecutor should've spoken up the moment I put my client on the stand, which she did not. Further, I object to playing the raw audiotape because it is completely prejudicial. It's like the victim would be speaking from the grave, and it will unduly inflame the jury."

"Your Honor," Linda said, in a quieter tone. "This jury is entitled to the truth, and there is no better way to get the truth than through Anna's own words. It's not hearsay because it comes in under the exception and it doesn't violate the confrontation clause because the defendant had a chance to cross-examine at the PFA hearing. At the heart of this case is a credibility contest, but I'm hamstrung here because the victim is dead—"

Judge Gardner cut her off with a hand chop. "Ms. Swain-Pettit, your request is denied. The audiotape is a different matter than the transcript. It goes too far. Mr. Owusu, your objection is sustained."

"Thank you, Your Honor." Thomas turned from the dais, and Noah knew they had just dodged a bullet. It was a rare victory for them, but at least they had points on the board. Except that the jury had heard they were being deprived of Anna's own words.

"Thank you, Your Honor." Linda signaled her paralegal. "Dr. Alderman, I am calling to the screen Commonwealth Exhibit 52, a transcript of the PFA hearing."

Chapter Twenty-eight

Maggie, Before

Maggie drove while Anna sat plugged into her phone, but she knew from driving Caleb around that moms were Uber without the tip. They approached Lower Merion High School and the district administration building, a massive low-profiled rectangle with several different wings, encircled by well-trimmed hedge, mulched beds of forsythia, and a lush lawn. An American flag flapped on a tall pole, and in front was a sign painted by the theater students advertising the spring show, *Oklahoma!*

"I love *Oklahoma!*" Maggie said, glancing over. "Have you seen it?"

"No."

"The song, 'Oh, What a Beautiful Mornin' is from *Oklahoma!* It *is* a beautiful morning, isn't it?" Maggie smiled, trying to be cheery. In fact, it was cool and sunny, and this morning when she'd checked the garden, she'd spotted buds on her peonies, balled like tiny fists.

Anna started texting, and Maggie looked over, wondering.

"Anna, if you don't mind my asking, who are you texting?"

"I'm not, I'm using my app. It's called Calm. Ellen turned me on to it."

"How does it work?"

"You choose what you're interested in, like calming your thoughts, reducing anxiety, helping you sleep, or building self-esteem."

"So what did you choose?"

"All of the above." Anna smiled.

"I had no idea they had apps like that."

"I have a ton." Anna started scrolling through her phone. "Pacifica, Chill, Relaxed State, Nervana. Jamie really loved Nervana. She was into the breathing and meditation apps like Headspace. Her parents worried she'd commit suicide, but she never would. They had her on the suicide-prevention apps like Crisis Care and some others."

"There are apps for suicide prevention?" Maggie felt a pang for teenagers in so much pain. From her postpartum days, she knew how it felt to have anguish you couldn't wish away.

"They used an app that searches your social media for the words 'kill myself' or 'kill yourself.' It even searched her texts and emails, like, if she said KMS in a text it meant, kill myself. KYS is kill yourself." Anna frowned. "I don't think they had the right to do that. They invaded her privacy."

"I guess sometimes you have to protect your child from herself."

"But maybe if they hadn't pushed her, she wouldn't have left school." Anna looked at the high school as they rounded the curve. "Do you think I'm too dressed up?"

"No, you look great." Maggie glanced over, and Anna had on one of her new boho dresses, a flowy affair in dark blues. Her brownish hair swung shiny to her shoulders, complementing her lovely blue eyes.

"It was dumb to dress up. I look like a tryhard."

"What does that mean?" Maggie smiled. "I try hard."

"It means you're thirsty."

"I'm thirsty, too!" Maggie said, and they both laughed. She turned into the entrance, steered toward the parking lot, pulled in, and they walked to the school, which was modern and newly renovated, with tan stone and four large panels of glass above an overhang for the main entrance.

Anna looking this way and that. "That must be the student lot. I can't wait to go car shopping."

"We will, in time." Maggie had forgotten to talk to Anna about the new car. They entered the school's bright entrance room, with its large black rug that read LM in maroon letters, then went to the main office, another large, bright room with a long counter of light wood. The school staff worked on sleek desks behind the counter, and a waiting room held maroon-padded chairs organized in a square.

They went to the counter, and a blond staff member approached them with a smile. "May I help you?"

"Yes, I'm Maggie Ippoliti, and I have an appointment to register my daughter, Anna Desroches."

"Great, Maggie." The staffer turned to Anna. "Anna, I'm Judy, and welcome to Lower Merion. Did you bring your papers?"

"I did, right here." Maggie dug in her purse and extracted a thick folder of documents that James had emailed them. "Here's her immunization records, transcript, Social Security card and birth certificate, and bills showing proof of residence. I also filled out the Parental Registration Statement."

"Thank you so much. I'll get these photocopied." Judy took the folder and turned to Anna. "We'll get you into classes tomorrow. I'm going to introduce you to your guidance counselor, and she'll go over your schedule with you, then give you a quick tour."

"That sounds great."

"Thank you," Maggie said, then they were taken down a hallway blanketed with colorful college pennants to the Guidance Center to meet Brittany Holt, a young brunette in a Lilly Pulitzer dress. Brittany's office was covered with inspirational posters and a metal rack of pamphlets: Straight Talk for Teens About Alcohol, 37 Scary But True Facts About Drugs, and When Is It Rape? Maggie eyed the titles, realizing that she had a whole new list of things to worry about, while Brittany and Anna talked about her course schedule.

When they were finished, Brittany stood up. "If you have time, I'd like to show you around."

"Sure, thank you," Anna answered, and Maggie followed them out of the office and into the large hallway area packed with students plugged into iPhones and carrying backpacks, purses, and gear bags.

Brittany nodded. "This is a really busy time, changing from A lunch to B lunch. The bus schedule determines our hours, and the high school gets the earliest pick-up."

"My old school was much smaller." Anna scanned the scene, nervously.

"Are you planning on taking the bus or driving, Anna?"

"Driving."

"Then you'll need a parking permit. You can apply for one in the office." Brittany turned to Maggie. "Don't let our size worry you, as a parent. Even though we have a lot of students, we have an excellent student–teacher ratio."

"That's great." Maggie smiled, and Brittany led the way past a collage with scenes of the school, which read Enter To Learn, Go Forth To Serve next to a placard of a bulldog, the school mascot. Students checked Anna out, but she looked down. Brittany pointed out the gorgeous Bryant Gymnasium donated by the basketball-playing alum Kobe Bryant, then the well-appointed library, display cases of trophies, and a banner that read Governor's Award for Excellence in Academics. The tour ended at the cafeteria, which was massive, with students laughing, talking, and eating at long gray tables, between two all-glass walls.

"Oh, there's those girls from *Phrases*." Anna pointed at one of the tables, and Maggie saw a table of three girls, all wearing funky clothes like the ones at Circa. She recognized the girl in the middle from the Facebook picture.

Brittany glanced at her phone. "There's still ten minutes. Let's take a peek inside, shall we?"

Maggie nodded. "Great idea. Anna, you can say hi to those girls, introduce yourself."

"No, thanks," Anna answered quickly. "I don't want to go in."

Maggie looked over. "You sure, honey? I'd like to."

"I don't need to." Anna met her eye meaningfully, then turned to Brittany. "Can I use the bathroom?"

"Of course." Brittany pointed. "The ladies' room is on the left."

"Be right back." Anna edged backwards, and Maggie watched her go, guessing that Anna didn't want to be introduced with her mother.

Brittany leaned over. "She's a very smart, sweet girl, but she seems quiet."

"I know." Maggie felt defensive on Anna's behalf. "I think she's overwhelmed. The school she came from was more sheltered. She'll get used to it in time."

"Right, I saw Congreve online. It's much smaller. But don't worry, I'll keep an eye on her."

"Thanks. She's worried about making friends."

"She needs to join something. That's the best way."

"We talked about that. She likes poetry." Maggie pointed to the *Phrases* table. "They're the Poetry Club, right?"

"That's one name for them." Brittany sniffed.

"What do you mean?"

"Strictly between us?" Brittany leaned closer. "And this is just my opinion, okay? That table is the Island of Misfit Toys."

"Really," Maggie thought back to the pamphlets in the guidance office. Drugs. Alcohol. Suicide. She fell into a troubled silence as Anna returned with a smile.

Brittany turned to her. "Anna, it was wonderful meeting you."

"You too, thanks so much." Anna shook her hand. "I'll see you tomorrow."

Maggie extended a hand to Brittany. "Thank you so much. We really appreciate your time."

"You ladies are welcome to stay for lunch. It's Pizza Day."

"That's okay, thanks," Anna answered quickly. "We have errands to run."

We do? Maggie thought, but didn't say.

Chapter Twenty-nine

Noah, After

TRIAL, DAY 5

Linda signaled to her paralegal. "Dr. Alderman, please direct your attention to Commonwealth Exhibit 52, which is the transcript of the PFA hearing."

Thomas jumped up. "Your Honor, I object to the admission of the transcript as hearsay, violative of my client's constitutional right to confrontation, and unduly prejudicial."

Linda turned back to the judge. "Your Honor, the transcript is admissible as a hearsay exception under rule 804(b)(1) in that it is former testimony that was given as a witness at trial who is now unavailable, due to death. The defendant had a full and fair opportunity to examine the witness at the hearing, under *Commonwealth v. Bazemore*."

Judge Gardner nodded. "The objection's overruled."

"Thank you, Your Honor." Linda signaled again to her paralegal, and the screen came to life with a portion of the transcript:

Mr. Carter: Ms. Desroches, what happened when you went out for a driving lesson with your stepfather on Thursday night, April 27?

Ms. Desroches: He took me driving in the parking lot behind the shopping center, and it was after

dark. It was just the two of us in the car, and
on the way over, he said some inappropriate things
to me. They were compliments but over the line.
Mr. Carter: Like what?
Ms. Desroches: Like that I was beautiful, and I
had great eyes, nice hair, and I had great dimples
like my mom.
Mr. Carter: How did that make you feel?
Ms. Desroches: I thought it was nice at first, but
then it started to make me very uncomfortable. I
mean, he's my stepfather. He was acting like we
were on a date.

Linda faced Noah. "Dr. Alderman, you were present when Anna testified about these inappropriate remarks, were you not?"

"Yes."

"You testified that you didn't make any such remarks, isn't that right?"

"No, that was not my testimony," Noah answered, without hesitation. Linda was trying to trip him up, but it wouldn't work. Thomas warned him that his trial testimony had to be consistent with his PFA testimony, so Noah had memorized the PFA transcript. Surprisingly, his memorization skills from med school weren't rusty.

"What *did* you say to Anna in the car?"

"I might have said, 'you look nice,' but that was it."

"You never told her she had great eyes?"

"No."

"You never told her she had nice hair?"

"No."

"You never told her she had great dimples?"

"I said that, too." Noah felt on edge. He tried not to look at the back row for Maggie. He would be pointing her out to the media.

"Isn't it true that you intended your compliments to be seductive?"

"No."

"But you intended it to be pleasing and flattering, did you not?"

"Yes."

"So you were trying to flatter Anna, weren't you?"

"No, not *flatter* her." Noah was about to say *per se*, but caught himself. "I was trying to be nice."

"You were trying to get Anna to like you, isn't that right?"

"Yes."

"So that you could seduce her, isn't that right?"

"No."

"Dr. Alderman, weren't you *grooming* her?"

"Objection, Your Honor!" Thomas rose. "The prosecutor is using an inflammatory and prejudicial term."

Linda faced Judge Gardner. "Your Honor, that term could not be more relevant to this case."

Judge Gardner nodded. "Overruled."

"Thank you, Your Honor," Linda said, turning to Noah. "Dr. Alderman, weren't you trying to *groom* her?"

"No, I wouldn't use the term *grooming*."

Linda nodded. "Oh I see, you took the hint from your counsel, didn't you?"

"Objection, Your Honor." Thomas half-rose. "Counsel is testifying and trying to—"

"Sustained," Judge Gardner said, before Linda could even argue.

"Dr. Alderman, please direct your attention to the next section of Commonwealth Exhibit 52." Linda signaled to the paralegal, and the screen changed.

Mr. Carter: Let's return specifically to the night of April 27, when you went out for your driving lesson with your stepfather. Do you recall what happened that gave rise to your petition?

Ms. Desroches: Yes, I'm sorry. That's what you asked me before. I'm a little nervous. It's so weird to be here. I never was in court before, and it's hard to say these things, out loud.

Mr. Carter: Of course. We understand. That's okay.

Ms. Desroches: What he said was, um, sexual, and it's weird to say in front of everybody, especially him, since he's looking at me like that.

Mr. Carter: You mean your stepfather is looking at you a certain way in the courtroom, right now?

Ms. Desroches: Yes, he's glaring at me. I know he's mad I filed the petition but I want him to stop doing -

Mr. Carter: Let the record reflect that the Defendant is attempting to intimidate this witness. Your Honor, I ask that the Defendant be removed from the courtroom immediately.

Mr. Owusu: Objection, Your Honor. I'm sitting next to my client and he is doing no such thing.

Mr. Carter: But Your Honor, Defendant's attorney cannot see his client's face from his vantage point.

Mr. Owusu: Your Honor, I object to Petitioner's request. These are grave allegations, and the Defendant intends to take the stand. He cannot exercise that right if he has not been permitted to hear the testimony.

Mr. Carter: Your Honor, Defendant is in no way entitled to intimidate this young woman, taking unfair advantage of their disparate positions and power. Not only is he her stepfather, but he is older and a doctor.

The Hon. Jane Hamilton: I will permit Defendant to remain in the courtroom. Dr. Alderman, I was not looking at you, so I cannot determine if you were making menacing faces -

The Defendant: I wasn't, Your Honor.

The Hon. Jane Hamilton: Please don't interrupt me. I wasn't asking for a response, sir. You're not under oath and you may not testify from counsel

```
table. I warn you that I will not allow the
intimidation of any witness who comes before me
seeking a Protection From Abuse order against a
domestic abuser. My courtroom always will be a
safe place for them, and I will not allow it to be
violated in any way, shape, or form. Mr. Carter,
you may continue your direct examination of the
witness.
```

Linda straightened. "Dr. Alderman, you recall that exchange, don't you?"

"Yes." Noah remembered being startled when Anna referred to him directly from the stand, and the judge's explanation characterized him as a domestic abuser in front of the jury. He heard them shifting, and the courtroom sketch artist flipped a page of brown paper, her pastel chalk between her teeth.

"Weren't you making faces at Anna to intimidate her?"

"No."

"So when she said that, she was lying?"

"Yes."

"Dr. Alderman, you previously testified that you had *some* anger at Anna for filing the Petition for the PFA, didn't you?"

"Yes."

"You had *some* anger because you claim Anna falsely alleged that you had attempted to engaged in sexual misconduct with her, isn't that right?"

"Yes."

"You had not heard the specifics of these allegations before Anna testified about them at the PFA, isn't that correct?"

"Yes."

"So if they were untrue, as you claim they are, then they would have come as a surprise to you, wouldn't they?"

"Yes."

"Isn't it possible that when you heard those allegations against you for the first time, your facial expression reflected *some* anger?"

"I don't know, I can't say. I don't know what my face looked like that day."

Linda's eyebrow lifted. "Then you can't know that you *didn't* look angry, can you?"

"Well, no."

"So then, isn't it entirely possible that you *did* look angry when you heard Anna's testimony, isn't that correct?"

"I . . . suppose so." Noah had just contradicted himself. Linda had hog-tied him with his own words.

"So then Anna *wasn't* lying when she said that your expression was angry, was she?"

"No."

Linda signaled to her paralegal. "Let's move on."

Chapter Thirty

Maggie, Before

"What errands?" Maggie asked Anna, who perked up as soon as they left the school building.

"Can we go to the Land Rover dealership, please? Just for fun? It's only fifteen minutes away."

"How do you know that? You've only lived here a day." Maggie smiled, surprised. She reached for her keys and chirped the Subaru unlocked.

"I Google-mapped it." They climbed into the car, shutting the doors behind them.

"You can't really want a Land Rover, can you?" Maggie reversed out of the space. "My first car was an old Mazda, bought used. It was bright orange. I named it Tangerine. I figured I'd rather be a tangerine than a meatball."

Anna smiled crookedly. "But I like Land Rovers. Dad drove one and so did my grandparents. They say they're the safest cars, like a tank."

"But they're so expensive. How much is a Land Rover?"

"The Range Rover is $75,000, not *that* expensive."

"Honey, that's expensive, in my book." Maggie spared Anna the Value of Money lecture because she was about to deliver the Meeting New People lecture.

"But can't we go look, just for fun?"

"Okay, for fun." Maggie took a right turn on Montgomery Avenue, heading toward the dealership. "So what do you think of the school?"

"It's crazy *big*."

"Don't worry. You'll be fine."

"I hope so." Anna looked out the windshield, biting her nails.

"Why didn't you want to go in the cafeteria? Because I was with you?"

"No, I just wasn't ready."

"Okay." Maggie thought about what the guidance counselor had said, about the Poetry Club being the Island of Misfit Toys. "You know, those *Phrases* girls seem nice, but it's good to keep an open mind to different sorts of people. I saw a lot of nice-looking kids in the cafeteria."

"Okay, but can we talk about the car? So, they come standard with all these driving aids, like the command driving position . . ." Anna yammered all the way to the dealership, marked by a silvery sign and man-made hillock topped by a new Land Rover, demonstrating off-road capabilities that no high-school junior would ever need.

"We're just having fun, remember?" Maggie pulled in and turned to Anna, but she was already climbing out of the car.

"Sure, I texted the guy."

"What?" Maggie grabbed her purse hastily and got out of the car to see Anna waving to a young African-American man in a green polo shirt and khaki pants.

"Hey, Simon!" Anna called out to him.

"Perfect timing!" Simon called back to Anna, shaking her hand as Maggie arrived.

"I'm Maggie Ippoliti, Anna's mother." Maggie shook Simon's hand.

"Great to meet you." Simon held up a clunky ignition key. "Ready to go? I'd be happy to take you guys out. Maggie, I'd rather you drove since Anna doesn't have a valid PA license and she's a minor."

"Let's go!" Anna said, excitedly.

Maggie hesitated. "Simon, that won't be necessary. We wouldn't want to take your time."

"Nah, it's fine. Follow me." Simon handed Maggie the key and led them to a glistening black Range Rover parked at the head of the line. "This is the Range Rover Sport HSE, in Narvik black."

Anna clapped. "Beautiful!"

"Very nice." Maggie glanced at the sticker, and the bottom line was $75,000.

"Everybody into the pool." Simon climbed in the backseat, Anna took the passenger seat, and Maggie hoisted herself into the driver's seat. The car interior was a buttery-tan leather with perforated seats, a black cockpit with large dials, and matte-silver trim.

Anna ran a finger on the dashboard. "This feels soooo good."

Simon poked his head between the front seats. "Take a look at the simplicity of the cabin. Those are quality finishes. Of course, the air-bags are behind there too, but you'd never know it."

Maggie plunged the thick key into the ignition, nervously. She hadn't expected to test-drive anything, much less a house on wheels.

"The Range Rover has a four-by-four capability but the ride is very smooth, truly a luxury ride. Now Maggie, reverse out. You've got room."

"What if I hit something?"

"You won't. The big windows make for great safety and visibility. Check the camera."

Anna touched her arm. "You got this, Mom. No fear."

Mom. "No fear," Maggie repeated. She steered the big car out of the lot and turned cautiously into traffic on Lancaster Avenue.

Simon gestured. "Go up two blocks. Take a right. Then we'll be on the back roads."

Maggie's fingers gripped the wheel. "Got it. Are we having fun yet?"

"Totally!" Anna bounced. "This is the cushiest seat ever!"

"It sure is," Simon said, from the backseat. "You can go anywhere you want to and have total comfort every step of the way."

"And it's safe," Anna added.

"Correct," Simon said, as if cued. "I know a lot of parents worry about safety. There are distracted drivers everywhere. People texting. Eating in their cars. Reading Facebook."

"You're making me more nervous," Maggie interjected, steering the big car.

"Not to worry. The car has every feature possible to keep us completely safe. Turn right here."

"Thanks." Maggie reached the corner and steered uphill onto a two-lane road.

Anna held on to the plastic hand strap. "Give it more gas."

"I'm fine at this speed."

"Don't you want to open it up?"

"It's open enough." Maggie kept an eye out for deer or squirrels.

"Mom, go for it. It has a six-cylinder engine, four-wheel drive."

"So you could drive up Everest?"

Anna laughed, giddy. "Here, the road is straight now, you can go faster. Just to see what the car can do."

"She's right," Simon interjected from the backseat. "Anna knows as much about this car as I do. She could do my job tomorrow."

Anna beamed. "Simon, don't you think she should go faster?"

"I'm not going any faster," Maggie answered, firmly. "I don't own this car."

"Don't worry, Mom. I do."

"What are you talking about?" Maggie glanced over, confused. "Anna, we're not buying this car."

"You don't have to. I already did. Surprise!" Anna grinned.

"Are you *serious*?"

"Yes, James wired them the money. Right, Simon?" Anna faced the backseat, and Simon popped his head between the seats.

"Yes, I got the wire this morning. The deal's done."

"Wait, what, hold on." Maggie felt so dumbfounded that she pulled over to the side of the road. "Anna, what are you talking about? You can't buy a car when you're seventeen."

"Yes, you can." Anna nodded, delighted. "And I did."

"She can't do that, can she, Simon?" Maggie turned to the back-seat, and if Simon was surprised that Maggie hadn't known, it didn't show.

"Yes, she can. We do it all the time. It's the Main Line. She couldn't finance the car at her age, but she's not doing that. We can't let her drive it off the lot because we prefer she have a valid Pennsylvania license. But it's hers."

"Really?" Maggie felt like an intruder into SuperRich World. Noah wouldn't pay cash for a Range Rover, even if they could. She struggled to get up to speed. "What if I said she couldn't have it? Would you take it back?"

Anna interjected, "No, Mom, I want it!"

Simon shook his head. "Sorry, all sales are final. We'll help you sell it, if you wish. I could speak with—"

Anna interrupted, "But Mom, it's an awesome car, don't you think?"

"This is crazy, honey." Maggie didn't know where to begin. "You said we were coming for fun."

"I know, I wanted to surprise you." Anna's face lit up.

"But we can't even get it home."

"Not a problem." Anna turned excitedly to Simon. "You said you'll deliver it. You said that, right?"

"You deliver a car, like a *pizza?*" Maggie asked, aware that the Range Rover's being delivered was the least significant of facts.

"Of course," Simon answered with a grin. "Welcome to the family."

Chapter Thirty-one

Noah, After

TRIAL, DAY 5

"Dr. Alderman, please direct your attention to Commonwealth Exhibit 52."

Noah turned to the screen, cringing inwardly.

Mr. Carter: What took place during your driving lesson on April 27 that gave rise to this petition?

Ms. Desroches: It was kind of dark and my stepfather Noah and I were in the parking lot, and no one was around. Well, maybe there were a few cars but they were far away, and I was practicing trying to get in and out of the space by the stanchion, like, where the light was.

Mr. Carter: And were the two of you alone in the car?

Ms. Desroches: Yes. I asked Noah if my stepbrother Caleb could go with us, that's his son, but he said no, that I needed to concentrate. Anyway, I was reversing out of the space, and he was showing me how to use the rearview mirror on the outside, so my head was turned away, and all of a sudden, I felt, like, his hand up my dress on my thigh. I was so surprised I knocked my phone off the console.

Mr. Carter: Did you say anything?

Ms. Desroches: No, I was so startled and I was about to say something but I didn't know what to say, so I, like, pretended it wasn't happening.

Mr. Carter: Did he say anything?

Mr. Owusu: Objection, calls for hearsay.

Mr. Carter: Your Honor, as you know, PFA hearings don't adhere strictly to the rules of evidence, and his client is free to rebut this testimony when he testifies.

The Hon. Jane Hamilton: Overruled.

Mr. Carter: Thank you, Your Honor.

Mr. Owusu: Thank you, Your Honor.

Mr. Carter: Do you remember the question? It was, "Did he say anything?"

Ms. Desroches: He said, "How does that feel?" And he moved his hand farther up, you know what I mean.

Mr. Carter: Anna, I know this is difficult, but you have to explain what you mean.

Ms. Desroches: But it's so awkward and I feel so weird.

Mr. Carter: I understand that, but please try to explain it more particularly.

Ms. Desroches: He moved his hand closer up my thigh, like, close to my underwear, and he said, "I can teach you a lot of things more important than driving. Your first time should be nice, and I know how to do that."

Mr. Carter: And what did you say, if anything?

Ms. Desroches: I didn't know what to say, I was so shocked, and I said, "What are you doing?" and he acted all innocent and pulled out his hand. He said, "I thought you dropped your phone." And I

said, "Don't do that ever again or I'm telling
Mom."

Mr. Carter: And what did he say, if anything?

Ms. Desroches: Nothing.

"Dr. Alderman, you recall the incident to which Anna is referring, don't you?"

"No, that isn't what happened," Noah answered, consistent with
his testimony in the PFA hearing.

"Didn't you take Anna driving on the night in question?"

"Yes."

"Isn't Caleb your ten-year-old son?"

"Yes." Noah felt a deep pang, thinking of Caleb. He only saw his
son twice a month, when Maggie's best friend, Kathy, brought him
to MCCF. They kept the conversation light, but Caleb was always
nervous, wide-eyed at the other inmates in the visiting room, who
would cry or even fight with their families. Worse, Noah could tell
that Caleb saw him differently, acting more guarded, which was
understandable. It tore Noah's heart out to think of what he had
done to Caleb, and his only consolation was that the boy was home
with Maggie, who loved him to the marrow.

"Dr. Alderman, isn't it true Anna requested that Caleb come along
on the driving lesson, but you declined, saying she had to concentrate?"

Noah hadn't been asked that in the PFA hearing. "Yes, that is true.
But the real reason I didn't ask Caleb is because my wife asked me
to take Anna out alone, so we could spend time together."

Linda's eyes flew open. "Your testimony is that you took Anna
driving alone at your *wife's* request?"

"Yes." Noah ignored the spectators in the gallery, turning their
heads to look at each other.

"You didn't testify as to that in the PFA hearing, did you?"

"No, because I wasn't asked specifically."

Linda frowned in an exaggerated way. "So you may have been
asked, but it wasn't specific enough, is that your testimony?"

"Yes," Noah said, knowing it was the wrong answer but the only one he had.

"So you're testifying now that the reason you took Anna driving without Caleb was because your wife asked you to?"

"Yes."

"But that's not what you told Anna, is it?"

Noah blinked. "No."

"Dr. Alderman, when Anna asked you if Caleb could come, you told her that he couldn't because she had to concentrate, isn't that right?"

"Yes."

"So you lied to Anna, isn't that right?"

"Yes." Noah heard shifting behind him in the jury box, not that he needed that to let him know how badly his testimony was going. And Maggie was in the courtroom.

"Isn't it true that you put your hand on her thigh?"

"No, that's not what happened."

"Dr. Alderman, please answer yes or no. Did you or did you not put your hand on Anna's thigh?"

"It's not susceptible to a yes or no answer, and I can explain." Noah spotted Thomas looking at him in disapproval, but it couldn't be helped. "What happened was I put my hand on her leg, maybe on her thigh but certainly not under her dress, because her phone dropped from the console and fell in her lap. She said, 'Oops, my phone fell,' and I went to get it. My hand may have been in her lap, but I was reaching for the phone and I didn't get it, so I stopped."

"So even though Anna told the truth about Caleb, she was lying when she said you put your hand under her dress?"

"Yes."

"And even though Anna told the truth about Caleb, she was lying when she said that you told her that you could teach her for her first time?"

"Yes."

"Dr. Alderman, weren't you referring to her virginity?"

"I didn't say anything like it."

"But you know if Anna was a virgin?"

Noah wondered if Maggie remembered their conversation. None of this had come out at the PFA hearing. It had been more broadbrush. He didn't know whether to lie or tell the truth. The truth would get him in worse trouble, so he lied. "I believe she was."

"How did you know?"

"My wife told me."

"Dr. Alderman, didn't you proposition her sexually during the driving lesson?"

"No."

"Your testimony is that you put your hand in Anna's lap to get her phone?"

"Yes, I thought she wanted me to."

"But she didn't ask you to get her phone, did she, even according to your version of the incident?"

"No, but I thought it was implied. She said, 'oops, my phone fell.'" Noah realized they hadn't asked this at the PFA hearing, either.

Linda frowned. "Dr. Alderman, your testimony is that you think it's *implied* that when a young girl's phone drops into her lap, you are entitled to *plunge* your hand between her legs to retrieve it?"

"Objection, Your Honor." Thomas jumped up. "That mischaracterizes my client's testimony."

Linda faced Judge Gardner. "Your Honor, that's the substance of what Dr. Alderman just testified to."

Judge Gardner shook his head. "Sustained. Ms. Swain-Pettit, I'm going to ask you to rephrase."

"Thank you, Your Honor," Thomas said, sitting down.

"Your Honor, I'll strike the question and ask another." Linda turned to Noah. "Dr. Alderman, isn't it true that you used the dropped phone as an excuse to put your hand into Anna's lap?"

"No."

"Isn't it true that you had growing lustful urges toward Anna?"

"No."

"Let's explore that further," Linda said, motioning to her paralegal.

Chapter Thirty-two

Maggie, Before

Maggie drove home from the dealership with Anna, glancing in the rearview mirror to see Simon in the black Range Rover, followed by another black Range Rover, like a caravan of Bulgarian diplomats.

"Are you mad at me?" Anna asked, shaky. "Please, don't be mad."

"I'm not mad, but I wish you hadn't done it." Maggie chose her words carefully. She was trying to build their relationship and she didn't want to hurt their new closeness.

"I thought I was doing a good thing."

"Why?" Maggie kept her tone even. "You didn't tell me."

"Because it was a surprise."

"But not a good one."

"Why not? I'm being responsible. I needed a car, did the research, and bought one. And I looked into the insurance and if I didn't have my own insurance, you'd have to put me on yours."

"So you called James and got the money?" Maggie remembered that James had told her Anna wanted a car and barely used funds from the trust.

"No, I texted him."

Maggie hid her reaction. She lived in a world where teenagers texted for eighty-thousand-dollar cars. "Did you tell him what it was for?"

"Sure."

"Did you tell him that I didn't know about it?"

"No, he didn't ask." Anna pursed her lips. "Please don't fire him. It's not his fault. It's my fault. I didn't want to burden you guys."

"It's not a burden, it's our job as your parents." Maggie felt more confounded then angry. "We talked about this. We were supposed to make that decision as a family."

"Maybe that's the problem," Anna said, after a moment. "I never had a family before. I've been on my own all my life. I don't consult with anybody. If I need something, I get it."

"Maybe that's true." Maggie felt sympathy, and guilt. Anna had learned to be on her own because she'd been abandoned, by both parents.

"I *never* spend money. But I wanted the car, I told you. I'm not a brat."

"I'm not saying you are."

"I thought you would think it was adult of me," Anna said, hurt. "Remember when we went to dinner in Congreve, and you told the waiter to give you the check? You beat me to it, and I thought, that's so smooth. So I said to myself, 'I'm just going to beat her to the check.' That's why I took care of it."

"I see." Maggie felt touched that Anna wanted to be like her.

"I think the kids at school are really going to like it."

"I don't want you to get a car because you think it will help you make friends."

"That's not the reason I did it, but that's okay, don't you think?"

"No, I don't, honey," Maggie answered, gently. "You don't want the kind of friends who like you because you have a cool car."

"But I saw Land Rovers in the student lot at school and on Facebook. It'll fit in."

"You'll make friends. You could have given it a chance. You could have given *yourself* a chance."

Anna sighed. "I can sell it, if you really don't want me to have it."

"It's not that I don't want you to have it, and if we tried to sell it now, we'd get a fraction of its value."

"So can we keep it, please? I promise I won't do anything like this, ever again. Really."

"Only if you understand my point." Maggie looked over when they stopped at a red light, and Anna looked back at her, her mouth turning down at the corners.

"I do. I totally understand, and I'm really sorry."

"Okay."

"So you're not mad anymore?"

"No."

"Cool." Anna smiled.

Maggie felt better to see her happy. "Did you ever drive such a big car before?"

"No, we used compact cars at Congreve to make it easier to pass the test."

"So Noah can take you out in it, then?"

"Yes."

"Great," Maggie said, though Noah had texted her while they were at the dealership, **bad news, be home late.** She'd called him back but no response.

All told, she wasn't looking forward to the evening.

Chapter Thirty-three

Noah, After

Linda signaled her paralegal, and another transcript portion appeared on the screen. "Dr. Alderman, please direct your attention to Commonwealth Exhibit 52."

Noah read:

Mr. Carter: Anna, how would you characterize your relationship to your stepfather?
Ms. Desroches: When I first moved in, I felt nervous around him and I told my mom that, and then I realized that he has two sides to him, like, a light side and a dark side. He showed my mother and his son his good side, and I'm sure his patients think he's a nice doctor. But his dark side comes out when he's angry or when he's out of control. Then, he snaps. He's very controlling. I think his anger at me started when he couldn't control me or when I wouldn't give in to, you know, what he wanted. My friend at school, Samantha, calls him Dr. Jekyll and Mr. Hyde.
Mr. Carter: And Samantha is?
Ms. Desroches: Samantha Silas.

Thomas rose. "Objection, Your Honor. This is not only hearsay, it's double hearsay and completely unreliable. We have no opportunity to cross-examine Samantha Silas or determine the factual basis for her opinion. I objected to its admissibility at the PFA hearing and I'm renewing my objection."

Linda faced Judge Gardner. "Your Honor, you have correctly ruled that the transcript from the PFA hearing is admissible."

Thomas shook his head. "Your Honor, this is not a PFA hearing, but a murder trial. Rules of evidence are strictly observed here to guarantee the constitutional protections due my client. I let it go earlier, because it wasn't as important as this. This portion regarding Samantha Silas should not be admissible."

Judge Gardner frowned at Linda. "Ms. Swain-Pettit, do you know if Samantha Silas is available?"

"I do not, Your Honor. If defense counsel insists, we can strike Samantha Silas's statement from the record."

Thomas pursed his lips. "Your Honor, that won't unring the bell."

Judge Gardner sighed. "The objection is sustained in part and overruled in part. Stenographer, please strike from the record the statement regarding Samantha Silas's opinion. The transcript is otherwise admissible, and the jury can determine the weight they will give this testimony." He turned to the jury. "Ladies and gentlemen, please disregard that last statement regarding the opinion of Samantha Silas."

"Thank you, Your Honor." Thomas sat down heavily.

"Thank you, Your Honor," Linda said, signaling again to her paralegal, and a new transcript appeared on the screen.

Mr. Carter: Is there an example you can recall in which the Defendant became angry or out of control, which would help the Court understand the basis for your testimony?

Ms. Desroches: Yes, I needed a car to get to school and I bought one with my own money, as a cool surprise. My mother didn't love it at first,

but we talked it over and she said from now on I
should talk to her about it, and that was that. But
my stepfather saw the car in the driveway when he
came home and he freaked out.

Mr. Carter: What do you mean by "freaked out?"

Ms. Desroches: He became angry and abusive. He
yelled at me, telling me that I was in his house
now and I had to follow his rules and I had to ask
his permission before I did anything and everything.
That's exactly what he said, too. And he yelled at
my mother and my stepbrother, then he sent me
upstairs and I hadn't even eaten yet, and later I
heard him and my mother fighting.

Mr. Carter: Did the fighting turn physical?

Ms. Desroches: No. He's much smarter than that.
He's manipulative. And when he doesn't get what he
wants, he becomes angry and out of control. That
night, he banged the table so hard that a glass
broke. That's what I mean, like Samantha said, he's
Dr. Jekyll and Mr. Hyde.

"Objection!" Thomas said, then he and Linda started fighting
again, but Noah tuned them out, stricken. He remembered every detail of that night. He knew he'd been out of control, and if he could
explain himself to the jury, he could convince them that he wasn't
Dr. Jekyll and Mr. Hyde.

Noah had been at work when he got the call that one of his favorite patients, a fifteen-year-old named Mike Wilson, had died. Mike
was allergic to bee stings and always carried an EpiPen with him.
Mike even had great parents, Dina and Steve, who always reminded
him, *No pen left behind.* Noah had made up the slogan himself to
help his young patients.

But on this one day, Mike had left to play soccer from a friend's
house, leaving the EpiPen. Mike had gotten stung on the field, gone
into anaphylactic shock, and died. Noah had rushed to the emergency

department, answered Dina and Steve's heartbreaking questions, and comforted them while they cried.

Noah had left the hospital with their agonizing questions in his ears—*did he feel pain, what was it like, did he suffocate to death*—then had driven home and found the black Range Rover in his driveway. He'd spotted the temporary tag taped to the window, and in that moment, it had become clear to him that he couldn't control anything, neither the allergens, nor Mike or his other patients. Not even his own family.

What the hell's in the driveway? Noah had shouted as soon as he'd walked in the door.

Babe? Maggie recoiled, surprised. *There's no need to yell. It's Anna's car, and I already talked to her about it. She bought it with her own money.*

That's not the point! She bought it without permission!

We've settled that already and—

She has to ask permission! Noah had shouted, slamming the table. A glass fell over and rolled onto the floor, breaking on the hardwood. *Anna, go to your room right now! You have to ask my permission for anything and everything!*

Suddenly Noah came out of his reverie because Linda and Thomas were leaving the dais. He didn't know what they'd decided. Thomas caught Noah's eye and tilted his chin upward, in a victorious way. The projection screen went abruptly blank.

Judge Gardner turned to the jury. "Ladies and gentlemen of the jury, we're going to strike from the record not only the statement regarding Samantha Silas, but that transcript portion in general. Court stenographer, please strike that portion from the record."

Noah's heart sank, understanding that he would never be able to explain why he had acted that way.

"Let's move on, Dr. Alderman," Linda began.

Chapter Thirty-four

Maggie, Before

Maggie knew that Noah was upset the moment he walked in the door and she knew why. She'd called the office when they'd gotten home, and they'd told her that Mike Wilson had died. Everyone was upset, and Maggie knew that Noah would take it badly, since he'd adored Mike. But even so, she would never have expected him to come home so angry. He'd yelled at Anna about the Range Rover, and she'd run upstairs while Caleb had hustled outside with Wreck-It Ralph, leaving Maggie alone with Noah in the dining room.

"Maggie, how could you let this happen? What's the matter with you?"

"Noah, really?" Maggie tried to get her bearings. She stepped back against the table, set for dinner. She'd tried to make everything special. A salmon fillet with fresh dill and rosemary potatoes roasted in the oven, filling the air with its distinctive aromas. She'd cut peonies from her garden and put them in a glass vase, and the late-day sun filtered through the windows.

"What, *really*?"

"Look, I know you're upset about Mike, and I'm so sorry but—"

"This isn't about Mike."

"Yes it is." Maggie knew Noah better than he knew himself, which was probably what most wives thought, and they were right.

"It is not!"

"Stop yelling, you're acting crazy."

"The hell I am, the *hell* I am! Do you know how *outrageous* that is?" Noah motioned at the driveway. "That a seventeen-year-old buys a brand-new Range Rover, just because she wants one? Do you know how much those cars cost?"

"Yes, but that's no reason to holler."

"Evidently, I have to because nobody listens! I told you that she was going to get that car. I gave you the heads-up. You dragged your feet on this, and look what happened! Who's in charge here?"

"Noah, lower your voice or I'm not going to talk to you anymore." Maggie swallowed hard, shaken.

"We are a family. She is supposed to be a part of this family. She joins us, we don't join her. We set the rules, not her."

"We didn't have a rule that you can't buy a car, and anyway, that's not what you're upset about." Maggie could see that his eyes were bloodshot, and he must've been upset after the hospital. "I heard you went to meet Dina and Steve. How are they?"

"This isn't about them, either. This is about Anna and how we live our lives." Noah motioned to the driveway again. "And *that* is *not* how we live our lives. We don't blow money like that."

"It's her money—"

"The point is she has to ask us if she can buy something that big. She lives under our roof and she has to learn our values. That's what parents do. They teach their children values."

"She's never been part of a family before. She's learning—"

"She's running the place. She even took my parking space. I can't even park in my own driveway."

"Noah, we talked about it, and it won't happen again."

"You're damn right it won't. That car's going right back to the dealer."

"No, all sales are final, and I told her she could keep it." Maggie was trying to reason with him, despite the resentment building in her chest. "We can teach her our value system, no matter what she drives. She made a mistake, and that's part of the learning process."

"Oh really? There's a *learning process*? When did it start? Because the good ship 'begin at the beginning' already sailed."

"I'm sorry, I let it get away from me."

"You sure did, honey."

"Stop it. Don't be so snide." Maggie didn't like the way he was looking at her, with contempt. "And really, is it the end of the world? Did she lie, cheat, or steal? No, she bought herself a car because she's used to being on her own. She's not used to asking anybody for permission because nobody's ever been there to ask, most of all *me*. And it's not why you're upset anyway."

"Will you please stop telling me how I'm feeling!" Noah scowled. "I'm feeling the way anybody would feel, any father, any *man* who came into his house and saw that it was completely out of control."

"It's in control. Maybe not your control, but my control."

"Oh please. She's got you wrapped around her little finger. You're overcompensating out the wazoo. What's she buying next, a house?"

"*Basta!*" Maggie stalked out of the dining room. "Clean up the glass you broke, before Ralph steps on it."

"Fine!" Noah shouted after her, and Maggie stormed up the stairs, fighting tears. She reached the second floor, went to Anna's door, and knocked quietly.

"Honey?" Maggie called softly.

Chapter Thirty-five

Noah, After
TRIAL, DAY 5

Noah sat on the witness stand during another conference with the judge at the dais. This time the courtroom clerk had misnumbered some exhibits, and Thomas, Linda, and Judge Gardner were fixing them, leaving Noah waiting awkwardly, his hands linked in his lap. He didn't know what to do with himself, like someone eating alone in a restaurant, except that at the end of the meal he could go to prison for the rest of his life.

Noah couldn't stop thinking about the fight over the Range Rover, which now marked him as Dr. Jekyll and Mr. Hyde. After Maggie had gone upstairs, he'd cleaned up the broken glass, gotten a beer, and looked outside the kitchen window. Caleb had been playing with Ralph in the backyard, and Noah had heard him talking to the cat. When Caleb had been younger, he had practiced counting in front of Ralph, who didn't seem to mind that Caleb had apraxia and his 1, 2, 3, 4, 5 sounded like *pa, poo, pee, bah, pi*.

Noah had thought about how much he loved his son and what it would do to him if he lost Caleb, the way Dina and Steve had lost Mike. Even the way that Maggie had lost Anna, gone from her life, only an infant. He felt a wave of guilt that he had treated them all so badly.

Noah had gone out the back door and crossed the lawn to Caleb, with his beer in his hand. *Hey buddy.*

Hey Dad, Caleb had answered, and Noah walked around to the front of Caleb so they could see each other.

I'm sorry I yelled, buddy.

It's okay, Caleb had said, but it had come out like *zoky,* unintelligible to anyone else, which meant he was stressed, not taking the time to formulate a motor plan and form his words more clearly.

Want to go inside? It's getting dark.

That's okay, Caleb had said, but it sounded like *thzoky.*

What if we skip dinner and have ice cream? I think there's mint chocolate chip in the freezer.

No.

Mind if I keep you company?

No.

Good. Noah had taken another sip of beer, then sat down on the grass, cross-legged. Ralph had come over, sniffing the sweating beer bottle, and Noah stroked the cat's back. Ralph's tail curled into a question mark.

He doesn't like that. Pet under his chin.

Okay. Noah scratched Ralph under his chin, and the cat squinched up his face, wrinkling his nose.

He drooled and purred, Caleb had said, but it was barely intelligible. The letter R was difficult for kids with apraxia and other speech disorders. Noah remembered they were behind on their target words this week and at this rate, they'd never get to *accident, badges, antiseptic,* or *emergency.*

Noah said, *I really am sorry I threw that fit. I'm going to say I'm sorry to Maggie and Anna too.*

Not Anna. She got a car. She didn't ask.

Yes, that's true, but two wrongs don't make a right. I'm the father and I have to act like one.

You're not her father.

No, that's true, Noah had said, surprised. *I'm not her biological father, but I'm her stepfather.*

Caleb had fallen silent, looking away at the cat, and Noah had realized that he might have been overlooking Caleb's reaction to Anna's moving in.

What do you think about that, Caleb?

Caleb hadn't answered.

Does it make you happy or sad? You can tell me, buddy.

Still no reply. Caleb always shut down when he was stressed. He'd known his speech wasn't up to the task.

Son, don't worry about how the words come out. Just tell me. I can understand you. I thought you liked her.

She doesn't like me.

Why do you say that? I think she does. I know she does. You guys had a good time with the trains. Noah had touched Caleb's bare arm, chilled in the cooling air. It had been a cold spring, and the backyard smelled of soggy mulch.

She said a curse.

What was the curse?

We were in the car. She said, "Don't effing touch the buttons."

Caleb, that was wrong. Noah had flashed on the night at Bed Bath & Beyond, when Anna had asked him if he wanted to know how soft she was. Maybe he hadn't misheard her. Maybe this was a game she played. Or maybe Caleb had been lying out of jealousy.

Dad, don't tell Mag. Mag loves her.

Caleb, Maggie loves you, too, you know. She loves you very much.

I know. She always tells me.

Good. Noah had given Caleb a hug, and in time they had gone inside, and the courtroom came back into focus and Noah wasn't in his backyard anymore. Thomas, Linda, and Judge Gardner were still huddling, leaving the jury in suspended animation and Noah on the witness stand, wondering if anything would have been different if he'd told Maggie what Caleb had said.

But what had happened next was so much worse, it had gone forgotten.

Chapter Thirty-six

Maggie, Before

"Can I come in?" Maggie asked Anna, through the closed door.

"Okay," Anna answered, her voice shaky, and Maggie slipped inside the room to see Anna cross-legged on her bed with her laptop open, her lovely blue eyes shining with tears.

"Anna, I'm sorry."

"No, I'm sorry." Anna wiped her cheek, leaving pinkish streaks. "I'm so stupid. I never should've bought the car. What an idiot."

"You're not an idiot." Maggie came over, sat on the edge of the bed, and patted Anna's leg.

"Yes, I am, and I bought it because it was cool. That was stupid, too. I bet those girls in the Poetry Club will hate that car. I don't know what I was thinking."

"Say to yourself, 'lesson learned,' and be done with it. That's what my mother would say." Maggie smoothed a strand of Anna's hair from her face.

"Are you mad at me, now that Noah is?"

"No, and he'll calm down. I'm sorry he behaved so badly. A patient of his died today. I would have told you, but you and Caleb were having so much fun in the car."

"Look, that's sad, but I heard what he said. He thinks I'm a spoiled brat." New tears shone in Anna's eyes, and Maggie's heart went out to her.

"No, he doesn't."

"I didn't realize it was his parking space. I should've told them not to park in the driveway."

"I swear to you, that's not what's bothering him. We'll get this sorted out."

"I'm worried we won't." Anna sniffled. "There's no way he's taking me driving now. I don't need the lesson anyway. I can get used to the car on my own."

"No, he wants to."

"It's not only about the car." Anna's lower lip trembled. "I made a mess of things. I was just emailing James to see what my options are."

"What are you talking about, options?" Maggie felt a note of worry.

"You know, like, emancipation. Noah doesn't want me here." Anna's eyes glistened. "You might, but he doesn't. Coming here was a big mistake."

"Don't say that, that's not true." Maggie squeezed Anna's arm, as if she could hold her in the house. "You're jumping the gun, honey. It's only the first week."

"But I didn't want to mess things up for you. I just wanted to be with you and get to know you. I wanted my mom." Anna's eyes spilled over, and Maggie gave her a hug.

"And I'm here."

"I'm messing up your family."

"You *are* my family." Maggie released Anna, then motioned her up. "Come with me. Right now."

"What?" Anna moved the laptop.

"You'll see." Maggie took Anna's hand, led her out of the bedroom, and into the master bedroom. The room was a soothing blue that complemented a blue-chintz quilt, headboard, and curtains, a custom-made splurge. Maggie gestured to the bed. "Please, sit down."

"Why?"

"You'll see." Maggie crossed to the closet, opened the door on the left, and rummaged on her side, which was markedly messier than

Noah's side, though in her own defense, she had dresses, shoes, sweaters, scarves, purses, and skirts, and he had testosterone. She retrieved the fancy blue Lanvin shoebox from the top shelf and brought it over to the bed, opening the lid.

"What's this?" Anna shifted on the bed, leaning over the box, and Maggie sat down next to her, putting the box on her lap and digging inside.

"These are my keepsakes from when you were born." Maggie picked out the item on top, a plastic baby bracelet that read Ident-A-Band. "Here, from the hospital."

"Oh my God, really?" Anna looked over, and Maggie read aloud what was written on a piece of paper inside.

"'Girl of Maggie I. Desroches, 3/6/2000, 8:12 pm, BKF.' That's you." Maggie felt her heart lighten, thinking back. "You were born at eight o'clock at night. Can you imagine your wrist was ever that little?"

"No." Anna giggled. "I'm surprised you kept it."

"Your baby bracelet? I bet all mothers do. It's precious."

Anna slipped it over her index finger. "So little!"

"You were only six pounds when you were born."

"Is that fat or skinny?"

"Skinny. Fat was my department." Maggie smiled.

"What does BKF stand for?"

"Bolton, Kraus, Finer. That was my OB group. Dr. Finer delivered you. He was great." Maggie felt a twinge, thinking back. Dr. Finer had been a wonderful OB, the doc who confirmed her diagnosis of postpartum psychosis, but she didn't want to think about that now.

"Look." Anna slid two fingers inside the bracelet. "That was my entire wrist."

"If I rested you on my arm, you could fit almost completely on my forearm and hand."

Anna smiled. "What happened the night I was born? Did it hurt?"

"Well, that day I felt kind of tired—"

"Were you throwing up?"

"Not past the first trimester." Maggie threw up the whole

pregnancy, but enough already. "So I'd read somewhere that the way to induce labor was to stay really active, so I went food shopping, and I was in the produce aisle when my water broke. I basically peed myself in front of the green peppers."

Anna squealed, covering her mouth. "That's so embarrassing! Then what happened?"

"I didn't know what to do, I just froze, then I realized that I had to get to a hospital."

"Did you call Dad?"

"No, he was out of town." Maggie kept her smile on, even after she remembered that Florian had been in Palo Alto, allegedly trying to raise venture capital. She would learn later that he'd cheated on her with a blond Stanford senior, and Kathy would joke that he'd raised adventure capital.

"So what did you do?"

"I took a cab to the hospital, and Kathy met me there. You were born on your due date."

"Dad wasn't there?"

"He came later," Maggie answered, diplomatically. "He got the red eye out of San Francisco and was there just in time to say hello."

"Aw." Anna smiled, and Maggie returned to digging in the box. She pulled out a wrinkled white envelope, and on the front she had written in faded ballpoint, *Anna's First Curl.*

"You saved my *hair*?" Anna laughed.

"Sure. My mother saved my first curl, too. I have it somewhere, I think in my jewelry box." Maggie didn't add that her mother had also saved her teeth, gross little nuggets bundled in a Kleenex and wrapped with a rubber band.

"Can I see my curl?" Anna shifted over.

"Of course. You had such pretty hair, it was so soft and fine." Maggie unsealed the back of the envelope, yellowed with age.

"When was the last time you opened this?"

"I never have. I vowed to myself that I wouldn't open it until I got you back in my life. I've never even gone in this box."

"Aw." Anna smiled softly.

"And now we get to do it together." Maggie swallowed hard, unglued the back flap, and looked inside the envelope. There was a flattened C-shape of a brownish curl, and all of the memories came flooding back, like a wave of emotion. "Wow."

"Let me see."

Maggie felt herself choke up, but kept it together. "I remember that I used to play with that curl while you were nursing. I used to curl it around my finger."

"I nursed?"

"Yes, for about three months." Maggie shook the curl into her palm, then moved her hand into the waning sunlight, which caught the reddish highlights amid the light brown strands.

"So much red! I don't have that much anymore, do I?"

"No, your hair's browner now. Mine got darker, too, from when I was little."

"Dad had a lot of red in his hair."

"Yes, he did." Maggie shook the curl back into the envelope, thinking back to the time she had first met Florian. His hair was the best thing about him. It took her a decade to learn that looks didn't matter. The fact that Noah was handsome was just gravy. He was a good man, and he probably already felt lousy about the way he'd acted, which he should.

"What else is in there?" Anna peered into the box, plucked out the cotton knit hat they'd given her in the hospital, and popped it on her head. "Cute?"

"Very!" Anna put the hat back in the box, and they went through the pink card that had been on Anna's bassinet, an unofficial birth certificate with her footprint, a cottony-white receiving blanket, and an old color photograph of Maggie as a young mother, sitting with a happy infant Anna in her lap, the both of them facing the camera.

Maggie felt a warm rush of love, showing the photograph to Anna. "And here we are."

"Aww. Who took the picture? Dad?"

"No, Kathy."

"I'd like to meet her."

"You will." Maggie smiled. "She's your godmother."

Anna eyed the picture. "I look more like you than Dad."

"Yes, you do." Maggie smiled, returning her attention to the photo. The resemblance between mother and daughter was unmistakable, in the dimples and the grin, which was happy with a side order of goofy.

"It was a long time ago, wasn't it?"

"Yes, it was, and that's the time that we lost." Maggie put the photo in the box, replaced the lid, and looked directly at Anna. "And that's why your being here means so much to me. I prayed you would come back in my life and you have. So don't worry about any of this fussing with Noah, okay?"

"Okay." Anna nodded, with a shaky smile.

Maggie patted the box. "This is where we started. And this is where we belong. Together."

Chapter Thirty-seven

Noah, After
TRIAL, DAY 5

Noah waited on the witness stand while Thomas, Linda, and Judge Gardner were still conferring. He retreated to his memories, mentally escaping the courtroom. Even bad memories were better than a murder trial, if you were the defendant.

Noah was thinking back to the night of the Range Rover fight, after his talk with Caleb. Noah had put Caleb to bed while Maggie was in their bedroom with Anna. He had gone back downstairs to clean up and by the time he'd gotten upstairs, Maggie had gone to bed, facing away from him.

Noah had undressed and slipped into his side of the bed, linking his fingers across his chest like a dead man, which was how he'd felt. Maggie hadn't been sleeping, but she'd been waiting for him to talk first, playing marital chicken.

You awake, babe? Noah had asked softly.

What do you think?

I'm sorry. I really am. Noah had turned over, but Maggie hadn't. She had on a T-shirt, though she always slept naked this time of year, and so did he. He'd always liked that about them as a couple.

That was terrible, Noah. You behaved terribly.

I know, and I'm sorry. I just lost it. It was only partly because of Mike. But that wasn't all of it. Noah had still felt he'd been right about the

Range Rover, but he hadn't wanted to start all over again. *No matter what I think about her getting the car, I shouldn't have yelled like that. At you, Anna, or at Caleb. I'm sorry.*

It was terrible. Maggie hadn't turned around. *She thinks she's not welcome here. And I don't blame her. You're not making her feel welcome.*

I know and I'm sorry.

You have to apologize to her.

I will.

I'm going to make a special dinner tomorrow night, Indian food. She told me she loves it. And it's her first day of school. You can apologize then.

I'd be happy to, Noah had said, meaning it. His father had been one of those men who would never say he was sorry.

Can you imagine how she feels? She moves in here, having lost her father, having no sense of place at all, moving to a new state and a new family, and the welcome she gets is you yelling at her?

I understand.

We don't yell at our kids. That's not our values, as you say, is it?

No, I know that. Noah had heard the shakiness in her voice and realized that she might've been crying earlier. He'd put a hand on her shoulder, but she hadn't moved. Normally, she would've turned over and they would've hugged or had make-up sex. That wasn't happening tonight, so he didn't even try. He'd removed his hand.

She was crying in her bedroom.

I'm sorry. Noah had found himself counting, that had been the fourth time he'd said he was sorry.

And what about the driving?

I'll take her. It had galled Noah that he'd be teaching Anna to drive in that car, but whatever.

What if she doesn't want you to, now? The car is obviously a sore spot.

I'll convince her, I'll say I'm sorry. Noah had ticked it off in his head. *Fifth time.*

I thought it was a chance for you guys to get close. I thought it was something you could share. Now it's all ruined.

It's not ruined, Noah had said, though it was Anna's fault, not his. *She was looking up lawyers, too.*

Why? Is she going to sue me?

It's not funny.

Okay, fine. Noah had heard irritation creep into his voice. He'd been trying to stay patient, but there was a limit. Mike Wilson had died today. Dina had been so distraught she'd had to be sedated. Steve had asked Noah if Mike had suffered before he died. Noah hadn't had the heart to tell him the truth.

Anna's thinking about whether she should emancipate herself so she doesn't have to live here. Because you're not succeeding in making her feel welcome, and I feel like I'm cleaning up after you. Even Caleb is really trying to be nice to her. You should've seen the two of them, laughing in the car.

Noah had stayed silent. He'd thought about what Caleb had said in the backyard.

You have to make this right, Noah. We need to earn her trust in the beginning. Some things you just can't come back from. Sometimes there's just too much damage done.

I know, and I'm sorry, Noah had said again, losing count of his apologies. He'd felt exhausted, the awful events of the day catching up with him. His eyes had begun to close, and he'd fallen into a restless sleep.

Noah looked over when he noticed Judge Gardner shifting backwards into his tall chair, then swiveling to face the jury.

"Ladies and gentlemen, my apologies." The judge gestured to the courtroom deputy. "Please take the jury into the jury room while counsel and I sort this out. We'll recess for twenty minutes."

Chapter Thirty-eight

Maggie, Before

"Come in, honey!" Maggie opened the front door for Kathy, who held a cardboard carrier with two large cups of coffee and a bag of doughnuts.

"Good morning." Kathy grinned, stepping inside in her fleece top with jeans. "This is so exciting! Anna is moved in and everything?"

"Yes, isn't it amazing? I'll show you her room in a minute. Coffee and doughnuts first." Maggie led her into the kitchen, where she pulled out two stools at the island. Wreck-It Ralph sat at the far end, which was permissible, if vaguely unsanitary.

"Meanwhile, you got a new car?" Kathy sat down, setting the coffees and food on the island. She opened the bag and took out a doughnut oozing strawberry jelly.

"It's not ours, it's Anna's. She bought it herself, with cash."

"*What* cash?" Kathy's eyes flared with surprise.

"Wait'll you hear." Maggie sat down next to Kathy, took a sip of coffee, and launched into an update on Anna's arrival, her inheritance, the Island of Misfit Toys, and the Range Rover fight.

Kathy's brow knitted. "Noah yelled at you? That's not like him."

"I know, he apologized." Maggie was trying to let it go. "It's because of Mike."

"Give him time. He's trying. He gave her his home office. He'll have to adjust to having Anna here, and that can't be helped or rushed. So cut him a break."

"You're right." Maggie took a final sip of coffee. "Maybe tonight will get us back on track. It's her first day of school, and I'm making Indian food. Noah's going to apologize to her, too."

"Good. You need to settle into each other, that's all." Kathy rose. "Show me her room. I'm dying to see."

"I have to go get paint chips today so she can choose a wall color. I'm thinking blue, but you can let me know what you think." Maggie rose, taking the lead, and they went upstairs to Anna's room. Anna had unpacked and moved in all of her things, and Maggie felt pleased at how the room looked, with the pretty bed, bureau, and bookshelf full of textbooks, novels, and volumes of poetry.

"What a transformation!" Kathy walked to the bed, touching its frilly canopy with her fingertips. "I love the canopy."

"She picked it out."

"And how cute is this?" Kathy went over to the bookshelves. "So many books!"

"I know. She's a big reader." Maggie scanned the hardbacks of the entire Harry Potter series, took one off the shelf, and flipped through the pages. A line of Hermione's dialogue was underlined, where Anna had written a margin note that read, awesome! "Aw, she likes Hermione."

"Don't we all?" Hermione is Nancy Drew with a British accent."

"She really likes poetry. That's her thing." Maggie replaced the Harry Potter book and slid out a volume of Sylvia Plath.

"Sylvia Plath? Now there's a fun gal."

"She was a good poet."

"But she dies in the end. I know, I saw the movie. Gwyneth Paltrow, my girl crush."

"I didn't know that about you." Maggie looked over with a smile.

"Now you do. I subscribe to Goop. How else will I know where to eat in Barcelona?"

"You're not going to Barcelona."

"What if I do and I'm hungry?"

Maggie replaced the Sylvia Plath book. "Anna wants to join the Poetry Club at school, like I was telling you. The Misfit Toys."

"Don't sweat it. Teenagers choose their friends. You can't help it."

"What if they choose the wrong ones?"

"Then you'll deal." Kathy slid one of the textbooks off the shelf. "You say she gets good grades?"

"Yes." Maggie had been so proud to see Anna's transcript from Congreve, emailed by James. "Even in math."

"Oh look at this." Kathy thumbed through an algebra textbook and plucked a piece of paper from the pages, chuckling. "They pass notes in class, like we did."

"Really?" Maggie leaned over to see the note. "I recognize Anna's handwriting from the Harry Potter book. It's the second line."

"The one with smaller print." Kathy nodded, and they read together:

Please God make it stop
It won't be on the midterm anyway
She's the worst teacher in the history of teachers
Boogie alert—check her left nostril
OMG too funny
She's literally wearing mucus
What a hag! She could be a Wiccan
LOL guaranteed

Maggie smiled. "I remember when we used to make fun of teachers."

"Now I'm the teacher, and kids are making fun of me. Meanwhile, do I have a boogie in my left nostril?"

Maggie laughed, returning her attention to the note. "I wonder if this is between Anna and her friend Jamie, who left school."

"Left school? That's too bad for Anna." Kathy replaced the note, flipped through the other pages, and pulled out another note. "Oh look, here's a second."

Maggie looked over. "This time, the first line is Anna."

She spits when she talks
That's part of her charm
I bet she chews with her mouth open
I know she does
How
High tea on parents weekend, remember? She ate a raspberry scone.
You can't unsee that.
I wasn't there
Oh right sry
So there are advantages to having no parents
Take mine

Maggie felt a wave of guilt. "The poor kid. How much does it suck to be on Parents' Weekend with no parents? I should've been there for her."

"You can't own everything. Sometimes people are working against you, and Florian did that, and he won." Kathy put the book back, and another note fell to the rug.

Maggie bent down to pick it up.

I'm so over this place and my family. I'm leaving
For real?
Yes
When
Tomorrow night after dinner. PG and Connie are getting me a bus ticket.
My parents would know if I put it on the amex.
Don't go
I have to. I'll be happier. PG agrees.
Don't. You're my one and only friend ☹
I'll stay in touch
Promise
I promise

"Oh no," Maggie said, taken aback. "This must have been between Anna and Jamie, and it looks like Jamie ran away. I didn't get that impression from Anna when we talked about it."

"Maybe she didn't want you to know?" Kathy arched an eyebrow.

"I wonder if Jamie has been in touch with Anna since she ran away."

"She might have lied." Kathy pursed her lips.

"I hate to think that."

Kathy shrugged. "It happens. Jamie was her only friend from school, right?"

"Yes, but she said they weren't that close."

"They look close from these notes." Kathy shot Maggie a knowing look. "Maybe Anna lied to you about that too."

"Right." Maggie had to admit it made sense. "We don't know if Jamie got in touch with Anna after she left."

"But she promised to. That matters with kids."

Maggie mulled it over. "If Anna knows where Jamie is, we should tell Jamie's parents."

"Agree. Also, Connie or PG, whoever they are, might know where Jamie is, since they bought the bus ticket for Jamie."

"Right. They're probably on the poetry magazine. That was the circle of friends. PG has to be initials, doesn't it? Unless it's a nickname."

"We can look for the Congreve Poetry Club on Facebook. Maybe they have a page." Kathy slid her phone from her pocket.

"They might not. The school keeps the privacy settings high. Anna's therapist said they discourage social media."

"What's the name of the poetry magazine?" Kathy scrolled through her phone to Facebook.

"*The Zephyr.*"

"*The Zephyr?* Gimme a break. Do these people lack a shit detector?" Kathy typed in the search function, and no organization appeared, only a list of people with their profile pictures. "There's no page for *The Zephyr* at Congreve, so you were right.

Meanwhile, people are actually named Zephyr? Who names their kid Zephyr?"

"Gwyneth Paltrow?"

Kathy looked up. "Hater."

"Maybe there are other notes?" Maggie reached for another textbook.

Chapter Thirty-nine

Noah, After
TRIAL, DAY 5

"That was a mess-up," Noah said, when Thomas entered the attorney's conference room.

"Which mess-up are you talking about? There were so many." Thomas sat down. His skin looked shiny in the fluorescent lights overhead.

"I'm trying."

"I know but she's scoring off you." Thomas sighed heavily. "I stalled to slow her down, break her rhythm. It's like basketball. She had a hot hand."

"I had no idea." Noah would never get over the gamesmanship in a courtroom. "What should I do while you guys are talking with the judge?"

"Just sit there being quiet. It's when you talk you get in trouble."

"Ha." Noah forced a smile, knowing Thomas was trying to cheer him up.

"Just keep on keepin' on."

"It's because Maggie—" Noah started to say, then stopped himself. Thomas wouldn't know that Maggie had been in the courtroom.

"What about Maggie?"

"I haven't seen her yet. Have you?"

"No, but Tim is keeping an eye out. She's not there."

"Oh." Noah assumed that Maggie's disguise was working, to a total stranger. "What bothers me is that they're getting such a wrong picture of Anna, like she was perfect and wonderful. She was anything but."

"Noah, we've discussed this—"

"But she was hardly sweet and innocent." Noah shook his head, disgusted. "That testimony about the night I lost my temper? I get why you objected, but I could've explained that. That was the day my patient died. It was awful."

"Were you negligent?"

"Of course not." Noah recoiled.

"What difference would that have made, that your patient died?"

"I was upset that day, I wasn't myself. Don't you think that if they knew that shouting was atypical for me, that would make them question that I'm a control freak, intent on controlling Anna?"

"You want to prove that you only yelled this one time and that Anna is manipulative?"

"Yes."

"That's blaming the victim, and it never works. It's the legal equivalent to speaking ill of the dead. In addition, it only gives you more of a motive to kill her. If she was ruining your family, you wanted to take revenge for that, or put a stop to it. When she filed for that PFA against you, the cat was out of the bag on your happy home life."

"We had a happy home until her."

"I can't prove that unless you let me call Maggie."

"No." Noah felt frustrated, trying to make him understand. "They don't know how selfish Anna really was. Like there was this one time, Maggie was going to make this nice Indian dinner, and I was going to apologize. We were sitting at the table waiting, and Anna doesn't come home. Maggie's calling everywhere, even hospitals. Anna didn't call or answer Maggie's texts."

"And?" Thomas blinked, unimpressed.

"And then she waltzes in late, saying she got a ride home, and that was that. No apology for not answering the texts."

"Noah, this is minor."

"But it's indicative of who she really was. It was rude and selfish."

"You sound like a control freak right now."

"It's not about control, it's about what a family is. And she bullied Caleb, too. She told him to get out of her car when he touched the radio."

"My nephew does that. Drives me nuts."

"She was using us."

"For what?" Thomas asked, skeptical. "What did she need from you? She had all the money in the world. She didn't need anything from you guys."

"I could never figure that out." Noah racked his brain. "I have no answer."

"And that's why it wouldn't make sense to bring up to a jury."

"They're not understanding what it was like, living with her. She wanted her own rules."

"In other words, a typical teenager."

"It sounds that way, but it's not. The only one she listened to was Maggie. We fought constantly over her. Caleb regressed because of the stress. She ruined our lives. She ruined our family."

"And you wanted to get her back for that, so you strangled her with your bare hands."

Stunned, Noah didn't say anything.

"You have my point. That cannot be our theory of the case because it gives you ample motive, even more than the failed seduction. And it plays into the picture they're painting of you as Dr. Jekyll and Mr. Hyde."

Noah flashed on a bigger fight with Anna, when Anna had lied to him and Maggie about her friend Jamie, but Noah couldn't prove it was a lie anyway. He wondered if she was a pathological liar or a sociopath, but it didn't matter now. She couldn't do him any more damage, and telling the truth would only convict him.

"And a week after this was the barbecue, correct?"

"Yes, the infamous barbecue." Noah realized that Maggie would probably be back in the courtroom because she would want to hear what he said about that night. "That was Maggie's idea, too. She wanted to introduce Anna to our friends. Most of them didn't even know she had a daughter. She'd been ashamed to tell anyone."

"Because she lost custody?"

"Yes, it weighed on her." Noah thought back, pained. "Maggie has a soft heart, a wonderful heart. It killed her that she lost Anna. All Maggie wanted was to have Anna back, then the barbecue blew everything up."

"Linda's going to get to that next."

"I figured." Noah dreaded it. "But then she's finished with me, right?"

"Not quite. She's not done until you lose consciousness."

Noah assumed it was a joke. "Any advice?"

"Whatever you do, don't get angry."

"Okay," Noah said, but he was angry already.

Chapter Forty

Maggie, Before

Maggie and Kathy sat on the floor of Anna's room, eyeing the notes between Anna and Jamie, which were laid out in front of them. There were nine, mostly from the algebra textbook, about teachers, calories, schoolwork, and hair products. The only note that concerned Jamie's running away was the one they had found already.

"Oh boy." Maggie couldn't deny the evidence, staring her in the face. "So it looks like Anna probably knows where Jamie ran away to."

"Right." Kathy met Maggie's eye, gravely. "They might even be in touch, too."

"I guess Anna lied to me." Maggie sighed, and Kathy smiled sympathetically.

"That's how you know you're a parent of a teenager. You got lied to."

"I got the impression from Anna that Jamie had left recently, definitely in this semester."

"But we don't know the exact date."

"No." Maggie scanned the notes.

"The note about Jamie's leaving was the most recent, because it was farthest back in the book. I flipped through the book back to front."

"Okay." Maggie turned to the laptop. They had Googled Jamie

Covington and Congreve, hoping to find an article about her running away in the local newspaper, but there had been nothing. Maggie assumed that it hadn't been newsworthy enough or that Congreve or Jamie's family had kept it out of the press.

"I can't believe we can't figure out who PG is, or Connie." Kathy picked up a copy of *The Zephyr*, which had been among Anna's notebooks on her shelf, and turned to the front page. It had a masthead and a black-and-white photo of the staff, captioned Nora Brady, Simona D'Artiel, Sofia Belovic, Jamie Covington, Larissa Cabot, Rachel Dinatello, and Leah Rosenstein.

"Jamie's so cute, it's a shame she was so troubled. She had everything going for her." Kathy pointed a manicured fingernail at Jamie, who stood out with her Goth looks.

"And the picture's black-and-white, so we can't tell what hair color she has. They're trying too hard. Tryhards." Maggie finally understood the term.

"But none of these girls is PG or has the initials PG, and there's no Connie."

"So PG is either a nickname of a staffer, or they aren't staffers. I think PG is a nickname. It sounds like one."

"Or they could be girls in their dorm or somebody in some other class or activity."

"But I get the impression that the circle of friends is small and tight. There's nobody else even mentioned in the notes except for PG and Connie."

"Is it possible that PG is a guy?"

"It's a girls' school, so that seems unlikely." Maggie double-checked the note that mentioned PG to see if it used the pronoun he or she, but it didn't use either. "Anna was lonely, and I'm getting the impression that anybody she'd be close friends with, like Jamie, wasn't seeing anybody either."

Kathy hesitated. "Do you think they're gay? Anna or Jamie?"

"No, I don't get that impression from Anna. I don't know about Jamie. Okay, I'm going to assume that PG is a girl. And none of the other notes mention a boyfriend or a guy."

"So let's stay with our original assumption, that they're lonely girls and they're friends."

Maggie realized something. "I wonder if Jamie's running away was another reason Anna reached out for me."

"Right."

"Anna's been going through more of a rough patch than I thought."

"Funny that the therapist didn't mention Jamie to you, isn't it?"

"No, I'm not sure if the therapist realized how close Anna and Jamie were either. We talked about the fact that Anna didn't have any friends."

"Do you think that Anna kept it from the therapist or the therapist didn't mention it to you?"

"It doesn't make sense that Anna would keep it from the therapist, so I bet the therapist didn't mention it to me. It is confidential." Maggie mulled it over. "I feel so terrible for Jamie's parents. They have to be told about this."

"I know." Kathy nodded. "We could try to find them in white pages.com."

"But that goes by state, doesn't it?" Maggie looked over. "We don't know where they live."

"True. Maybe Facebook." Kathy searched in her phone, typing quickly. "Damn. Covington is a such a common name. We could start looking, but I should probably get going."

"It doesn't change what I'm going to do anyway." Maggie rallied, determined. "I have to talk to Anna about this. She has to tell us where Jamie is. I can't sit on it. I would never do that to another family. I want to talk to Noah first, then we can sit Anna down together, after dinner."

Kathy pursed her lips. "You have to. Jamie's a young girl. Anything could happen. Anna will understand."

"Not right away. She's going to be pissed."

"Oh well. Comes with the territory."

"Suddenly my trip to Benjamin Moore doesn't seem all that pressing."

"Are you kidding?" Kathy stood up and helped Maggie to her feet. "There's nothing like a fan deck to lift a girl's spirits."

"Wanna come with me?"

"Wish I could but I can't. I'm getting snacks for the boosters, so I have to go buy oranges and bottled water. I'm going to sneak in some soft pretzels, too."

"Nice."

Kathy smiled slyly. "Best. Snack Mom. Ever."

Chapter Forty-one

Noah, After
TRIAL, DAY 5

"Dr. Alderman, you and your wife held a barbecue on May 6 to introduce Anna to your friends, isn't that right?"

"Yes."

"Please read Commonwealth Exhibit 52 and then we'll discuss it." Linda signaled to her paralegal.

Noah turned to the screen to see a transcript he could've recited from memory:

> **Mr. Carter:** Anna, please tell the Court what happened after the barbecue.
>
> **Ms. Desroches:** It happened after everyone had gone home, the guests I mean, but before that, my stepfather gave me wine. He handed it to me during the party, when he was walking by, and he said, "Drink up." It was in a red Solo cup, so I thought it was a Diet Coke or something like that. But when I looked at it, I saw it was wine.
>
> **Mr. Carter:** But you're only 17, under the drinking age, isn't that right?
>
> **Ms. Desroches:** Yes.
>
> **Mr. Carter:** Did you drink the wine?

Ms. Desroches: Yes, I figured it was okay because he gave it to me.

Mr. Carter: Did you feel the effects of alcohol?

Ms. Desroches: Totally, because I hadn't eaten much.

Mr. Carter: So what happened afterwards?

Ms. Desroches: Everyone went home, and I was alone in a powder room near the staircase. The toilet wouldn't stop running. My mother was upstairs putting Caleb to bed, and I thought Noah was outside, dealing with the grill.

Mr. Carter: Okay, go on.

Ms. Desroches: I heard Noah coming down the hall and I called to him to fix the toilet. And he came in, and I showed him it was running but he reached for me and—God, this is so horrible.

Mr. Carter: We understand.

Ms. Desroches: Anyway, he pressed me against the wall and kissed me, and I could feel that he had, you know, in his pants—

Mr. Carter: An erection?

Ms. Desroches: Yes, and while he kissed me he grabbed my breast and made a groaning sound that was really disgusting.

Mr. Carter: Did he say anything?

Ms. Desroches: Yes, he said, "I'm crazy about you. You have to let me fuck you."

Mr. Carter: Then what happened?

Ms. Desroches: All of a sudden, I heard my mom on the stairs, and I called out, "Mom, help!" And I ran out of the bathroom and to her.

Noah waited for his question, sensing a collective repugnance in the courtroom. The testimony shone on the screen, so it couldn't be ignored. *You have to let me* hovered over his shoulder.

"Dr. Alderman, you were drinking the night of the barbecue, weren't you?"

"Yes."

"How much did you have to drink?"

"Three beers, with a hamburger and a hot dog."

"Were you affected by your alcohol consumption that evening?"

"No." Noah had never heard the courtroom so silent. He knew the gallery and the jury were still reacting.

"Isn't it true that you gave Anna wine that night?"

"No."

"Did you give her anything to drink?"

"Yes."

"What did you give her?"

"A red Solo cup with Diet Coke."

Linda smirked. "Dr. Alderman, isn't it possible that you were mistaken and that you gave her wine instead of soda?"

"No."

"Did you say 'drink up' when you handed her the cup?"

"Yes."

"So Anna lied when she testified it was wine, is that your testimony?"

"Yes."

"Dr. Alderman, isn't it true that you forcibly kissed her and embraced her while you had an erection?"

"No."

"No." Noah could hear the jurors shifting. The gallery glanced at each other with nervous half-smiles. The sketch artist stared at him so hard she could have been memorizing his features, and reporters scribbled in their notebooks.

"Did you forcibly kiss her and embrace her while you *didn't* have an erection?"

"No." Noah knew Linda was repeating the words to mortify him and shock the jury. It may have been shocking the jury, but he was beyond mortification.

"Isn't it true that you grabbed her breast?"

"No." Noah remembered that Anna was wearing the blue-checked sundress she had worn the first day, without her jeans jacket.

"It's her word against yours, isn't that right, Dr. Alderman?"

"Yes."

"Except you're here, and she's dead, isn't that right?"

"Objection, Your Honor!" Thomas half-rose.

"I'll withdraw it, Your Honor," Linda said, before Judge Gardner even ruled. She faced Noah. "Dr. Alderman, isn't it true that you told Anna that you wanted to 'fuck her'?"

"No."

Judge Gardner frowned. "Counsel, find a euphemism, please."

Linda pursed her lips. "Dr. Alderman, isn't it true that you propositioned her for the second time?"

"No, I never propositioned her, either time. I heard Anna calling from the bathroom, so I went in and she said the toilet was running." Noah told it exactly the way he had told it at the PFA hearing. "I bent over, took the lid off the tank, and looked inside, but everything seemed fine. I heard my wife coming down the stairs, and when I turned around, Anna was against the wall, and her bra strap was out. She called out, 'Mom, help!' then ran out of the bathroom."

"So according to you, Anna is lying about this entire incident?"

"Yes."

"Why would Anna make up such a lie about you?"

"I don't know."

"Wouldn't Anna have every motive to say nice things about you, in gratitude for your giving her a home, isn't that right?"

"Yes."

"So why would Anna make up such a lie when it would also cause her to end up in court for a PFA, which you could see she was plainly uncomfortable testifying about?"

"I have no idea." Noah knew Anna wasn't uncomfortable at the PFA hearing. She had *acted* uncomfortable, but she wasn't.

"So even you have no idea what her motive would be for making up such a lie, is that correct?"

"Yes." Noah realized that the only answer to the question was yes, but it made it look like an admission.

Suddenly in the back of the courtroom, the deputy stood aside, and the door opened. A woman in a jeans jacket left the courtroom. It was Maggie, and she was gone.

Chapter Forty-two

Maggie, Before

Maggie sealed the leftover Indian food into the Tupperware tub, and Noah was upstairs practicing target words with Caleb. Anna had missed dinner, not answering any texts. In the meantime, Maggie had told Noah about the notes, and he'd agreed to let Maggie do the talking when they spoke to Anna about it, tonight.

"Anna?" Maggie heard the front door opening and went to the family room, where a beaming Anna was setting down her book bag, her hair flowing loose to her shoulders.

"Hi, Mom. Sorry I'm late, but guess what, I think I made a friend!"

"That's great!" Maggie hated to rain on her parade, first thing.

"Her name is Samantha Silas, and she's in the Poetry Club. And guess what else? They said I could join *Phrases*! I'm in!"

"Wonderful, honey." Maggie got to the point. "But why did you miss dinner? I made vegetarian."

"Sorry." Anna puckered her lower lip. "I got caught up with Samantha. She gave me a ride home. I should've called."

"Yes, but lesson learned, right? Next time, you will." Maggie let it go. They had bigger fish to fry tonight.

"We ate at a pizza place called Morrone's. Samantha took me, and the food is awesome. And the kids are so much nicer here!"

"Really?" Maggie sat down, gesturing to the chair. "Tell me every-thing."

"Okay, sure." Anna's face lit up, and she plopped on the chair, crossing her legs in the long dress. "The Poetry Club is so much better. Anybody can join. You don't have to submit. Samantha was showing me some of her poetry, and it's really amazing."

"That's wonderful." Maggie worried about the Island of Misfit Toys. "Is she one of the girls in the cafeteria yesterday?"

"Yes, she's a badass. She has *sleeves.*"

"Doesn't everybody?" Maggie asked, confused.

"No, *tattoo* sleeves." Anna giggled. "She knows a really authentic Japanese artist."

"You're not going to get a tattoo, are you? Please don't."

"Don't worry." Anna grinned.

"Thank God," Maggie blurted out, and they both laughed.

"I'm really sorry I missed dinner." Anna's expression softened. "You made vegetarian?"

"Yes, Indian, but even Ralph didn't beg for it." Maggie felt the ease between them return. "Did Samantha miss dinner, too?"

"No, she gets her own dinner. Her parents are divorced, and her mother is never home. Samantha doesn't have, like, *any* rules."

Terrific, Maggie thought, but didn't say, and Noah started down the stairs.

"Hi, Anna!" he called out, cheery. "How was the first day of school?"

"Great." Anna looked up at him. "Sorry I missed dinner."

"Sure, next time just give us a call." Noah crossed to the couch and sat down beside Maggie, loosening his tie. "Anna, listen, I'm really sorry about last night. I behaved terribly. I was out of sorts and I took it out on you and your mother."

"Thank you, I appreciate that." Anna smiled shakily. "And I'm sorry that I didn't ask before I bought the car."

"That's great, thanks. And if you need a driving refresher, I'd like to take you. It'll be fun."

"Okay, great." Anna smiled, happily.

"Then it's settled. First lesson is when?"

"Thursday night?"

"You got it." Noah nodded, smiling back.

"Great!" Maggie felt they'd cleared one hurdle, but had one more. "Anna, there's something else we wanted to talk to you about. It's about your friend Jamie Covington at Congreve."

"Sure, what?" Anna cocked her head.

"I think you told me that she left school, right?"

Anna hesitated. "Yes, why?"

"I don't know if 'left school' means ran away, but if she ran away I'm sure her parents are worried about her, don't you think? I'm just wondering if you know where she is. Do you?"

"No." Anna's smile began to fade.

"Are you sure about that, honey?" Maggie tried to soften her tone, but Anna reacted almost instantly, with a frown.

"What are you trying to say?"

"If you know where she is, then we have to tell her parents. She's a runaway. Anything could happen to her. It's dangerous."

"I don't know where she is. I told you we weren't that good friends."

"Are you sure about that?"

"What are you saying? Where's this coming from?" Anna looked bewildered, her gaze shifting to Noah. "Is this from you?"

"No, not him," Maggie rushed to answer. "I'll tell you what happened. I was showing your room to Kathy—"

"Why?"

"I wanted to show her your bed and everything. We were going to talk about wall colors. She's my best friend. Kathy, your godmother. Remember I told you about her last night?"

"Okay," Anna said slowly.

"I picked up one of your textbooks, and this fell out." Maggie pulled from her pocket the note about Jamie leaving school and PG and Connie buying her a bus ticket. "From the note, it seems like you know where Jamie went, or PG and Connie do, because they bought—"

"You read that note?" Anna frowned deeply. "That's my personal property."

"I'm sorry. I only found it by accident, but there is an overarching concern here, honey. Jamie's safety."

"Are you saying I'm lying, Mom?"

Maggie felt her gut twist. "Anna, if you, PG, or Connie know where Jamie went, then her parents have a right to know that. I wouldn't feel good withholding that information from them, and you shouldn't either."

"I *don't* know where she went." Anna's fair skin mottled with emotion. "Jamie said she wasn't going to tell me because she knew her parents would ask us all and she didn't want to put me in a bad position. I'm a bad liar. I get nervous when I lie and it always shows."

Maggie hadn't considered that as a possibility. "You're saying that Jamie didn't tell you on purpose? You discussed that with her?"

"Yes, totally. She didn't tell anybody because she knew that we would all be asked, not just by her parents, but Ellen, the House-master, and the Head of School. She knew it would happen, so she didn't tell us."

Noah interjected, "Are you sure, Anna?"

"*Yes*," Anna answered firmly.

Maggie touched Anna's hand. "Honey, I believe you didn't know, but PG or Connie must know. They bought Jamie the bus ticket."

"I don't know if they did. They told Jamie they were going to, but I don't know if they did."

"Who's PG and Connie?"

"Girls at school."

"Don't you think we should ask them, or at least tell Jamie's parents to ask them?"

"They already did, and they said they didn't know."

"Well, was that the truth?" Maggie dialed back her tone. "I just think of Jamie's mother and how she must feel, not knowing how her daughter is."

"You don't know Jamie's mother." Anna scoffed. "Jamie's a total Parker, just like I was. Her parents only come to Parents' Weekend for show."

"Honey, I still don't feel comfortable withholding that information. Why don't we call PG or Connie and ask if one of them bought the bus ticket? If so, then she'll know where Jamie went. If not, that's the end of it."

"I don't want to." Anna pursed her lips. "I don't want to start calling those girls. Please don't make me. PG and Connie weren't friendly to me anyway. They're mean girls, straight up." Anna's eyes started to well up. "Mom, I really wish you hadn't gone in my room. This is my business."

Noah interjected, "Anna, what you're saying would make sense if this was the only note, but it wasn't. There were others."

Maggie stiffened. Noah had just busted her.

Anna's head swiveled to Maggie. "What's he talking about? How does he know that?"

Maggie felt stricken. "I did find some other notes—"

"What, did you search my room?" Anna jumped to her feet, wounded. "Why would you do that?"

"No, I didn't search your room. I looked in your textbooks, concerned about Jamie."

Noah interjected, "Anna, we weren't born yesterday. You must know where Jamie is. I don't believe that she kept it from you to give you deniability. So why don't you just tell us, and we can call her parents."

"You're accusing me of lying?" Anna grabbed her backpack and purse, then edged toward the staircase.

Maggie stood up. "Noah, Anna, wait—"

"Anna, hold on." Noah rose. "You wouldn't be the first person who lied to protect a friend—"

"I'm not lying, Noah! You didn't want me here in the first place!" Anna reached the staircase and started upstairs.

"No, I just want you to tell the truth and I—"

"You're the liar, Noah!" Anna called back, hurrying upstairs. "You're the one who said you wanted me here and you don't!"

Maggie went to the bottom of the stairs. "Anna, wait!"

"I'm *not* the liar, Noah! *You* are!" Anna yelled from the top of the stairs, before her bedroom door slammed close.

Chapter Forty-three

Noah, After

TRIAL, DAY 5

Noah sat on the witness stand next to the enlarged picture of Anna on an easel. Nobody would believe that such a fresh face concealed a ruthless, deceitful heart, especially Maggie. They had been in the family room after Anna had run upstairs, when they'd confronted her about her missing friend, Jamie.

You called her a liar, Noah! How could you do that?

Honey, I said she was lying, I did not call her a liar. There's a difference.

No there's not. And I don't think she's lying.

She knows where Jamie is.

You don't know that.

Yes I do. I know when a kid's lying, and she's lying.

Noah, really? She's my daughter, and what she said made sense. I should've thought of it before. Jamie didn't tell her where she was going, on purpose.

To give her deniability? What teenager thinks like that? No way. You had her dead-to-rights with the notes.

Why did you tell her I found the other notes?

What's the matter with that? She has to tell us where Jamie is. There's a girl out there on the streets. You know bad things happen. We just lost Mike.

Noah, Jamie is not Mike. This is not about Mike.

I know that, Noah had said, finding himself in the confounding position of making the opposite argument he had made in their last argument. They'd been fighting so much he hadn't been able to keep track.

I told you I would do the talking.

I let you. Noah hadn't begun to understand how he and Maggie had gotten so far apart. He hadn't been able to remember the last time they'd agreed on anything. *Maggie, you have to think about Jamie. She's missing.*

She's not missing, she ran away. It happens every day. It's not Adam Walsh time.

Her parents don't know where she is. To me, that's missing. We should call the school and ask them for the contact information for Jamie's parents. We could call Jamie's parents and tell them—

What? To call Anna? To give her a hard time?

Maggie, I'm not gonna pretend this didn't happen. We could call the school and get Jamie's information. Or PG and Connie's. How hard can that be to figure out?

I'm not doing that.

Why not? Don't you care about Jamie?

I care about Anna more, and so should you.

Any parent would be heartbroken if their kid went missing, even if she'd run away. Can you imagine?

Yes, Noah, I can imagine that just perfectly. Maggie's eyes had brimmed with tears. *Because I've been doing that for the past seventeen years, and if you keep this up, I'm going to lose her for good.*

Babe, listen, Noah had reached out to her, but Maggie had pushed his hand away.

Noah, I don't know who you are lately. When did you turn into such a control freak?

But for that, Noah had no answer, except one that was unsayable: After Anna.

Chapter Forty-four

Maggie, Before

The morning dawned gray and chilly, and Maggie got out of her car at the Lenape Nature Preserve, breathing in fresh air. She hadn't slept, and Noah hadn't either, though they lay back to back, neither saying a word. Anna had fallen asleep in her room with her clothes on, and the sight of Anna's lovely face, set in profile against the pillow, had reminded Maggie so much of when she was a little baby. The memory had come rushing back of how sweet Anna had been as an infant, and how Maggie used to watch her sleep, hanging on the crib rail and breathing in her powdery smells, listening to her soft breathing, realizing that her new baby was a miracle, belonging to her, *made* from her.

Maggie sank into a bench, wiping her eyes. She couldn't fathom how everything had gone so wrong so fast. She spotted Kathy's car on the road and felt as if the cavalry were on the way. Kathy honked hello as she pulled into the parking lot, and Maggie rose. Kathy parked, got out of the car, and gave Maggie a big hug.

"That bad, eh?" Kathy whispered, and Maggie smiled tearfully, letting her go.

"Kath, on a scale of one to terrible, it was catastrophic."

"Oh no." Kathy put an arm around Maggie's shoulder and guided her to the walking path. "Tell me everything."

Maggie fell in step and filled Kathy in on everything that had happened during the fight with Anna, then the fight afterwards with Noah. It took her half the meadow to get the entire story out, and they were passed by a few runners.

"Oh boy." Kathy sighed heavily. "I'm sorry it went so badly."

"She was so hurt. And Noah called her a liar." Maggie shook her head as they walked along. "And I don't know what to do about Jamie."

"Here's my brilliant idea, and I truly think this is a great compromise for you. Let's say that Anna is not lying to you."

"Do you think she is?"

"Honey, I don't know for sure, and it truly doesn't matter. You guys don't call anybody. No kid that age is going to let you call the school or call anybody's parents, and I doubt that the school will give you the parents' contact information anyway."

"You're right."

"But there has to be a way that Anna can get a message to Jamie and Anna should ask Jamie to call her parents."

"That's not a bad idea."

"And you know what else? You guys need to start having fun. It's supposed to be a nice weekend. Why don't you go down the shore?"

"But it's only April."

"Who cares?" Kathy smiled, chugging along the path. "You need a change of scenery. You're in that house fussing all the time. You need to go somewhere different, where your roles aren't set."

"I love it!" Maggie felt her heart lift. She pictured Anna and Caleb playing on the beach.

"And you know what else? I think you should throw a party for Anna. Something easy, like a barbecue. She moved in, and so far, it's been a source of conflict. Why not flip that? Celebrate! Your daughter is back in your life!"

"But nobody even knows I have a daughter." Maggie felt a wave of shame that she knew well, like an old friend, or an old enemy.

"So it's time to tell them, don't you think?" Kathy looked over, her expression frank. "That's ancient history, and you didn't do anything wrong. I think you should introduce Anna to everybody."

"So, in other words, I'm coming clean?" Maggie thought of their friends, parents in Caleb's class, and Noah's partners and their wives.

"Yes, why not?" Kathy patted her back. "Everybody loves you, Maggie. Nobody's going to think about the past, we're just going to be happy that she's here."

"I guess you're right," Maggie said, as they walked the final stretch around the field. "I like the statement it makes to Anna. That we're happy that she's in our family and we want her to meet our friends, like you."

"Exactly! I can't wait to see her!" Kathy grinned, then stopped walking. "Wait. Did you tell her that I searched the textbooks, too?"

"No."

"I owe you one," Kathy shot back, laughing.

Chapter Forty-five

Noah, After

"Dr. Alderman, you discussed the incident that had taken place in the bathroom with your wife, didn't you?"

"There was no incident, it didn't happen."

Linda blinked. "Did Anna inform your wife of the *alleged* incident in your presence?"

Noah cringed inwardly, remembering the awful scene. Not many people know exactly the moment their marriage ended, but he did. "My wife was upstairs with Caleb, and Anna and I had been in the bathroom—"

"Please answer the question. Did Anna inform your wife of the alleged incident in your presence or outside of it?"

"I was there. It was in my presence."

"Where did the conversation take place?"

"In the hallway outside the powder room. Anna left the bathroom and as soon as she got into the hallway, she started crying. My wife had just come downstairs and saw Anna there, crying."

Linda snorted. "Are you saying that Anna left the bathroom and burst into tears, all of a sudden?"

"Yes."

"You're saying Anna *faked* spontaneous tears?"

"Yes."

"Anna didn't have acting lessons before she came to live with you, did she?"

"Not that I know of." Noah heard the jury shifting in their seats.

"Dr. Alderman, please direct your attention to Commonwealth Exhibit 52." Linda signaled her paralegal, and another portion of the transcript came onto the screen. The gallery craned their necks, and Noah read about the worst night of his life:

Mr. Carter: Anna, tell us what happened after you left the bathroom.

Ms. Desroches: I just started crying, and then my mom came down the stairs. I ran to her and she hugged me and I said, "Noah won't leave me alone and he grabbed me and kissed me and said this horrible thing to me, and you have to help me because this has to stop."

Mr. Carter: What did she say or do?

Ms. Desroches: She looked totally shocked and she went white in the face. I thought she was going to faint. She was just, like, stunned. I felt so bad for her because I knew she didn't suspect anything and I never told her about what he did on the driving lesson.

Mr. Carter: What did she say or do?

Ms. Desroches: My mother looked at Noah and she said, "Noah, is this true?" And he said I was lying, making the whole thing up. Then she asked him if he had been drinking and he said yes but he wasn't drunk or anything. And she was really shocked and upset, but she was trying not to cry and she said, "Anna, go upstairs, I want to talk to Noah."

Mr. Carter: And what happened next?

Ms. Desroches: I ran upstairs, but when I got in my room I thought to myself that I couldn't have

```
him do that to me anymore. I really wanted to stay
living with my mother, but he has her totally
fooled. And I didn't want to have to move out and
I had nowhere to go. So I figured that I needed to
help myself.
```
Mr. Carter: What do you mean by "help myself"?
Ms. Desroches: I went online and it was really
```
easy and you could download the Protection From
Abuse form, and they had a FAQ and all. I filled
the form out and here we are. I know that he
didn't want the truth to come out. But I had to
stand up for myself. I'm just really glad that
there's courts like this where you can go if you're
a girl and you want to protect yourself from
abusers.
```

"Dr. Alderman, have you read this testimony?"

"Yes." Noah tried to find his emotional footing. He remembered everything about that night so vividly. Maggie had been so hurt, her eyes widening with shock and betrayal.

"Isn't it true that Anna's testimony was exactly what happened that night?"

"No."

"What did Anna say that wasn't true?"

"It's true that's what she told Maggie, but what she told Maggie wasn't true."

"Pardon me?" Linda made a face of exaggerated confusion. On the dais, Judge Gardner frowned as if he hadn't understood either. Noah sensed that the judge's demeanor had changed toward him after the sexually explicit testimony.

"Anna lied about what happened in the bathroom."

"But your wife believed Anna, didn't she?"

Noah hesitated. "I don't know."

"Well, you discussed what had happened in the bathroom with your wife, when you were alone, didn't you?"

"Yes."

"And didn't you deny to your wife what Anna said happened?"

"Yes."

"And after your denial, your wife didn't embrace you and say 'forget about the whole thing,' did she, or words to that effect?"

"No."

"She didn't accuse Anna of lying, did she?"

"No."

"She didn't ask Anna to leave the house, did she?"

"No."

"Isn't it true that the one she asked to leave the house was you?"

"Yes."

Linda lifted an eyebrow. "Let's take a new look at that Petition, Dr. Alderman."

Chapter Forty-six

Maggie, Before

The sky was still cloudy, but the air was fresh and cool, and Maggie waited on her front step, since Anna was due to be dropped off by Samantha at six o'clock. She was baking an eggplant parm for dinner, and Caleb was upstairs doing his homework. Maggie had taken him to the speech pathologist, but he hadn't done well on his target words, *bandage, accident, emergency*. The stress in the house was affecting him, but she hoped they could put it behind them.

A yellow-and-black MINI Cooper pulled up at the curb, with Anna in the passenger seat. Maggie rose to meet them, checking out Samantha, who had short hair dyed bright red, big blue eyes, and an easy grin, looking cute and funky in a vintage flowy dress.

"Hi, honey!" Maggie gave Anna a quick hug when she got out of the car, hoisting her backpack and purse to her shoulder.

"Hi, Mom. Why are you out here? I texted you."

"I know. I thought I'd come meet Samantha."

"Oh, okay. Mom, this is Samantha Silas." Anna gestured at the car, and Maggie peered inside.

"Great to meet you, Samantha. Would you like to have dinner with us?"

"No, thanks. I have, uh, somewhere to go."

"Then it's a rain check?"

"That would be great."

"Bye, Samantha!" Anna called out, waving.

"See you," Samantha called back, then pulled away.

Maggie fell into step next to Anna up the front walk. "She seems nice, and that was good of her to give you a ride home."

"Right." Anna looked away, and Maggie took her hand when they reached the top of the stairs.

"Honey, can we sit down and talk?"

"But I have so much homework and I fell asleep early last night so I'm behind."

"Please." Maggie sat down, tugging Anna gently beside her. "I have some apologizing to do. I'm sorry. I was concerned about Jamie."

"I understand." Anna looked more sad than angry. "You're just trying to do the right thing."

"Yes, exactly." Maggie felt pleased. "The question is how do we accommodate Jamie's safety and your privacy. So Noah and I are not going to call the school or her parents."

"Good, thank you." Anna met Maggie's eye, pained. "I know you won't understand this, but those girls, they never really liked me. They tolerated me, even Jamie. If you called the school or Jamie's parents, it would be so embarrassing."

"I get it. That said, here's a compromise. I'm going to ask you to get in touch with Jamie and ask her to go home or, at least, to call her parents."

"But I don't know if I have her number." Anna frowned. "She probably got a new phone."

"Try her old one or ask around to see if anybody has her new number. Try and see if you can call PG, Connie, or somebody on *The Zephyr*. If you get that message to her, I would sleep better at night."

Anna groaned. "So you want me to start calling people from Congreve? They'll just snark me."

"If something terrible happened to Jamie and you hadn't tried to help find her, you'd never forgive yourself."

"Okay, I'll do it," Anna answered, with a sigh.

"Great, and I'm sorry things have been so rough lately." Maggie gave her a hug, feeling close to her again.

"I know, it has been *so* hard." Anna broke the embrace, her eyes searching Maggie's. "I hate all this drama. I thought it was going to be hard at school and easy at home. But instead it's easy at school and hard at home."

"We're going to fix that." Maggie ignored the ache in her chest. Hearing Anna say it made it worse. "Listen, I have an idea. Do you like the beach?"

"I love it." Anna perked up. "I used to go with my grandparents. They had a house in the south of France."

Maggie smiled. "We're talking the south of New Jersey, as in Avalon."

Anna burst into laughter. "Hey, fine with me, I would do that."

"We'd make it a family day, just us four."

"Okay." Anna wriggled her shoulders. "I can get my tan on."

"It'll be fun." Maggie sensed Anna was trying. "And next weekend, on Saturday night, I'd like to have a barbecue to introduce you to our friends. You're the guest of honor."

"Me?" Anna smiled, surprised.

"Yes." Maggie started to feel better. "I think it's time that our friends met you, don't you? Ask Samantha to come, too."

"That's so nice. I will." Anna beamed, then looked past Maggie toward the street. "Oh, here comes Noah. This is awkies."

"No, don't worry. I have an idea." Maggie watched as the Audi SUV pulled up in front of the house, then Noah cut the ignition and got out, shouldering his messenger bag.

"Quite the welcoming committee!" Noah walked up the flagstone path with a smile, and Maggie smiled back.

"Noah, I decided that we need a reset. I'd like you to meet my daughter, Anna."

"Okay. Anna, pleased to meet you." Noah grinned, extending his hand to her.

Anna hesitated, then shook his hand. "Pleased to meet you, too, Noah."

"Anna, I'm the kind of a guy who means well, but sometimes I say dumb things in the heat of the moment. I'm sorry."

Anna managed a smile. "I'm the kind of girl who overreacts and slams doors. I'm sorry, too."

Maggie interjected, "Anna has agreed to try to get a message to Jamie, telling her to call her parents, so we don't have to call the school or anybody else."

"That's great." Noah turned back to Anna. "I'm still up for that driving lesson, if you are. Tomorrow night? Eight o'clock?"

"Perfect."

"It's a date." Noah turned to Maggie. "And by the way, who are you?"

"Your loving wife." Maggie kissed him on the cheek, but she felt a new remoteness from him. She hoped they could set it right this weekend.

"Caleb, I'm home!" Noah called out, as they went inside.

Chapter Forty-seven

Noah, After
TRIAL, DAY 5

"Dr. Alderman, you testified earlier that the Petition in question was filed by Anna, didn't you?"

"Yes."

"Please direct your attention to paragraph three of the Petition."

Noah turned to the screen and read:

> **I am filing this petition on behalf of:**
> **__ Myself**
> **X̲ Another Person**

"Dr. Alderman, you see that the box that's checked is Another Person, isn't that correct?"

"Yes."

"Let's look farther down in paragraph three."

Noah watched the screen change, and it read:

> **Indicate your relationship with plaintiff:**
> **__x_ Parent of minor plaintiff**
> **____ Applicant for appointment as guardian ad litem of minor plaintiff**

____ Adult household member with minor plaintiff

____ Court-appointed guardian of incompetent plaintiff

"Dr. Alderman, the box that is checked is parent of minor plaintiff, isn't that correct?"

"Yes."

"The parent referred to is your wife Maggie Ippoliti, isn't that
correct?"

"Yes."

"So your prior testimony was misleading when you stated that the
Petition was filed by Anna, wasn't it?"

"No."

Linda frowned. "Dr. Alderman, wasn't the Petition filed by both
Anna *and* your wife Maggie?"

"No." Noah and Thomas had discussed how to handle this line of
questioning. "Anna's handwriting is at the top. Anna wrote her name
in the Plaintiff box and my name in the Defendant box. Anna filled
out the form."

"But doesn't this form clearly show a box checked, indicating that
the Petition was filed by a parent of a minor plaintiff?"

"Regardless, it was filed by Anna. My wife had to sign only because
Anna was a minor."

"Dr. Alderman, are you suggesting that your wife didn't agree with
the allegations that Anna made in the Petition?"

"Yes, they were Anna's allegations, and my wife only signed to
enable Anna to file, like a cosigner."

Linda's eyes flew open. "Is a young girl trying to protect herself
from sexual abuse like somebody getting a *car loan*?"

"No, I was trying to explain. It's an analogy."

Linda nodded to her paralegal. "I'm going to call to the screen the
very last page of the Petition. Please read it yourself and we'll discuss it."

Noah turned:

VERIFICATION: I verify that I am the Petitioner designated in the present action and that the facts and statements contained in the above Petition are true and correct to the best of my knowledge. I understand that any false statements are made subject to the penalties of 18 Pa.C.S.A. section 4904, relating to unsworn falsification to authorities.

Margaret Ippoliti
Anna Desroches

"Dr. Alderman, isn't it true that two signatures appear there, Anna's and your wife's?"

"Yes."

"Your wife was smart enough to understand that she was subjecting herself to penalties of perjury if she signed a Petition she believed to be false, wasn't she?"

"Yes."

"So isn't it true that your wife's signature on the Petition shows that she believed the allegations to be 'true and correct'?"

"No, because you have to consider that the PFA Order was not issued. After the hearing, my lawyer and I went to the attorneys' conference room to await Judge Hamilton's decision, but there was a knock on the door. We assumed it was the bailiff telling us that the judge had decided, but it was my wife. She initiated a settlement, which I think shows that she was ambivalent about whether Anna's allegations were true."

Linda scoffed, her impatience plain. "Dr. Alderman, isn't it true that you settled Anna's Petition because you knew that Judge Hamilton was going to issue a PFA Order against you?"

"No."

Linda shot him a skeptical look. "Why would you settle if you thought you were going to win?"

"I settled because it made sense for all of us."

"Dr. Alderman, wouldn't it have been a disaster for your medical practice as a *pediatric allergist* if a PFA Order had been issued against you for sexual abuse of Anna, *a minor?*"

"Yes."

"So it was consistent with your self-interest to settle, was it not?"

"Yes," Noah had to admit.

"And isn't it true that under the settlement, Anna agreed to withdraw her Petition, and you agreed to leave the home voluntarily?"

"Yes."

"And you rented a carriage house in Haverford the very next day, which ultimately became the crime scene, isn't that correct?"

"Yes." Noah cringed.

"Dr. Alderman, isn't it true that Anna did not seek nor did she receive any money damages in return for withdrawal of her Petition against you?"

"Yes." Noah didn't elaborate, though Linda knew full well that damages weren't available in PFA actions.

"So isn't it true that the only thing that Anna stood to gain by her PFA Petition is that you would leave the house?"

"Yes."

"Why would Anna want you out of the house if you hadn't sexually abused her?"

"I don't know," Noah said, hearing the jury shifting.

Chapter Forty-eight

Maggie, Before

Maggie passed that night feeling apart from Noah, who worked in the basement while she was on her laptop in the bedroom. Both kids were on their laptops in their bedrooms. By bedtime, she realized that none of them had looked at anything but a computer for the entire night, but they all needed a cooling-off period, especially her.

The next morning, Noah left for work, Caleb took the bus to school, and Anna was picked up by Samantha. Maggie went to Mike Wilson's funeral, where she sat with Noah, though they arrived separately since he'd come from the office with the others. She and Noah greeted a grief-stricken Dina and Steve Wilson in the receiving line, and Maggie continued to feel withdrawn during the heartbreaking service, though she didn't reach for Noah's hand and he didn't reach for hers. When the service was over, she kissed him dryly on the cheek, but he barely met her eye.

In the afternoon she busied herself painting color samples on white canvases to make it easier for Anna to choose a bedroom color, then she prepared dinner, spaghetti with pesto sauce and a fresh Caprese salad, thick slices of beefsteak tomato and soft buffalo mozzarella covered with chopped fresh basil, drizzled with overpriced balsamic and olive oil. Anna texted **be home at 6 and stoked to drive** ☺, which made Maggie feel better.

They all sat down to dinner at the usual time, but other than that, nothing else about the mealtime was typical. Noah seemed unusually silent, perhaps the aftermath of Mike's funeral, and Caleb was also quiet. Maggie carried the conversational ball, asking both kids about their school day, but only Anna responded with enthusiasm, then she and Noah left together for the driving lesson.

"How did it go, guys?" Maggie said, coming from the kitchen when she heard the front door opening. She'd just finished baking choco-late chip cookies and arrayed them on a serving plate next to four small plates and napkins, expecting they'd all eat cookies and yam-mer away, like an impromptu family party.

"Okay," Anna answered, entering the house with a frown.

Noah came up behind, puzzled. "What do you mean, Anna? You did very well."

"Thanks." Anna hoisted her purse to her shoulder and headed for the stairwell, but Maggie intercepted her.

"Want a snack, honey? I made cookies."

"Sorry, I better get to work. I'm so behind, I'll be up all night."

"But I want to hear about your lesson. How did it go? How was the car?"

"Fine, I really should get to work." Anna pursed her lips, going upstairs. "See you later."

"Where's Caleb?" Noah asked, sliding his tie off.

"Upstairs, doing homework." Maggie took a step closer, keeping her voice low, even after Anna had gone. "What happened? She seems bummed."

"She seems fine to me." Noah left for the kitchen, and Maggie followed him, bewildered.

"How did she do?"

"Great, but she really shouldn't drive on the street until she gets a Pennsylvania license." Noah crossed to the kitchen island, took a few cookies and a napkin, and turned to head down to the basement.

"Where did you take her?"

"The strip mall behind the Chinese restaurant." Noah slid his phone from his back pocket and thumbed the screen.

"Was she nervous?"

"No." Noah kept scrolling, and Maggie knew he was checking his email, which was always test results, nothing urgent.

"Were you nice about the car?"

"Yes."

"You didn't give her a hard time?"

"No." Noah read his phone screen, and Maggie felt her temper flare.

"Excuse me, but can you look at me for two minutes? I'm trying to figure out what happened."

Noah looked up, his mouth tight. "Nothing happened. What could have happened?"

"You didn't bring up Jamie again, did you?"

"No." Noah met her eye directly. "Babe, can we have *one* night when we don't fight? Is that too much to ask?"

"Fine," Maggie answered, stung. "It's just that the driving lesson was the fun thing that was supposed to get you two back on track."

"I'm trying my best, honey."

"I don't think you are." Maggie felt her resentment boil over. "She came home unhappy."

"She's *not* unhappy."

"She's not bubbling over with excitement, now is she?" Maggie couldn't believe he was arguing this point, when it was obvious.

"You're making something out of nothing." Noah turned away, opening the basement door.

"Really?" Maggie watched him disappear into the basement, then she put some cookies on the plate, poured a glass of milk, and went upstairs to Anna's room, where she knocked on the door. "Anna, can I come in? I've got carbs."

"Sure," Anna answered.

"Hi," Maggie said, opening the door to see Anna sitting cross-legged on her bed, having changed into a gray T-shirt and Congreve gym shorts. Her laptop and textbooks were spread around her, and her new bedside lamp filled the room with a soft glow.

"Aw, cookies. Thanks." Anna set the laptop aside, and Maggie handed her the plate and milk.

"Hey, what do you think of your paint selection?" Maggie gestured to the canvases she'd lined up on the wall, showing a paint sample with the name of the color on each one, so they didn't forget.

"I know, that was so nice of you." Anna got up and went over to the canvases. "I like Nottingham Green. What do you think?"

"Me, too, but live with it for a day or two. The colors change depending on the light, and give the blues a chance."

"You think blue would be better?" Anna turned to her, more relaxed than she had been when she came in, which did Maggie's heart good.

"It might be, but it's your choice."

"Thanks." Anna took a bite of cookie. "Mmm, this is awesome."

"By the way, were you able to make any progress with Jamie? Like, find her new number or text her?"

"No, not yet." Anna shook her head. "But I will, I promise. I was so busy today trying to get everything done and then the driving lesson."

"Sure, I understand." Maggie had to trust that Anna would keep her word. "So how did it go? Was it okay?"

"It was fine." Anna flopped on the bed. "But I don't need Noah to take me anymore. I'll use a driving school for one or two more lessons. I just signed up online."

"You don't want Noah to take you?" Maggie sank into the bed, disappointed. "What happened?"

"Nothing." Anna hesitated. "Why, did Noah say something happened?"

"No, but why do you want a professional? Was he too critical? He's usually patient, even if he's, well, picky."

"No, he's fine."

"Did he give you a hard time about the car?"

"No."

"Did he bring up the Jamie thing?"

"No. It's nothing he did." Anna pursed her lips. "It's just that I felt kind of uncomfortable."

"Why?"

"I don't know, but I just felt, uncomfortable. Maybe because of all the drama." Anna looked away. "I think it's better this way, really, Mom."

"You sure?" Maggie asked, worried that the rift between Anna and Noah was getting worse.

Anna turned away, eyeing the canvases. "That was so thoughtful of you to do that."

"It was fun," Maggie said, troubled.

Chapter Forty-nine

Noah, After
TRIAL, DAY 5

"Dr. Alderman, let's briefly review your testimony, shall we?"

Noah nodded, not knowing whether he should answer. It sounded as if Linda was about to end her cross, and it couldn't come soon enough. He straightened in his chair.

"Dr. Alderman, Anna Desroches moved into your home on April 22, isn't that correct?"

"Yes."

"And she was murdered only eighteen days later, on May 10, is that correct?"

"Yes."

"You thought she was beautiful, didn't you?"

"Yes."

"And you complimented her on her looks during your driving lesson, did you not?"

"Yes."

"And after you learned that she stood to inherit $50 million, you offered to give her driving lessons, is that correct?"

"Yes."

"And when Anna asked you if your son Caleb could go, you lied to her about the real reason he couldn't go, telling her that it was because she had to concentrate, isn't that correct?"

"Yes."

"Anna would later claim that you touched her inappropriately on the thigh during that driving lesson, isn't that correct?"

"Yes." Noah realized that Linda was taking him methodically through the most damning facts of his case. She was simply dismantling him, the way a butcher breaks apart a chicken carcass, piece by piece, wedging back the legs and wings until the joints break, then tearing the limbs off.

"About a week after that driving lesson, on May 6, you and your wife held a barbecue at your home, and after the barbecue, Anna claimed that you kissed her and tried to touch her breast, isn't that correct?"

"Yes."

"And on Monday after the barbecue, on May 8, Anna filed a Petition for a Protection From Abuse Order, signed by both Anna and your wife, isn't that correct?"

"Yes."

"But before Judge Hamilton could reach her decision, you reached a settlement whereby Anna agreed to withdraw the Petition and you agreed to leave the home, isn't that correct?"

"Yes."

"You moved out of your home, and only two days after that, on Wednesday, May 10, a text was sent from your phone to Anna's phone, asking her to come to your house, isn't that correct?"

"Yes."

"Anna was strangled to death that very night on your front porch at about that time, isn't that correct?"

"Yes."

"You called 911 from the scene, did you not?"

"Yes."

"And you spoke to the dispatcher for a little over a minute?"

"Yes."

"And one minute after you hung up with 911, you called your lawyer, with whom you spoke for twelve minutes, isn't that correct?"

"Yes."

"Dr. Alderman, you're aware that your DNA, hair, and threads from your clothes were found on Anna's body, isn't that correct?"

"Yes."

"You are also aware that Anna's DNA, hair, threads from her clothes were found on your clothes, isn't that correct?"

"Yes."

"Your wife didn't visit you in prison while you were incarcerated, isn't that correct?"

"Yes." Noah assumed Linda had checked the prison's visitor logs.

"Your wife didn't testify in your defense at the PFA hearing, did she?"

"No."

"And she didn't testify in your defense at this trial, isn't that correct?"

"Yes."

"Dr. Alderman, given all of these facts, which are undisputed, how do you expect anybody on this jury to believe that you are anything but guilty of Anna's murder?"

"I—" Noah started to say, then realized he had no way to finish the sentence.

"Your Honor, I have no further questions," Linda said flatly, then strode back toward counsel table.

Noah felt a wave of nausea wash over him. He had expected to feel relief, but he knew how badly it had gone.

"Thank you." Judge Gardner looked at Thomas. "Mr. Owusu, do you have redirect examination for the witness?"

"No, Your Honor. Thank you." Thomas half-rose, shaking his head, and Linda looked over at Thomas, pausing just before she sat down, but her expression remained professional.

Noah assumed that Thomas was declining redirect because if he accepted, then it would give Linda the opportunity for recross. Thomas was putting Noah out of his misery, like shooting a wounded animal.

None of them knew Noah was dead inside.

Chapter Fifty

Maggie, Before

Maggie closed Anna's bedroom door, simmering. She went down to the basement to find Noah at his computer with his headphones on, reading an array of test results. He'd reassembled his desk, bookshelves, and filing cabinet in the same arrangement as his former office upstairs. Maggie felt a twinge, appreciating his initial sacrifice, but things had gone so wrong since then. She touched his shoulder to get his attention, and he slid off his headphones.

"What's up?" Noah asked, over his black reading glasses.

"Anna is getting a professional driving teacher. She doesn't want you to take her anymore."

"Really?" Noah blinked. "Did she say why?"

"That she felt nervous around you."

"I thought it went well."

"It obviously didn't."

"Maggie, what do you want me to do?" Noah slid off his reading glasses and tossed them on the desk.

"I want you to help me get to the bottom of this."

"She changed her mind. Teenagers do that."

"Noah, why are you acting this way?" Maggie felt like they didn't even know each other anymore.

"I'm acting how I always act."

"No, you're not. You're kinder than this. You're a great father."

"I took off tonight for her. I'll be up for three more hours to make it up." Noah gestured at the glowing screen. "I have to get ready for the conference. Remember? In Miami."

"But still, if you're going to take the time to take her, it doesn't take longer to be nice." Maggie had forgotten there was a medical conference of the NAAAI, or the National Academy of Allergy, Asthma, & Immunology. The office always sent Noah, who loved to geek out at the latest in allergy advances.

"You're killing me, babe. What do you want me to do?"

"How about *care*?" Maggie shot back, giving way to anger. "Noah, what's going on? Tell me how you feel. The kids can't hear. We can yell as much as we want."

"Okay." Noah pursed his lips. "This house has been in an uproar since she got here, and all you do is make sure that she's happy. Has she even called to find Jamie yet?"

"She hasn't had a chance."

"Right." Noah rolled his eyes. "She follows her own rules. You fill her every need. You're jumping through hoops for her."

"Of course I am. I'm trying to show her I'm happy she's here. What about you?"

"So what I'm doing isn't good enough?"

"No, it's not."

"Well, that's nice." Noah returned his attention to the computer and slid his reading glasses back on, his mouth a bitter twist. "I'm not going to fight with you anymore. I have work to do. I have to moderate a panel. I'm leaving Sunday morning until Thursday night. I decided to stay for the closing sessions. I can pick up three CME credits, and Anthony Fauci is speaking, the NIAID Director. He identified AIDS, you know."

"I know," Maggie said, though she hadn't been exactly sure. "You're going to stay 'til closing?"

"Yes, I wanted to anyway, and given what's going on here, it makes sense."

"So you're running away." Maggie folded her arms.

"No, I'm doing my job."

"Did you remember we have the barbecue on Saturday? I emailed the invitations, and you're leaving me to prepare by myself." Maggie knew it wasn't what was really bothering her. It was just what she could get him on.

"I'll be home in plenty of time to help."

"I can't leave things until last minute. Food shopping, going to the beer distributor, getting the extra chairs and folding tables from the garage, cleaning up in the backyard, that has to be done in advance."

"I'll be here for the heavy lifting. Leave it for me." Noah squinted at the screen, evidently dismissing her.

"Fine," Maggie turned angrily away. Something was going on with him, but she didn't know what. She climbed the stairs, starting to wonder about the conference. And why he was staying longer.

And then she realized. He would see *her*.

Jordan.

Chapter Fifty-one

Noah, After

Noah sat at counsel table, as the Commonwealth witness was about to take the stand. He couldn't help but think that the prosecution had produced enough evidence to convict him. Thomas had warned him that he would feel the worst by the end of the Commonwealth's case, and even though Noah had been prepared, it was cold comfort.

Linda stood at the front of the courtroom waiting while her witness was sworn in, a slim Indian woman dressed in a trim blue suit, with steel-rimmed glasses and her dark, glossy hair in a short pageboy.

"Please state your name for the record," Linda said pleasantly, as the witness sat down.

"Dr. Lydia Kapoor."

"And please tell the jury your occupation."

"I am the assistant coroner for Montgomery County." Dr. Kapoor was probably fifty-something and she gave off an air of experience and clinical authority.

"How long have you been in that position?"

"Approximately seven years."

"And in that time, how many autopsies would you estimate you have performed?"

"We perform about 220 autopsies per year." Dr. Kapoor pressed up her glasses.

"And did you perform the autopsy on Anna Desroches, the victim in this case?"

"Yes."

Noah could see the jury shifting in their seats, anticipating the testimony to come. The gallery was beginning to crane their necks, and his attention was caught by a woman he recognized instantly. It was Jordan.

Noah faced front, masking his surprise. He hadn't seen Jordan since the NAAAI conference in Miami last May. It never occurred to him that she'd come to his trial, and she looked terrific. She had a gorgeous face with big green eyes, a cute nose, and a dazzling smile. Great hair, longish. Of course a killer body. She worked for Astra-Zeneca, and he remembered when they met at the NAAAI conference in Dallas. His buddies had told him to stop by Jordan's booth, since he was a widower.

Meanwhile, Linda was asking, "Dr. Kapoor, did you produce a report in connection with Anna's autopsy?"

"Yes."

Noah tuned her out again. He'd found himself strolling along the trade floor, a massive grid of blue-draped booths staffed by reps hawking meds, instruments, coding software, and billing systems, dispensed with logo T-shirts, crappy pens, totebags, and stress balls in company colors, plus jellybeans, Hershey's Kisses, and in season, candy corn.

The autopsy report came on the screen, and Linda faced the witness stand. "Dr. Kapoor, what is your conclusion about how Anna died?"

"By manual strangulation."

"What is that process, in layman's terms?"

"The air supply through the trachea, or windpipe, is cut off by the hands of another person, leading to hypoxia, or lack of oxygen, and death. The obstruction of the windpipe produces a sound called stridor, which is a wheezing, grating noise unique to death by strangulation."

Linda paused while the jury reacted, aghast, and Noah stopped listening, preoccupied by Jordan. She'd approached him on the floor of the tradeshow, flashing her fitness-instructor smile, extending a hand.

I'm Jordan Nowicki. Pleased to meet you.

Noah, he had said, as if he didn't have a last name. She would tease him about it later, in bed. (*I swear, you were tongue-tied. It was like you never talked to a woman before.*)

What's your specialty, Dr. Noah?

Noah is my first name. My last name is Alderman.

I know. I can read your name tag. You're so serious. I think I'll call you No-ha. So what's your specialty, No-ha?

I'm a pediatric allergist. Noah fumbled the answer, even though it was the first question that every rep asked, probably from the handbook. (*Get them talking about themselves, establish a rapport, then pitch your crap.*)

Oh, that must be so much fun, working with children. I love kids.

Yes, it is fun, Noah had said, finding his bearings. It was the second thing every rep said to him, especially the single women. (He always heard the subtext, *I would be a good mother to your son. Ask me out.*) It never worked because he couldn't bear to think of another woman taking Karen's place. But Jordan had been so distinctly unqualified for that, being so young, that Noah had felt it was okay to be with her.

Jordan had touched his arm. *I have a little brother who has asthma, and I love his allergist.*

Actually, the majority of my practice is asthma patients.

That's so awesome! You guys save lives!

No, not really, Noah had said. It was obvious flattery, but if she had a brother with asthma, she was kind of right.

My little brother wasn't diagnosed until he was nine. He almost collapsed at a track meet. He has stress asthma. My mom thanks God every day for his allergist.

That's nice, Noah had said, realizing how young she must have been, just from the way she said *my mom*. He would find out later that she was twenty-three to his forty, and petite, five-one to his six-one, so she was looking up at him like an Allergy God. Karen would've laughed her ass off, and normally, so would Noah, but he didn't feel like laughing, looking down at Jordan. He did feel like smiling, however.

No-ha, where are you from?

Philadelphia.

Jordan's lovely face had lit up. *I knew I liked you! It's because we both have a Philadelphia accent!*

I beg your pardon, Noah had shot back in a mock English accent, and Jordan had burst into laughter like he was the funniest man on the planet. He'd known she was selling him, but after Karen's illness and death, the chemo protocols, the radiation burns, the counting of millimeters and cells, Jordan had felt like the first day of spring after a long winter, a new flower in bloom. He remembered even now that she smelled great.

Noah hadn't felt ready to ask Jordan out, even after she'd plied him with T-shirts and keychains, but he'd thought about her through the panel he was moderating, Childhood Asthma: It's All About That Bacteria. And that same night, he'd run into her at the elevator, and she had asked him to have a drink at the rooftop bar. He'd said yes, and, two scotches later, he'd taken her to bed. And the next morning, he had missed the Chronic Rhinosinusitis panel, but he didn't mind at all.

Noah remembered every detail of her, in bed. They had spent so much time there, her with the rowdy enthusiasm of a healthy young girl, and him trying to remember pleasure, laughter, and light, trying to find a way back into life itself. Somehow her youth had been all of that for him, and Jordan hadn't been looking for marriage or kids. At least that was what she'd said in the beginning.

Noah remembered she'd wanted to meet Caleb, but he'd kept putting it off. His partners had found out about her when she'd dropped by the office in her Miata, with its WE ARE PENN STATE bumper sticker. She'd brought him his phone, which he'd left at her apartment, and when he'd introduced her around the office, he'd been kidded later. (*She might not be wife material, but she sure as hell is babysitter material.*)

Noah thought back to the breakup, which he'd felt terrible about. He hadn't seen Jordan as a stepmother for Caleb, given that she'd had a brother the same age, and by then Noah had realized that their fling was all about him—his conversation, his schedule, his plans. For a while it hadn't been the worst thing, because nothing had been about him since Karen had gotten sick. He hadn't known what he had been missing until he met Jordan, and he was grateful to her, but that didn't mean that they should be, or could be, married.

Then Noah had met Maggie at the gym, a funny, curvy, curly-headed woman who was always joking with the trainers at the sign-in counter, and he'd found himself on the treadmill next to her. She'd engaged him in nonstop chatter that drew him out by sheer force of will. He'd known that if they started dating, it would matter, so he'd broken up with Jordan.

Noah thought back with regret for how he had handled things. Jordan had taken the breakup hard, so he'd been surprised when she'd been so friendly to him at the NAAAI in Miami, last May. And after what had happened there, it didn't make sense that she'd come to his trial. He wondered how long she had been here. How had he missed her? And what if Maggie came?

Noah didn't have time to worry because Linda was signaling for a new exhibit, and he knew what it had to be.

He braced himself.

Chapter Fifty-two

Maggie, Before

Monday morning, Maggie walked the grassy track at the Nature Preserve next to Kathy, filling her in on what had happened with Anna and Noah. The air was filled with the chirping of crickets and birds, which usually calmed Maggie down, but not today.

Kathy looked over, her brow knitted. "So what do you think happened on the driving lesson?"

"He's not the most patient teacher, and it made her nervous."

"I hear you." Kathy huffed and puffed, carrying her foam-covered hand weights.

"And now he's gone to a conference, and you know who's going to be there? Jordan."

"The fetus?"

"Yep." Maggie smiled at Kathy's nickname for Noah's old girlfriend, Jordan Nowicki, a young rep who was drop-dead gorgeous. "She's not a fetus anymore."

"So she's crowning."

"I wonder if she's still single."

"Nah, I bet she got herself a hubby. Her biological clock is ticking." Kathy matched Maggie stride for stride. "My biological clock is a Casio. That's how old I am."

"If she's there, she'll find him. I swear she was a stalker. He never saw it, though."

"Men are dumb. Even smart men are dumb."

"He told me they started dating when she ran into him at the elevator by accident. What are the odds?"

Kathy snorted. "She probably rode the elevator all damn day."

"I met her when she came to the office to drop off his tie. She said he'd left it at her place a *year* ago."

"What, knotted to the bedpost?"

"Yeah, right." Maggie laughed. Noah had no interest in anything kinky in bed, which was fine with her. Sex was great, and she could never understand why people couldn't leave well enough alone.

"She brought him his tie, after a *year*? Obsess much?"

"Totally." Maggie warmed to the story. "She goes to the front desk and asks if she can see Noah. In the middle of the day, mind you. He has appointments all afternoon. And she's so gorgeous that every mom in the waiting room hates her on sight."

"What is it with these reps? Do you think they have a beauty contest?"

"Anyway she made a big thing that she couldn't just leave the tie at the desk, then the receptionist called me over and introduced me as Noah's fiancée."

"Oh, burn!"

"It was sad, truly."

"Boo-hoo, bitch. Call me after gestation."

"She was hurt, but she tried to cover it up."

"She's too young to hide her emotions. She'll learn."

"Kath, I have to admit, when I met her, she looked *so* damn young. I didn't think he was like that."

"Oh please. Men love young things. It's fresh eggs. They can smell them."

"She even asked to see my engagement ring."

"Did you stick it in her face?"

"No. She called me later, to say it was nice to meet me. The temp had given her my cell number because she was a rep." Maggie thought back to how happy she and Noah had been, in the beginning. They'd gotten engaged only six months after they had met. She'd known it was right, or at least she'd thought it was. "Marriage is a funny thing, isn't it?"

"I smell philosophy."

"You don't know what's going to happen in a marriage. In your life. You have to be able to deal with it."

"Quite true." Kathy pumped her arms.

"Like with Anna coming. I would've guessed Noah would be great."

"I said, you just have to give it time."

"That's the thing, everything is happening so fast. He said the house is in an uproar, and he's right."

"It's not the worst thing for him to take a week off right now. It'll give the house time to settle."

"I hope so, especially for Caleb. I'll give him extra attention this week, and we have the barbecue Saturday night. You guys are coming, right?"

"I wouldn't miss it. What do you want me to bring, the Ina Garten corn salad?"

"Yes, you make that great."

"You have to make those deviled eggs I love. Kick it old-school."

"That's me." Maggie felt a rush of comfort, having a friend she knew so well that she knew her best dishes. Girlfriends were a blessing.

"And don't worry about Noah in Miami."

"I can't help it. If Jordan's there, she'll seek him out."

"So what? He wouldn't cheat on you."

"She's younger and thinner."

"He loves you, silly."

"Right, I keep forgetting," Maggie shot back.

Chapter Fifty-three

Noah, After
TRIAL, DAY 4

Noah stiffened at the enlarged black-and-white photo of Anna in death, which showed her face, neck, and bare shoulders. Her eyes were fixed open, gruesomely, since the sclera around the irises was black with blood. Her skin had a gray pallor, contrasting with the dark bruises encircling her neck like a lethal choker. Linda, Thomas, and the courtroom clerk were working through the details of admitting and labeling the photo, which took a horribly long time, whether inadvertently or on purpose.

Noah let his thoughts travel backwards to the Miami NAAAI conference, which was after he'd married Maggie, Anna had moved in, and everything had gone south. He'd found himself again on the trade floor, knowing at some level that he was looking for Jordan, and as he'd headed toward AstraZeneca, he'd spotted her chatting up another rep.

They'd been laughing, Jordan throwing her head back, her hair bouncing, her lipstick a fresh pink, her throat open. He'd recognized her suit, a pinkish tweed that was tightly tailored. She used to wear a silky white top underneath, she'd called it a *cami*. And he'd flashed on the bra she'd have on, a lacy black push-up that she joked was her *conference bra*. Her skirt had been short, and she'd had on high heels, like always. He remembered them lying on the rug next to the bed like a pair of lethal weapons. He used to trip on them on the way to the bathroom, but he'd never complained.

Noah had approached her, and she'd done a double-take when she saw him, which she'd masked with another pretty laugh. He'd watched her touch the other rep on his upper arm, her fingertips brushing his biceps, but she'd been dismissing him. The rep had probably believed Noah was a sales target, but Jordan had known better.

Jordan, hey, Noah had tried to sound casual, which was impossible. He was born formal.

Hi, good to see you again. Jordan's dark eyes had glittered in the way he recognized from before, connecting with him directly, not bothering to hide her interest.

How are you?

How's married life?

Fine, good. Noah had noticed she didn't answer the question.

I don't believe you. You still look No-ha to me.

No, it's fine. Noah had swallowed hard, unmasked. Jordan had been right, but he couldn't tell her that.

I've missed you, Jordan had said, which was something he had always liked about her. She was strong in her own way, which was darker than Maggie's way. Still he tried not to compare the two women. He loved Maggie. He'd never loved Jordan.

You look busy, Noah had said instead. He hadn't missed Jordan until Anna had stirred everything up, not only the fighting but problems he hadn't wanted to acknowledge in his marriage. Something had been missing. He'd realized what it was, looking down at Jordan who was looking at him, her smile so lovely, her *cami* gapping in her cleavage. In her eyes, he felt like a man again, not a dad or a doc. He hadn't felt like that since the early days with Maggie, when they'd clawed each other in bed. But after the forty-pound bags of mulch, the double coupons, and the parents' nights, they'd lost something that no amount of date nights could fix. He couldn't say exactly when, because time was a funny thing, backwards and forwards, from the tradeshow to the courtroom and somehow all the same. Somewhere along the line he'd lost himself. He'd become a husband, not a man.

No-ha, wanna meet me for a drink later?

Why not?

Come to my room at eight, number 317. I'll bring the scotch. You bring the ha.

Noah had felt an unaccountable thrill. Of course she'd remembered he drank scotch. She was what his mother used to call *a man's woman.*

Suddenly another group of doctors had come over, and he'd watched as Jordan's expression had changed, the sexy warmth morphing to a cheery professionalism, and it had struck him that maybe there had been a face that she'd reserved only for him, that she did still love him. He'd left the trade floor and attended the afternoon session and the breakout, taking notes, sipping iced water from the ugly plastic pitcher, eating butterscotch candies, and checking his phone to see if Jordan had texted. She'd been an inveterate texter, being young.

Noah had moderated the final panel feeling more alert than he had in weeks, on top of his game. He'd handled the question-and-answer session with dispatch, then had an obligatory beer with his buddies, but begged off going to the evening speaker. At eight o'clock, he'd knocked on the door of Jordan's room, not completely surprised when she'd opened it wearing only a hotel bathrobe.

I knew you'd come, Jordan had said, taking him by the arm, phone in hand, and Noah had let her close the door behind him, and she'd come fully into his arms, standing on tiptoe to kiss him and press herself against him, her breasts naked against the laminated name badge with its red satin Moderator ribbon.

Ouch, Jordan had said, stepping back. *Your name tag scratched me.*

Oh, sorry. Noah had spotted a red welt above her magnificent breasts, and it had broken the spell. He wasn't a guy who cheated in a hotel room, surrounded by a cheap coffeemaker, a scummy remote, and Spectravision. He'd had a laminated name badge with a red ribbon. He was the Moderator of Panel 2508, Childhood Asthma &

Environment; Problems at the Playground. He was the guy they counted on for order. The guy who made sure nobody monopolized the session. The most responsible guy, of all. *That* guy.

What's the matter, No-ha? Jordan had asked, confused.

I don't know what I'm doing here.

Yes you do. Jordan had stepped toward him, raising her lovely arms, closing her eyes and opening her mouth for a kiss, but Noah had caught her wrist, stopping her.

No, don't. I'm remarried. I'm a father.

You were a father before. Jordan had slipped her right arm inside his jacket and pulled her body against him, but he'd held her off, his hand on her shoulder, more firmly.

Jordan, I'm sorry, I shouldn't have come. I can't do this.

Yes, you can. Nobody has to know, just you and me.

Still I can't. Noah had felt the words spilling out, he'd known he'd been talking to himself.

Come on, No-ha. Just this once.

No, I love my wife and Caleb. I have a new stepdaughter, Anna. We're giving her a big party Saturday night, it's a whole thing—

But No-ha, I know how to make you feel good—

I can't. Noah edged back and reached for the doorknob. *I shouldn't have let you think this was going to happen.*

But you can't walk out on me—

I can't stay. Noah had slipped out the door, but Jordan had grabbed it and held it open.

Noah, you'll regret this! Jordan had shouted, but he hadn't looked back.

"Dr. Kapoor," Linda was saying, snapping Noah into the present. "How long would it take to strangle a young woman like Anna Desroches?"

"It takes approximately two to five minutes to strangle a person by hand, unless that person had drugs or alcohol in their system, or was unconscious."

"Were alcohol or drugs found in Anna's system?"

"No."

"What did you conclude about whether Anna was conscious or not, when she was strangled?"

"I concluded she was conscious."

The jury fell silent. Noah could see them, curling their upper lips in disgust, imagining the scene.

"Dr. Kapoor, what findings do you expect if a person is conscious when they are strangled?"

"There will be a struggle, and I would expect to find fingernail marks from the victim on their own neck, from where they were trying to pry off the hands of their killer."

"Did you find such fingernail marks in this case, on Anna's neck?"

"No, because the victim's fingernails were so short, bitten to the quick on some fingers. In addition, typically in a strangulation case, I would be able to take scrapings from under the fingernails of the victim and I would expect to find DNA of the perpetrator underneath the fingernails, in the form of skin cells. Because of the shortness of the victim's fingernails in this case, I was not able to obtain any such scrapings."

"What, if anything, do you typically find on the hands of the perpetrator in a strangling case?"

"Typically, I would expect to find fingernail marks from the victim on the perpetrator's hands, unless the perpetrator was wearing gloves."

"Do you know if any such fingernail marks were found on the defendant?"

Thomas half-rose. "Objection, Your Honor. This witness did not examine Dr. Alderman."

Linda frowned. "Your Honor, I said, 'if she knows.'"

Judge Gardner nodded. "Overruled." He turned to Dr. Kapoor. "You may answer, if you know."

"I do not believe fingernail marks were found on the defendant."

"Dr. Kapoor, did you draw any conclusions from that fact?"

"I concluded that either the victim's fingernails were too short to scrape him or he was wearing gloves."

Thomas jumped up. "Your Honor. Objection, speculation."

Linda scoffed. "That's within her expertise, Your Honor."

Judge Gardner shook his head. "Overruled."

Thomas sat down with a heavy sigh, and Noah kept his game face on.

Linda returned her attention to the witness. "Dr. Kapoor, based on your autopsy, did you reach an expert medical opinion with respect to how Anna was strangled?"

"Yes. My opinion is that she was strangled by another person, most likely an adult male."

"What is the basis for your expert medical opinion?"

"My examination and expertise tells me that the pressure applied to the throat sufficient to cause death would have been in the range of strength possessed by most adult men."

"Would you place the defendant in that range?"

"Yes."

"What, if anything, could you determine about the perpetrator's hands from the bruising on Anna's neck?"

"I was able to rule out people with larger or smaller hands. The size of the hand that caused the bruising was average, and there were no distinctive fingermarks that would identify it, so the majority of the adult male population would match it."

"Again, would you consider the defendant's hands to be within the average range?"

"Yes."

"Thank you, I have no further questions." Linda faced Judge Gardner, who turned to Thomas.

"Cross-examination, Mr. Owusu?"

"Yes, thank you, Your Honor." Thomas rose and strode toward the witness stand. "Ms. Swain-Pettit, I won't be needing the autopsy photo."

"Whoops, I forgot." Linda motioned to her paralegal, though Noah didn't believe for a minute that she'd left it up by accident.

Thomas stopped in front of the witness stand. "Dr. Kapoor, you testified that your office performs about 220 autopsies per year. How many of those have been on homicide victims?"

"Probably ten."

"Ten total?" Thomas lifted an eyebrow.

"Yes."

"And you aren't the only assistant coroner who performs autopsies, are you?"

"No."

"How many others are there?"

"It varies, two or three."

"How many homicides generally occur in Montgomery County, per year?"

"It varies between three and five. Except last year, we had eleven."

"So in fact, the overwhelming amount of your experience is not on homicide victims, isn't that correct?"

"Yes." Dr. Kapoor frowned.

"And even so, how many of those homicides were by manual strangulation?"

"I'd have to think about that. Most are by gun or knife."

"Would you say less than five are by manual strangulation?"

"Yes."

"Would you say less than three are by manual strangulation?"

"Yes."

Thomas stood taller, and Noah could read his mind. He had hit paydirt. "Dr. Kapoor, how many autopsies have you personally performed on victims where you found the cause and manner of death as homicide by strangulation?"

"One."

Thomas allowed himself a theatrical frown. "So the opinions you gave during your testimony regarding what you expected to find in a manual strangulation were not based on your actual experience, isn't that correct?"

"Yes." Dr. Kapoor pursed her lips unhappily.

"And, you testified that in your opinion, whoever killed the victim by strangulation was most likely an adult male, isn't that what you said?"

"Yes."

"Isn't it true that you have no idea of the age of that male?"

"Yes." Dr. Kapoor pressed her glasses higher on her nose with an unpolished fingernail.

"The killer could also have been any size or weight, could he not?"

"Yes."

"Furthermore, the killer could have been a very fit woman, couldn't she?"

"Yes."

"In fact, you can't tell from the bruising whether the murder was committed by a man or a woman, can you?"

"No."

"Dr. Kapoor, isn't the most you can say for certain is that Anna was strangled by a person who was strong enough to strangle her with their bare hands?"

"Yes."

"And you testified, did you not, that you could not determine the size of the killer's hands by the bruises on Anna's neck, isn't that true?"

"Yes."

"The most you could say for certain is that the hand was average in size, isn't that correct?"

"Yes."

"What is the average hand size for men?"

"Between six and eight inches."

"I would assume that women's hand sizes are generally smaller than men's, isn't that correct?"

"Yes."

"And isn't there an overlap between hand sizes for men and women?"

"Yes."

"So in fact, you could not say for certain whether the hands of the killer belonged to a man or woman, isn't that correct?"

"Yes."

"Dr. Kapoor, you also testified that there were no fingernail marks from the victim found on the defendant, isn't that correct?"

"Yes."

"And you further testified that because there were no fingernail marks on the defendant, you concluded that either the victim's fingernails were too short to make a mark or that the defendant was wearing gloves, isn't that correct?"

"Yes."

"But isn't it possible that there were no fingernail marks on the defendant because he did not commit the murder in question?"

"Yes."

"Thank you, I have no further questions." Thomas strolled back to counsel table and sat down with a satisfied smile, and Noah contained his happiness, because Thomas had warned him not to react. It was one of the best moments the defense had had, and Noah felt a surge of new hope. The jury was nodding, and VFW Guy lifted his grayish eyebrows in surprise.

"Your Honor, I'd like to call my next witness," Linda said quickly.

Chapter Fifty-four

Maggie, Before

Maggie felt excited that the barbecue was finally here, especially after the week she'd had. She'd been on her own with Caleb, who'd gotten a bad cold, then Anna, who got the same cold but had tons of homework. Maggie had been busy at the office, then at night had gone shopping, driving herself crazy to find paper plates that were nice enough and heavy plastic forks, not the flimsy white ones. She realized she was worrying more than usual because of what had happened with Noah before he'd left for the conference.

He'd stayed in only light touch with her through the week, texting at night and calling only once, toward the end. He'd said he'd been too busy to call, but there was a rift between them. They were tacitly agreeing to table the conversation, the way married people do after more serious fights, but that left her only with an uneasy feeling that there was a disturbance in her field. Noah had remained remote even after he'd gotten home late Thursday night, and she had spent Friday and Saturday setting up the tables, chairs, tablecloths, and box lanterns to string from the trees, which looked artsy instead of cheesy.

The party started with the sun dipping behind the treeline and the garden looking perfect. Everybody arrived on time, and Kathy helped Maggie refill platters and pour drinks throughout the evening.

Noah had manned the grill as if it were his fiefdom, but kept a distance from Maggie and Anna. There was plenty of wine and beer, and Maggie made sure everybody had champagne to toast Anna, overjoyed that the welcome was unalloyed happiness, despite the past.

Maggie would have felt like everything was falling into place, if only Noah had been in sync, but he wasn't. She noticed him drinking, which typically made him frisky later, though she doubted they'd be having sex tonight, or if they did, it would be one of those big-talk-then-sex sessions, which she liked more than he did. Either way, Noah didn't have much to say to Anna and only once did Maggie see him hand her a drink, so he was making an effort.

Darkness fell as the meal was served, everybody ate their fill, and the approved playlist went into its umpteenth loop while the guests went home, leaving Maggie, Noah, Caleb, and Anna. Noah had wanted to scour the grill, so Maggie had taken Caleb up to bed, and Anna had said she would clean up the kitchen. Maggie had been coming downstairs when she heard Anna shouting in unmistakable distress.

"Mom, help!"

"Anna!" Maggie almost tripped as she ran down the stairs, reaching the bottom just as a disheveled Anna came running toward her, the front of her sundress revealing her bra strap.

"Mom, this has to stop, I can't take it anymore, I just can't!" Anna burst into tears, running into Maggie's arms.

"What?" Maggie hugged her tight, dumbfounded. "Honey? What happened?"

"Babe?" Noah came out of the powder room, stricken, and Maggie realized that he had been in with Anna.

"Mom, you have to stop him! He tried to kiss me! He keeps coming on to me—"

"*What?*" Maggie asked, astonished. Her mouth went dry. Her heart hammered. She looked at Noah in shock. "What is *going on?*"

"Maggie, listen—"

"Mom, you have to know the truth!" Anna let her go, tears spilling from her eyes. "You have to get him to stop! I can't take it anymore, I can't!"

"*What* did you say?" Maggie said, still unable to believe her ears. Noah stepped back against the open door of the powder room, and Anna headed for the stairwell, grabbing the banister.

"You ask him, Mom! Ask him about the driving lesson, what he tried to do! I can't live with him!"

"Anna, wait!" Maggie felt her mouth hanging open. She couldn't close it, she was so thunderstruck. She whirled around to face Noah in disbelief. "Is this *true*?"

"Maggie, she's crazy. I don't even know what she's talking about."

"Noah, what's going on here?" Maggie tried to get a grip. "What's she talking about with the driving lesson? What happened?"

"You can't believe any of this—"

"I don't know what's going on, I don't know what to believe! She's saying you came on to her? Did you come on to her? To *Anna*?"

"Of course not!"

"Then what happened? Did you try to kiss her?"

"No!"

"What happened during the driving lesson?" Maggie found herself backing toward the stairway. She couldn't believe it was true, but he'd been behaving so strangely. "Is it possible? Are you lying?"

"No, of course not, it's not!" Noah raked his hands through his hair. "This is insane!"

"Is that why she doesn't want you to take her anymore?" Maggie didn't believe it, but what if she was in denial? She had made the same mistake with Florian, before. He'd been cheating on her, but she hadn't believed that either.

"Maggie, I swear, I don't know what she's talking about."

"What happened in the bathroom?" Maggie struggled for emotional footing. "Just tell me!"

"She told me the toilet was running, and I went to fix it and when I turned around she said I was trying to kiss her."

"Did you try to hug her or anything?"

"No, nothing. Nothing like that."

"Have you been drinking?" Maggie knew the answer. She had seen him.

"I had a few, yes, but—"

"Did you have too many? Are you out of control? Are you drunk?"

"Of course not!"

"But you know how you get when you drink."

"Not ever, never, with *Anna*. She's a kid! *Your* kid!"

"She's not a kid, she's a young woman." Maggie thought of Jordan, down at the conference. Jordan had been young, too. "Did something happen at the conference? Did you see Jordan in Miami?"

"No, she wasn't there."

"Did you go to the AstraZeneca booth? Did you go to the trade floor?"

"Yes, but I didn't see her there."

"Was she registered?"

"How do I know? I didn't look up the registrations."

"Who was there for AstraZeneca? We know those reps. Were ours there? Michelle and Chase?"

"I have no idea."

"But you like younger women." Maggie's mind raced, and she felt dumbfounded and appalled, both at once. *Fresh eggs*, isn't that what Kathy had said? But *Noah* with her *own daughter*?

"Maggie, I love you. I'm married to you."

"Did you hit on Anna? Is this a weird younger-woman thing?"

"Maggie, don't get crazy, none of this is true."

"Why would she lie?" Maggie threw her hands up in the air. She felt tears come to her eyes, but she held them off. "Why would she, Noah? She just moved in here. She wants a family!"

"I don't know."

"We just had a big party. Everything was nice. The only weird part of the party was you. You didn't talk to her."

"She didn't come up to me, either. She avoids me. I think she wants me out of here, out of my own home."

"No, I think it's the other way around. I think you want *her* out of here. And it's my home too. And now *this*?" Maggie felt herself fighting to understand what was happening. She could hear Anna crying upstairs, and Noah was still shaking his head, his lips parted.

"Maggie, I would *never*."

"I don't know if I believe you!" Maggie blurted out, her heart speaking out of turn, and for the first time, she heard truth.

"How can you say that?"

"How could I not?" Maggie reached for the banister. "I'm going to ask her what happened."

"Go ahead, she'll just lie to you."

"What if you're the liar, Noah?" Maggie shot back, hurrying up the stairs.

"I'm not!" Noah called back. "She is!"

The bedroom was dark, and Maggie leaned against the headboard, holding Anna close as her sniffling subsided, just like she had held Anna when she was a baby, crying from colic, fatigue, or the myriad mysteries that made babies unhappy. Maggie had loved the sensation of cuddling her baby girl, a warm bundle in a flannel onesie, and when Anna would finally stop crying, Maggie would feel rewarded, affirmed that she had done something right. Mothers had a sacred duty to love, protect, and comfort their children, but after Maggie's postpartum psychosis had crept over her, darkening those peaceful, happy moments, she felt stricken that she had failed Anna. And if Anna was telling her the truth, Maggie was failing her all over again.

Maggie closed her eyes, anguished. Anna had said, between sobs, that Noah had tried to molest her on the driving lesson and in the powder room downstairs. The very notion turned Maggie's stomach and shook her to her very foundations. She tried to collect her thoughts but her mind reeled. She didn't know who to believe. She couldn't conceive that this was happening under her own roof. She'd read the news about young women being preyed on by their stepfathers. She knew it happened everywhere, even in the nicest homes, like her own. She closed her eyes, tried to slow her heartbeat, and prayed that she could sort out what was true from what was false.

Maggie heard Anna's breathing settle into a soft rhythm and realized her daughter had fallen asleep in her arms, just as she had back in Congreve. Maggie thought back to that night, remembering her silent vow to never let Anna down again. A wave of guilt washed over her, and a sadness so deep she felt it to her very marrow. Tears came to her eyes, and she bit her lip not to cry. She couldn't understand any reason Anna would lie. Even Noah had no answer for why Anna would lie. People didn't lie without reason, did they?

Maggie's gaze fell on her phone when it lit up with a notification for an incoming text. She didn't recognize the number, and the notification showed a tiny photo with writing too small to read. She picked up the phone and opened the text. The photo was of Noah, caught in motion, leaving what looked like a hotel room. A banner across the photo read:

Enjoy your party, Maggie? Hope he wasn't too tired.

Maggie stared at the phone, stunned. Who was this from? What was Noah doing in the picture? In a hotel room?

Maggie read the text again, her eyes still wet. She enlarged the photo. It was definitely Noah.

Maggie eased Anna off her chest, shifting her onto the bed.

Anna half-woke, murmuring, "Love you."

"Love you, too," Maggie whispered, then headed for the door.

Chapter Fifty-five

Noah, After
TRIAL, DAY 3

Noah straightened as Linda called her next witness to the stand, an attractive African-American woman in her mid-thirties dressed in a loose-fitting black pantsuit. She had a pretty face dominated by oversized wire-rimmed glasses, and she wore her hair short, with little gold hoop earrings. She smiled for the courtroom clerk, who swore her in.

Linda stood in front of the witness stand. "Please state your name for the record, if you would."

"Patricia Evans."

"Thank you, and what is your occupation?"

"I'm a criminalist in the Forensic Services Unit in Montgomery County."

"And do you have a degree in criminology?"

"Yes, I have a criminal science degree from Drexel University."

"And how long have you been a criminalist?"

"Approximately four years."

"Ms. Evans, can you tell the jury, in layman's terms, what a criminalist does for Montgomery County?"

"We collect, document, preserve, and interpret physical evidence using scientific techniques, in order to support law enforcement in its investigation of crime."

"And did you collect evidence relating to the murder of Anna Desroches?"

"Yes, I was called to the crime scene that night."

"Please describe for the jury the fiber evidence you collected at the scene."

"Certainly, to begin . . ." Evans launched into her testimony, but Noah already knew the fiber evidence. They had found two white threads from his oxford shirt on Anna's dress, and they had found a blue thread from her checked dress on his khaki pants. Noah remembered that sundress, which she'd worn to the barbecue that had turned into a nightmare. It had only gotten worse after Maggie had come down, after having listened to Anna.

Noah! Maggie had charged downstairs into the basement. Her face had been red, her eyes had glistened with angry tears. She held her phone in the air like a flaming torch. *What the hell is this?*

I don't know what you mean. Noah hadn't been able to see what was on the phone.

This is a text I just got. It looks like a picture of you in a hotel room. This is you, isn't it? Maggie had thrust the phone at his face.

Maggie, hold on. Noah had put up his hands, reflexively. It had looked like him in the photo, going out a door. But he hadn't known who had taken it or when.

Who took this photo?

I don't know.

Oh, come on! This is a hotel room. I enlarged the photo. You can see the notice on the back of the door. It says checkout time is noon. What time did you check out, Noah?

I don't know, Noah had started to say, then he'd seen the phone number that had sent the text, a number he recognized. Jordan's. She must've taken the photo as he was leaving her hotel room in Miami. He remembered she'd had a phone in her hand, but he hadn't realized she'd taken a picture of him.

Noah, is this recent? When was this taken? Who took it?

Babe, I can explain—

So start explaining. Because I'm getting a suspicion that this is from

Miami and it was taken by you-know-who. Maggie's eyes had flashed with fury. *How does she know about our party tonight? How could she know that unless you told her? What the hell were you doing in her hotel room? You just told me that you didn't see her down there!*

Maggie, listen, I'm sorry, but nothing happened. Noah had tried to take her arm, but she'd smacked it away.

You just told me you didn't see her.

I'm sorry—

So you saw her? So you lied before? You really did? Maggie's eyes had widened, her worst fears confirmed. *I believed you, Noah! I believed you and I thought you were faithful to me! You told me you didn't see her down there, but you did, didn't you?*

Yes but—

What am I supposed to think about this? What did you do?

I didn't sleep with her, I didn't even kiss her.

Bullshit! You were in a hotel room! She got a picture of you leaving!

Because I didn't stay. I wouldn't stay and she was mad—

Noah, what were you doing in her hotel room in the first place? And why did you lie to me about it? How am I supposed to believe you? And what is going on with you?

*Maggie, wait—*Noah had put his hands up again, seeing that she had been losing control. Tears had spilled from her eyes. Mucus had bubbled in her nose.

Noah, my daughter cried herself to sleep! She told me that you've been trying to molest her! You're telling me you didn't! How am I supposed to believe you now?

Maggie, what does Anna have to do with it? These things aren't related—

Yes they are! How stupid do you think I am? You have no credibility with me! You're, like, a predator!

No, I'm not!

You've got a thing for young girls. Jordan was always too young for you! It's disgusting!

I know that, she was a mistake, it was after Karen—

Stop using Karen for an excuse! I'm so sick of hearing about your grief! How inconsolable you were! I'm the one who picked up the pieces! And now, when I finally get what I want, my own daughter coming home, this is how you repay me? This is what you do? Attack her in a bathroom?

No, I'm telling you, don't connect these things—

How can I not, Noah? I thought you never lied to me, but you lied to me tonight. That text is proof!

I did lie to you about that, but I'm not lying about Anna—

Liars lie, Noah, that's what they do! I don't know what happened to you. I don't know if you're going through a midlife crisis. I don't know if the fact that I brought Anna home made you crazy, maybe got you thinking about young women again. Maggie's lips had curled into a sneer of revulsion. *Noah, you're forty-three! A father. A stepfather. It's disgusting! She's underage! I should turn you in to the police, do you know that?*

Maggie, wait! Noah had said, panicky. He'd taken a step toward her but she'd moved back into the hallway. *Maggie, listen, you're getting this wrong. I've never lied to you before—*

Before when? Before tonight? Before Jordan? Before Anna?

Honey, you can't, you have to believe me—

The hell I do! Maggie had pointed a shaking finger at him, crying harder. *Get out of this house tonight, Noah! I don't care where you go! Go see Jordan! Bring her some effing carbohydrates!*

Maggie, no, please—

I don't want you in this house! I need to think and I need to talk to my daughter!

Maggie, please, just let me explain—

There's nothing more to explain. You don't have anything more to say, do you? Maggie had put her hands on her hips, her eyes boring into him. She'd been looking at him as if she'd never seen him before.

Maggie, stop, slow down, I'm not what you think—

That's what I'm worried about. Now get out!

"I have no further questions, thank you, Ms. Evans." Linda turned to Judge Gardner, and Thomas rose.

"Your Honor, I have cross-examination."

"Proceed." Judge Gardner gestured, and Linda returned to her seat as Thomas came forward.

"Ms. Evans, you testified that you found certain threads of the victim's on Dr. Alderman, and conversely, you found certain threads of Dr. Alderman's on the victim, isn't that correct?"

"Yes."

"It's true, isn't it, that your experience and expertise do not reveal to you how those fibers were exchanged, now do they?"

"That's true," Evans answered, after a moment.

"And in your expert opinion, isn't it possible that those fibers could have been exchanged while Dr. Alderman was engaged in efforts to resuscitate Anna?"

"Yes."

"You also testified that you found certain hairs of Anna's on Dr. Alderman, and conversely, Dr. Alderman's hairs were also found on Anna, isn't that correct?"

"Yes."

"And again, in your expert opinion, isn't it possible that those hairs could have been exchanged while Dr. Alderman was engaged in attempts to resuscitate Anna?"

"Yes," Evans answered after a moment.

"Your Honor, I have no further questions," Thomas said, turning away.

Noah felt like cheering, but he kept it inside. Thomas had scored off an important witness.

But Noah didn't know if it was enough to save him.

Chapter Fifty-six

Maggie, Before

Maggie sat in the backyard in the dark, having texted Kathy and asked her to call ASAP. She could imagine what Kathy would be doing right now, hurrying the boys to bed, letting the dog out one last time, and twisting the deadbolt on her front door, believing she had locked the danger outside, keeping her family safe. Maggie would've been doing the same things, assuming that the bad guys were outside, somewhere else, not under her roof. But she would never think that again.

Maggie eased back on the chaise lounge, clutching her phone. The barbecue smells hung in the air, and the lanterns were still lit, strung from tree to tree along the back fence. The folding chairs and card tables had been put away in the garage, and the cast-iron racks rested atop the grill, since Noah always insisted on cleaning them. It was almost impossible to believe that a man so picky about a barbecue grill could be the same man who would molest his stepdaughter.

Maggie couldn't believe she was thinking about a divorce, but she was. She loved Noah, or who she thought Noah was, but the foundation of their marriage was shifting beneath her very feet, like a domestic earthquake, the tectonic plates of their very lives, disjointed and broken.

Suddenly her phone rang, and the screen lit up with picture of Kathy in a tiara, from her last birthday. Maggie picked up. "Kath—"

"OMG, that party was so great! I'm so happy for you!" Kathy sounded like she expected a gossipy rehash, juicy fun for them both.

"Thanks, but something's the matter."

"What's up?"

"It's bad. Very bad. Are you somewhere you can talk?"

"Yes." Kathy's voice darkened. "What's going on?"

"I don't know where to start," Maggie began, but tears came to her eyes. "I can't say it."

"What do you mean? What is it?"

"I can't."

"Maggie. It's okay. Whatever you did, I love you."

"It's not me." Maggie wiped her eyes on her shirt. She had put on a blousy black top and black capris for the party, her Cool Mom Outfit. It seemed pathetic now.

"What's the matter, honey?" Kathy's tone softened.

Maggie prepared to say words she could never believe would come out of her mouth: "I think Noah may have molested Anna."

"What?" Kathy gasped, shocked. "You *can't* be serious."

"It's so awful," Maggie found herself whispering. She couldn't admit it aloud, even to herself.

"Molested?"

"Tried to kiss her and touch her breast, in the bathroom."

"No!" Kathy gasped again.

"Yes." Maggie was still whispering.

"How do you know?"

"I don't for sure. But I think . . ." Maggie swallowed hard, struggling to stay in emotional control. "I didn't believe it myself. I wouldn't have believed it. But then I got a text and he saw Jordan in Miami. He was in her hotel room."

"He saw her, the fetus?" Kathy asked, in confusion.

"Yes. He told me he didn't see her but then she sent a text, and he had to admit that he lied."

"What does that have to do with Anna?"

"Let me explain," Maggie said, launching into an account of everything that had happened, the words gushing as if she was bleeding them. She texted Kathy the photo of Noah in the hotel room, and after Kathy had gotten the photo, her tone hardened, which made Maggie's chest tighter. "Kathy, you think he did it, don't you? The picture convinced you, I can tell."

"I can't believe this, and I didn't, but this photo . . ." Kathy let the sentence trail off.

"What's the *matter* with him?" Maggie asked, anguished.

"God knows. How's Anna?"

"Sleeping."

"Where's Noah?"

"I don't know and I don't care."

"And Caleb?"

"Asleep. I'm hoping he didn't hear anything. I'll check on him later and tell him that Noah had to go in to work." Maggie edged forward on the chair, trying to collect her thoughts. "Do you think Noah would do something like that? To Anna?"

"I wouldn't have before, but I don't think it's impossible, not since I've seen that photo. Something must be going on with him."

"He tried to molest my *daughter*." Maggie rubbed her face, feeling a wave of pain. "I can't let him back in the house."

"No, you can't."

"I have to protect Anna. I owe her that, as my daughter." Maggie heard herself saying the unthinkable. "I don't know what this means for me and Noah. For our marriage. I just can't bring myself to believe he would do such a thing. Anna didn't even tell me the first time it happened, at the driving lesson. She didn't want to upset me. I don't know if she would've said anything if he hadn't tried it again."

"I'm glad she did, even though it's awful."

"I am too." Maggie sighed, weepy. Heartbroken.

"Even if he didn't do it, you have to err on the safe side. He should move into a hotel or rent something, for a while. You need to get her to a therapist, and him too. Do you think he'll agree to that?"

"He has to. I'll make it a condition to his coming home." Maggie couldn't believe that her life had gone from blissful to disastrous in a single week. She held back her tears.

"Maybe the pressure's getting to him?"

"What pressure? The pressure isn't any different than it has been before."

"Maybe Anna moving in, or Mike, that patient he lost? Or is it his own grief, over Karen? Somehow it's setting him off."

"Setting what off?" Maggie racked her brain. "What if he just has a thing for younger women?"

"Honey, I'm so sorry this happened. Do you want me to come over?"

"No, thanks. I want to keep things as normal as possible here. I feel so terrible about Anna." Maggie felt tears coming back, but held them at bay. "She loses her father and reaches out to me and now look what happens. It's so awful."

"I know, but you can't help that. You didn't do it."

"I brought her here. I thought everything would be so great."

"It's not your fault."

"Remember I met with her therapist? I told her how great everything was going to be. This is so shameful."

"You didn't know. You couldn't know."

"What if I should have? What if this has been happening with him for a long time? What if Anna isn't the first and neither is Jordan? I'm afraid to look at his computer but believe me, I want to."

"Don't."

"Why not? I know his passcodes. He has them on a pad."

"What do you expect to find?"

"Pornography? Pictures of young girls? Emails?"

"Don't, don't, don't."

"What if he goes online and meets young girls?"

"If he does that, he'll have deleted the history."

"You believe her then."

"I hate to say this, but I do."

"I do too," Maggie heard herself say, burying her face in her free hand. Agonized, she couldn't speak for a minute. She didn't know if Noah had committed a crime or not. She wondered if she needed a lawyer. She wondered if she should call the police. She would handle this the best way for Anna. That was her job as Anna's mother, especially because she had let her down before.

"You still there? I should come over."

"No, really." Maggie's mind reeled. "How can I stay married to him?"

"Honey, you're going to have to take it a step at a time. If he wants to stay married to you, he's going to have to do what you say."

"Right." Maggie told herself to take control of the situation. She couldn't let it victimize her. Anna was the victim, after all.

"You can do it."

"Can you believe he would do this? To Anna? To me? To this family? He's destroying everything, *everything*."

"He'll figure it out, with professional help."

Maggie sighed. "I feel so tired."

"Go to bed. Call me if you need anything."

"I will. Thanks for everything. Love you, Kath."

"Love you too, honey. We'll get through this. Sleep tight."

"You, too." Maggie pressed End, sat up, and glanced back at the house. The light was still off in Anna's bedroom. Caleb's light was off as well, so the second floor of the house was dark, the roof a shadowy outline against a dark sky. Clouds covered the moon, and there wasn't a star in sight. Ambient light from the neighboring houses made a hazy glow in the air, and Maggie could hear televisions playing in other people's family rooms.

She wondered how many of those families had such horror under their own roofs. She read about them in the newspaper and online. She never thought she would be one. In truth, she used to judge some of those mothers. How could you not know your teenage son stockpiled guns? How could you not know your daughter was pregnant? How could you *not* know? Only the terrible mothers didn't know what was happening in their own homes.

Then Maggie realized that she had already been adjudicated a terrible mother.

Unfit, was what the court had said. And here she was now, unfit all over again, seventeen years later, *unfit, unfit, unfit*.

She looked up at the black sky without knowing why. An appeal to God? For guidance? For help? A silent prayer? For forgiveness? But all she saw was darkness. She rose on shaky knees and walked toward the house.

Because she was a mother, and she had a job to do.

Chapter Fifty-seven

Noah, After
TRIAL, DAY 2

Noah straightened in his seat as the Commonwealth's next witness was sworn in, Detective Andrew Hickok. Thomas nicknamed him Detective Peacock, and it was clear why. His dark suit was well-tailored, and his dotted tie shone like real silk. He had dark hair layered in an expensive cut around a square-jawed face with brown eyes, a straight nose, and a salt-and-pepper mustache that was carefully trimmed. Overall, Detective Andrew Hickok had the demeanor of a complete law-enforcement professional, at home on the witness stand.

Linda smiled at the detective, her regard plain. "Please state your name for the record, sir."

"Detective Andrew J. Hickok."

"Detective Hickok, would you briefly tell the jury your credentials?"

"Yes. I started as a patrolman with the Philadelphia Police Department, then joined the Homicide Unit of the Philadelphia Police Department. I moved to Montgomery County and joined the Detective Bureau as a detective."

"And how long have you been with the Montgomery County Detective Bureau?"

"Sixteen years."

"How many homicide investigations have you participated in?"

"Over a hundred."

"And did you have anything to do with the investigation of Anna Desroches's murder?"

"Yes. I was lead investigator."

"Did you go to the crime scene on the night of the murder?"

"Yes, after I had obtained the warrants I thought I would need."

"And what was taking place at the crime scene?"

"Patrol officers were establishing a perimeter, and Dr. Kapoor and her team were with the body on the porch. She told me her initial finding on cause and manner. Criminalists from the Forensic Services Unit were taking photographs and collecting evidence from the scene, including the cars, house, driveway, and porch. In addition, a patrol officer had confiscated the defendant's cell phone and gave it to me."

"Detective Hickok, did the cell phone provide any evidence related to this investigation?"

"Yes, after I obtained the proper warrant."

"What was that evidence?"

"We found a text that the defendant had sent to the victim earlier that night."

"I'm going to show you a document and ask you to please identify it for the jury." Linda retrieved a paper from counsel table, then placed it in front of Thomas, Judge Gardner, and then the detective, who read it and looked up.

"This is the text that we found on the defendant's phone. The text was sent at 6:55 P.M. on May 10, the night of the murder."

"Your Honor, I'd like to mark this as Commonwealth Exhibit 43." Linda glanced back at Thomas, who nodded.

Judge Gardner nodded. "So admitted."

Linda signaled, and the text appeared on the screen.

> Anna, will you meet me at my house @915 tonight? I'm sorry and I want to work this out. Please don't tell your mother.

"Detective Hickok, did you consider this text relevant to your investigation?"

"Yes, it was highly suggestive of guilt. The literal terms of the text, the fact that the meeting place was at the defendant's home, and that defendant was present on the scene at the time the victim was murdered and was the one to call 911."

"And what did you do next?"

"We proceeded with our investigation through the night."

"And what, if anything, did you conclude?"

"We concluded that defendant had committed the murder of Anna Desroches."

"On what did you base your conclusion?"

"We had ample evidence. In addition to the defendant's text to the victim, we considered the existence of a PFA Petition that had been filed by the victim against the defendant on Monday, May 8, only two days before the murder."

"Detective Hickok, excuse me, why was that relevant?"

"It showed that the defendant had attempted to engage in prior sexual misconduct with the victim, supporting our theory that the defendant lured the victim to his home for another attempt at sexual misconduct, was rebuffed, and killed the victim in a fit of rage or a crime of passion, which generally occurs by strangulation."

"Did you consider other evidence to form your conclusion that the defendant had committed the murder?"

"Yes, we also considered the autopsy report and the trace evidence of hair, fibers, and DNA evidence that had been collected and analyzed by the criminalists, all of which supported our theory."

Linda cocked her head. "Isn't it true that typically, in a strangulation murder, the victim will fight back, leaving so-called defensive wounds on the perpetrator?"

"Yes."

"Did defendant have any such defensive wounds?'

"No."

"Did that undermine your conclusion that the defendant committed the murder?"

"No. Defensive wounds typically occur on the arms, and the defendant was wearing an oxford shirt with long sleeves at the time he was taken into custody."

Noah listened, his chest tight. Detective Hickok was coming off as smoothly credible, and Linda was preemptively asking questions that she anticipated Thomas would be asking on cross-examination. Unfortunately, Detective Hickok had an answer.

Linda paused, head still cocked. "Isn't it also true that typically, in a strangulation murder, the defendant will get the victim's skin cells underneath his fingernails, during the struggle?"

"Yes."

"Did the defendant have Anna's DNA under his fingernails?"

"No."

"Did that undermine your conclusion that the defendant committed the murder?"

"No. We knew that he was a doctor and had access to gloves, and his text to the victim demonstrated planning, so he could have had the gloves with him."

"Detective Hickok, were gloves found on the defendant's person when he was taken into custody?"

"No."

"Did *that* undermine your conclusion that the defendant committed the murder?"

"No. He could have disposed of the gloves before he called 911."

"Did you or anyone else find any gloves on the property?"

"No, but because we determined that the homicide was by manual strangulation, we didn't conduct a search, as we would have for a murder weapon. In addition, the other evidence of guilt was so overwhelming that it justified the charge."

"Did you find any fingerprints of the defendant's on Anna's neck?"

"No, our Forensic Unit doesn't have the capability to take fingerprints from skin or fabric."

"Detective Hickok, what did you do next in your investigation?"

"My partner and I met with an assistant district attorney and presented the evidence. He determined that the evidence was sufficient to charge the defendant, and we placed him under arrest and in the morning, he was arraigned." Detective Hickok turned to the jury. "That's a fancy word for formally charged."

"Thank you, Detective Hickok. I have no further questions." Linda smiled, obviously pleased, and returned to counsel table.

"I have cross, Your Honor," Thomas said, already on his way to the stand, as Linda passed him without a glance, then sat down.

Judge Gardner nodded. "Please proceed, Mr. Owusu."

Thomas stood at a distance from the stand. "Detective Hickok, when you went to the crime scene, weren't you aware that Dr. Alderman had already been brought in for questioning in connection with the murder?"

"Yes."

"And weren't you also aware that Dr. Alderman had told the 911 dispatcher that he had discovered the body?"

"Yes."

"And finally, weren't you aware that Dr. Alderman was the subject of the PFA Petition?"

"Yes."

"Detective Hickok, you testified that you investigated through the night, didn't you?"

"Yes."

"And what time of the night did you reach your conclusion that Dr. Alderman committed the murder?"

"By about four in the morning."

"So you and your partner had decided, only seven hours after the crime, that Dr. Alderman was guilty, isn't that correct?"

"Yes."

"You didn't interview any other suspects that night, did you?"

"No."

"You didn't seek any other suspects, did you?"

"No."

"Didn't look for a *single* other suspect, did you?"

"We had a prime suspect."

Thomas stood taller. "Detective Hickok, I'll repeat the question. You didn't look for a *single* other suspect, did you?"

"No." Detective Hickok tilted his chin up, in the slightest defiance.

"Do you know the term 'confirmation bias,' as applied to law enforcement?"

"Yes."

"Please define the term for the jury."

Detective Hickok turned to the jury. "Confirmation bias means that once you reach a conclusion about a perpetrator, you seek facts that support the conclusion and ignore facts that do not."

"Detective Hickok, did you consider the possibility that the killer could have come from a neighboring house?"

"No."

"Why not?"

"It seemed less likely."

"Less likely than Dr. Alderman, that is?"

"Yes."

"But wasn't Dr. Alderman's carriage house in view of the main house, where his landlord lived?"

"Yes."

"Wasn't the landlord home on the night of the murder?"

"Yes."

"The landlord's name was Scott Ropsare, is it not?"

"Yes."

"But didn't Mr. Ropsare have a view of Dr. Alderman's carriage house?"

"Yes."

"So isn't it true that Mr. Ropsare could have seen Anna Desroches pull up in her car, get out, and wait on Dr. Alderman's porch?"

"Yes." Detective Hickok blinked.

"Nevertheless, you didn't take Mr. Ropsare in for questioning, did you?"

"No, but I did knock on his door and speak to him. I asked him if he had seen anything unusual or suspicious, and he said he had not."

Thomas frowned. "My question was, you didn't take him in for questioning, did you?"

"No."

"Were you aware that Mr. Ropsare had a 2015 conviction for aggravated assault against his former wife?"

Detective Hickok's lips flattened. "Yes, I learned that the next day."

"But you *still* didn't go back to pick Mr. Ropsare up and take him in for questioning?"

"No."

"Because you had already charged Dr. Alderman with the crime, isn't that correct?"

"Yes."

Noah thought it was a masterful demonstration of confirmation bias and he wondered if Thomas would risk another question. The jurors were listening, and Noah sensed that they were getting the point.

Thomas paused. "Were you aware that Mr. Ropsare committed suicide six months ago, only one month after the murder of Anna Desroches?"

Detective Hickok blinked, twice. "No, I was not."

Noah's mouth dropped open. He hadn't known that either. He had only met Ropsare once, and Thomas hadn't told him that the landlord had committed suicide. The jury reacted with surprise, and VFW Guy shifted forward, newly intrigued.

"I have no other questions, Your Honor." Thomas turned and headed back to counsel table, his expression solemn. He sat down next to Noah, picked up his pen, and wrote on his legal pad:

Boom! I didn't tell you because I wanted your reaction. I got it. You're not as good a liar as you think.

Linda shot to her feet and hurried forward to the stand. "Your Honor, I have redirect, if I may."

Judge Gardner nodded. "Proceed, counsel."

"Detective Hickok, are you confident that the defendant committed the murder of Anna Desroches?"

"Yes."

"Do you believe that confirmation bias played any role at all in your investigation?"

"No, not in the least."

"I have no further questions, Your Honor."

Chapter Fifty-eight

Maggie, Before

Maggie barely slept Saturday night, but rose early on Sunday as usual, fed Ralph, and made batter for pancakes before the kids got up. She couldn't bring herself to believe that Noah had molested Anna. She'd gone back and forth about it in her mind, all night. She remembered what he'd said, that he hadn't done anything to Anna and whatever had happened with Jordan was unrelated. She supposed it was correct in the abstract, but it still didn't sit right with her. Still, she couldn't turn off her feelings for him so fast. She loved Noah, even though she didn't know if their marriage could survive. They'd been so happy, before.

Caleb came downstairs with a sleepy smile, in his oversized Phillies T-shirt. He accepted her explanation that Noah had gone back to the conference, and their conversation had centered on whether she should make banana or blueberry pancakes. Anna came down later with puffy eyes and bedhead, in a Congreve T-shirt and gym shorts. She said nothing about Noah in front of Caleb, and Maggie felt the two of them sharing a terrible secret throughout breakfast, which passed with silly speculation about whether SpongeBob was cute or weird-looking.

After breakfast, Anna and Caleb went to their respective rooms, and Maggie checked on Anna around lunchtime, only to find her dozing with the laptop open and her textbooks around her. Maggie closed the door and let her sleep, then went to Caleb's room, helped him with his homework on the book *Wonder,* and played apraxia Mad Libs with *bandage, accident,* and *emergency.* Caleb had backslid, but she didn't make a point of it, and he didn't mention Noah.

Maggie went through the rest of the day as if she were sleepwalking, puttering in the kitchen, watering the garden, and eyeing Noah's laptop in the family room, wondering if she should search it. She succumbed around four o'clock, logging on. She checked his browser history, which hadn't been deleted. She scanned the sites, but none of them were pornographic, only Noah-like searches of medical websites, online banking, pollen indexes, and abdominal exercises. She checked their bank accounts, but no suspicious checks had been sent to any random escort sites, nor were there any unusual cash withdrawals. After that, she went to the basement and searched his desktop computer, but that turned up nothing pornographic, mercifully.

Maggie was coming up from the basement when she heard footsteps on the stairwell, so she hurried into the kitchen and rushed to the sink to fake-drink a glass of water.

"Mom?" Anna said, entering the kitchen holding a packet of papers.

"Hey honey, how are you feeling?" Maggie gave her a big hug, freer to be real since Caleb wasn't around.

"I feel better, now." Anna hugged her back, then thrust some papers at Maggie, who assumed they were homework until she read the top: **PETITION FOR PROTECTION FROM ABUSE**

"Wait, what is this?"

"It's called a PFA. I'm going to file it on Monday against Noah, but I need you to sign it because I'm under eighteen."

"What are you talking about?" Maggie read the allegations on the form, her stomach turning.

"I can't take it anymore, I told you. I won't live in the same house with him."

"Anna, you don't have to do this," Maggie rushed to say, anguished and torn. "I've already decided what we're going to do. I haven't had a chance to talk to you about it yet. I'm going to tell him to see a therapist. He won't be allowed back until we all—"

"No, I won't ever live with him. I need a Protection From Abuse Order. I learned about it online and I called the hotline, so I know what to do next."

"Anna, this is what people do when they're abused by their husbands."

"Or by their parents. Their stepfather."

"Anna, really?" Maggie struggled to think clearly. "Don't you need a lawyer?"

"No. The woman on the phone said I could just file it on an emergency basis, first thing Monday morning. I already emailed and called the judge's chambers. I'm trying to get a hearing. I'm going to tell the judge that Noah sexually assaulted me." Anna met Maggie's eye directly. "I'm not going to take this, not one more minute. If I wanted to, I could call the police on him, but I'm only doing the PFA."

"But honey, I'm handling this." Maggie collected her thoughts. "He's not going to come home until we know that you can be safe. I mean, we can deal with this ourselves."

"I don't want to. What he did was wrong."

"Anna, what's the rush?" Maggie shuddered, thinking of Noah being arrested. "Why can't you give us a chance to settle this as a family?"

"Look, I know you love Noah. That's the problem, right?" Anna flopped onto a stool at the kitchen island, still one of three. Maggie hadn't even had a chance to order an extra one.

"Right. Yes, I do. He's my husband. Obviously, my emotions are conflicted right now."

"But you believe me, don't you?" Anna blinked, her blue eyes widening, and they reminded Maggie so much of her own mother's eyes, in the frank way in which they looked back at her, in the way that eyes could be a clear view of someone's soul, like a pair of binoculars focused inward on the human heart.

"Yes, I believe you," Maggie answered, and Anna's expression warmed, her gaze softening, and her mouth curving into a weary smile. She raised her arms and gave Maggie a hug.

"Thank you so much."

"I'm so sorry about all this." Maggie released Anna from the embrace.

"I'm sorry, too. I keep thinking, maybe I did something wrong, or wore something, to give him the wrong idea."

"Of course you didn't, honey. You're the victim." Maggie felt heartbroken to think that Anna was blaming herself.

"Then why would he do it? Has he done something like this before?"

"No, I would never have thought in a million years that he would try anything inappropriate with you. If I thought that, I wouldn't have brought you home. In fact, if I thought that, I wouldn't have married him in the first place."

"That's what I thought." Anna smiled, reassured.

"I don't know why he did it either. I can't give you any answers."

"So why don't you want me to go to court?"

Maggie hesitated. "Because I think we can handle it as a family, the way I said."

"No." Anna shook her head, her lips setting firmly. "The lady on the phone said that's what the moms always say."

"Who's this lady? What's her name?"

"I didn't ask her. She said the moms never want to go to court because they're in denial."

"I'm not in denial," Maggie said, though she wondered if she was, partly.

"And she said abusers don't take it seriously unless you get a PFA, so that's what I want to do."

"Anna, I really think that's taking it too far—"

"You do?" Anna's eyes flew open, pained. "You know what *I* think is taking it too far? When your stepfather sticks his tongue down your throat. Or puts his hand up your dress."

Maggie recoiled, disgusted. "I know, I'm sorry."

"I think that's really why he wanted to take me driving, so we could be alone together, without you."

"That can't be, it was my idea and—"

"Mom, I don't want to make you feel worse." Anna sighed, frowning. "You don't have to sign the PFA papers. I'll call James. He'll know somebody here who will help me."

"That's not necessary—"

"Yes, it is. Either Noah moves out or I do. If you don't want to sign the papers, then I'll get myself declared emancipated and move out." Anna straightened, determined. "Either way, I'm going to file for a PFA. I want to stand up for myself. I want to send a very clear message to him that what he did was wrong."

"He knows that, Anna."

"Mom, here's the thing." Anna touched Maggie's arm. "My whole life, I had nobody. It was just me, on my own. Dad left. You left. It was me, on my own. I can take care of myself."

"But you don't have to do that anymore. You have me."

"Do I? Noah is your husband. You just told me you love him."

"But I can protect you—"

"You didn't before," Anna shot back.

"I didn't know, how could I know?" Maggie heard herself sounding like those mothers on television, the ones she used to judge. She felt *unfit, unfit, unfit.*

"If you care, then go to court with me. Back me up. Sign the papers." Anna picked up a pen off of the kitchen island and held it out to Maggie.

"Anna—"

"Please, Mom?"

Maggie eyed the pen in Anna's outstretched hand, feeling a stab of anguish. She had to choose between Anna and Noah, right this minute. She felt bewildered that it had come to this so quickly. She didn't know what to do. She felt ripped down the middle in a familial tug-of-war. If Anna got a PFA against Noah, there would be no going back for her marriage.

Maggie slid the pen from Anna's hand.

Chapter Fifty-nine

Noah, After

TRIAL, DAY 1

Noah sat stiffly at counsel table while Linda gave her opening argument, saying buzzwords like *heinous murder, innocent young woman,* and *abundance of evidence,* and Thomas countered in his opening argument, firing back buzzwords like *rush to judgment, presumption of innocence,* and *reasonable doubt.* They reminded Noah of the target words he used to practice with Caleb, *accident, bandage, emergency,* but those days were over.

Noah controlled his emotions, trying to wrap his head around the fact that he was standing trial for a murder he hadn't committed. The truth was he hadn't killed Anna, but that didn't seem to matter anymore. He had learned that the only thing that mattered in the American legal system was what you could prove, and the Commonwealth had tons of proof against him, ironically, even though he hadn't done it. He hadn't sent the text to Anna that night, he hadn't molested her in the car or the bathroom, and his fibers, hair, and DNA had gotten on her body when he'd tried to save her life.

Linda stood before the dais. "Your Honor, the Commonwealth calls its first witness, Officer David Simon."

"Please proceed." Judge Gardner nodded, and Noah watched as a tall, lanky, uniformed police officer was sworn in. VFW Guy looked at the cop with admiration, but an African-American accountant in the back row lifted an eyebrow.

Linda moved to the front of the stand. "Please state your name for the record."

"Officer David Simon."

"And your occupation?"

"I'm a patrolman with the Montgomery County Police Department."

"And were you called to the crime scene on the night in question, Wednesday, May 10?"

"Yes."

"And what did you do upon your arrival?"

"We exited our vehicle and were met by the defendant."

Linda took Officer Simon through her direct examination, asking him about what had happened when he'd met Noah at the carriage house, an account that Noah didn't need to be reminded of. He had cycled over and over it in prison, mentally retracing his steps, wondering what he had done wrong or could've done differently, rewinding everything back to the night of the murder.

That night, Noah had driven home to his carriage house, which he'd rented on the fly. It was a tenant cottage behind the main house, where his landlord lived, and Noah thought it would be nicer for Caleb to visit him or move in, if it went that far. Noah had gotten home and pulled into the driveway, surprised to see Anna's Range Rover.

Noah had gotten out of his car, mentally preparing to see Anna. He'd wanted to confront her for her lies about him. He'd wanted to know why she'd been so hell-bent on ruining him, breaking up his family, destroying his life. He had to know *why*. Noah had walked the path to the porch, but it was too dark to see anything. His eyes hadn't adjusted to the darkness until he was almost standing on top of Anna, who was lying faceup on his porch floor, her arms flung wide.

Noah hadn't understood, his brain refusing to accept the obvious. He'd thought she had fallen asleep. He hadn't known why she was even here. He hadn't known how she'd even gotten the address, maybe from Maggie. None of it had made sense.

Anna, what are you doing?

He'd knelt over her, reaching reflexively in his back pocket for his phone. He'd slid it out, switched on the flashlight, and shined it in her face. Her eyes had been bulging, the sclera red with blood. Petechiae had dotted her eyelids and underneath her eyes, vivid against the pallor of her skin, blanched in death. Horrified, he'd pressed two fingers under her chin, which was still warm. There had been no pulse.

Noah had gone into action, administering chest compressions and fumbling to dial 911 at the same time. A female dispatcher had picked up, and Noah had thought of the 911 tapes they played on the TV news, which Maggie always hated. That had been the moment he'd realized that the police were going to think he had killed Anna.

Noah had to admit, he'd been thinking of himself. That's why he felt so guilty now. Even though he hadn't committed the murder, he hardly felt innocent. Anna had been his first thought, but his second thought had been *they are going to arrest me for this murder.* He never would've thought that before the PFA hearing. Before then, he'd thought that law led to justice and good guys never got convicted. But he'd learned quite the opposite that day, because the judge was going to issue that PFA against him if they hadn't settled it. And he would have been found to have sexually abused Anna, which he hadn't done, either.

Noah had kept up the compressions, all the time looking around, paranoid, on alert, wondering who could've killed Anna, why, or if they were still around. Where they could've come from, and how. The lights had been on in his landlord's house and in the house to the back, but it was another five hundred yards to the back neighbor's privacy fence. Noah hadn't seen anyone else, and there had been no other cars in the driveway, so somebody must've come on foot or gotten dropped off in a car.

Noah had kept the compressions going and tried to talk to the dispatcher, but all he could think of was *they are going to arrest me for this murder.* He had rushed the 911 operator off the phone and called Thomas, telling him everything that happened. Noah hadn't been sure that even Thomas had believed him. They both had known the police were on the way and that Noah would be taken in for questioning. Thomas had told him what to do, but Noah started thinking about Maggie. Anna was dead, and it would kill Maggie. All she'd ever wanted was Anna, and now Anna had been murdered. Strangled. On his front porch. What would Maggie think? Would Maggie believe he hadn't done it?

The police had arrived, Officers Simon and Pettigrew, and Noah had told them what Thomas had advised him to say, *I came home, I found her here, and that's all I know.* And then after that, *I'm not going to answer any further questions on the advice of counsel.*

But all along, Noah had wished he could say the only thing that mattered to him. But he couldn't.

I didn't do it.

Chapter Sixty

Maggie, Before

Maggie hadn't known it was possible to feel numb for hours, but it was. She felt numb all day Sunday, refusing to acknowledge to herself that she'd signed Anna's PFA form, that Noah had molested Anna, or that she was going to be in court for a PFA hearing, caught in the middle between her husband and her daughter. Maggie went through the motions of her day, doing laundry, serving dinner, spraying countertops, and helping Caleb with his homework, then saying good night to Anna, who told her that she hadn't heard about the hearing yet.

Maggie couldn't bring herself to say, "Fingers crossed!"

By the next morning, Anna had gotten a lawyer, who called the law clerk of the emergency judge and got them a hearing, which found Maggie in a courtroom, unable to look at Noah sitting at counsel table, his face front. She continued to feel numb throughout Anna's testimony, as awful as it was hearing what had happened. She listened as Noah testified, but even afterwards, she wasn't sure who was telling the truth.

Afterwards, Anna's lawyer had said that he believed the judge was going to issue a PFA Order against Noah, and Maggie had come to life. She couldn't let it happen to Noah, but more importantly, she couldn't let it happen to Caleb. The guilt, and the bullying, would have killed the boy. Maggie had persuaded Anna and her lawyer to let her broker a settlement, which Noah and his lawyer had accepted, then they'd all gone home. Separately.

Maggie didn't go to work on Monday and she told them she was taking another week off, assuming that Noah would keep his mouth shut about the PFA hearing. She felt so lost, knocking around the empty house, taking Caleb to his speech pathologist, and trying to figure out how to tell him that Noah wasn't at a medical conference, but was never coming home. She'd have to call a family lawyer and see if she had any rights to Caleb, whom she'd always intended to adopt, but hadn't just yet. On Tuesday morning, Maggie walked with Kathy, but their Talk & Talk didn't help the way it usually did. Kathy nagged her to call a therapist, but Maggie couldn't make herself do it yet.

On Wednesday after dinner, Anna said she was going over to Samantha's, driving the Range Rover alone for the first time. Maggie didn't love the idea, but let her go and sat by herself in the family room with a novel open on her lap and the TV playing a Bravo *Housewives* reality show. Later, Maggie heard a car out front, assuming Anna was home in the Range Rover. She looked out the window, only to see a police cruiser parking in front of her house.

Maggie rose, alarmed. *Anna was in an accident, she must have been in an accident, oh my God no, please no.* She hurried to the front door, telling herself she was overreacting until she saw two policemen walking to her door. She knew from TV and movies that there was only one reason that police came to see you like that, but she couldn't even hold that thought in her brain for very long, defaulting to a thousand possibilities. *They must have the wrong house. They just want to tell me something. They're collecting for that circus they do every year. They're interviewing the neighbors. Maybe there's a burglar in the neighborhood. It could be anything. Anna wasn't in an accident. They could have the wrong house. It's just some giant colossal mistake.*

Maggie flung open the door. "Yes, hello, Officers."

The policemen took off their caps, tucking them in the crooks of their arms. "Are you Mrs. Ippoliti?" asked the one officer, his voice gentle.

"Yes, yes—"

"We found your address on a temporary registration in a Range Rover, which is registered to one Anna Desroches. Do you know—"

"Yes, that's my daughter, is she okay?" Maggie felt her throat constrict, she could barely get the words out. "She wasn't in an accident, was she? Please tell me she's okay. It's a new car, and she hadn't practiced—"

"May we come in?"

Maggie gasped, *this is really happening,* and tears of fright sprang to her eyes. Somehow the police came in, and she sank onto the couch and the police asked if they could get her some water, but she shook her head *no* and tears spilled from her eyes before they could even tell her anything, and all she could keep saying, over and over, was *I never should have let her buy the car, I never should have let her buy the car.*

The police officers told her the unthinkable, that Anna had been murdered, that her body had been found at Noah's, and that Noah had been taken in for questioning in the crime.

"No, no, *no!*" Maggie shouted, her thoughts flying. *They were lying. Anna wasn't dead. Noah didn't kill her. There were so many lies in her life. This was the worst lie of all. It wasn't true, it was a horrible, horrible lie. Her husband could never kill her own daughter. It wasn't possible. How dare they.*

Suddenly Maggie jumped up, seized the startled police officer by his arms, and started shaking him back and forth, a woman unhinged, desperate, out of her mind. His cap fell out from under his arm, and the other police officer intervened, trying to soothe and contain her, but Maggie flailed back, lashing out with her fists, but when they finally held her still, doubled over in tears, she emitted a scream she never heard coming from herself or any human, one so primal that Caleb had come racing downstairs wild-eyed.

"Mag, Mag, what?" Caleb screamed, already crying, stricken with fear.

"Baby!" Maggie cried out, to him, to Anna, to her tiny baby girl, *it couldn't be true, Anna couldn't be dead, Noah couldn't do such a thing, how could she tell Caleb that his father had killed Anna, it couldn't be true, it just couldn't.*

Maggie collapsed to the floor with Caleb, hugging him tight as they cried together, clinging to each other until the police officers finally left, shaken and disturbed.

Chapter Sixty-one

Noah, After
TRIAL, DAY 10

Noah faced front at counsel table, and the jury returned to the courtroom, entered the jury box, and filed into their seats. The foreman was carrying a piece of paper, the verdict slip. He handed the slip to Judge Gardner, who read it, then looked up.

"Will the defendant please rise?" asked the judge.

Noah stood up, his knees weak. His heart hammered. His mouth had gone dry. He was in a waking nightmare. He was about to hear the jury's verdict for a crime he hadn't committed.

Judge Gardner peered at the spectators. "Ladies and gentlemen in the gallery, members of the media, I admonish you that there will be no outbursts, conversation, or discussion of any kind after I read this verdict. I will hold anyone who violates this order in contempt. In addition, please remain in your seats after the verdict is read. You may not leave your seats until I adjourn Court and we are no longer in session."

Noah felt pressure building in his jaw. He clenched and unclenched it, but it didn't help. It had been a long trial and an even longer incarceration, and earlier, he'd told himself that the verdict didn't matter because he'd already lost everything he loved. Now, he realized he'd been wrong. In fact, the opposite was true. The verdict mattered more than anything else. His life was on the line, right this minute, and for him, time stood still.

Judge Gardner cleared his throat, reading from the slip, "We, the jury in the matter of *Commonwealth of Pennsylvania v. Noah Alderman*, Docket Number 18-3277, find the defendant Dr. Noah Alderman guilty of first-degree murder in the death of Anna Ippoliti Desroches."

Noah reeled from the impact, as if he'd been hit by a truck. Thomas stood beside him, rock-solid. The courtroom fell deathly silent except for some coughing.

Judge Gardner set the verdict slip down. "Dr. Alderman, would you like to make a brief statement?"

Noah hadn't discussed that with Thomas, so he was on his own. "Yes, Your Honor, I would," he answered, finding his voice.

"Please do so, Dr. Alderman."

"I didn't kill Anna," Noah stated simply. He said it for Maggie. She wasn't here, but she would read it in the newspapers. His beloved audience of one.

He would never know if she believed him, but it was the truth.

Chapter Sixty-two

Maggie, After

That very night, Maggie and Kathy left in stricken silence for the county morgue, after leaving a heartbroken Caleb with Kathy's husband, Steve. Kathy did the driving, and Maggie kept all of the possibilities alive in her mind because she wouldn't believe that Anna was dead until she had seen her body. *There could have been some mistake, there must have been some mistake, a giant and colossal mistake, it happens in the world, it could be somebody else's daughter, not my daughter, though it shouldn't be anybody's daughter, a life ended at seventeen.*

The sight of Anna's body reduced Maggie to her knees. Her only daughter was gone, her skin gray and cold, her eyes closed, and her body covered by a sheet. One of the morgue employees had said *strangulation,* and Maggie almost fainted on the spot, though she didn't need to be told. Purplish bruises encircled Anna's neck, a sight so grotesque that Maggie could barely look. An odd darkness covered the back of Anna's neck and shoulders, which Maggie realized was her daughter's lifeblood, pooling inside her very body.

Maggie felt an uncontrollable fury aflame inside her, a rising rage that Noah had done this to her baby girl, her only one. She covered her mouth not to cry out, but sobbed against Kathy, new tears of agony and grief. She couldn't do anything to get Anna back. She couldn't understand what had happened. She'd hadn't dreamed Noah was capable of such violence, such cruelty.

Maggie let Kathy guide her from the morgue and back home, and after that, Kathy had practically moved in, taking care of Maggie and Caleb and fending off reporters. Noah was charged with murder the next day, and Caleb kept asking for his father and crying. Maggie tried to explain everything to him, then let him stay home from school. She didn't want him bullied, now that their family was in the papers, LOCAL DOC CHARGED IN MURDER.

Kathy babysat while Maggie made Anna's funeral arrangements, chose the casket, the flowers, and Anna's boho dress for her to be buried in. They held a brief memorial service at the funeral home, and Maggie and Caleb sat in the front row next to Kathy and her family. Behind them were their circle of friends, who had just been at the barbecue, stunned and stricken by the unthinkable turn of events. A pastor gave a generic eulogy, but Maggie crawled into a mental shell to avoid feeling the worst pain of her life.

At the end of the service, a woman in a navy-blue dress approached her. "Excuse me, are you Maggie Alderman?"

"Ippoliti," Maggie corrected her, though she never had before.

"I'm so sorry for your loss."

"Thank you," Maggie answered, guarded. She suspected the woman was a reporter. "And you are?"

"You don't know me, I'm Chris Silas, Samantha Silas's mother. Our daughters were friends."

"Oh, yes." Maggie remembered Samantha, with the MINI Cooper and the tattoos.

"This must be so difficult for you."

Maggie couldn't begin to respond, so she didn't try. "How's Samantha? It must be hard for her, too."

"She ran away." Chris's face fell.

"What do you mean?"

"She's gone. She's run away before. This time I think it was because of Anna, you know, her death."

Maggie felt a stab of sympathy. She hadn't even thought of the ripple effects of Anna's murder. "I'm so sorry to hear that. Samantha's a very nice girl."

"You met her?"

"Yes, when she dropped Anna off, and she came to our barbecue, too." Maggie couldn't begin to remember that night. The powder room. Anna crying. Noah's lies. The photo from Jordan's hotel room.

"Thanks. Appreciate it." Chris smiled, sadly.

"Did you tell the police?"

"Yes, but no luck. I'm hoping she'll come back soon." Chris patted Maggie's shoulder. "You take care. I have to get to work."

"Thanks," Maggie said, withdrawing to the comfort of her shell.

Chapter Sixty-three

Noah, After

Noah sat hunched over on the bus seat, shackled at the wrists and ankles, which rendered it impossible to sit up straight. His back ached after the long ride in that position, but he ignored it. The Department of Corrections bus was unheated, and a few windows were stuck open, letting in frigid air and smoky exhaust. It was dark by the time they'd left SCI Camp Hill, which served as the Classification and Evaluation Center for the Pennsylvania prison system. He'd been bused there from the courtroom, and now he'd been shaved, deloused, classified, processed with an inmate ID number, and given a wristband with a barcode and a GPS tracker. He'd been assigned to SCI Graterford, which was Pennsylvania's largest maximum-security facility, housing four thousand convicted felons, like him.

Except that he was innocent.

Graterford was located on a thousand-acre parcel about thirty miles from Philadelphia, and it had been built in the 1920s, one of the older prisons in the system. It was at 105 percent overcrowding, second-highest in the state, but its replacement, SCI Phoenix, was already under construction on the same parcel, behind schedule and overbudget at a cost of $400 million. Noah knew the statistics because he'd read the inmate manual in the library at SCI Camp Hill, undoubtedly the only inmate to have done so.

His only goal was to survive, though for how long he didn't know. He hadn't been sentenced yet, and he was just trying to survive another day, though he wasn't sure why. He was fine not knowing why, for now. It was instinct. Every living thing fought to stay alive. People. Animals. Plants. Cells. Viruses. Allergens. He felt reduced to his primal self, following his only reflex. Survival.

He inhaled, and the exhaust fumes nauseated him, but he ignored that, too. He kept his head to the glass, which was covered by a wire lattice, and he looked out as they rumbled along the highway. Families in SUVs and minivans passed them, and he could see the kids buckled into their car seats and watching videos, the fathers straight-arming the wheel, and the mothers in the passenger seats, reading Facebook on their phones. He didn't permit himself to think of Maggie or Caleb. Or Anna. Or even Wreck-It Ralph.

Inmates filled the bus, all hunched over in shackles, sitting nearest the window like he was, spread out to avoid contact with each other. None of them appeared to be first-timers, since nobody was crying or talking. They all knew the unwritten rules, which they made and communicated by actions. Stay in your lane. Mind your own business. Don't discuss your case with another inmate or they'll use the information against you or trade it to reduce their own sentence. Above all, find your kind. There was safety in numbers.

Noah knew that would be his immediate problem, since he doubted there were other pediatric allergists at Graterford. He had no group to join. He was a generic white guy, but not a white nationalist. He wasn't black, Hispanic, or Asian, which were automatic groups. He wasn't a gang member of any stripe, another automatic group. He wasn't a Jesus freak or a "girlfriend," inmate slang nobody needed to spell out. He was on his own, which made him vulnerable.

Noah kept his eye out the window. His bid at Montgomery County Correctional Facility hadn't prepared him for what lay ahead because MCCF was a minimum-security facility. That was kindergarten compared to Graterford, with its general population of murderers, drug-dealers, arsonists, rapists, burglars, robbers, addicts, schizophrenics, and psychopaths. Graterford would be "hard time," not "smooth time" like MCCF. And Graterford housed the only Death Row in the state.

The bus crossed the border into Skippack Township, signified by a small green sign, and in time, they turned off of Route 73 onto an unmarked single-lane road that traveled downhill. It lead to Graterford, and massive lights made a white halo as bright as a major-league baseball stadium. Noah shifted up in his seat to see the prison, and so did the others, blinking from the sudden brightness after the long, dark drive. He wondered if they were all thinking the same thing.

This is the last time I'll see it from the outside.

Graterford was a massive conglomeration of buildings, and Noah could see only the lit office complex in front because the entire prison was encircled by a thirty-five-foot high concrete wall, barbed concertina wire, and guard towers with smoked-glass windows.

They traveled to the prison and were hustled out of the bus, shuffling along like a line of hunchbacks because of the shackles. They were ordered into an intake area, where they were unshackled, stripped, showered, and examined, then changed into a reddish-brown shirt with yellow trim and baggy pants with white prison slippers. They were photographed, cuffed up, and given a toilet kit, mattress, blanket, sheets, and towels, then split up by cellblock.

Noah was ordered to go with a burly CO, or corrections officer, in a black uniform with a name tag that read EVESHAM. They walked through dull white cinder-block corridors. The fluorescent lights flickered dully, and the floors were of worn concrete. The overheated air smelled antiseptic and dirty, both at once. The only sounds were the crackling of the walkie-talkie holstered on CO Evesham's black utility belt and the jingling of his keys. The long hallway ended in a locked sally port, and stenciled letters above it read, CELLBLOCK C.

CO Evesham detached his key ring. "Stand back, Dr. Alderman," he ordered, getting ready to unlock the door.

Noah obeyed.

CO Evesham turned to him, then said under his breath, "They're expecting you."

Noah blinked, surprised. "What do you mean?"

CO Evesham didn't reply, unlocking the door.

Chapter Sixty-four

Maggie, After

Maggie sat hunched at the kitchen island, her mail spread out and her laptop open to the bank's website. She was supposed to be paying bills, but the task seemed overwhelming. Everything seemed overwhelming since Anna's death, and Maggie knew she was stuck in the familiar mire of depression. She felt herself going under, being sucked down, the muck clogging her nostrils and filling her mouth. She wondered if she deserved to die that way, suffocated like Anna.

Maggie's gaze strayed to the window, and she watched raindrops batter the glass. She couldn't bear to think that Anna was under the ground, and cold rainy days like this made her regret leaving her there. She had visited Anna's grave often before the trial, but then reporters had started following her. Now, three days after the guilty verdict against Noah, the media was finally losing interest and only one news van sat parked at her curb. Her neighbors probably hated her, for that and everything else, and she was considering moving, but Caleb didn't want to.

Maggie had made him her priority since Noah's arrest, trying to keep the house running as normally as possible, drilling him with his target words, and getting him to his appointments with his speech pathologist, as well as weekly sessions with a child psychologist, to help him cope. He'd wanted to visit Noah in jail, and his therapist thought it would be better if Kathy took him, which was fine with Maggie. She'd kept him home during the trial, with Kathy babysitting the time Maggie had gone to court. He was going back to school next week and was upstairs reading with Wreck-It Ralph.

Maggie missed Anna so badly, feeling the loss of everything her daughter could have been, could have had, and could have grown up to be. She agonized over the fact that not only was Anna dead, but Noah had killed her. Still, sometimes at night, alone in bed, Maggie admitted to herself that there was a tiny part of her that just couldn't believe Noah had done it. It just didn't seem like something he could do, despite his conviction and the evidence against him. And he'd said he hadn't done it, in court. She'd read it in the newspaper. She knew that Caleb had some doubts, too, though his therapist and Kathy thought that was denial.

Maggie didn't know if she loved Noah anymore. She loved the Noah she used to know, but she didn't know if he was real or fantasy. She'd been working part-time doing billing for a law firm, and one of the lawyers had helped her prepare divorce papers, which she had yet to file.

Suddenly her phone rang, and the screen lit up with a number from an area code she remembered. Congreve's. Maggie knew it wasn't James because she had emailed him about Anna's death. He had emailed back, saying that he would deal with the trust and the estate, since Anna had been killed before Florian's will had even been probated. By the terms of Anna's will, her money went to a variety of charitable causes, which would take months to distribute.

The phone rang again, and Maggie answered it, out of curiosity. "Hello?"

"Hello, is this Maggie Ippoliti?" a woman asked, her voice vaguely familiar.

"Yes, who's calling?"

"This is Ellen Salvich from the Graham Center at Congreve Academy. We met last year. I was Anna's therapist."

"Oh, yes." Maggie felt guilty she'd never contacted Ellen. She'd been too embarrassed and ashamed. She hadn't known how to explain. *I'm sorry, but my husband killed my daughter, whom I told you I would take wonderful care of.*

"I just saw in the newspaper, online, what happened—"

"I'm so sorry, I should have called you."

"I was away until recently. I took a leave from school. My father was in hospice in Scottsdale and he passed last week. I'm just now getting back."

"I'm so sorry." Maggie felt an instant kinship with anybody who had lost anybody.

"Thank you. Are you in a position to talk? It's important, and you might find it shocking."

"Yes, go ahead," Maggie said, though nothing could shock her anymore.

"When I came home, I saw a newspaper story online about your husband's conviction for murder. They have his picture, next to Anna's. Anna's name is under the caption. I'm looking at it right now."

"Yes." Maggie sighed, pained. "He was convicted of her murder. I really should've called you, I thought about it so many times."

"No, that's not why I'm calling. This picture in the newspaper, which says Anna Desroches in the caption, is not a picture of Anna Desroches. This is not the Anna I knew and treated. She looks like Anna, but it's not Anna."

"I don't understand what you mean."

"I'm texting you the photo that's in the newspaper, which reads Anna Desroches." Ellen finished the sentence, and Maggie's text alert chimed.

"Hold on a sec, okay?" Maggie put Ellen on speaker, then scrolled to her texts. On her phone screen was a photo of Anna, slightly pixilated. Just looking at it hurt Maggie's heart. "Yes, that's Anna."

"No, it's not. That's my point. The girl identified as Anna Desroches in the newspaper is not the girl that I know as Anna Desroches. Or that we know as Anna Desroches at Congreve. As I say, she looks similar, but it's *not* Anna."

"I don't know what you mean." Maggie couldn't understand what she was being told.

"Hang on, I'm texting you a photo of my patient, your daughter Anna Desroches. It's a picture I took of us together, on her birthday last March."

"Okay," Maggie said slowly, and in the next moment, her text alert chimed again and a photo popped onto her phone screen. It showed Ellen, grinning with her arm around a young girl with blue eyes, a big smile, and dimples. The girl looked a lot like Anna, that is, the Anna that Maggie had known as her daughter.

"Maggie, are you there? Are you okay? I warned you, it's shocking."

"I don't understand," Maggie said, repeating herself. She couldn't tear her eyes from the photo. "Are you saying this is Anna, in this photo with you?"

"Yes, exactly." Ellen's tone turned adamant, even urgent. "This is your daughter, Anna Ippoliti Desroches, with me. It's a selfie. As I said, we took the picture last March on her seventeenth birthday."

"I'm confused. Is Anna with you now?" Maggie didn't understand. It didn't make any sense.

"No. She's missing. Anna is missing. She must have disappeared over Spring Break, last year."

"Wait, what?" Maggie's mind reeled. "So the person that I thought was my daughter wasn't my daughter?"

"Yes, the last time I saw Anna was before Spring Break, on April 3 at our regular Monday appointment, and we talked about her reaching out to you. We talked about everything I told you when we met at Graham Center."

"So then what happened to her?"

"We don't understand what happened or how. But we know that the person in the newspaper is not Anna. Even though the girl in the newspaper looks like Anna and seems about the same age, it's not Anna."

"It's really *not* Anna?" Maggie felt stunned. She squinted at the selfie. "*This* is my daughter? In the photo with you? So the girl I took home was only *pretending* to be my daughter?"

"Yes, we believe she must have been."

"What's her name?" Maggie asked, dumbfounded. "Who is she? Was she?"

"We don't know. I just discovered this a few hours ago, myself, and I went to the Head of School Morris Whitaker and Assistant Head of School Jack Amundsen. I'm with them now. We've already contacted the Congreve and the Maine State Police."

"My God." Maggie thought back to her visit to Congreve, that night. "But I walked her to her dorm. She went inside and packed while I went to see you. Didn't anybody wonder who she was and why she was taking Anna's things?"

"We wondered that ourselves, so we contacted the students, who are now seniors. One of them remembered the girl because she looked like Anna. The imposter, for lack of a better term, told them she was a paralegal sent over by James Huntley, a lawyer in town."

"I know him. He handled Anna's trust."

"Yes, we checked with him. He's on vacation in Florida but we reached him there. He did not send over a paralegal, and he had no knowledge of this. He concurs that the girl in the photo is not Anna." Ellen cleared her throat. "In addition, our records show that our registrar received an email from Anna's email address at 9:02 A.M. on Friday, April 21, telling them she was withdrawing from Congreve that very day. We do not know if that email came from the real Anna or the imposter. We assume word got around at Parker, and that's the reason that no one questioned the imposter when she packed Anna's room. She left campus that night, with you."

"An *imposter*." Maggie's head was spinning. She had so many questions, but only one mattered. "Where's the real Anna? Where's my daughter?"

"We don't know. You may want to fly up. There's a snowstorm predicted but if you hurry, you can get in. Text me when you arrive. Come directly to the Administration Rotunda."

"I'm on my way, bye." Maggie hung up, then rose, texting Kathy. "Caleb!"

Chapter Sixty-five

Noah, After

Noah didn't know what CO Evesham had meant by *they're expecting you*, but it couldn't be good. He walked behind CO Evesham along the second tier of Cellblock C, which was fully 250 feet long, with two tiers of cells on either side. The cells were full, two inmates to a cell, and they were locked at this hour, almost lights out. Noah kept his eyes front as they passed, fixed on CO Evesham, whose meaty build strained the seams of his black uniform with epaulets and gold-and-black PADOC patches.

Inmates came to their cell doors, leaning their elbows on the crossbars, yelling, "Hey, doc," "Yo!" and one inmate called, "The Doctor is in!" to laughter. It wasn't like on TV, with inmates hollering lurid things like "fresh meat," but the reality was more sinister. Noah sensed an undercurrent rippling down the cellblock as he passed, like a dark undertow rolling beneath the surface.

"This is you." CO Evesham stopped at a cell toward the end of the row, where his cellmate, an older inmate, was lying on the bottom bunk, reading an old Louis L'Amour paperback, his legs crossed at the ankles. The man was about seventy years old, short and slight, with wispy gray hair, a straight nose that held a crooked pair of bifocals, and a benign grin, though appearances could be deceiving in prison. At MCCF, it had been the old gangsters that were the real threat, ordering the dirty work that the young ones did.

"Go in and turn around," CO Evesham said, and Noah obeyed as the CO unlocked the cell, then uncuffed him. Noah dumped his mattress and sheets on the top bunk, and CO Evesham locked the door and walked away.

"I'm Noah Alderman," he said, and the old man stood up, extending a withered hand.

"Mike Smith, but they call me Peach because I'm wrinkly." Peach leaned a knobby elbow on the bed frame.

"Hi, Peach." Noah unrolled the mattress, glancing around. The cell was six by twelve, and the walls were grimy white cinder block. A long skinny window was set lengthwise at the end, and underneath was Peach's shelf, which held toiletries, paperback books, and oddly, a magazine collage of Tony Bennett.

"You look like Dr. Kildaire, from the TV. You old enough to know Dr. Kildaire? Good-looking guy. A doctor. Dr. Kildaire."

"Right, Dr. Kildaire." Noah sensed Peach was the chatty sort. He set his toilet kit on a narrow metal shelf next to an open toilet and a urinal.

"You got in late. Normally they don't do intake this late. They tell you your job assignment?"

"No." Noah unfolded his single sheet and tucked it around the thin mattress.

"You gotta get a good one. I work in the leather shop. I make boots. That's the best. There's a waiting list. The only people who work there are lifers. They gotta die for something to open up."

"What else is a good job?" Noah got the sheet on, and the buzzer sounded, reverberating in his ears.

"Try laundry." Peach eased back into his bunk. "Garment sucks. Kitchen sucks. Wood shop's decent. Friend of mine works there. He can put in a good word. He knows people."

"Thanks." Noah finished making his bed, then went to the sink, brushed his teeth, and washed up. He'd already relieved himself at intake. It was one of the things he hated most about prison, the lack of privacy. He would have to come to a *place of acceptance.*

"You don't talk much."

"I'm tired." Noah climbed up into his bunk, stretched out, and clammed up, in prison mode. Suddenly another buzzer sounded, and the lights went off abruptly.

Peach clucked. "Damn, I wasn't at the end of the chapter. It's good you got here. I could do a lot worse."

"It's mutual." Noah looked at the ceiling. He could hear men talking, praying, and singing, the noises echoing in the dark cellblock. He heard a congested cough nearby, but he couldn't see who it was because there were walls between the cells. He diagnosed it reflexively, as sinusitis.

"I been here twenty-one years. It's no picnic, but you get used to it. People get used to anything. Put your hand over the side."

"What?"

"You heard me. Put your hand over the side."

"Why?"

"Just do it. I ain't gonna hurt you."

Noah let his right hand drop and felt Peach give him a paper bag. "What's in it?"

"What's in what?"

Noah shifted onto his side and looked inside the bag, in the dim light from the window. It was a makeshift first-aid kit with a roll of gauze, a small bottle of Betadine, dental floss, and a heavy industrial needle, glinting in the half-light. The needle was contraband, which could get him thrown into the RHU, the Restricted Housing Unit, or solitary confinement.

Noah asked, "Peach, why did you give me this? Are you setting me up?"

"Don't be stupid."

Noah's thoughts raced. He'd been right about the undercurrent. Something was going to happen.

"Get some sleep, doc."

Chapter Sixty-six

Maggie, After

Maggie pulled up in front of Kathy's house with Caleb in the backseat. She'd told him only the basics about why they were going to Congreve, not wanting to confuse him. Happily, he was plugged into his earphones and immersed in a video game on his phone.

"Hey girl." Maggie opened the car door, letting Kathy in, bundled in a parka and snowboots.

"Maggie, hi. Hi, Caleb." Kathy climbed, closing the door. "I can't believe this, can you?"

"Amazing." Maggie hit the gas, and they took off in the pouring rain. She'd booked three seats on the next flight, and with any luck, they'd get to Congreve by dinnertime. "I'm still trying to figure it out."

"Me too." Kathy looked over, her eyes alive with animation. "I mean, the real Anna could be alive."

"I know." Maggie had thought of nothing else, newly energized. "But where is she? Why would anybody do this? And who was the imposter?"

"I don't know." Kathy shook her head.

"She was impersonating Anna. They look a lot alike." Maggie tore through the suburban streets in the rain, the windshield wipers pumping frantically, matching her mood.

"I know. I saw from the picture you texted me."

"I'm embarrassed to say I didn't recognize my own daughter." Maggie kept her eyes glued to the traffic, which was light.

"You couldn't. The last time you saw her, she was a baby. Florian kept the pictures. You couldn't see the way her face changed over time."

"You would think a mother would know." Maggie had been kicking herself ever since Ellen had called.

"I wouldn't have. It's crazy how much alike they look."

"It happens. I get people all the time that say they know somebody who looks like me." Maggie had been thinking nonstop, but was happy to have Kathy as a sounding board. "It must have to do with Anna's inheritance. Maybe that's what was behind this whole thing. Maybe that's why the girl was pretending to be Anna."

"That would make sense. I was thinking that's why she bought the Range Rover right away."

"Yes!" Maggie blew through a yellow light. "I think I see how the misidentification happened. I didn't bring the imposter with me when I went to see Ellen the therapist, or James the lawyer. I went to see them alone. So they would have no idea that the girl I was talking about wasn't the real Anna, because they didn't see her."

"So the girl you had dinner with was the imposter, right?"

"Yes, but she must have known the real Anna pretty well. She knew a lot about her, like that I was her mother and I had been writing to her, and she knew that Anna wanted to reach out to me. The real Anna had told her therapist that, too. So the imposter must have been a friend of Anna's."

Kathy frowned in thought. "Hmm, a lookalike friend. But I guess they didn't have to look that much alike."

"Right." Maggie took a left, heading toward the expressway.

"Do you think the imposter went to Congreve?"

"It seems the most likely." Maggie accelerated into the fast lane.

"You know what else I was thinking? Remember those notes between Anna and Jamie that we found in Anna's textbooks, way back when, before the murder?"

"Yes." Maggie had forgotten about Jamie, after Anna died.

"I was thinking, it's really strange that Jamie disappeared, isn't it? I wonder if that has something to do with it?"

"What though?" Maggie turned left, hitting the expressway in record time. The windshield wipers flapped madly, and the defroster blew on max. The sky was pewter-gray, pouring rain. She'd checked online, and they'd be racing to Congreve ahead of the snowstorm.

"I don't know. Jamie's last name was Covington, right?"

"Yes," Maggie answered, and it was all coming back to her. "And PG and Connie were going to get her a bus ticket."

"Right," Kathy said, urgently. "We have to tell the people at Congreve about that. We have to find Jamie, PG, and Connie and see what they know. Maybe it's connected to Anna's disappearance."

"Yes, how can two girls go missing and nobody worry about it?" Maggie accelerated, struck by a sudden memory. Anna's funeral was over seven months ago, but a thought was coming back to her. "Oh my God, do you remember at Anna's funeral? That woman who came up to me at the end?"

"No, who?"

"Anna—the imposter Anna, that is—made a friend at Lower Merion named Samantha Silas. Her mother spoke to me at the end of the funeral." Maggie tried to think back. "She told me that Samantha ran away after Anna was murdered because she was so upset, and that she had run away before."

"For real?"

"Yes." Maggie felt her chest tighten, making a connection. "Anna's only friend at high school, Samantha, runs away? And before that, Anna's only friend at Congreve, Jamie, runs away? And now Anna, the real Anna, my daughter, is missing? Doesn't that seem coincidental to you?"

"It does. I mean, what are the odds?" Kathy's eyes rounded.

"I think that's definitely something we should tell them. Ellen said they called the police, and we should lay it all out for them."

"Yes, it gives them a place to start their investigation."

"Yep." Maggie bore down, steering through the rain. "It worries me though. I hate to think that Anna is missing. What's happening with these girls?"

"We're not cops."

"No, but we're moms on a mission." Maggie looked over with a tense smile, and Kathy smiled back, equally tense.

"What happens to Noah, if this is true? He was convicted of killing Anna, but Anna isn't dead."

"I was wondering about that too. I don't know what it means, le-gally. They don't just let him go. I mean, that girl was murdered." Maggie gripped the steering wheel. She glanced in the backseat to make sure Caleb wasn't listening, and he was still ear-plugged into the video game. "Kathy, do me a favor, get my phone out of my purse, look up Neil Seligman, and call him? He's one of the criminal lawyers I know from work. He might have the answer."

"I'll do it, you drive." Kathy started digging in her purse, found the phone, and pressed in Neil's number. "Got it."

"Put him on speaker, okay?" Maggie drove while Kathy switched the phone to speaker, and it rang twice.

Neil picked up. "Hello?"

"Neil, this is Maggie Ippoliti. Got a minute?"

"Of course. I was thinking of you, reading about your husband's conviction. This must be a very difficult time for you."

"Yes it is, thank you. Do you have a minute to talk?"

"Of course."

"Neil, I'm in a car with my best friend Kathy, and I have a ques-tion for you about my husband. Can I speak to you confidentially, as an attorney?"

"Certainly."

"There's been a surprising development in his case, and I'd like to get your opinion." Maggie launched into the story about the phone call from Congreve and learning that the girl whom Noah had been convicted of killing wasn't Anna. Caleb kept playing his video game, and they sped past billboards on the way to the airport. Trucks and vans sprayed water and road salt.

"So what do you think, Neil?" Maggie asked, when she was finished.

"Noah doesn't get out of jail free. The fact that he was convicted of killing someone—let's call her Jane Doe, but she was in reality, Susan Smith—is not relevant to his conviction, if the only new fact is just a mistaken identity."

"I figured." Maggie felt a pang.

"Under the doctrine of transferred intent, the intent to murder may be transferred where the person who was actually killed was not the intended victim. Think of it like a situation where someone shot at another person's head with the intent to kill him, and that person ducked, and a third person was killed. You follow?"

"Yes," Maggie and Kathy answered in unison.

"It's still first-degree murder, despite the fact that the shooter did not intend to kill that person. The same would be true if someone put poison in someone's coffee cup with the intent to kill that person, and a third person drank the coffee and died."

"I understand." Maggie saw they were closing in on the airport.

"So Noah is still guilty of first-degree murder. It's not legally relevant if he was mistaken about the identity of the person he killed. Now, where the mistaken-identity issue could be helpful is if Noah can present substantial evidence that the person thought to be Jane Doe was actually killed by someone who wanted to kill Susan Smith and that person knew Jane Doe was Susan Smith. However, it would require evidence and not just speculation."

"I get it, thanks."

"Good, I'll get back to my brief. See you at work. When do you come back?"

"Next week, when Caleb goes back to school. Thanks again, bye." Maggie hung up.

"You're getting carried away, girl." Kathy looked over with a frown. "Just because somebody was impersonating Anna doesn't mean that Noah didn't kill her."

"It could." Maggie felt her pulse quicken as she drove.

"But it doesn't necessarily, and I don't want you to get your hopes up."

"I like my hopes up. They've been down so long."

"But it'll be worse later." Kathy glanced at Caleb, then lowered her voice. "Face it, Noah killed that girl, whoever she was. He was convicted. There was a lot of evidence against him."

"But think about it. We know now that the girl was impersonating Anna. Doesn't it make you wonder if she was lying about Noah?"

"Lying when she said that he was abusing her?"

"Yes, why not?" Maggie shot back. "She was lying about everything else. She was lying about who she was. She was pretending to be my daughter when she wasn't."

Kathy looked unconvinced. "Noah lied about Jordan in the hotel room."

"True." Maggie sped ahead in the rain, spotting the airport ahead.

"And what about the text he sent Anna? He lied about that."

"What if he didn't? What if she sent it herself the way he said? What if he was telling the truth, all along?"

"He wasn't. You're getting kooky." Kathy shook her head.

"But it really makes you think, doesn't it?" Maggie's heart lifted. "Stranger things have happened, haven't they?"

"Yes they have, and to you."

"Tell me about it!" Maggie found herself smiling for the first time in a long time, heading to the airport exit.

Chapter Sixty-seven

Noah, After

Noah didn't realize he'd fallen asleep until he awoke to noises in the hallway. Shuffling, whispering, and panting. He sat up in alarm. It was still nighttime. He could barely see in the darkness. Inmates were opening his cell door.

"Doc, get down here!" Peach whispered.

Two men rushed in like shadows, dragging a third inmate to the far side of the cell under the window. Noah heard rapid breathing and knew the man was in deep trouble.

He grabbed the brown bag, jumped off his bunk, and hustled to the men against the far wall. He crouched over the injured inmate, who lay on his back, his head against the wall, his mouth open.

The man's chest heaved noisily with each breath. He was barely conscious. His eyes fluttered, the pupils rolling back in his head. Blood soaked his shirt, spreading at a catastrophic rate.

"Doc, you gotta help him!" one of the inmates whispered, his eyes wide.

"I'm outta here!" the other inmate said, bolting out of the cell.

"What happened?" Noah felt the injured inmate's neck for a pulse. It was weak. The skin was clammy. The body shook. The man panted, in shock.

"He's cut in the chest! You gotta fix him up!"

"Peach, get a flashlight. I need to see." Noah leaned closer to the injured man, patting his face. "Buddy, stay with me."

"Doc, sew him up! You got the stuff, right?"

"Peach, a flashlight. Hurry." Noah raced to unbutton the injured man's shirt, and a stream of blood geysered into the air.

"Doc, he's bleedin' like crazy!" The inmate recoiled. "You gotta sew him up!"

Noah grabbed a towel off the rack, balled it up, and pressed it down on the injured man's chest. He had to stanch the bloodflow so he could examine the wound. He could feel the warm blood pulsing into the towel under his palms, coming at regular intervals. The knife must have severed an artery.

"Here's light!" Peach aimed a cone of jittery brightness on the man's heaving chest.

"Stay with me, buddy." Noah moved the towel to look at the injured man's chest. It was a gruesome sight. One four-inch gash near the heart, severing the aortic artery. Two cuts puncturing the left lobe of the lung, bubbling air and blood. Noah replaced the towel and pressed down to stop the loss of blood.

"Doc, what are you waiting for! Sew him up!"

"I can't. I can't move the towel. He needs surgery."

"So do it!"

"It doesn't work that way—" Noah started to say, but the inmate shoved him in fury. He fell backwards, scrambling to keep his balance. The soaked towel came off the injured man's chest. Noah lunged forward, grabbed it, and pressed it back down.

"Doc, sew him!"

The injured man stopped breathing. His eyes traveled heavenward, then stopped there, fixed.

Noah started chest compressions on top of the towel. "We have to call somebody."

"Sew him, come on!"

"Listen, you can't just sew the skin. He'll bleed out internally.

There's not enough blood to keep the heart pumping. That's why it stopped." Noah kept compressing the chest. He didn't feel the arterial pulse anymore.

"Doc, sew him up!" The inmate thrust the needle at Noah.

"It's not going to do any good." Noah's hands were slick with blood. He couldn't have threaded the needle with dental floss if he tried. "If you don't call the CO, he's dead. Call or I will."

"Doc, if you call the CO, *you're* dead."

Noah felt for the injured man's pulse as he pumped. It was gone. The man was dead. Noah hadn't been able to save his life. He hadn't been able to save Anna either. But he kept pumping, not knowing whom he was trying to save. Himself.

"Guard!" Noah hollered, but it was too late.

For both of them.

Chapter Sixty-eight

Maggie, After

Maggie steered the rental Honda through the snow-covered streets of Congreve, down the main drag that she remembered from last April. It had been chilly then, but it was freezing now, 4° at 6:23 P.M., according to the red digital numbers on the bank sign. It was already dark, and snowflakes gusted in the frigid wind. There was little traffic except for plows and salt trucks, and the sidewalks were deserted except for one or two hardy souls. The shops and restaurants were closing, their lights going off in their storefronts.

Maggie drove carefully in the storm, which had gummed up everything at the airport. Flights were delayed or canceled with Thanksgiving only days away. Luckily, the holiday left vacancies at the Congreve Inn, and she had booked two rooms, though they were going directly to the school. Caleb slept in the backseat, tired from the excitement of the plane ride.

"Do you believe this weather?" Kathy asked, marveling. "Mainers are better than we are."

"What do you mean?" Maggie looked over with a smile.

"They're stronger. They're tougher. I couldn't live here. I'd die of laziness."

Maggie chuckled, driving along, and the windshield wipers flapped madly, struggling to keep the flakes at bay. They passed bundled-up residents operating snowblowers, clearing their sidewalks and driveways before too much snow accumulated.

"Is that the school, at the end of the street?" Kathy pointed.

"Yes." Maggie felt her juices flowing. She had texted Ellen from the airport and told her when to expect them, and they were right on time. Directly ahead lay Congreve Academy's ornate wrought-iron gate, which was propped open. The school's brick buildings looked picturesque in the falling snow, and a white blanket covered the rooftops. Nobody was outside except for maintenance men operating snowblowers and shoveling.

"Whoa," Kathy said, as they reached the entrance. "This is the preppiest snowglobe ever."

"I know." Maggie braked at a lit security booth, which was brick and had a window on the side.

An older security guard slid the window aside. "May I help you ladies?" he asked, blinking against the snow.

"Yes, we're here to meet with Ellen Salvich, in the Admissions Rotunda. I believe she's with Head of School Morris Whitaker and Assistant Head of School Jack Amundsen."

"Fine, drive straight ahead." The guard gestured, and Maggie drove forward, spotted a sign, and steered in that direction. Ahead was a red-brick building that was completely round, topped by a domed rotunda covered with snow. Palladian windows dominated the façade, and lights were on inside and under a small white portico that covered the entrance. She pulled into a small parking lot that had already been plowed, empty except for two BMWs.

Kathy looked around. "No cop cars? I thought the cops would be here."

"So did I." Maggie parked, then turned around to wake Caleb up. "Honey, Caleb? We're here."

"Okay," Caleb said sleepily, rousing. "Where are we again?"

"We're at Anna's old school and we're going to meet some people and talk." Maggie chose her words carefully, not to give him too much information. "You can come to the meeting, but I think it would be better if you waited in the waiting room. Is that okay with you?"

"Yes, can I bring my phone?"

"Yes. Do you have to go to the bathroom?"

"No."

"You thirsty? You wanna bring your water bottle?"

"No."

"Okay, let's go." Maggie and Kathy collected their purses, Caleb got his phone, and they got out of the car and ran toward the entrance with their heads down against the icy flakes. They flung open the door and found themselves in a circular waiting room with Congreve-blue sofas and chairs, cherrywood end tables, and an empty reception desk.

"Hello, I'm Morris Whitaker, the Head of School." Whitaker smiled as he entered the room from an attached office. He was tall and thin, maybe sixty-something, with a lined face behind horn-rimmed glasses. He had on a dark three-piece suit with a Congreve-blue bowtie, plus heavy Sorel snowboots. He extended his hand. "You must be Maggie Ippoliti. I saw you drive in."

"Yes, hi, I'm Maggie," she said, shaking his hand, and introducing Caleb, who shook Whitaker's hand, and Kathy, who introduced herself.

"Ladies, come into my office and meet some folks. I put on a pot of fresh coffee."

"Thank you. Caleb's going to wait here." Maggie gestured Caleb into a chair, and he sat down.

"Fine." Whitaker led them into an office where there were two other middle-aged men in dark suits and rep ties. They both wore wire-rimmed glasses, but one was short and one was tall. Ellen Salvich, Anna's therapist, wasn't present, which surprised Maggie.

"I thought Ellen would be here."

Whitaker smiled politely. "There was no need. She gave us the information we need."

"I was hoping the police would be here, too. Ellen told me you were calling them."

"Chief Vogel of the Congreve Police was here, but he was called away. It's a small police force, and the storm is placing a heavy demand on its manpower and resources." Whitaker gestured to the other two men. "Please, meet Jack and Roger."

"Welcome, I'm Jack Amundsen," said the tall one, shaking Maggie's hand. "Assistant Head of School. I'll be sitting in tonight."

"Roger Baxter," said the short one. "General Counsel and a member of the board."

"Great to meet you," Maggie said, and they shook hands, introduced themselves to Kathy, then settled in chairs with coffee around a circular cherrywood table, which was nestled among bookshelves filled with reference books, awards and citations, and a group of family photos. A large matching desk was on the far side of the office.

"Well, Maggie." Whitaker cleared his throat, his hooded hazel eyes meeting hers with concern. "First, let me say that I'm so sorry about this situation. We commenced an investigation as soon as Ellen brought it to our attention."

"Thank you." Maggie sipped her coffee, served in a blue Congreve mug. "I've been racking my brain myself and I think I have some things figured out."

"Really, what would that be?" Whitaker cocked his head, and Maggie launched into an explanation, including the notes with Jamie they had found in Anna's textbook, about PG and Connie buying the bus ticket for Jamie, and even about Samantha's disappearance at Lower Merion.

"Of course," Maggie finished by saying, "my main concern is that Anna's missing and has been missing since April."

"That's our primary concern as well." Whitaker nodded quickly.

"Did you know Anna?"

"Somewhat. She was on the quiet side, so perhaps I didn't know her as well as some of the more extroverted students."

"Do you know anybody in the student body who looks like Anna?"

"Not offhand." Whitaker nodded, this time in the direction of the lawyer. "Roger, why don't you take the reins?"

"Of course. Maggie, thank you so much for this information." Roger flipped a page of a legal pad on which he had been taking notes with a gleaming Mont Blanc pen. "Here is the chronology we have, from Ellen."

Maggie got her phone to take notes, and so did Kathy.

"As you know, your ex-husband Florian Desroches was killed in a plane crash on March 8. Ellen saw Anna for her weekly appointments, on Mondays, except for Monday, March 13 because Anna was at her father's funeral in France. The last time Ellen saw Anna was April 3, because of Passover and Easter Monday. So we don't know when Anna went missing exactly, but we know that it had to be after April 3. I strongly suspect it was during Spring Break."

Maggie tapped it into her phone. "Okay, and just so you know, the imposter called me on Easter Sunday, April 16, and I met her for dinner on Friday, April 21, and brought her home on April 22."

"Thank you, I'll make a note of that."

Maggie blinked. "Maybe you can fill in some other dates for me. When did Anna return from the funeral in France?"

"We received a call on Thursday morning, March 9, from a French lawyer representing your ex-husband, notifying us of his death." Roger flipped back through his notes, then consulted a page. "We summoned Anna out of class and notified her. She left school the same day, on Thursday, March 9, and she returned to campus on March 15."

"And she went to class as usual at least until Spring Break, which was April 10 through April 18?" Maggie had looked up the school calendar on the website.

"Yes, though during Spring Break, she doesn't go to any regular classes."

"But she boarded here, so she was still here. Have you asked the other students who board?" Maggie thought for a minute. "The imposter told me that the boarders live in Parker Hall and that they're made fun of, because they're parked there. So I wonder if any of them stayed during Spring Break. Maybe they'd remember seeing Anna that week. They must've. Did you speak with them?"

"We attempted to, however, we want to keep this discreet, as I'm sure you understand. There's no reason to alarm the students or the parents."

Maggie blinked. "I think there is, for sure. They should know if someone is preying on the campus."

"But there's no evidence of that."

"Anna may have been abducted."

"Or she went missing, and that was almost eight months ago, it's being investigated, and there's certainly no immediate danger."

Maggie worried they were being dismissive. "Have you had a student go missing since Anna?"

"No."

"What about a student running away?"

"No, and this week, most of our students have already left for Thanksgiving break, which is until November 27. Thanksgiving is Thursday, the twenty-third, and classes ended today."

"But what about the ones who haven't? I can't believe that they all go away for Thanksgiving, especially not international students. Or maybe they couldn't get out because of the storm? Maybe their flights were delayed or canceled?" Maggie had questions and felt like she wasn't getting answers. "And what happened to Jamie Covington? Have you been looking for Jamie as well? Or was she found? Did she go home? Was it foul play?"

Roger shook his head. "To the best of our knowledge, Jamie hasn't returned. Her parents consider her a runaway. They do not suspect foul play."

"And what about PG and Connie, who bought the bus ticket for Jamie? Could we find them? Do you know who's nicknamed PG?"

"No."

"How about Connie?"

"No." Roger glanced at Whitaker. "Do you know a PG or Connie, a Constance? Maybe a senior?"

"I'd have to check into that, and I will."

Kathy frowned, shifting forward in her seat. "We think a great place to start investigating would be with the staff of *The Zephyr*. Have you spoken with any of those girls? It was only last year, and not all of them would have graduated. Even so, you probably have their home addresses."

Roger nodded. "We have already begun to ask those questions, but as Morris says, it is a holiday break and not everyone is around."

Maggie was losing patience. "Gentlemen, I don't think we're on the same page. My daughter Anna disappeared from the school, going missing sometime during last April, Spring Break. She could've been abducted, even kidnapped. And it's possible that whatever happened to her also happened to her friend Jamie, also a student. Aren't you going to do anything about it? Why are you so calm? Why aren't the police here?"

Roger raised a palm, coolly. "On the contrary, we're very concerned. As we say, the state and local police were here, but they were called away due to the storm."

"What about the FBI?"

"We saw no need to contact them. We reported it to the appropriate police, state and local."

"But this is a matter that may involve three missing girls, one from Pennsylvania and two from here. Why not call the FBI?"

"You may, if you wish. Their closest satellite office is in Bangor." Roger's tone turned official. "I would remind you, in this regard, that Morris received an email from your daughter at 9:02 A.M., on Monday, April 10, withdrawing from Congreve effective immediately."

"But you don't know if that was from Anna or the imposter."

"It was completely reasonable for us to assume that the email came from Anna, and it's still a reasonable assumption."

"So?" Maggie didn't like the change in his manner, which had turned distinctly lawyerly.

"I have reviewed this matter, and in my opinion, our legal responsibility for Anna Desroches terminated as of that email. We did not believe, nor can we reasonably have believed, that the email came from anyone but Anna Desroches, and after that point, Anna Desroches was no longer a student at Congreve."

"Are you serious?" Maggie asked, getting angry. "Are you saying you're not responsible because she wasn't a student here, technically, after the email?"

Kathy interjected, "Roger, don't you care about the fact that Anna is missing? We can get lawyers, too. You want the lawyers to battle it out or do you want to find Anna? And Jamie, too. Or do you want to be another private school that doesn't protect its female students?"

Roger bristled. "Ladies, as I have said, Congreve had no control or knowledge of Anna's leaving." He turned to Maggie. "In fact, the responsibility for her departure lies completely with you, since you were the one who took her from campus, and though we—"

"Now wait one minute—"

"—understand your emotionality in the circumstances—"

"You think I'm emotional?" Maggie interrupted again, angry. "This is me, calm. You haven't seen me emotional. Do you even have a heart? You're going to blame me for the fact that someone took my daughter and impersonated her? You're going to stand on some legal technicality so you don't have to care about her?"

Kathy nodded. "Yeah, Roger, I'm a teacher and I know you stand in the position of a parent here, *in loco parentis.* You're responsible for her and you should be ashamed of yourself."

Roger picked up his legal pad, rising. "We have done everything that we are responsible to do and we will continue to do so."

Whitaker rose, his expression softer. "Ladies, I'm doing everything that I can reasonably do and so is my staff. But you have to understand, a snowstorm like this stretches everyone to the limit. Chief Vogel will get back to you at his earliest, I promise you."

Roger added, "Yes, he will, though I would caution you to remember that this is a missing person case that is almost eight months old. It is simply not going to be resolved tonight. My advice is to see if there are any rooms at the Congreve Inn, hunker down during the storm, and by the end of the week, I'm sure you will hear from the Chief. We gave him your contact information."

Maggie rose, fuming. "Thanksgiving is the end of the week. Nobody's rushing around except to buy turkeys. It's snowing. That's what I'm hearing from you. Will you at least call Chief Vogel and tell him the information I gave you? Maybe he has some ideas or leads."

"Will do." Roger nodded.

"Tonight? As if a life depended on it? Because it could. Did you even file a missing persons report or should I do that? Just tell me the process."

Roger pursed his lips. "The process is more informal than what you're used to, in larger cities. We spoke with Chief Vogel, and you can follow up, but as I said, later. All of the area police are being deployed to deal with the snow emergency, and this matter may be dealt with after the storm, in just a day or two."

Kathy stood up, touching Maggie's arm. "Honey, you know what? Maybe they're right. Maybe we should just go to the hotel, check in, take a shower, and wait it out."

Maggie turned to her, confused. "Why should we let them off the hook? They have all the information. They're barely lifting a finger, and that's okay with you?"

Kathy put an arm around her. "Maggie, listen. We've had a long day, and this has been upsetting. We can call the Chief after a good night's sleep. I think we need to decompress and debrief."

"You do?" Maggie asked, nonplussed.

"Yep, let's get Caleb and go." Kathy shouldered her purse and started shaking everybody's hands. "Gentlemen, thank you so much. We know you'll do your best to find Anna and that you'll stay in touch with us."

"Thank you." Roger smiled tightly, shaking Kathy's hand.

"Yes, thank you." Whitaker shook Kathy's hand, then offered his hand to Maggie. "Maggie?"

"I'll be damned if I'll shake your hand!" Maggie snatched up her phone and purse.

"Gentlemen, thank you, bye." Kathy tugged Maggie from the office, collected Caleb from the waiting room, and hustled them all out of the Administration Rotunda into the cold and dark.

"You want to go to the *hotel*?" Maggie stopped her under the portico, zipping up her coat.

Kathy looked back slyly. "How long have you known me, girl? I got an idea."

"What is it?"

"Race me to the car."

"Me first!" Caleb called out, taking off.

Chapter Sixty-nine

Noah, After

Noah experienced the night as a horrible blur, COs running into the cell, taking the dead inmate away, locking down the cellblock, and taking him, Peach, and the other inmate into the security wing for questioning. Police and prison officials interrogated Noah for hours, and he told them what had happened, except about the contraband needle. He'd grabbed the needle off the floor during those first moments of confusion, palmed it, and dropped it in the hallway outside the cellblock.

They finished questioning Noah by dawn, deciding not to write him up because they credited his account that he didn't know about the fight or that their cell door was unlocked. He hadn't been given a chance to coordinate his story with Peach, but they'd been in jail long enough to know not to snitch. The higher-ups knew that Noah had just arrived at the prison, which gave credence to his story, and they had an internal problem, since a CO must have intentionally left their cell door unlocked. Noah assumed it had been CO Evesham, unless a different CO had done it after he and Peach had fallen asleep. He'd heard the stories of guards who would leave a cell door unlocked at night, looking the other way so the inmates could fight, sell drugs, or have sex. In any event, it wasn't his problem.

But during the process, Noah had had the realization that he had no control over *anything*. He had always been the guy who had everything in control, even in medical school. That was what his notetaking had been about, and the belief that hard work would lead to success and happiness, as if to control the process was to control the outcome. But there was no logical relationship between process and outcome, in life. And it had taken everything that had happened to him to arrive at that understanding, starting with Anna's moving in and ending at Graterford, being questioned about another life he hadn't been able to save. But learning that lesson had cost him Maggie, Caleb, and his freedom.

His *family*.

By morning, Noah was permitted to shower and change, with a CO posted. But Noah didn't trust even him. The COs would be no friends of his, now that he'd caused one of them to be disciplined or fired. He began to feel shaken by the violence he'd seen. He couldn't get the images out of his head, and now that he knew he had no control, he felt even more vulnerable.

He was escorted to breakfast late and hustled down the hall to the cafeteria. By then, the prison was no longer on lockdown, because lockdown at mealtimes was a logistical nightmare, since inmates had to be fed in their cells, requiring extra manpower that strained personnel and budget.

Noah entered the cafeteria and joined the back of the line, grabbing a tray, plastic cutlery, and a napkin, glancing behind him, reflexively. The cafeteria was a long rectangle with stainless steel tables and the same grimy cinder-block walls. COs were stationed along the wall, entrance, and exit, and Noah guessed they had extra guards because of the murder, but it didn't reassure him.

The line shifted forward, and so did Noah, moving his tray along and eyeing the powdered eggs, gloppy chipped beef, and white bread. He lifted his plate and accepted the food, and out of the corner of his eye, he could see inmates beginning to notice him, their heads turning to check him out. Noah was willing to bet they knew more about the murder than he did. Only during his interrogation did he find out the name of the inmate who had been killed. Jeremy Black.

Noah reached the end of the line, taking a carton of milk. He turned to the tables, which were beginning to empty, the inmates looking back at him as they left, their expressions hard. He spotted an empty table on the left, so he walked over, sat down with his tray, and dug into his eggs, which were lukewarm and oversalted.

Noah started on his chipped beef, and a brawny inmate sat down across from him with his tray. The man's head was shaved and tattooed with tribal markings, and he had narrow-set brown eyes and a lower lip that jutted forward from an underbite.

"Hey," the inmate said quietly.

"Hi." Noah gulped down another forkful of chipped beef. The guards were looking over, their heads turning.

"Name's John Drover."

"Noah Alderman." Noah could see the guards coming over, but he didn't understand why.

"I know. You let my homie die."

Chapter Seventy

Maggie, After

"You're so smart, Kath." Maggie rallied, steering the rental car toward the gate. The snowfall seemed heavier, the flakes flying into their headlights in the darkness.

"I'm an *educator*, baby." Kathy cackled, thumbing through her phone, the screen illuminating her features from below.

"That was fun!" Caleb giggled in the backseat.

"What's your idea?" Maggie asked Kathy, driving through the gate.

"Keep going, and I'll fill you in. We need them to see us leave, in case they're watching. Pull over anywhere when you get into town."

"Okay. I'm going to call Ellen." Maggie reached for her phone, pressed the number, and the call was answered. "Ellen?"

"Yes, Maggie, hello." Ellen sounded more distant than she had earlier in the day.

"Ellen, hi, we just came from the meeting, and I was surprised you weren't there." Maggie drove ahead, and traffic had lessened as they passed the lovely homes. Nobody was outside snowblowing or shoveling in the frigid night.

"Frankly, they asked me not to be. I probably shouldn't be taking this call."

"I thought so." Maggie felt herself get angry all over again. "What's their problem? You're just trying to help. I appreciated how concerned you were when we spoke. Don't they care?"

"Yes, but unfortunately, legalities intervened. I think they're realizing that they've been somewhat lax about security at the school. Our remote location lulls us into complacency. They're very concerned about liability."

"I'm not going to sue anybody. I just want to find my daughter."

"I understand that, but their response is an institutional one. The board and the lawyers are advising them now."

"But I'm worried about Anna. Aren't they?"

"I really can't say more. I should go. I wanted you to know that I care about Anna, and they're going to do the best they can. I'll make sure they do."

"Just let me ask you this, Anna's friend Jamie Covington went missing from school too. Did you treat Jamie?"

"I can't answer that."

"Does that mean you did? It must."

"I've been asked not to speak with you directly. Roger wants the information to flow through him."

"Can you just text me Jamie's parents' contact information? I won't say where it came from."

"No, I can't do that."

"But I think Jamie was helped to run away by people named PG and Connie. Do you know them? I'm thinking they might know where Anna is. I keep thinking they're connected because—"

"Please, I shouldn't stay on the line. Take care, Maggie. Good-bye." Ellen hung up.

"Damn." Maggie ended the call and entered the town of Congreve, which was hunkering down for the storm. The shops had closed, switching their lights off.

"Pull over here. It won't be long before we go back."

"We're going back?" Maggie parked in front of a boutique with darkened windows. Snow hit the windshield, and the wipers flapped madly.

"You're darn tootin'." Kathy nodded, eyeing the phone. "We're going to snoop around."

"Good, I say we start with Parker. Somebody has to be there."

"Agree, and look. This is a virtual tour of the school. It's on the Congreve website." Kathy held up the phone screen, which depicted a bird's eye view of the campus, with its classy brick buildings surrounded by lush green plantings, hedges, and trees.

"Notice they don't show it in winter."

"They're not that stupid." Kathy swiped right, then left, navigating around the campus. Names popped up next to each building, with a description of its use. "See? Daley Auditorium, Palumbo Lab Center, the Janet Baker Library. Parker Hall."

"I know where Parker is. I was there."

"But do you know this?" Kathy navigated to a white Victorian house with turrets, its eaves painted violet, lavender, and mint green. She read the pop-up description aloud, "'This is Steingard House, home to the school's award-winning poetry magazine, *The Zephyr*.'"

"Nice. I see how to get there from the entrance. Take a hard left and go straight." Maggie noted the street that ran in front of the Victorian house, which was on the far west side of campus. Dickinson Way.

"We have to wait until the suits leave the Administration Rotunda. Whitaker and Amundsen live on campus, and the map shows their houses. They live on the east side of campus, near the lake."

"So they won't see us. What about the security guard?"

"We'll make up something. Say I left something in the office or wanted to take a picture or something. We couldn't look more harmless, two moms and a little boy."

"I'm not little!" Caleb called from the backseat, and Maggie thought he heard more than she'd generally suspected.

"And the lawyer, I doubt he lives on campus."

"No, he lives under a rock." Kathy looked up. "But he has to drive by us when he leaves. This is the only street out of the school, right?"

"Right. When he drives by, the meeting is over. The lawyer is always the last to leave."

"How do you know that?"

"I learned it at work. Once the lawyer leaves, the conversation isn't privileged anymore, so the meeting's over."

"Whoa."

"I know things, too," Maggie said, checking the rearview.

Maggie, Kathy, and Caleb hurried up the path to the front door of Parker Hall, which had been salted and shoveled, leaving drifts almost waist-high on either side of the sidewalk. They had waved their way past the security guard at the gate, who must have recognized the car from before and hadn't even bothered to open the window, maybe because of the snow.

Maggie remembered Parker Hall, a lovely brick mansion, and there were plenty of lights on inside, so some of the Parkers must have been home. Maybe somebody could help them. They reached the covered entrance doors, which were wood with small glass windows, and through them they could see an entrance hall with Shaker benches, brass floor lamps, and another Oriental rug in front of a curving paneled staircase.

"Somebody's home." Maggie knocked again.

"Is there a Housemaster or something like that?"

"Yes, I think so." Maggie knocked harder, then looked around for a buzzer or intercom, but there wasn't one. She looked over at a lit window on the first floor, but she couldn't see inside because the shade was pulled down. She made a megaphone of her hands and shouted, "Hello, on the first floor, can you come to the door? Please?"

"Hey look!" Kathy said, and Maggie turned to see a young student in Congreve sweats, padding into the entrance hall in moccasins. She wore hip black glasses, and her hair was up in a long ponytail.

Maggie called to her, "Please let us in, we're two frostbitten moms! And a big boy!"

The student came to the door, opening it with a smile. "Are you parents or something?"

"Yes, hi, I'm Maggie Ippoliti, and this is my son Caleb and best friend Kathy. We're from Pennsylvania, and my daughter lived here. Her name was Anna Desroches. *Is* Anna Desroches."

"I'm Madison Leone. What's the problem? Did your car break down?"

"No, but to make a long story short, my daughter went missing last year and we're looking for her. She lived here. Did you know her?"

Madison frowned, buckling her smooth forehead. "No. What class was she in?"

"She was a junior last year."

"Oh, I wasn't here then. I transferred in this year."

"Do you know anybody who can help us? I just want to ask a question or two. We're trying to find her."

"I would have told you that Kurt and his wife can help you. He's our Housemaster. But he and his wife went away for Thanksgiving. I'm taking care of their cat."

Kathy interjected, "We're working with Morris Whitaker on this, so it's okay."

Madison nodded. "Right, I know what you're talking about. They were here today, talking to Sofia about Anna. Sofia lived upstairs, next door to Anna. I know about it because I heard them talking. My room is on the first floor, right over there." She pointed. "I hear everything. That's how I heard you knocking."

"Oh." Maggie realized that Sofia must have been the student who told Whitaker that the imposter had posed as a paralegal. "Is Sofia around? Maybe we can talk to her."

"No, she left for the holiday."

Maggie wanted to pick Madison's brain, too, just in case. "If you're new, you didn't know Jamie Covington, did you?"

"No, that name doesn't sound familiar."

"Do you know if a girl named PG lives here? Or Connie? These were friends of my daughter's."

"No, I never heard of them."

"Do you know who else we can speak to? Anybody who might know Anna, Jamie, PG, or Connie?"

"Sure, hold on." Madison took a phone from her sweatpants pocket and thumbed in a text. "I'm asking Genevieve, she's a senior. She'll be right down. She knows everybody."

"Great, thanks." Maggie turned to the staircase, and in a few moments, a short African-American student in a red sweater and jeans descended and approached them.

"Hey, I'm Genevieve," she said, with a sweet smile. She wore her hair pulled back, and silver bracelets jangled on her forearm. "How can I help you?"

Maggie smiled back. "I'm looking for my daughter, Anna Desroches. Did you know her?"

"Yes, but not well. You're her mom?"

"Yes." Maggie realized that until this very moment, she hadn't met another student who knew Anna, the real Anna. She didn't want to get emotional now, so she suppressed the thought.

"I heard she went to live home with you, didn't she?"

"Yes, she did, but to make a long story short, she's gone missing."

"Oh, I'm so sorry to hear that." Genevieve frowned. "She's a nice girl."

"Thank you," Maggie said, touched. "This is going to sound strange, but did you happen to know a student who looked like her? A lot like her?"

"No."

"We're also trying to find somebody who knew her friends Jamie Covington, PG, and Connie."

"I knew Jamie. She left school last year."

"Right. Have you heard from her since then?"

"No, but we weren't that friendly."

"Do you know a PG or Connie?"

"No, what's their last names?"

"We don't know."

"Were they seniors?"

"We don't know." Maggie had an idea. "Do you happen to have a yearbook?"

"Sure, come with me."

Chapter Seventy-one

Noah, After

"I didn't let anybody die." Noah rose, and two COs flanked Drover and lifted him bodily off the bench.

"Let's go, Mr. Drover." The COs hustled Drover from the cafeteria, and a third CO walked around the table to Noah and motioned him upward.

"Dr. Alderman, come on. Leave the tray." The CO motioned Noah up, and he went without complaint. He'd be safer in a cell anyway.

"Can I go back to my cell?"

"No. They're still working on it."

Noah swallowed hard. They'd told him last night that his cell would have to be examined and photographed for evidence, since it had become a crime scene.

The CO led him toward the cafeteria exit. "This way."

"So where am I going?"

"Block time. You don't have a job yet."

Noah flashed back on his old life, when he'd travel for a conference but his hotel room wouldn't be ready. He used to be so annoyed, back then. He'd make a fuss at the reception desk. He couldn't believe that it had taken prison to make him realize that he'd been a bit of a jerk.

The CO led him to the left, down an empty hallway. Drover and the other COs were nowhere in sight.

"So John Drover knows Jeremy Black?"

"Yes." The CO faced front, walking beside him.

"Are they in the same gang or something?"

"You doing a documentary?"

Noah let it go. "Which cellblock is Drover in?"

"C," the CO answered.

"But I'm in C."

"Oops," the CO said, walking.

Chapter Seventy-two

Maggie, After

Maggie, Kathy, and Caleb knocked on the door to Steingard House, which had a small window of frosted glass. A light was on inside, which cheered Maggie, who was trying to stay positive. They had searched the Congreve yearbooks and hadn't seen any Connies or PGs, though there had been photos of Jamie, and more importantly, of Anna. Maggie had taken pictures of Anna's photos with her phone, and it had helped her explain what was going on to Caleb.

"Here comes somebody." Maggie straightened up as a shadowy figure grew closer on the other side of the frosted glass, and the door was answered by a tall, slim student who had her blond hair piled in a twist. She had a long face, prominent cheekbones, and wore an oversized Harvard sweatshirt with black leggings and black Dr. Martens.

"Hello, can I help you? I'm Mercer Cooperman, one of the editors on *The Zephyr.*"

"Yes, thanks." Maggie introduced herself, Caleb, and Kathy. "I'm Anna Desroches's mother, and she was a student here until last year. I'm afraid she's gone missing. We've spoken with Morris Whitaker, and they're dealing with the police, but we want to ask a few questions too, on our own."

Kathy interjected, "It's a mom thing."

"I get it. My mom would too. Come on in. I've just put the Winter Issue to bed. It was supposed to be published before Thanksgiving, but poets don't follow deadlines." Mercer opened the door, admitting them to a funky entrance hall with a pair of lime-green-velvet armchairs, next to a wood coffee table piled with books.

"Thanks so much. Are you a senior, Mercer? Did you know Anna?"

Mercer shut the door. "Yes, I met her once or twice. I'm so sorry she's gone missing."

"You met her?" Maggie asked, encouraged. "Here or at Parker? Or in classes?"

"I think I had French Lit with her, but mostly, she'd stop by the office with Jamie Covington."

"Yes, they were friends." Maggie felt like they were onto something. "Did you know Jamie?"

"Not well, she was kind of a loner. Is she coming back to school?"

"I don't know. Do you know where she went?"

"No, I just heard she dropped out of school." Mercer puckered her lower lip. "She was so talented."

"Do you know PG or Connie, who were friends of Jamie's and Anna's?"

"Hmm, not Connie, but PG sounds familiar." Mercer frowned in thought. "Oh wait, I remember PG. She was a friend of Jamie's. She called herself PG for Ponygirl, after Ponyboy."

"Who's Ponyboy?"

"Ponyboy from *The Outsiders*? The novel? We read it in middle school."

Kathy interjected, "I know that book. My sons read it in Language Arts. Ponyboy is the hero. He's the poor kid in the town, one of the Greasers, and the rich kids are called the Socs."

Caleb looked up. " 'Stay gold, Ponyboy.' "

"Right!" Mercer grinned down at him. "That's from the book."

"Good for you, honey." Maggie hugged Caleb to her side. "Mercer, are you saying you remember PG? Did you meet her?"

"No, she didn't go here, but I remember Jamie talking about her because of the Ponygirl story."

"Do you know where PG is? Where did she go to school?"

"I assume she went to public school, Congreve High. She was a waitress at Eddie's. I think that's where Jamie met her. Jamie liked to eat there to get off campus, but it's bad food. Everything's fried."

"Is Eddie's in town?" Maggie felt her heart start to pound.

"No, it's in Tipton, one town north. It's Eddie's Diner, like a truck stop but nicer."

"How long does it take to get there?"

"Twenty minutes in nice weather, but in this snow, an hour. Mainers will tell you a place is 'just down the road.' But that means, like, hours."

"We'd better go. Thank you so much." Maggie reached for the doorknob. "You've been so helpful."

"Yes, thanks," Kathy said, right behind her.

"We got a break!" Maggie started the engine, excited.

"We sure did!" Kathy rubbed her hands together.

"Stay gold," Caleb said again. "She was nice. And pretty."

"Yes she was." Maggie pulled away from Steingard House and steered to the exit gate. The campus seemed completely deserted, and nobody was around snowplowing or shoveling at this hour. They drove past the Administration Rotunda, now darkened. "I wonder if Whitaker even called Chief Vogel."

"Me, too."

"Only one way to find out. Would you mind looking up the number of the Congreve Police Department for me, and I'll call?"

"Not at all." Kathy retrieved Maggie's phone, scrolled to the Internet, and found the number. "Here."

"Thanks." Maggie accepted the phone and pressed Call. The call rang and rang, then was answered.

"Congreve Police," a woman said. "How may I assist you?"

"Hi, I'm Maggie Ippoliti and I'm the mother of a girl named Anna Desroches, a seventeen-year-old student at the Congreve School who went missing last April. I believe that Chief Vogel has been in touch with Morris Whitaker about it today. May I speak with Chief Vogel? It's important."

"He's out right now. I'm just taking the phones on account of the storm. I'm not a patrol officer."

"Does he have a deputy or someone I can speak to?"

"He's out too, sorry. They all are. There's only three patrol officers, and one part-timer we share."

"May I have Chief Vogel's cell-phone number?"

"I'm sorry, I don't have that information. You can look him up if you want to. He's in the book."

Maggie looked over to see Kathy already scrolling through her phone for Chief Vogel's home number. "Do you happen to know if he filed a missing persons report for my daughter with the town or the state police?"

"I don't know about a report, ma'am. Like I say, I'm just picking up phones. We're stretched pretty thin."

"Okay, will you give him a message that I called?" Maggie drove through the snowy streets of Congreve.

"Certainly. What did you say your name was again?"

Maggie repeated her name, spelled her last name, then said, "Can you tell Chief Vogel that he can call me on my cell anytime, no matter how late? I'm staying at the Congreve Inn and heading out to Eddie's Diner in Tipton. There's a waitress there named PG who may know something about Anna's disappearance."

"Oh, Eddie's?" The woman perked up. "That's *real* good food. Try the flounder. It's double batter-dipped."

"Thank you, bye now." Maggie hung up and handed Kathy back the phone. "In the meantime, will you do me another favor? Look up the FBI in Bangor and let's give them a call."

"You're on fire." Kathy took the phone, scrolled through, then pressed Call and handed the phone back to Maggie. "While you were on with the Congreve police, I Google-mapped driving directions to Eddie's. I'll set my phone here so you can see. It's a straight shot north."

"Thanks." Maggie held the phone, listening to it ring. She slowed behind a snowplow as they passed the Congreve Inn. She didn't want to think about the night she had taken the imposter there, with the canopy, the room service, and the *Top Gun* tears. Maggie had bought the whole thing.

"I also checked Yelp. Eddie's gets five stars, and they say it has great showers. I like a restaurant with a good shower."

"Me, too. I order the soap on the side."

"It must be a trucker thing."

Maggie heard a click, and the phone was answered. "Hello?"

"Special Agent Tony Delgado here. To whom am I speaking?"

"Hi, my name is Maggie Ippoliti and I'm the mother of a seventeen-year-old, Anna Desroches, who went missing from Congreve School last April. I wonder if you can help me."

"Ms. Ippoliti, it's after business hours, and I'm on desk duty. This sounds like a matter for the local police, not the FBI."

Maggie didn't know the FBI kept business hours, but whatever. "They've already been contacted, but I think the FBI should get involved, too. There are two other girls who have gone missing, Jamie Covington from Congreve and Samantha Silas from Ardmore, Pennsylvania."

"Covington? I remember hearing about that case. That wasn't a missing persons case. My recollection is she was a runaway."

"Maybe that's what people were saying about it earlier, but I have new information that suggests that it wasn't." Maggie drove behind the snowplow. "Jamie Covington was a friend of my daughter's, and they were also friends with another girl named PG, who waitresses at Eddie's Diner in Tipton."

"Your daughter went missing in April?"

"Yes, but we just found out about it, and I want to find her."

"I can have my supervisor call you during business hours tomorrow."

"But do I have to wait until then? Can't you help me? I'm driving to Tipton to speak with PG."

"You're headed to Tipton now? That's treacherous weather up north, Ms. Ippoliti. You shouldn't be on the road."

"Special Agent Delgado, forgive me if I'm concerned enough to drive around tonight. I'd do that for my *cat*, for God's sake." Maggie looked in the rearview to see Caleb giving her the thumbs-up.

"The Governor is about to declare a snow emergency."

"He hasn't yet." Maggie accelerated when the snowplow turned off the road and she drove straight onto a single-lane highway leading out of town, mounded with snow on either side.

"Ms. Ippoliti, you're not going to do your daughter any good if you get into a car accident, or cause one. I'll have my supervisor call you."

"Please do, as soon as possible, at this number. It doesn't matter how late it is."

"Will do, Ms. Ippoliti. But please get off the road and leave the policework to the professionals."

"It's not policework, Special Agent Delgado." Maggie steered into the storm. "It's what any mother would do."

Chapter Seventy-three

Noah, After

Noah was released into Cellblock C, where inmates were talking or playing cards at tables with checkerboard tops and stainless-steel stools affixed to the concrete floor. An old TV was mounted underneath the first tier of the cells, playing on mute, and inmates were watching on closed captioning or with old earphones. Another line of inmates stood at two phones, waiting to make calls. There were more COs than Noah would have expected, and he looked up to see COs and officials clustered in front of his cell on the second tier.

Noah scanned the inmates for Drover, but he was nowhere in sight. Drover could have been in his cell, since inmates were permitted to stay in their cells during block time. After last night, Noah couldn't believe that prison officials would leave both him and Drover in the same cellblock, but changing cells in prison was an administrative problem like any other, and it took time.

Noah spotted Peach and walked toward him, looking around. He didn't think any trouble would break out when there were so many officials on the second tier, but still. He reached Peach, and they shook hands. "You okay? They didn't write you up?"

"No." Peach half-smiled. "I owe you, Dr. Kildaire."

"Not a problem."

"What'd you do with it?"

"Dropped it in the hallway outside. They'll find it sooner or later, but they can't link it to C." Noah glanced over his shoulder. "Where's John Drover's cell?"

Peach hesitated. "205. Top tier, catty-corner to us on the other side. Don't look now."

"Is he there now?"

"No. He didn't come back yet."

Noah wondered if they had already changed Drover's cell assignment. "Tell me about him."

"He runs a gang from Coatesville. It doesn't matter where he is, anyway. He's got people."

"Why does he think I let Jeremy die?"

"Because he ended up dead. They get each other's back." Peach pursed his thin lips. "Jeremy was in the RHU more than he was out of it. Kid was so damn young. Mouthy, disrespectful, always in fights, and the last one, he pissed off the wrong guy. Drover got the first-aid kit to you for backup."

"Who killed Jeremy?"

Peach frowned. "I can't tell you that."

"Yes you can." Noah needed to know as much as possible to protect himself. He didn't have a weapon, and information was the next-best thing. "Tell me. Or I'll tell them about the needle."

"You're learning the ropes." Peach smiled, admiring. "Jimmy Williams."

"Is Williams on C too?"

"Yeah, 207." Peach glanced behind him. "Dr. Kildare, you got trouble. Drover's going to blame you no matter what."

"So what do I do?"

"Watch your back. You're on your own. They'll split us up."

"Right." Noah could see that Peach wasn't unhappy about that, which made sense. If Noah was a target, his cellmate would be collateral damage.

"Think I can get them to move me to a different cellblock?" Noah had been running possibilities in the back of his mind.

"It won't make a difference. Drover's guys can get you anywhere."

"Not anywhere," Noah said, looking around for a CO.

Chapter Seventy-four

Maggie, After

Maggie, Kathy, and Caleb stepped inside Eddie's Diner, looking around. The room was an empty square with a drop ceiling and harsh fluorescent lighting, and in the front half was a cluttered store selling trucking supplies, lights and lenses, reflectors, headphones, air fresheners, tools, and hardware next to a cash register packed with cigarettes, chewing tobacco, gum, candy, and Tristate Megabucks Maine Powerball tickets. The air smelled like dry heat and stale cigarettes, and black-and-white photos of tractor-trailers lined the walls, interspersed with handmade signs: **Whoopie Pie Our Specialty** and **Brake for Moose, It Could Save Your Life**.

Kathy looked askance at the moose sign. "Does that really need to be said? What's the alternative? See a moose and hit the gas?"

Caleb laughed, and Maggie hugged him to her side. "You hungry, honey?"

"Yes."

"Good, the restaurant's in the back." Maggie led them past a fuel desk toward the back half of the store, which contained long wooden tables with wooden chairs and benches, in picnic-style seating. Color enlargements of a rocky seacoast, a lighthouse, and a wide river hung on the walls, and there were a few booths along the back wall next to the kitchen. The restaurant was empty except for a family with three young children, digging into pancakes and eggs.

Kathy said, "I love breakfast for dinner. How about you, Caleb?"

"I do too. I like pancakes."

"I don't see a waitress." Maggie looked around, hopeful. She knew the odds weren't good that PG would be working tonight, but they could get lucky.

Kathy gestured at the room. "Guys, where do you want to sit? You want a view of the snow or the chewing tobacco?"

Caleb pulled out a chair. "Here."

"You got it." Maggie pulled out a chair for her and Caleb, and Kathy sat across from them, unzipping her coat.

"It wasn't a bad drive. Except that we didn't kill any moose." Kathy took laminated menus from a condiment carousel on the table and slid them to Maggie and Caleb. "Here's your menus. I say we have the Chateaubriand with potatoes Dauphinoise and the molten lava cake for dessert. Then, of course, we shower."

Caleb giggled. "I want pancakes."

"You would think a waitress would come out." Maggie twisted around to the kitchen entrance, and Kathy waved at her.

"Yoo-hoo, are you even listening? I'm giving you my best stuff here. You were in outer space the entire drive."

"Sorry." Maggie rubbed her face, trying to keep her emotions at bay. All she could think about was whether Anna was dead or alive, her real daughter. It was as if she were getting a second chance, all over again. A waiter appeared from the kitchen, and walked toward them with the weary smile, deflating her hopes. She doubted there was another waitperson here tonight, given the conditions.

"Hello, ladies," the waiter said, crossing to their table with a smile. He looked about eighteen years old, with clear blue eyes and a short haircut. He was wearing a white polo shirt with jeans, with a name tag that read BOB. "Can I get you some water? Or a nice hot coffee?"

"Coffee would be great for me," Maggie answered, putting the menu back. "I'll have the pancakes and so will my son."

Kathy put her menu back, too. "Same for me, thanks."

Bob nodded. "We use maple syrup from Hurricane, Maine. Up near Québec. It's the best. You folks from New York?"

"Pennsylvania," Maggie answered. "Bob, I'm here because my daughter was friendly with a waitress here, named PG. Do you know her?"

"No." Bob frowned. "But I've only been here three days. She might be on day shift."

"Do you think anybody else would know her? Are there any other waiters or waitresses on tonight?"

"No, just me."

"How about the chef, or anybody else? Would they know her?" Maggie gestured to the general store. "Or maybe in front?"

"I'll ask the cook."

"Great, thanks. Can you let me know what he says before you bring the food?"

"No problem. I'll be right back." Bob ambled back to the kitchen, but Maggie couldn't wait. She rose, patting Caleb on the head.

"I'll be right back, honey."

"I figured." Kathy smiled as Maggie got up, hustled back to the cash register, and waited for the clerk, an older man, to get off his cell phone. His eyes were hooded, and reddish capillaries covered his longish nose. He was bald with gray stubble, and his sunken cheeks were bracketed by deep lines. His frame was slight but wiry, and he had on an old black T-shirt and jeans.

"Miss, you need somethin'?" he asked, though he didn't hang up the phone, but merely held it against his chest.

"Yes, I'm looking for a waitress named PG. Do you know her?"

"PG? Sure."

"Terrific!" Maggie said, thrilled. "She's a friend of my daughter's, and I was trying to find her. I don't even know her last name."

"It's Tenderly."

"PG is a nickname, right?"

"Yes. Her real name is Patti."

"I heard PG stands for Ponygirl."

"Ha!" The man chuckled, which turned into a smoker's cough. "You're telling *me* something now. I didn't know that. I didn't even know she liked horses."

Maggie didn't bother to explain. "I know she's not here, but do you know where she lives?"

"Sure, right down the road. Broom Lane, it's called. Go straight, take the second left. What'd you want to go see her for?"

"My daughter was a friend of hers, and we can't find her. I'm hoping PG will know where she is."

"Sorry about your daughter." The man *tsk-tsk*ed. "Mark my words. She'll come back."

"I hope so."

"PG might be able to help you. She's one smart girl. Makes friends where'er she goes."

"That's nice." Maggie sensed it made it more likely that PG would have information about Anna.

"She lives with her granny. Elma."

"Where are her parents?"

"Her mother was never worth a damn. Never even met her father. You know how it is, with the pills."

"They were addicts?"

"And drunks. Goes hand-in-hand, far as I can tell." He shook his head. "PG, she's a good girl. The tips she made here, she give to Elma. Always nice to me, the customers, tourists. She'd ask after my wife and she'd buy a Powerball, ever'day. She even baked me a chocolate cake for my birthday."

"Doesn't she work here anymore?" Maggie felt confused, noticing that he'd starting using the past tense.

"No, she don't. Hang on a minute. Lemme show you the cake she made me. Wrote my name on it and everything." The man swiveled around on his stool, shuffled through a pile of papers, then turned back with a photo, showing it to Maggie. "Here we go."

Maggie looked down at the photo. She froze at the image.

"You see, there's me, and PG, and the cake, and she wrote 'Happy Birthday, Sammy' in red, so it shows up on the chocolate."

Maggie couldn't speak. She felt her heart hammer. She recognized the girl in the photo. PG had short hair, big blue eyes, and a pretty smile that brought out her dimples. She looked a lot like Anna except for her haircut. The truth stared back at Maggie. PG was the girl she'd taken home, who'd impersonated Anna.

"Ain't that a nice cake?"

Chapter Seventy-five

Noah, After

Noah went up to the nearest CO, who was standing against the wall under the first tier. He was a huge forty-year-old with a brushy mustache, and his name tag read BOCANEGRA. "Mr. Bocanegra, I'm Noah Alderman and I'd like to speak with Deputy Warden McLaughlin."

"Pardon me?"

"I'd like to speak with Deputy Warden McLaughlin. I met with him last night." Noah was kicking himself. If he had known about Drover before, he would have dealt with it last night. But then again, now he had a bargaining chip.

"Uh, he's busy. Please, move along, Dr. Alderman."

"It's important. Can you contact him right away?"

"I'll make a note of it. We'll get back to you." CO Bocanegra half-smiled.

"This is very important. Can you take me to his office, and I'll wait there until he's available?"

"Like I said, I'll inform him of your request. We'll get back to you about an appointment."

"This can't wait." Noah knew the inmates were straining to hear the conversation. He was blowing his cover, but he had nothing to lose. On the contrary, the more public he went, the safer he'd be.

"It will have to wait, Dr. Alderman. We just got out of lockdown. There was a murder on this block last night, as you well know." CO Bocanegra glanced upward to Noah's cell. "You see the bigwigs up there. We have our hands full. So please, move along."

"Okay, fair enough, thanks." Noah turned on his heel, walked through the inmates, and strode to the staircase. He climbed to the second-tier stair in full view of the entire cellblock, heading to his cell. The inmates were beginning to look up, pausing their conversations and their card games.

Noah strode toward his cell, until his path was blocked by a big CO with a name tag that read KELLY. "Excuse me, Mr. Kelly—"

"Your cell isn't ready yet."

"I know that, I want to see the bigwigs."

"What do you mean?"

"Whoever is the most important person in there, that's who I want to see." Noah raised his voice, channeling the huffy doctor he used to be in his former life, the pediatric allergist who would be *damned* if he'd wait for a hotel room when he needed to prepare for his panel, which he was *moderating.*

"You mean Deputy Superintendent DeMaria?"

"Deputy Superintendent DeMaria is fine with me. I want to be transferred out of this prison."

"That's not possible—"

"It has to be possible," Noah said, raising his voice. "I'm in danger and I demand to be transferred immediately."

"Are you freaking kidding?"

"If you don't transfer me out and something happens to me, I'm going to make sure you're held liable." Noah let his gaze fall pointedly to the name tag. "Mr. Kelly, I'll make sure you're named as a defendant, individually and personally."

"Doc, hold on—" CO Kelly put up his hands like a traffic cop.

"I'm a target in this prison. And now that I said that, you're on notice. You're a witness to this statement. It's on camera." Noah gestured at the security camera, mounted a few cells over. He could see over CO Kelly's shoulder that two other COs were coming, with a frowning administrator in a gray suit and tie. "That video will be Exhibit A. Mr. Kelly, you're all going to be held liable if you don't transfer me immediately."

"I'm Deputy Superintendent Bill DeMaria. What the hell's going on here?"

"I'm Noah Alderman, and I'm in danger as a result of the Jeremy Black murder. I was threatened at breakfast. I'm going to be attacked and I'm not about to sit on my thumbs. I'm requesting to be transferred out of the prison."

Deputy Superintendent DeMaria scowled. "Not exactly, Dr. Alderman."

Chapter Seventy-six

Maggie, After

Maggie parked on Broom Lane, which turned out to be in a rural area. Snow covered the pastures like a white sheet, and there were no other houses except the Tenderlys' dilapidated farmhouse. It was of grimy clapboard, and so small that it seemed engulfed by the snow drifting against its side wall and accumulating on its sagging porch roof. A TV flickered in the front window of the house, and there was no car parked in the driveway. If there was a walkway from the street to the front door, it hadn't been shoveled.

"Let's go." Maggie turned to talk to Caleb, who'd plugged himself back into his video game, but Kathy stopped her, with a hand on her arm.

"Maggie, wait. We need to talk before we go in. You ranted about PG all the way here."

"I can't help it. She pretended to be my *daughter*. And worse, what did she do to Anna? Where's Anna? I want to know. It drives me crazy, to think she could have done something to Anna."

"Well, she paid a price, didn't she?"

"That's true. Sorry." Maggie dialed it back. "Why would she pretend to be Anna? It had to be because of the money, didn't it?"

"It seems like it would be a factor, doesn't it? Let's talk it over before we go off half-cocked."

"My mother used to say that."

"Mine did, too. That's why we get along. Because we became them and now we are them and we are also each other."

Maggie smiled. "Okay. So we agree the money had to be a factor. We learned PG played Powerball. She lived in a place like this. She had friends who went to a fancy private school. Maybe she wanted to be like them."

"And somehow she meets Anna, right?"

"Yes, and Jamie, and maybe Connie, at Eddie's. Or maybe Connie works at Eddie's, too. And Anna is lonely, so maybe PG gets to know her while she waits on her and finds out that she's a rich girl."

"And they both notice the similarity in their appearance."

"Then, as luck would have it, Florian dies in the plane crash." Maggie could visualize basically how it had happened. "Suddenly Anna stands to inherit millions of dollars, and like we said, PG must've been close enough to the real Anna to know she was thinking about reaching out to me."

"Yes, or Jamie could've been the one to tell PG. You know how girls talk."

"Like us."

"Right. And then Spring Break comes up, and there's no therapist and no classes, so Anna's not seen by anybody. She doesn't officially exist for a week. Most of the Parkers are away, and it's the perfect time for PG to strike."

"So what do you think PG did?"

"I don't know, but it scares the crap out of me." Maggie felt her gut twist. "Worst-case scenario, PG kidnaps or hurts Anna, then gets ahold of me, and like a fool, I come running, taking her in while my own daughter is God-knows-where."

"You weren't a fool. Anna was planning to reconnect with you or it wouldn't have worked so well."

"Do you think Anna's alive?" Maggie almost couldn't bear to give it voice, but she had to. It was the only question in her heart. "She has to be alive, doesn't she?"

"Yes, I believe that."

"I don't think PG killed her, do you? Not a seventeen-year-old girl." Maggie thought aloud, reassuring herself. "It doesn't sound like PG. PG is a girl who brings her tip money home to her grandmother. Who bakes cakes for people. She's a girl with dreams. She's not a murderer."

"Right, and maybe she even got Anna's approval. Anything could have happened." Kathy shrugged. "Maybe Anna wanted to take a break, figure things out after her father died. My Aunt Michelle traveled for six months after my uncle died. Partly it was an escape and partly it was clarifying."

"Really."

"Yep." Kathy shifted up in her seat. "Anna could've done that. She had the money. Maybe she and PG planned it together. She could have had it squirreled away. The lawyer and the therapist thought Anna was coming home with you. They wouldn't have questioned anything. And PG was smart enough to tell the housemates that she was cleaning out Anna's room on the lawyer's instruction. It's really the perfect escape. Like the prince and the pauper, they switch identities."

"But why?" Maggie didn't think it made sense.

"Maybe Anna just wanted to live on her own for a while, to see who she was. To get away from Congreve, which she hated anyway."

"What about Jamie? What does this have to do with Jamie?"

Kathy shrugged. "Possibly, nothing. You heard the FBI. They said Jamie was a runaway. Everyone is telling us she's a runaway."

"And what about Samantha, from Lower Merion?"

"Same thing. Her mother said she runs away. These are troubled kids. Borderline, lonely, vulnerable. It's sad. I feel for them." Kathy sighed heavily. "We live in a complex time, and kids keep secrets. Boys, too. I'm close to mine, but I know they keep things from me. I know they sneak a drink. Probably experiment with pot, or worse. I want to be all over it but you can't get in their face or they'll back away forever. Then they're lost for good."

"Lost for good," Maggie repeated, turning to the house. "I hope I haven't lost Anna for good."

"Let me put it this way, honey. We're not giving up without a fight."

"Agree," Maggie said, setting her jaw. "Do we tell the grandmother that PG is dead?"

"No, it's not our place. If she's alone, she might want her family around."

Maggie flashed on going to the morgue, seeing Anna. Rather, PG. She didn't wish that pain on anybody. "If I told her PG was dead, I'd have to tell her that Noah was convicted of her murder, whether he did it or not."

"Honey, he *did* it," Kathy said, keeping her voice low.

Maggie didn't reply. "Let's go. Caleb?"

Chapter Seventy-seven

Noah, After

Noah sat on the floor in the isolation cell, trying to figure out how long he had been here. He was in the ACU, or Administrative Custody Unit, for inmates that were in danger from other inmates. They had given him lunch through a slot in the door and then dinner, a while ago. The twelve-by-six cell was a white, windowless box that had a cot, urinal, toilet, and sink.

Noah rose. Sooner or later, Deputy Warden McLaughlin would have to see him. They couldn't keep him in the ACU forever, and even in the RHU, he'd have been entitled to a release hearing in seventy-two hours. There was no practical difference between the ACU and the RHU. Solitary confinement was the same, no matter what you called it.

He went to the heavy metal door and pounded hard. It was painted white but scuffed in places, and dented along the bottom, from being kicked. "Mr. Stanislavsky!"

There was no answer, so he pounded again. "Mr. Stanislavsky!"

There was still no answer, so he kept pounding. Suddenly he heard heavy footsteps in the hallway coming to his door, and in the next moment, the eye-level slot was slid open.

"Knock it off, Dr. Alderman," CO Stanislavsky said, frowning.

He was lanky and tall, with wire-rimmed glasses. "I told you, I'll let you know as soon as the Deputy Warden is ready."

"I want to talk to my lawyer," Noah shot back, changing tacks.

"You don't have phone privileges yet. That account takes weeks to set up in the system. You just can't make a call."

"Yes, you can. Calls to lawyers may go outside the Inmate Telephone System. They're freely available and must be private and unmonitored, unlike the other calls. I don't have a phone card and I'll call collect." Noah knew the details because he had read the handbook, for which he patted himself on the back. The fact that he'd studied for prison could save his life.

"I'll be back when I see what I can do." CO Stanislavsky closed the eye-level slot.

Noah could hear the footsteps walking away, then a heavy door clanging shut. He leaned his forehead against the cell door. It felt cool and calming, like a cold compress in the overheated cell. He thought of Maggie, then realized why. Because she used to kiss his forehead.

He closed his eyes and wondered what she was doing now. He tried to think of what day it was. Tuesday, before Thanksgiving. He hated to think of what the holiday would be like for Maggie and Caleb. He prayed that they were okay, and it gave him some comfort to know that she and Caleb had each other.

Noah felt his eyes fill, but squeezed them tight. He thought about banging his forehead on the metal door, but it wouldn't do any good. He loved his wife, but he would never see her again. He would see Caleb again, but Kathy would bring him, like before. It tore Noah apart inside.

He heard the door outside opening, footsteps heading his way, and in the next moment the eye-slot was pulled open.

"Dr. Alderman," CO Stanislavsky said, "I'll take you to the phone. Deputy Warden McLaughlin can't see you yet. He's hoping to get to you tonight, if not, tomorrow morning. Cuff up."

"Okay." Noah backed up to the door, put his hands against the lower slot, which was opened, and through it, he was handcuffed.

"Come on." CO Stanislavsky unlocked the door and opened it, standing aside to let Noah out of the cell.

"Thanks," Noah said, stepping into the hallway, which was when he saw someone else standing against the wall. It was CO Evesham, who might have left his cell intentionally unlocked last night, so that Jeremy Black could be brought in after the fight.

Noah half-considered trying to get back in the cell, but it was locked. He felt the tightness of the cuffs on his wrists.

CO Stanislavsky frowned. "Something the matter, Dr. Alderman?"

"No," Noah answered, having no other choice, just yet. He couldn't tell if CO Stanislavsky was planning to ambush him with CO Evesham, or if one CO was plotting but the other wasn't, or if he was being paranoid. He braced himself and masked his fears.

"Let's go, Dr. Alderman," CO Evesham said, motioning him to the unit door.

Chapter Seventy-eight

Maggie, After

"Hello, is anybody home?" Maggie knocked at the Tenderlys' door, with Kathy and Caleb behind her. She knocked one more time, and the door simply opened. "It's unlocked."

"Whoa." Kathy shrugged. "Go in."

"Yeah, it's cold." Caleb shivered in his coat, holding his phone.

"Hello?" Maggie opened the door, and they entered the house to find Elma Tenderly sleeping in a recliner next to a brown sofa, which faced a TV playing QVC on mute. She looked to be in her eighties, and her head was turned sideways with her steely hair in a wispy ponytail. She had on a worn black sweatshirt with heavyweight jeans and patterned fleece socks.

"She's a sound sleeper," Kathy whispered.

"Like Ralph," Caleb added. "He never wakes up."

"Mrs. Tenderly?" Maggie stepped closer, and the old woman's hooded eyes fluttered open behind her bifocals.

"Oh, my, hello." Elma's lips curved into a confused smile. "Who are you?"

"Mrs. Tenderly, I'm sorry to barge in. My name's Maggie Ippoliti, and this is my son Caleb and my friend Kathy Gallagher. We were knocking for a while, and the door was unlocked."

"Oh, okay. Call me Elma. That's with an E, not an A." Elma straightened in her chair. "So are you folks lost or something?"

"No, we came from Eddie's Diner to talk about your granddaughter PG. I think she knew my daughter Anna, who went to the Congreve School."

"Oh sure, always happy to talk about my PG." Elma smiled, showing teeth missing on the sides. "Sit down, take a load off. I like company. I don't get much anymore."

"Thanks." Maggie sat down on the couch, and so did Caleb and Kathy. The end table was cluttered with crossword puzzles, pens, old newspapers, a pack of More 100s, a full ashtray, and an empty bag of microwave popcorn.

"Is it still snowing?"

"Yes."

"Oh, my. I thought it woulda stopped by now." Elma's rheumy eyes shifted to Caleb, and she smiled more broadly, her jowls slackening against her cheeks. "Oh, boy, aren't you just the cutest? How old are you?"

"I'm ten," Caleb said confidently, since he had practiced it many times.

"And what grade are you in?"

"Fifth."

"Do you like school?"

"It's okay." Caleb nodded.

"I see you got one of those phones. What you got on there?"

"Clash of Clans. A game."

"My oh my. Good for you!" Elma cleared her throat, with difficulty. "I'd love some tea. Caleb, would you get me some, so I don't have to get up? The kettle's full, all you do is turn the knob."

"Yes." Caleb rose and went to the kitchen.

"Thanks, Caleb." Maggie glanced back to make sure he was okay. The kitchen was small, and Caleb turned the knob on the stove, then sat down at the table to play his video game.

"Would you girls like some tea, too?"

"No thanks," Maggie answered, for both of them. "Is PG your only granddaughter?"

"Yes, she is."

"Do you have any grandsons?"

"Not from the same man. You know how *that* goes." Elma sighed. "Do you smoke?"

"No."

"Good. It's terrible for you. I want a cigarette but I can't have one. Not until bedtime. Sometimes I cheat." Elma smiled naughtily, showing dimples in her cheeks, which she must have passed on to her granddaughter, PG.

"Where does PG go to school?"

"Tipton High. She's a whip, that girl. Smart." Elma frowned. "I was fit to be tied when she dropped out, but there was no stopping her."

"When did she drop out?"

"January. Said school wasn't her thing. She's her own boss, that one."

"She was a waitress at Eddie's, wasn't she?"

"Yes, she got the job there. Liked it for a time, but she wanted to move to the big city."

"Which city?"

"Philadelphia, but they're all the same, aren't they? Tall buildings, too many people. No grass under your feet."

"Do you remember when she left for Philadelphia?"

"No." Elma shook her head. "It's been a while."

"Maybe April? Around Easter maybe?"

"Yes." Elma's rheumy eyes lit up behind her bifocals. "I remember because she came to visit me on Easter, to say good-bye. She brought me a hyacinth. I love hyacinth."

"So do I." Maggie glanced at Kathy, thinking that it confirmed that PG was the imposter. "Does she call you?"

"Sometimes. Not in a while. I try not to worry. She's a strong girl. Got a mind of her own. She wants to be president."

Maggie fell silent a moment, sad for Elma.

"You know what PG calls me? Not Elma, *Elmo.* Like the toy." Elma patted her head. "I had red hair when she was little, and she called me Granny Elmo. Her brother, too. They thought that was so funny. They would sit right there watching that show." Elma pointed at the floor. "*Sesame Street.* I put it on for them. Burton Ernie. I thought the puppet's name was Burton Ernie. They said, 'No, it's Bert *and* Ernie.'"

Maggie smiled. "I thought PG didn't have a brother."

"Her half-brother, Roy. He's older by three years. Roy and PG were thick as thieves when they were little. But he lost his way when he grew up." Elma frowned. "Fell in with the wrong crowd. They got him into trouble. He got locked up for a while."

"Elma, what's Roy's last name? Is it Tenderly?"

"No, Watson. He's a Watson, through and through. Him and his father, the low-lifers. *Low*-lifers." Elma shook her head. "I told my daughter, that man will get you in trouble. He'll steal anything ain't nailed down. He stole from me. He stole my check when it come in. He stole out my wallet. He stole my late husband's wedding band out my jewelry box!"

"Does Roy stay in touch with PG?"

"Yes, he says she's doing real good. She got an office job down there."

Maggie knew it was a lie, so Roy must have known that PG was impersonating Anna. "Did he say where the office job is?"

"Don't remember."

Maggie was thinking that it was time to go to the police and tell them about Roy and PG. Her purse was in the car, and she'd call when they left. "Where does Roy live, Elma?"

"Few blocks over, on East Road. He drops off my groceries every other week. He's got a good heart, that boy."

"What does he do for a living?"

"He's a truck mechanic."

"Is he married?"

"Oh no, no way. He plays the field. His friends, too." Elma frowned deeply. "I don't like them, not at all. Connie's the main one. Another low-lifer."

"Connie?" Maggie repeated, catching Kathy's eye. "Is Connie a man's name?"

"Yes, he's not from here. Konstantine. With a K."

"What's his last name?"

"I forget, I couldn't pronounce it anyway."

"Where does he live?"

"Oh, look, speak of the devil." Elma's head turned to the window, and Maggie rose and looked outside, alarmed to see two men running up the front walk, kicking up snow. The bigger man took the lead, and when they got closer, she could see him slide a handgun from his jacket pocket.

"He has a gun!" Maggie ran to the door, locked the old deadbolt, and pressed her hands against the door.

"A *gun*?" Elma repeated, shocked. "No!"

"Oh my God!" Kathy bolted to the door and tried to hold it closed.

"Open up, you *bitches*!" one of the men shouted, banging on the door.

And in the next moment, the hinges gave way.

Chapter Seventy-nine

Noah, After

"Where are we going?" Noah walked between CO Stanislavsky and CO Evesham. He scanned the hallway looking for escape routes, but there were none. The hallway was long, with security cameras mounted near the ceiling.

"We got a phone you can use," CO Stanislavsky answered, his tone noncommittal.

"Where is it?" Noah kept his tone equally noncommittal. He didn't want to alert them to the fact that he suspected anything. Adding to his nervousness was his complete disorientation. He wasn't familiar enough with Graterford to know where he was in the prison. Behind him was the locked door of the ACU and ahead of him lay another locked door.

CO Stanislavsky sucked his teeth. "We're improvising, since we can't take you back to Cellblock C. The muckety-mucks are still here because of the Jeremy Black murder and they're using up the conference rooms."

"So where are we going?" Noah asked again. They came to the end of the corridor, but there were no windows in the metal doors so he couldn't see what was on the other side.

They stopped, and CO Evesham extracted a jangling set of keys from his belt and unlocked the door. "Dr. Alderman, please stand aside."

Noah did as he was told. They hadn't answered his question. He worried they were waiting for the right moment. CO Stanislavsky kept sucking his teeth, apparently nonchalant.

CO Evesham unlocked the door, and Noah's heart began to pound. Adrenaline dumped into his bloodstream, his body alerted for fight or flight. He reminded himself he was bigger than he used to be. He could throw a punch if his hands were freed. He could sprint if he had to do that, too.

"Go ahead, Dr. Alderman." CO Evesham gestured him through the open door, and Noah passed through with CO Stanislavsky behind him.

"This way," CO Stanislavsky said, as they walked down another hall.

Noah fell into step. They went down a short flight of stairs, then entered another long cinder-block hallway, which felt stifling. They must've been closer to the boiler room.

Noah's heart thumped hard. He looked for a place to run, but there was nowhere. The security cameras were at regular intervals. He told himself they couldn't disable every security camera. Still he had no idea where they were. It seemed suspiciously off the grid.

"Where are we going?" Noah asked again, as they encountered another hallway and another set of metal doors, which CO Evesham moved to unlock and then held open.

"Stand aside, Dr. Alderman." CO Stanislavsky motioned to the corridor as the door swung wide open.

Noah was about to run for his life when he saw that CO Evesham was walking down the hallway to a metal door and just as he was about to unlock it, two female COs came out. They laughed when they almost collided with CO Evesham.

"Mark! What are you doing down here?" the one CO asked, a blonde whose name tag read LUNDY. She held a tinfoil tray of half-eaten vanilla sheet cake.

CO Evesham gestured at Noah. "Our celebrity inmate needs to talk to his lawyer, and the conference rooms are full."

"Oh Jeez." CO Lundy made a funny face. "We woulda cleaned up if we knew company was coming."

"Yeah," said the other female CO. "We woulda baked a cake! Oh, wait, we did!"

The COs laughed merrily, then stood aside as CO Stanislavsky gestured Noah forward, saying, "The phone is all yours, Dr. Alderman. Press nine to get an outside line. It's unmonitored. You have fifteen minutes. We'll wait outside."

"Go ahead, Dr. Alderman," CO Stanislavsky said, impatiently.

"Would you uncuff me, Mr. Stanislavsky?" Noah asked, turning to offer them his wrists.

CO Evesham burst into laughter. "Stan, you dumb Polack! How's he supposed to dial the phone?"

The COs laughed again, and CO Stanislavsky uncuffed Noah and closed the door behind him. The room was a small kitchen with a round Formica table and blue-Plexiglas bucket chairs. Against the wall was a wood cabinet, an old white microwave, and a tan landline. Noah crossed to the phone and pressed in Thomas's cell number. The call was picked up after two rings.

"Thomas, it's Noah Alderman."

"Noah, how are you?" Thomas asked warmly. "Where are you?"

"In a kitchen in Graterford. Did you read about the Jeremy Black murder?"

"Sure, yes."

"You gotta get me out of here," Noah said, then told Thomas everything that had happened, including naming Jimmy Williams as the murderer of Jeremy Black. When Noah finished, he asked, "So what do you think? Can you get me transferred?"

"I'll try. That information is gold."

"You can use it as leverage, can't you? I'll give them a statement. It makes me a snitch now, but it's my only chance."

"Will do," Thomas said, sounding concerned. "I'm hoping I can get you transferred, but the question is when. Prison bureaucracy is the worst."

"It has to be ASAP. I'm not safe here, not even in the ACU."

"I'll make some calls and start shaking the trees."

"Thanks, Thomas," Noah said, grateful.

"Hang tight. Good night."

"Good night." Noah hung up. He couldn't remember the last time anybody had wished him good night. He flashed on Maggie saying good night, then him spooning her in bed, wrapping his arms around her under their big blue comforter. On a winter night like this, she loved to be cuddled and she was always cold. She wore sweat socks to bed, and he thought it was adorable.

Noah suppressed the memory, crossed the room, and opened the door, but there were three COs standing there, Stanislavsky, Evesham, and a bearded one named Pinnella.

"Cuff up, Dr. Alderman," CO Stanislavsky said.

Noah stood his ground. "Why do I need three COs to escort me back to the ACU?"

"Because you threatened me," CO Evesham answered, recoiling as if he'd been startled.

"No, I didn't." Noah realized too late they were play-acting for the security camera.

Suddenly the three COs jumped him, bringing him to the ground, punching, kicking, and handcuffing him. Noah struggled to kick back. He torqued his body this way and that to escape the blows. He curled into a fetal position to protect his core. He absorbed punch after punch.

The last thing he remembered was a vicious blow to the head.

Chapter Eighty

Maggie, After

Maggie sat next to Kathy on the couch, terrified. Connie stood aiming a gun at them. He was a mountain of a man, fully six-foot-five with a broad chest and wearing a motorcycle jacket and jeans.

Maggie prayed Caleb was hiding. He hadn't come out of the kitchen. She couldn't imagine where he'd gone. The house was so small. Her heart hammered with fear. She told herself to keep it together. She had to get them out of this somehow.

"Connie, why'd you kick down the friggin' door?" Roy was holding the door up, trying to match the broken hinges. He was shorter than Connie, with a long, narrow face and grimy orange watchcap. His frame was slight enough to look lost in a Carhartt jacket.

"Shut up, Roy." Connie glowered. He had dark eyes set wide apart in a broad face with a strong jawline. His hair was a greasy black.

Elma sat in her recliner, agitated. "Connie, put that thing away. Roy, what's going on? What are you boys doing?"

"Shit." Roy struggled with the door. "Connie, you shoulda let us walk up like normal instead of a friggin' SWAT team."

"This is your fault, Roy." Connie's expression hardened to a mask of resentment. "That these bitches are here, askin' questions, makin' trouble. All your fault."

Elma shook her head, jittery. "Roy, make him stop. There's no call for this."

"Finally!" Roy turned from the door to Connie. "All you did was make work for me, dude. I'm gonna have to fix it later. My grandma's gonna freeze her ass off."

"No, she won't." Connie swiveled toward Elma, aimed the gun, and pulled the trigger. Fire blazed from the barrel. The gunshot filled the room, deafening. A crimson hole burst onto Elma's chest. She emitted a groan, then her head dropped forward.

Maggie tried not to scream, tears of fright springing to her eyes. She prayed Caleb stayed hidden. Kathy's hand flew to her mouth.

"No, no!" Roy rushed to Elma's side. "She's dead! You killed her!"

"Roy, come on." Connie shook his head. "She was a loose end."

"No, no, no!" Roy wailed, cradling Elma's lifeless body. "She wasn't! She didn't know anything!"

"She knows these bitches. You think she'd shut up about *them*?" Connie motioned to Maggie and Kathy with the gun. Smoke came from the barrel, filtering the cold air.

"I coulda explained it to her! She woulda listened to me!" Roy rose slowly, beginning to sob. He stared at Elma's blood on his hands. "Why'd you kill her, Connie? First PG, now her? She's all the family I got left, dude."

Maggie listened, horrified. So Connie had killed PG. Noah had been telling the truth. Tears rolled down Kathy's cheeks. Maggie had to do something. She racked her brain. She could hear the teakettle begin to whistle. She prayed it wouldn't tip Connie off that Caleb was there.

"Roy, man up!" Connie said, through gritted teeth.

"She was my grandma!" Roy shouted, sobbing. Suddenly he ran at Connie, reaching for his throat, his bloodied fingers grasping the air.

Connie raised the gun and fired. The bullet struck Roy in the neck, which exploded in blood and tissue. The gunshot reverberated, ear-splitting. Its force spun Roy around. He dropped to the floor.

Maggie fought terror to think. Connie was about to fire again. It gave her an opening. She wouldn't get another chance. The teakettle was whistling loudly. Her frantic gaze fell on the full ashtray. She picked it up and whipped it at Connie's face.

Connie's hands flew up reflexively. The gun fired into the air.

Kathy ran full-tilt into Connie's legs, knocking him off-balance. Connie flew sideways against the hard floor. The gun flew out of his hand and skidded into the kitchen.

Maggie dove for it and grabbed it, just as the back door flew open.

Caleb stood in the threshold, holding his phone high. "I called 911! I said it was an emergency!"

"You little bastard!" Connie raged, scrambling to his feet. "I'll kill you!"

"No!" Maggie fired the gun just as Connie lunged for Caleb.

"Bitch!" Connie fell, grabbing his leg in pain. Blood drenched his right thigh.

"Go, go, go!" Maggie grabbed Caleb by the shoulder and ran with him into the living room. Kathy yanked on the doorknob. The door fell to the side.

Maggie, Caleb, and Kathy bolted onto the porch, raced down the snowy stairs, and ran away from the house.

Suddenly the sound of sirens pierced the frigid air. Police cruisers zoomed toward them, red lights flashing.

"Help! Police!" Maggie dropped the gun as she ran. The three of them ran toward the cruisers.

"He's inside!" Maggie shouted, as the police cruisers swerved to a stop, spraying snow from their tires. Their doors flew open, and uniformed cops ran out, heading toward the house.

Connie ran limping to his truck.

Another police cruiser veered around the other corner, its sirens blaring and lights flashing. It halted, its big high beams cutting through the darkness, spotlighting Connie amid the snow flurries. Uniformed police jumped out with their guns drawn, blocking him in.

"Freeze!" the police shouted, coming up behind him. "Hands up!"

Connie stopped, trapped. Then he dropped to his knees in the swirling snow, raising his hands.

Chapter Eighty-one

Noah, After

Noah regained consciousness as he was half-walked and half-dragged down the hallway by COs Evesham and Stanislavsky. Pain arced through his skull. His ribs ached with every step. Blood ran down his forehead, warm and wet. He blinked to clear his eyes.

"You're not going to get away with this," Noah said hoarsely.

CO Evesham sniffed. "You refused to cuff up. You threatened my personal safety. You resisted in a dangerous manner. We're writing you up for misconduct."

"Everybody knows what you're up to, Evesham. I told them you were the CO who took me to my cell. You left the door open for Jeremy Black. You're going down for that."

"I locked the door. I had nothing to do with the door's being open. Must've been another CO who came after me."

"You're a liar."

"Wrong. The matter's been investigated and resolved. Officially." They reached the stairwell to the ACU, but instead of going up the stairs, they took a right down another hallway.

"Where we going?" Noah could barely hold himself up. Blood poured into his eyes. "You'd better be taking me to the infirmary."

"The RHU. You'll get my write-up later. You got Class I charges.

Threatening a CO with bodily harm, resisting arrest, and insubordination." They reached a maroon-metal door that read RHU, CO Evesham unlocked it, and they hustled Noah into a long hallway that had doors like the ACU isolation cells.

Noah thought about running. He was in too much pain. There was nowhere to run. He had no choice but to let them throw him in a cell. At least he would be safe.

CO Stanislavsky went to the first cell door and unlocked it. Noah stood aside. Blood ran down his face.

"Get in." CO Evesham opened the door, but the cell wasn't empty. Inside was John Drover.

And in his hand was a homemade shank.

Chapter Eighty-two

Maggie, After

Maggie, Kathy, and Caleb sat in the small waiting room of the homey Tipton police station, having finished giving their statements to a group of federal, state, and local law enforcement. Wooden chairs matched a table that held back issues of *People* magazine, and the air smelled like stale coffee. Maggie was waiting to find out about Anna. The authorities were still interviewing Connie, and she'd been told that he was making a complete statement in return for a plea deal.

The waiting area was separated from the office by an old-fashioned wooden door with a glass pane, and Maggie keep checking to see what was going on. Uniformed local police, assistant U.S. attorneys, local assistant district attorneys, and FBI agents flooded the small room, which held only a few wooden desks with outdated computers. Atop a line of battered gray file cabinets sat an old TV playing The Weather Channel on mute, next to stacked case files and a clutter of New England Patriots and Red Sox paraphernalia, including a David Ortiz bobblehead.

Maggie felt pure dread that the worst that happened to Anna, but she told herself to keep the faith, and she worried about Caleb, since the horrific scene at Elma Tenderly's. She was still amazed that he'd had the presence of mind to run out the back door and call 911 when Connie and Roy had burst into the house. She hadn't had a chance to talk with him about what had happened, and it had to have been traumatic. He seemed okay under the circumstances, sitting next to her with his phone in his lap. During the interview, he'd absorbed everything with wide-eyed interest. She would help him process it later, and he could talk about it in therapy, too, when they got home.

"How you doing, sweetie?" Maggie asked him, ruffling his hair.

"I'm okay." Caleb nodded with a smile.

"You must be tired." Maggie checked the wall clock. It was almost one o'clock in the morning.

"No, I'm fine."

Maggie touched his hand. "That was scary at the house, huh?"

"Yeah."

"I'm so proud of you, Caleb. You saved our lives, do you realize that?"

"Yes." Caleb grinned.

"I love you very much." Maggie gave him a hug and a kiss.

"I love you, too, Mag." Caleb looked up with a smile. "And I said *emergency*!"

"You sure did!" Maggie smiled, proud of him.

"Remember when I fell and cut my knee at school? It was an *emergency*?"

"Yes. You said it perfectly. You were amazing."

Kathy looked over, her eyes shining. "I agree, one hundred percent. Caleb, you were incredibly brave. You saved us."

Caleb grinned. "Mag *shot* the guy!"

Kathy flared her eyes, with a half-smile. "Yes, she did. Who knew?"

"Not me." Maggie shuddered inwardly. "And Kath, you tackled him."

Kathy winked. "Right? The boys taught me that. Lacrosse in the spring, and football in the fall. Go, team!"

Caleb grinned up at Maggie. "Did you ever shoot anybody before, Mag?"

"No, and I don't want to ever again. I wasn't trying to kill him, you know. I didn't want to." Maggie managed a smile, knowing she'd have some processing of her own to do, later.

Kathy put her hand on Caleb's. "Your mom shot only because he was going to hurt you."

"I know." Caleb looked up at Maggie. "You're a great mom."

"Aw, thanks, honey," Maggie said, feeling her heart melt. She knew he loved her, but he'd never said that to her before this very moment.

Suddenly, there was new activity in the squad room. The door to the interview room was opening, and men in suits were spilling out with laptops and legal files. The FBI types were putting on jackets, the lawyers their trenchcoats, and the police were donning bulletproof vests and leaving by the back entrance to the parking lot behind the station.

Maggie found herself on her feet. "They're going somewhere."

Kathy stood up. "Looks that way."

Caleb jumped up. "Here comes the Chief."

Maggie waved to Chief Vogel of the Congreve Police, who caught her eye as he threaded his way to the waiting room, zipping the blue insulated jacket over his uniform and putting on his blue cap. They had met earlier tonight, and she liked him. Vogel was a taciturn Mainer in his fifties, but he'd been concerned about Anna's case. He opened the door to the waiting room with a tense smile.

"Hello, folks," Chief Vogel said, shutting the door behind him

"Chief, what's going on?" Maggie met him at the door with Kathy and Caleb. "Is Anna okay?"

"I have some answers, but not all. I'm authorized to tell you only what you need to know. It's confidential police business, and we don't have much time to talk now."

"I understand."

"We are engaged in an ongoing police investigation. I'm telling you only because you are a victim's parent. One of the victims."

Maggie swallowed hard. Her heart started to thud in her chest. She prayed Anna was alive.

"A plea agreement is being finalized with Connie, full name Konstantine Rogolyi. Under its terms, Konstantine Rogolyi will be spared the death penalty and he will be spending life in prison without possibility of parole. In return, he agrees to plead guilty to the first-degree murders of Elma Tenderly, Patti "PG" Tenderly, and Roy Watson of Tipton. In addition, Konstantine Rogolyi is pleading guilty to several other charges, including numerous federal counts of sex trafficking."

"Sex trafficking?" Maggie's stomach turned over. She felt Kathy hold her arm, supporting her. She didn't know how much Caleb understood, but this wasn't the time or the place to explain.

"Yes. According to his statement, Konstantine Rogolyi was engaged with Roy Watson and others in a sex-trafficking conspiracy, in violation of the TVPA, or the Trafficking Victims Protection Act and other laws. Patti Tenderly, whom you know as PG, was an integral part of the criminal conspiracy. Patti Tenderly's role was to recruit victims like your daughter and lure them into meeting with Konstantine Rogolyi, Roy Watson, and others, who kidnapped and trafficked them." Chief Vogel's mouth set grimly. "Konstantine Rogolyi told authorities that there are seven victims being forced into prostitution, coerced under threat of violence. You may be unaware of this, but not all sex trafficking is international. On the contrary, domestic sex trafficking is on the rise in remote regions of the country like ours. In fact, state and federal law enforcement coordinate with many anti-trafficking groups, including women's groups and Truckers Against Trafficking."

"So does that mean Anna is alive?" Maggie felt a flicker of hope, setting aside her revulsion. "And you know where she is?"

"We have a reasonable basis to believe that she and the others are at a nearby location, but we cannot be certain. Konstantine Rogolyi told us that Patti Tenderly recruited Jamie Covington and your daughter Anna Desroches at Congreve. Patti Tenderly learned that your daughter was to inherit a trust fund at age eighteen. Seeing the similarity in her appearance with your daughter, Patti Tenderly befriended your daughter, trafficked her, and took the opportunity to steal your daughter's identity and move to Pennsylvania."

Maggie shuddered. "Because she wanted Anna's money?"

"Yes. In addition, she had to leave our jurisdiction to avoid detection, since she had already trafficked other victims here. More would have raised suspicion. Konstantine Rogolyi also told us that after Patti Tenderly moved to Pennsylvania, she trafficked one Samantha Silas, a junior at Lower Merion High School."

"All of the missing girls were trafficked?" Maggie felt absolute disgust, even as she tried to piece the story together. "Patti, or PG, worked so quickly."

"She had to, to take advantage of the school year to meet her victims."

"So why did Connie kill her? My husband was wrongly convicted of that murder."

"I'll explain, briefly." Chief Vogel glanced at the office, where the FBI, assistant U.S. attorneys, assistant district attorneys, and uniformed officers were leaving. "According to Konstantine Rogolyi's statement, Patti Tenderly intended to recruit victims in Pennsylvania using your daughter's identity until your daughter's trust fund and inheritance paid out, at eighteen years old. Then Patti Tenderly would have collected the money and left your home. However, she feared that your husband was going to change the terms of the trust so she didn't receive her payout until she was twenty-five. She didn't want to wait that long for the money, so she sought to eliminate him by making false allegations in a PFA against him."

Maggie put it together, appalled. "In other words, she filed the PFA to get him out of the house?"

"Yes, but she feared that you might eventually reconcile with him. She formed a plan to frame your husband for another incident of sexual assault, which she was going to use to charge him criminally and ultimately to force you to divorce him. Konstantine Rogolyi pretended to go along with her plan, meanwhile forming his own plan to kill her."

"How?"

"Unbeknownst to Patti Tenderly and Roy Watson, Konstantine Rogolyi felt that Patti was getting too big for her britches. So Konstantine Rogolyi went to your husband's house before your husband was due to arrive, killed Patti Tenderly, and left without being detected."

"Oh my God," Maggie said, horrified. "So where's Anna?"

"Konstantine Rogolyi has just given us information about a location in the vicinity where the victims are being trafficked. We intend to raid that location immediately." Chief Vogel glanced over as the law-enforcement personnel emptied the squad room.

"You mean you're going to find Anna now?" Maggie asked, her heart leaping.

"I think it's time for you to go to the Congreve Inn and wait to hear from us. Okay, folks?" Chief Vogel glanced at Kathy and Caleb. "I will call you at my earliest opportunity—"

Maggie interrupted, "If you're going to find Anna, I'm going with you."

Chief Vogel raised his palm. "Folks, I would prefer it if you waited at the hotel. We will be attempting to apprehend criminals who are armed and dangerous. The victims are in further danger once the operation begins. We want to avoid a hostage situation. This will be a major, coordinated operation of federal and state law enforcement."

"I'm coming, Chief." Maggie turned to Kathy. "Kath, I think you should take Caleb to the hotel, don't you?"

"Yes, agree. We'll go to the hotel." Kathy gave her a quick hug. "Good luck, honey. Be careful."

"Mag, I want to stay with you," Caleb said, taking her hand.

"Honey, no. You heard the Chief." Maggie kissed him and gave him hug. "Love you. See you as soon as I can, okay?"

Chief Vogel frowned. "Maggie, I'm advising you to wait at the hotel, too. Please."

"Thanks, but no," Maggie said. "I'm coming with you."

Kathy interjected, "Chief Vogel, you have to take her with. After all, you wouldn't have cracked this case if it hadn't been for her. You can thank her on the way."

Chapter Eighty-three

Noah, After

Noah realized with horror the COs were going to put him in the cell with Drover, like a cage match. Adrenaline poured into his system. His heart began to pound. His breath came short and choppy. He no longer felt pain. He broke a sweat. He didn't struggle because it would waste energy he needed.

"Uncuff me," Noah said, wanting a fighting chance.

"I don't think so, doc." CO Evesham shoved Noah inside the cell.

Noah staggered in and fell, handcuffed. The door clanged shut and was locked behind him. He scrambled to his feet, backing up. He willed himself not to panic.

Drover advanced slowly, brandishing the shank, a jagged piece of metal with an adhesive-taped handle.

Noah edged backwards, thinking fast. If he drew Drover close enough, he could kick the knife from his hands or kick him in the crotch.

Drover advanced, grimacing. He swiped the air with the knife, toying with Noah. His dark eyes glittered. "You killed Jeremy."

"No I didn't. I tried to save him." Noah backed closer to the door. Warm blood ran in rivulets down his face. He blinked it away. He was running out of space. He needed Drover to get closer still.

"You wouldn't sew him up." Drover swiped the air in the opposite direction.

"It wouldn't have helped." Noah felt his back against the door.

"I'm going to carve you like they carved him."

Noah heard shouting behind him. Heavy footsteps filled the hallway outside. Orders were being barked. "Get me out of here!" he called out, kicking the door.

Drover made his move, lunging at Noah with the knife.

Noah jumped out of the way, just missing the blade.

Suddenly the cell door flew open. The CERT team, or Corrections Emergency Response Team, burst inside. They charged in a phalanx at Drover in black riot helmets, protective eyewear, and heavy body armor.

Noah sprang aside. The lead CERT team member brandished a man-sized plastic shield, used it to shove Drover backwards, and pressed him to the floor while Drover struggled, yelling obscenities. The other CERT members disarmed and handcuffed Drover, armed with pepper-ball delivery-system guns. It took them only a matter of minutes to haul Drover to his feet and out of the cell, still hollering.

Noah wiped the blood from his brow, shaken, and Deputy Warden McLaughlin entered with another CO, his expression grim behind his glasses.

"CO Jimenez, uncuff Dr. Alderman," he ordered, turning to Noah. "Dr. Alderman, any injuries besides that cut on your forehead?"

"Maybe a broken rib, but I could have been killed." Noah tried to collect his thoughts. "You see what happened? I assume you spoke with my lawyer. I'm in danger in Graterford. You have to transfer me out of here."

"We'll do you one better." Deputy Warden McLaughlin smiled. "You're going to be a free man, Dr. Alderman."

"What?" Noah asked, bewildered. "How?"

"Your lawyer got a call from your wife. She's up in Maine with the FBI. They have a man named Konstantine Rogolyi in custody, and he confessed to the murder of Patti Tenderly on May 10. I just got off the phone with the assistant U.S. attorney in Philly, who confirmed the information."

"Really?" Noah felt stunned. He had no idea what was going on. May 10 was the date of Anna's murder, but he had never heard of Patti Tenderly. He wiped the blood from his face again.

"Let's get to the infirmary, doc." Deputy Warden McLaughlin put his hand on Noah's shoulder.

"But who's Patti Tenderly? And what's my wife doing in Maine? With the *FBI*?"

"I'll explain on the way."

Chapter Eighty-four

Maggie, After

Maggie gripped the plastic handle in the backseat as the police cruiser sped through the woods at night. Two uniformed officers in bulletproof vests sat in the front seat, silent except when they communicated on a radio. She was in the middle of a paramilitary operation of law-enforcement personnel, police cruisers, SWAT vehicles, and ambulances. Authorities were converging from all directions, flooding the roads to a secluded farmhouse in Tipton, near the highway exit and two truck stops.

Maggie kept her face to the window, trying to see through the driving snow and the darkness. Her heart hammered away. Every muscle in her body tensed. They passed through woods and finally reached open pasture. Every mile brought her closer to Anna. She sensed they were getting closer, racing down a curving country road. They accelerated behind the five other police cruisers, like the caboose on a runaway train.

The cruiser veered around a curve, following the others. The police in the front seat talked faster into the radio. Maggie caught sight of a farmhouse in the distance, a bright spot in the darkness. The cruiser zoomed ahead and so did the others in the line ahead, their red taillights burning through the blackness. The sirens remained silent, the light bars off.

The farmhouse got closer and closer. A light shone on the front porch and from every room, and the front of the farmhouse looked like the Tenderlys', but in back, were four mobile homes, also with the lights on.

Maggie swallowed hard. It made her sick to think that Anna and the other girls were being trafficked out of those trailers. She was horrified that Anna was inside, but she prayed Anna was alive. Where there was life, there was hope.

The police cruiser raced to the farmhouse behind the others. Suddenly all of the cruisers slowed to a stop at the same moment, then parked on an angle to the right, spraying snow. Maggie's cruiser was at the end of the line, about a hundred yards from the farmhouse.

The police in the front seat grabbed their long guns, jumped out of the cruiser, and knelt behind its open door, training their barrels on the farmhouse in the blowing snow. Police in the other cars were doing the same thing, and SWAT teams poured from boxy black vehicles in the front of the line, closest to the farmhouse.

Maggie's heart thundered. She couldn't see the farmhouse well enough. It was too far away and too dark. Flurries clung to the cruiser window. She rolled it down. Snowflakes blew into her face.

Even with the window down, the farmhouse was too far away for Maggie to see anything. It was too dark. Snow swirled everywhere. The porch light barely illuminated anything. She prayed silently. Any minute now, Anna could be rescued, taken hostage, or killed.

Maggie watched riveted as the SWAT team hustled to the farmhouse, splitting into three moving teams. One team broke down the front door with a metal ram and charged inside. A second and third team flanked the farmhouse, raced to the windows, and shattered them with their long guns.

Suddenly a fusillade of gunfire went off inside the farmhouse. The shots echoed through the snowy night. Light flashed in the windows.

Maggie felt her heart lurch. Anna was inside the house. She could have been shot.

Maggie got out of the cruiser, ducking behind the police officer in the driving snow. More gunshots blasted in the farmhouse. Lights flashed again in the windows.

Maggie had to see what was going on. She took off running to the farmhouse. Her legs churned in the heavy snow. Icy flakes bit her cheeks. She ignored the police calling her back.

A group of SWAT team members hurried from the farmhouse with two handcuffed men, hustling them onto the porch. Uniformed police and FBI agents rushed the handcuffed men to waiting cruisers.

Maggie stumbled in the snow but kept running. Ice bit her cheeks. Her breath grew ragged. She heard women screaming in the farmhouse. The sound cut to her heart, bringing tears to her eyes. She had to get to Anna.

Maggie kept running, snow swirling around her. Another group of SWAT team members hustled two more handcuffed men from the house, their heads down. Police and FBI agents clustered around them and hustled them to cruisers.

Maggie reached the front yard, where police personnel hustled this way and that. They jostled her, calling instructions.

"Miss, stop, get back, it's not safe!" one shouted, and a group of police blocked her path.

"My daughter's inside!" Maggie shouted back, but the police linked arms, forming a barricade.

Maggie watched the porch from behind them. Another SWAT team emerged from the farmhouse with two girls in parkas.

Maggie's heart leapt with hope. But neither girl was Anna. She told herself to get a grip. She remembered Chief Vogel's saying there were seven victims. There were five to go.

SWAT team members hustled out with two more girls in coats. Maggie's hopes soared again. She stood on tiptoe behind the police to see better. Neither girl was Anna. Only three girls were left.

Maggie began to panic. Anna had to be soon. Anna couldn't have been shot. Anna had to be alive.

SWAT team members brought out another two girls. Maggie jumped up and down. She felt a bolt of recognition. She knew one of the girls. It was Samantha Silas.

"Samantha!" Maggie called out, but Samantha didn't see her in the chaos and darkness before she was hustled off the porch.

Maggie started praying. Anna had to be next. She couldn't be dead. She had to be alive.

SWAT team members emerged from the house with a young girl in a coat, whom Maggie's heart recognized instantly, the way it was supposed to, even after all this time. A mother's heart, in the end.

"Anna! Anna!" Maggie cried, tears brimming in her eyes. She pressed against the police, but they wouldn't let her past. "That's my daughter!"

Anna turned to the sound, finally spotting Maggie as the police hustled her off the porch. "That's my mom!"

Maggie shoved the police aside to get to Anna, and Anna broke free of the SWAT team members to get to her. They made their way to each other, falling into each other's arms, clinging to each other in the blowing snow.

Maggie held Anna tight, finally holding her beautiful baby girl.

And vowing never, ever to let her go.

Epilogue

Maggie and Noah, After

Five months later, the sun was rising in a clear sky, shedding dappled light on the backyard. The Eastern Redbud tree was blooming with tiny pinkish-purple flowers, the forsythia bush had exploded in yellow stars, and the snowbells bowed their pure white heads. The Zephirine Drouhin rosebushes along the fence had grown sturdy canes with floppy green leaves, sending thinner tendrils curling around the wooden pickets and making a natural border dotted with hot-pink rosebuds, which released a sweet fragrance.

"What do you think of those roses?" Maggie asked, leaning back in the cushioned lounger.

"I think they're gorgeous," Anna answered, lying on the lounger beside her, with Wreck-It Ralph curled into a purring ball at her feet.

"I think they're *incredibly* gorgeous."

Anna smiled. "This is usually when you tell me that Zephirine Drouhin is one of the few varieties that are both thornless *and* fragrant."

"I was just about to, because I like to hear you pronounce Zephirine Drouhin."

"With my French accent?"

"Yes. Say it for me." Maggie was only half-kidding. She was so happy that she'd gotten Anna back, and that her daughter was recovering from her horrific ordeal with intensive therapy, support, and love. Anna had good days and bad, but this was one of the good ones, an Easter Sunday morning. Anna had taken the year off from school, and Maggie had stayed home to support her in her recovery. Fortunately, Anna had been spared a trial because the other co-conspirators had also taken plea deals. Jamie Covington, Samantha Silas, and the other four victims had been restored to their families.

"*Zephirine Drouhin*," Anna said, in French.

"Sublime." Maggie smiled, then heard Noah laughing by the bushes. She looked over to see him gesturing to Caleb, who was rifling behind the forsythia for the plastic eggs they had hidden, filled with M&Ms, Reese's Pieces, and other caffeinated treasures.

"Caleb, keep going!" Noah called out, laughing.

"Here? Or here?" Caleb raced back and forth with his bag.

"There!" Noah pointed beside the bushes. "Look there! There's more in that direction."

"Am I getting warmer or colder?" Caleb ran back and forth.

"Warmer!"

"Warmer here?" Caleb scooted to the right. "Or here?"

Maggie looked over at Anna. "How much longer is this going to take?"

Anna chuckled. "Noah hid the eggs too well. I told him he should have made it easier."

"When has Noah ever made anything easy?"

Anna looked over, her blue eyes shining. "He made everything easy for me. He's been wonderful to me, and I love him for it."

"Aw, he loves you, too. We both do." Maggie patted her daughter's forearm. She was so lucky that Noah and Anna were close, and that Noah had been completely exonerated. Maggie felt she'd redeemed herself for the past and had even adopted Caleb, so they had become a family. And Anna had fixed her trust so that it paid out later, and as part of the healing process, she'd established The Anna Fund, a charitable foundation to provide victims of sex trafficking with counseling, a safe house, and college tuition.

"Dad, you said *here,* not there!" Caleb giggled.

"No, I said *there,* not here!" Noah laughed.

"Noah?" Maggie called out, with a smile. "Will you guys be done by Christmas?"

"Doubtful!" Noah turned to Maggie, flashing a grin. The man still made Dockers look sexy, and she was more in love with him than ever. He had mellowed, and their marriage was stronger than before. Plus, when they fought, she always won. Because she'd saved his life.

"I found one!" Caleb jumped up and down, holding a yellow plastic egg.

"Great!" Noah ruffled his hair.

"Good job, Caleb!" Anna called to him.

"Only three hundred more to go!" Maggie shouted.

"Maggie, tell me where they are!" Caleb shouted back, with a smile.

"You really want to know?" Maggie shifted up in the chair.

"No!" Caleb took off running around the bush, resuming his egg search.

Maggie eased back in the chair. She wasn't truly in a hurry. She'd learned not to be so damn busy. She closed her eyes, delighted to feel the warm sun on her face, sitting with her family and surrounded by nature's beauty.

Maggie realized that life wouldn't be as much fun if we knew where its treasures were hidden. Sometimes you had to search for them. Sometimes you had to fight for them. And sometimes, they were at your feet.

Either way, they were waiting.

For you.

Acknowledgments

Here's where I get to say thank you, but because this book has a twist or two, I'll thank people here without explaining what they did to inform this novel. I owe them a huge debt of thanks, and all mistakes herein are my own.

Thank you to Steve Gordon, Patti Emmons, Dr. Lisa Goldstein, Matt Smyth of Land Rover Jaguar Main Line, educator Kathleen Buckley, and at my alma mater, Lower Merion High School, thanks to Doug Young, Anna O'Hora, and the great gang in administration. Thank you so much for all of your help to Jessica Kitson, Esq., and my brilliant goddaughter Jessica Limbacher, Esq., of Volunteer Lawyers for Justice. And thanks to my dear friend, legal genius Nicholas Casenta, Esq., Chief Deputy District Attorney of the Chester County District Attorney's Office.

Thank you to my goddess editor, Jennifer Enderlin, who is also the Senior Vice President and Publisher of St. Martin's Press, yet she still finds the time to improve every one of my manuscripts. And big love and thanks to everyone at St. Martin's Press and Macmillan, starting with the terrific John Sargent and Sally Richardson, plus Jeff Dodes, Lisa Senz, Brian Heller, Jeff Capshew, Lisa Senz, Brant Janeway, Erica Martirano, Tom Thompson, John Karle, Jordan Hanley, John Edwards, Jeanette Zwart, Anne-Marie Tallberg, Kerry Nordling,

Elizabeth Wildman, Talia Sherer, Kim Ludlum, Rachel Diebel, and all the wonderful sales reps. Big thanks to Michael Storrings, for outstanding cover design. Also hugs and kisses to Mary Beth Roche, Laura Wilson, Samantha Edelson, and the great people in audiobooks. I love and appreciate all of you!

Thanks and love to my terrific agent, Robert Gottlieb of Trident Media Group, for his dedication and enormous expertise, and thanks to Nicole Robson and Trident's digital media team.

Many thanks and much love to the amazing Laura Leonard. She's invaluable in every way, every day. Thanks, too, to Nan Daley for all of her research assistance to this novel, and thanks to George Davidson and Katie Rinda for doing everything else, so that I can be free to write.

Finally, thank you to my amazing daughter (and even coauthor), Francesca, for all of her support, laughter, and love.

AFTER ANNA
by Lisa Scottoline

Behind the Novel

• A Note from the Author: Taking Risks

Keep On Reading

• Reading Group Questions

A
Reading
Group Gold
Selection

Also available as an audiobook
from Macmillan Audio

For more reading group suggestions
visit www.readinggroupgold.com.

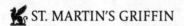 ST. MARTIN'S GRIFFIN

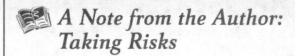

A Note from the Author: Taking Risks

Dear Readers,

I've learned you have to take risks in life and in writing!

My domestic novel *After Anna* was definitely risky for me because, as you just saw, the structure of this novel is unique. It's told in viewpoints shifting between the husband, Noah, and the wife, Maggie. I did that because I wanted to emphasize that they both have a different set of facts and a different take on those facts, as in any relationship, or marriage (not that I'm an expert, I'm divorced twice, but I remember it well! LOL). And not only that, Noah's story is told in reverse chronological order, and though that sounds complicated, it wasn't. I did it for an excellent reason, which is that Noah's story is told during a murder trial, and in a regular trial, the defense goes second, after the prosecution. If I had written the novel that way, it would've put the meaty, juicy part of the novel, namely, what really happened the night of the murder, at the back of the book, and I didn't want the reader to wait (and I hate waiting, too!). I like to get to the story fast, so I knew if I could do it this way, it would be so much more effective, and I think it paid off.

Yay!

After Anna was published to rave critical and reader reviews and it made me a #1 bestselling author, for the first time ever! I've been fortunate to be on the bestseller lists on a regular basis for the last two decades, but my ultimate dream has always been that for one week, my book would be the bestselling hardcover novel in the entire country, and with *After Anna*, my dream came true! Dear reader, you made that happen, and I thank you, from the bottom of my heart.

So, in truth, the real reason I take risks in my writing is for my readers. The greatest way I can thank you all is to work hard, keep it fresh, and take risks because I want to keep my books interesting for you. At the same time, it keeps me interested as I'm writing them. If I'm not intrigued, then you won't be either. So, I hope that you enjoyed *After Anna,* that you will continue to read my books, and that you think that my taking risks is worth it, too!

Thanks so much for your loving support. Every reader matters to me!

Love,

Lisa Scottoline

Reading Group Questions

1. *After Anna* is told in alternating perspectives and several different time lines. What did you think of this unique structure and what did it add to your reading experience?

2. Maggie was separated from Anna after suffering a severe bout of postpartum psychosis, an extreme form of postpartum depression. In the real world, as in *After Anna*, postpartum depression often goes untreated or is considered shameful. Why do you think there is so much stigma surrounding these illnesses? What can we do to help better support new mothers?

3. Anna was used as a pawn by her father, and he wielded his power and money, and even lied to Anna to keep her away from Maggie. What do you think his motivation was for doing it? What was your initial reaction when Maggie learned the truth about Anna's father? Were you instantly suspicious, or did you believe Anna's explanation? How did that affect your opinion of Anna throughout the rest of the novel?

4. Throughout the trial sections of the novel, damning evidence against Noah begins to build, from texts on his phone to official government documents. Were you convinced by the evidence? Why or why not? Did you think he was guilty—of murder or anything else?

5. When Anna enters their home, Maggie and Noah have to renegotiate their parental boundaries and the household rules. How do you manage this in your own household? How does Anna having a large amount of

money complicate this, and how do you think you would navigate a similar situation? Is there a right or wrong way to go about it?

6. On page 68, Anna's lawyer says, "Every girl needs a mother, doesn't she?" Whom do you turn to when you need mothering, whether your biological mother or someone else? Do you think we ever grow out of needing our mother?

7. When did you begin to get suspicious of Anna's erratic behavior? What struck you as particularly odd? How do you think your understanding of the novel would change if you read it again, knowing the outcome?

8. What do you think about the ethics of Kathy and Maggie looking through Anna's books for notes—are teenagers entitled to a certain level of privacy? Was it right, wrong, or more complicated than that? Why do you think this?

9. Near the end of the novel, Maggie thinks that she must push through, "because she was a mother, and she had a job to do." Where can you see this theme of what mothers would do for their daughters throughout the book? What kind of power do you think there is in a mother-daughter bond?

10. What did you think of the ending of the novel? Did you see it coming or were you completely blindsided? Did it change your understanding of the rest of the novel?

April Narby

Lisa Scottoline is a #1 bestselling and Edgar Award–winning author of thirty-one novels. She has thirty million copies of her books in print in the United States, she has been published in thirty-five countries, and her thrillers have been optioned for television and film. Lisa also writes a weekly column with her daughter, Francesca Serritella, for *The Philadelphia Inquirer,* and those stories have been adapted into a series of bestselling memoirs, the first of which is entitled *Why My Third Husband Will Be a Dog.* Lisa lives on a Pennsylvania farm with an array of disobedient pets. Visit www.scottoline.com or follow Lisa on Facebook, Twitter, or Instagram at @LisaScottoline.